In the
Presence of
Enemies

Also by William J. Coughlin

Death Penalty
Shadow of a Doubt
Her Honor
Her Father's Daughter
The Twelve Apostles
No More Dreams
Day of Wrath
The Stalking Man
The Grinding Mill
The Destruction Committee
The Dividend Was Death
The Widow Wondered Why
Cain's Chinese Adventure
(under the pseudonym Sean A. Key)
The Mark of Cain
(under the pseudonym Sean A. Key)

In the Presence of Enemies

William J. Coughlin

St. Martin's Press
New York

Design by Dawn Niles

Library of Congress Cataloging-in-Publication Data

Coughlin, William Jeremiah.
    In the presence of enemies / William J. Coughlin.
        p.   cm.
    "A Thomas Dunne book."
    ISBN 0-312-08818-3
    I. Title.
    PS3553.O7815   1993
    813'.54—dc20   92-29876
                                             CIP

First Edition: March 1993

10 9 8 7 6 5 4 3 2 1

For Ruth

In the
Presence of
Enemies

1

He wished desperately that he could think of something else.

A gray, seagoing freighter made its way slowly up the river. The squat, weathered boat was alone on the water except for a small sailboat going in the other direction. Clouds gathered in the autumn sky, although some slim rays of sunlight managed to poke through here and there, illuminating the darkening landscape in brief and erratic checkerboard patterns.

A senior associate, he enjoyed an office with a view, one of the perks of his rank within the firm. According to the standard firm joke, those windows, so high above the city, allowed an easy jump if the occupant failed to make partner.

The two boats, but for the ever-present gulls, were the only signs of life, for the core city was, as usual, deserted. It was Sunday and everything downtown was closed. Only an occasional car passed below and no one walked the vacant streets.

At night and on weekends, the city emptied. That had been the first real difference he had noticed after the move from New York. The empty avenues had reminded him then of those nuclear disaster movies showing imaginary cities with all life destroyed. To a New Yorker accustomed to crowds it was eerie, lonely.

Jake Martin had been a resident of the city almost five years, but the place, when it was deserted as it was now, still struck him just as eerie and, for him, just as lonely. He could not accustom himself to the desolation, nor the isolation. Others accepted it as normal, but it produced in him an ever-deepening sense of alienation.

Detroit. He had never imagined even visiting it, let alone living in the place.

"Jesus, it must be nice."

Jake swung his large leather chair, another mark of his rank, and turned from the window.

1

"What must be nice?"

Harry Fowler was a second-year associate, a pleasant, eager young man who was the only other Columbia law graduate in the firm. Harry had attached himself to Jake on the basis of their academic origin. Grinning, he now stood in the doorway dressed in running sweats, a mode of dress prohibited during work days.

"A window is nice," he said, "and the leisure to stare out of it."

"Someday all this will be yours."

"I'm packing it in for the day, Jake. Want to go someplace and grab a beer?"

"Where? Nothing's open."

"We could hop over to Greektown."

"Not for me. There's still a few things I've got to do."

Harry shrugged. "Like watching the river?"

"I was merely composing my thoughts."

"Let's get a beer. You probate and trust drones don't have deadlines like the rest of us. C'mon, I'll buy."

"Harry, you can write this down if you feel like it, but there is no lawyer, living or dead, who doesn't face deadlines."

Harry leaned against the doorjamb. "By the way, old man Armstrong said they decided to keep me for another year. I thought they would, but I was glad they made it official."

"When did he tell you?"

"Friday. Armstrong said the managing partners had gotten good reports on me."

"Congratulations. Is this a celebration?"

Harry shook his head. "Nope. I did that yesterday. Went to the game in Ann Arbor and then got ripped. I felt godawful this morning but I'm all right now, just tired. A couple of beers ought to take care of that. Come on with me, Jake."

"I'm working on a particularly ugly provision in a trust agreement. It's an involved thing and a mistake of even one word could cost millions. As we both know, I can't afford any kind of mistake, large or small, right at the moment."

Harry nodded. "No word, I presume?"

"None," said Jake.

"You'll make it. When you do, maybe you could get assigned to some other section."

"Why?"

"This probate crap has got to be dull."

"That depends on your definition of dull. Probate and trust brings in big bucks to this firm, real big bucks. It might lack the glamour of litigation and some of the other work around here, but this is where the goose lays her big golden eggs. Money is power, Harry, especially in this firm."

"Jesus," Harry grunted, "all you deal with is death, either before or after. It's like being in the funeral business except you don't have to handle the bodies."

Jake Martin shook his head and smiled.

"Death is American's growth industry. Didn't anyone ever tell you that? Take Detroit. Nearly five million people live in this area, and one hell of a lot of them are rich. This place has produced lumber fortunes, iron fortunes, car fortunes and even pizza fortunes. There are billions of dollars here, Harry, and billionaires. I couldn't believe it when I first came here, but this dirty shirt factory town on the edge of the Arctic Circle is richer than ancient Baghdad ever dreamed of being."

"So?"

Jake shrugged. "The local fat cats know they can't take it with them, but they're damned certain they want to keep it intact after they go. They don't want the government gobbling it up, and they don't want to risk the chance that it might go to the wrong relatives. This firm, our firm, makes sure that doesn't happen." Jake grinned. "And, when we perform our little magic, we keep a happy little slice for ourselves. Now that might not make for the high drama, I admit, but the size of the fees involved provides more than a little dignified excitement around here. As they say, Harry, someone has to do it. It's clean work, quiet, and the money's not half bad."

"Ah, the romance of probate." Harry laughed. "Why don't you jot down all this bullshit for a bar journal?"

"What for? As a swan song? The rule here, in case you've forgotten, is that all public writings must be cleared before submission for publication. This firm has a lock on the really big estate business in Detroit, my friend. If I put my probate philosophy in writing, the partners of this blue-blooded outfit would hire a socially acceptable hit man and I'd be history."

"Maybe," Harry shrugged. "Come on, one beer won't hurt."

"It's not the beer, Harry, it's the time needed to drink it. I don't have it. I'll take a raincheck."

After Harry left, Jake went back to staring out the window. The clouds had thickened, blotting out what was left of the sun, giving the scene even more of a cold, gray feeling.

Five years. No associate had ever been kept for more than five years with the law firm of Sperling Beekman. If a lawyer managed to last that long then a partnership was offered, or the door.

The final decision was up to the handful of senior partners who constituted the firm's management committee. They met, made their decision, rendered a verdict like a Roman emperor—thumbs up or thumbs down—and that was it. There was no appeal from that decision. It was as final as death.

Jake Martin was running out of time. Amos Sanders had hit the magic sixty-sixth birthday and was being forced into compulsory retirement, creating an opening for partner. But there were two other candidates besides himself for the vacancy.

Craig Dow, the rising star of the firm's litigation section, was actively campaigning, as was Cora Simpson. Dow, a four-year man, could be passed over. But Cora, like Jake, was in that fateful fifth year. If she lost, she too would have to leave.

Sperling, Beekman, Howe, Woods & Simon, known as Sperling Beekman by everyone, was one of Detroit's five major white-shoe firms. Six women already numbered among its forty partners, more than most of their competing law firms, so Cora's campaign for equality of feminine representation would have little or no practical effect. But Cora was from the University of Michigan, and that did worry Jake Martin. Sperling Beekman was known as a University of Michigan firm. Among the hundred-plus associates there were a few token members who, like Jake, were from the Ivy League, and a handful from other schools. But most of the partners, with a few exceptions, were University of Michigan people. And that was a definite plus for Cora.

Jake Martin was one of the few non-Michigan people ever to last the five years. But despite that he still felt like a stranger.

Swiveling away from the window, he picked up his notes. The trust language wasn't as difficult as he had led Harry Fowler to believe. And the work was almost done. It was just an excuse to keep from going home. Home was no longer like it used to be.

"Slow down, Eddie. We don't want to become our own customers, at least not yet. We're in no hurry. The lately departed will keep."

Eddie eased up on the station wagon's accelerator. The car's wipers beat a steady rhythm as they sped over the wet country road. The surrounding forest was thick with green pine, but the hardwood trees that managed life in the sandy loam were garbed in glorious autumnal reds and golds, radiant despite the rain.

"When we get there, Eddie, don't make an issue of it, but stay close to me, okay?"

Eddie glanced over at his employer. "Why?"

"I want a witness to everything that goes on."

Eddie's youthful face was pockmarked, a legacy from acne that had gone untreated. It bothered some people to work in a funeral home, but Eddie was grateful for the job. Any kind of steady employment was rare in the north, and he had found a strange satisfaction in the work.

"Do you think there's something fishy about the death? Murder, maybe?"

Harold Fleck smiled and shook his head. He valued Eddie and taught him everything he could about the funeral business. None of Fleck's children were interested in operating the only funeral home in Gladding, Michigan, the town that proclaimed itself to be the

4

"Heart of the North." Eddie, by default, had become a surrogate heir apparent, at least as far as the business was concerned.

"It isn't the death that bothers me, Eddie, it's the way they're handling the final arrangements."

"You sure it isn't murder?"

Fleck chuckled. "Quite the opposite, really. They've been trying to keep Gus Daren alive on the machines. It has something to do with his bank, I think, or maybe taxes. But whatever the reason, they sure as hell didn't want Daren to die."

"So what's the problem?"

"Slow down," Fleck said. "You'll see the entrance soon. It's just a small brass sign set in a big stone. Unless you're looking for it, it's easy to miss."

"I've seen it before."

Fleck raised an inquisitive eyebrow. "You've been here?"

Eddie shook his head. "I've driven by the entrance before. I've never been on the grounds, though I've seen the place from the lake. It looks like a log palace."

"It is a palace, log or not. I've been to Europe and I've never seen anything better." He pointed. "There it is."

Eddie swung the station wagon into the entrance and followed the winding road through the trees.

"They have a security station up a hundred yards or so. They know we're coming."

"You been here?"

Fleck nodded. "Once. I'm not exactly on the Darens' A list, but Mrs. Daren had me up here last year to discuss arrangements."

"A year ago?"

"Well, he'd had a second stroke. Should have finished him. I'm surprised he lasted this long. God, when I saw him last year he looked dead then. Mrs. Daren herself showed me his room. It was a fully equipped intensive care unit. He had enough machines and enough tubes running into him to launch a NASA rocket. As I figure it, he made it to sixty-eight. Not quite the Biblical seventy-year life span, but close. He was rich but it didn't do him much good, not at the end anyway. Money can buy a lot of things, Eddie, it can probably even buy some time, but nobody lives forever."

"What's she like?" Eddie asked.

Fleck smiled. "Ever see her?"

"Once, in town."

"What'd you think?"

Eddie shrugged. "Good-lookin'. But she's young."

"Good-looking hardly covers it, Eddie. She's out and out beautiful. Before she married Daren, she was a model. I'd guess she's only in her late thirties. Augustus Daren married only very beautiful women, and this was his fourth wife."

"She's rich now," Eddie said.

5

"Real rich," Fleck answered as the gate guard looked into their car, nodded, then waved them on.

"Jeez, the place looks like a golf course," Eddie said as the main house came into view, set off by an expanse of lush green lawn the size of a football field. "How the hell do they get grass like that to grow up here in this sand?"

"They imported the dirt and laid sod on top." Fleck answered. "Pull over there. That's the service drive. We're supposed to go in through the back entrance."

Beyond the house, Lake Bradford was calm. There was no wind, only the steady rain.

"We're not the only ones here," Eddie said, as he maneuvered into a spot between a battered sedan and a Mercedes. There were several other cars parked on the crushed gravel apron at the back of the house.

"Like I said, stay by me when we go in there."

"You told me that, but you never said why."

Fleck's face tightened into an inscrutable mask. It was his official funeral-home expression, worn like a dress uniform: digni-fied, but with a touch of sadness. "Mrs. Daren wants us to take the body and have it cremated tonight."

"But the crematorium ain't open on Sundays," Eddie said.

"It is now. I made arrangements. They'll be waiting for us."

"Is that legal?"

Fleck opened his door. "It is if she's done what I told her to do. That's Dr. Moran's car. I wanted him, as county medical examiner, here to certify the death. The county clerk should be here too so he can give me everything nice and official."

"Sounds pretty fishy to me," Eddie said, slowly climbing out of the car.

"That's why I want you along as a witness. It may all be legal, but it's still odd. I didn't ask why she wanted things done like this. I figure maybe she's one of those people who have a peculiar attitude toward death. There's a hell of a lot of them around, Eddie, and they're bad for business. But I suppose all this has something to do with probate. He had kids, grown kids. And there is one hell of a lot of money involved." He looked up at the sky as though the sheets of rain were a personal insult. "If any of this should end up in court, I want someone who can back up everything I say."

"You sure something illegal isn't going on here?"

"More or less. But if it is, I want to protect my license and reputation. So you make sure you're right at my elbow every minute we're in here."

Eddie ignored the rain as he opened the rear hatch of the station wagon and took out the canvas body bag. "How come we didn't use the hearse if we have to drive all the way over to the crematorium?"

6

"Mrs. Daren specifically asked, that's why. She thought the hearse might attract attention."

Eddie shook his head. "So what? Isn't she going to tell anybody he's dead?"

"Sure. But this is big news and I suppose she wants to do it in her own good time."

"So we throw the guy in the bag, take him a hundred miles and get him reduced to a couple of ounces of ashes and bones. It doesn't seem right."

"What do you mean?"

"This Daren was a big shot, right? He was a banker and famous. Now he's being sacked up and tossed out like garbage. He was somebody, you know. This just doesn't seem right."

Fleck allowed a small laugh, then quickly assumed his professional, sorrowful expression.

"From what I hear, Augustus J. Daren may have been no more than garbage, if you believe half the stories. Anyway, he's dead, so he can't care one way or the other what might happen to his remains."

As they approached, a maid opened the door.

"That still doesn't make it right," Eddie said quietly.

"Forget it. Just stay close."

Marie wasn't home when Jake got back to their apartment. He wasn't sure if what he felt was annoyance or relief. On the increasingly rare occasions when they found themselves alone together, they were both becoming more and more tense, like two strangers thrown together, both overly polite but both uncomfortable.

He put a frozen dinner in the microwave and popped open a can of beer. Flicking on the television, he listened for a moment as the commentator excitedly described the action of the two professional football teams on the field. The clock at the bottom of the screen showed less than a minute left to play. The Bears were on the five-yard line. He was interested until he heard the lopsided score. It was a blowout.

Jake turned off the television and idly went through the Sunday newspapers, but he found nothing of interest there. Having hardly noticed the dinner he'd just eaten, he tossed the empty plastic carton away and rinsed his plate.

Walking through the living room, he stopped and picked up the framed wedding photograph, vividly recalling that day when they had stood in front of the New York Federal Court, both of them grinning at the camera like two conspirators.

He was fresh from graduating from Columbia and she was a senior. The wedding had taken place in ten seconds at the dismal office of the New York City Clerk. They had been just one more couple in a moving line, shuffling through like the others, following a path of painted footsteps, being joined together in holy matrimony

7

quickly and impersonally in dingy, dour surroundings. But on that day their marriage was just as special to them as if it had been celebrated by an archbishop in an elegant cathedral. They had celebrated with beer and cold beef sandwiches at Pete's Tavern. Jake remembered being very happy then.

Marie looked so young in the photograph, giggling and bordering on chubby. Her full face, so fresh and eager, seemed alive with brimming good humor.

But she had changed.

Marie Chandler—she had kept her maiden name—had recently become a full partner in Brosner Whitley. Her short, jet-black hair was now worn regally long. Diet, plus membership in an expensive exercise club, had rendered her curvaceous form as sleek as a panther. Marie, who had gone about in jeans and sweaters, was always stunningly dressed now in Seventh Avenue's latest. And her humor, so wild and joyous, had become sharp and sardonic. While she was still eager, at least about her legal career, she was no longer innocently fresh. Marie, the girl from Michigan who had come to Columbia and who had persuaded him that their futures lay back in her native state, was not the same.

For her, perhaps the future did seem to be in Michigan. For himself, he wasn't quite so sure.

He looked at the photograph again. She had been merely pretty back then. At least he had thought she was. Now, five years later and at the age of thirty, everyone considered her a knockout, a sensational beauty.

Jake studied his own image in the photograph. He was thirty-eight now, but the Jake Martin of New York was little different from the Jake Martin of Detroit. Tall, thin, and even in the photo a touch awkward, he had a pleasant but unremarkable face, topped by light blond hair. But the hair was changing. It was beginning to thin at the top, and combing it over did little to cover the alarming retreat. Other than that, though, there was surprisingly little change in five years. He had been laughing when the picture was taken, a nice, full, hearty laugh. These days he seldom laughed like that.

At her insistence they had come to Detroit. They had found an affordable apartment in a stately, landmark building facing the river. In New York, such a place, with its eight high-ceilinged rooms and unobstructed view of the river, would have cost an unthinkable fortune. By New York standards they were living in royal splendor.

Money had only recently become a problem. Marie had to buy her partnership, taking out a $200,000 loan to do so. If he was offered a partnership at Sperling Beekman it would cost even more. Success had its price. If he made it, between the two of them they would end up owing more than half a million dollars.

But money was only a small problem. The marriage, if not dead, was dying, and they both knew it. If he got the partnership, then . . .

Jake cursed softly. Lately, he could think of nothing else, not even the problems between them. The quest for the partnership was like an obsession and seemed to blot out just about everything else. As he put the photograph back in its accustomed place, he released a sigh.

The apartment had a sun room, so-called, a glassed-in porch-like projection that looked out over the river. He took his beer and sat in the darkened room. Night had come, but clouds obscured the moon so that the river was discernible only in the reflection of lights from the Canadian shore.

Eating a frozen dinner in an empty apartment was not the bright and shining future he had imagined for himself. Like so many other Americans, he had envisioned a warm home, children, a loving wife, and a stable, successful career.

Children had been a cause of disagreement between them from the beginning. He wanted a family; she wanted to wait. And there was always one more reason to wait. It seemed to him that the more time passed, the more she wanted to put off starting a family. Now it wasn't even discussed. They slept in separate bedrooms. She said he snored. And their once robust sex life had dwindled away, a casualty of the immense pressure created by their two careers.

His income, now in six figures, would either skyrocket if he became a partner, or cease to exist if he wasn't selected. That was not his idea of a stable career. And if he was turned down for partner, he had no career potential in Detroit. Probate, unlike trial work, didn't lead to establishing a network of admiring opponents who might become possible employers. Even if he found something, he could never hope to come close to his present salary. If he went back to New York no big firm would be impressed by a lawyer who'd worked in Detroit for five years and had then been tossed out by a Midwestern law firm. And his age, thirty-eight, would be an additional liability. He was no longer a kid who could start easily at the bottom rung of a law firm.

And the prospect of being supported by his wife was intolerable.

He heard her come in the door.

"I'm in here," he called out.

Marie was outlined by the light coming from within the apartment. "What are you doing out there in the dark?"

"Contemplating the world and its woes. Have you eaten?"

"I ate at my parents'." She said it quickly, as if that ended the inquiry. Her parents, congenial when they had first married, seemed to have become chilly toward him, reflecting, apparently, their estimation of the change in the relationship between their daughter and himself.

9

"How are they?"

"Fine."

"I'm having a beer. Join me?"

"No, thanks. I have to review some files for tomorrow."

Once again, they both seemed reduced to an embarrassed silence, and then the telephone rang.

"I'll get it," she said, just a little bit too quickly.

He heard her in a brief conversation, then she called. "It's for you."

He smiled as she handed him the receiver.

"I'll be in my bedroom working," she said, without telling him who was on the line.

"Hello," he said.

"This is Donald Bellows. I'm sorry to have to call you at home, Jake; I hope I'm not taking you away from anything?"

"Not at all."

Bellows was one of the managing partners of Sperling Beekman, and head of the firm's probate and trust department. Seldom did he have anything to do with mere associates, instead chiefly devoting himself to attending to wealthy clients and the banks that managed their wealth.

"I just got home; I was at the office," he said, instantly regretting the statement, knowing he sounded like a schoolboy trying to make points with a teacher.

"That shows a good attitude, Jake." Although he was sixty-four years old, Bellows spoke in a soft, almost boyish voice. He looked much younger, a trim, tall man, as tall as Jake, with an office decorated by athletic trophies won in golf and tennis. Bellows seemed to be perpetually smiling, but his dark grey eyes were cold and stern, a feature that intimidated everyone, even his partners. He was the man to whom the other managing partners would turn when making the decision whether partnership should be offered to Jake Martin.

"What can I do for you, Mr. Bellows?"

"You probably haven't heard about it yet, but Augustus Daren has finally died. You might want to catch the eleven o'clock news. I suspect they'll do a short film review on his life."

"I'll watch it," he said, still wondering why Bellows was calling.

"This may sound unfeeling, since you worked so late today, but I wonder if you could come in early tomorrow?"

"Of course."

"Good. I want to put together a team to handle the Daren estate. You drew the will. It's possible that things might get a tad sticky, so I want the firm to be fully prepared." He paused and Jake could almost see those granite eyes. "A number of us," he continued, "have been impressed by your abilities, Jake. I would welcome your participation."

The gently spoken request had been a command, and they both knew it. "I'm honored to be asked," Jake responded.

"Good. We'll talk in the morning. I've been on the telephone with the widow. She is concerned that Daren's children may attack the will."

"Do you really think they might, Mr. Bellows?"

"Call me Donald, please. Yes, it's possible. Obviously this is all of great importance to the firm, Jake. We have handled virtually all of Daren's personal business, and we do represent Hanover Square, his bank, in a number of matters. His widow expressed full confidence in us, and we want to make absolutely sure we merit that confidence, don't we?"

"Of course."

Bellows chuckled. "Good. I'll see you in my office at seven o'clock. I even promise to provide coffee and doughnuts. This will just be a get-acquainted session mainly, an opportunity to explore some possibilities."

"I look forward to it."

"Good," Bellows said as he hung up.

Marie emerged from her bedroom. "What did Bellows want?"

He shrugged. "We're having a meeting in the morning. A client died."

"Who?"

"Augustus Daren."

"The banker?"

Jake nodded. "Yep. He's been on life-support for quite a while. It was no surprise."

"And Bellows wants you to handle it?"

"Part of it. He's putting together a team."

"This is your big break," she said.

He nodded slowly. "Maybe."

"They wouldn't assign you to something like this unless they trusted you completely."

She had changed into silk pajamas. He grinned. "Feel like celebrating? There's more beer."

"No thanks; I have work to do. Good luck tomorrow," she said, as she disappeared into her bedroom again and closed the door.

Once again the sense of emptiness seized him. He wanted her. If not as wife, then just as listener.

He sighed as he went to the kitchen. The nightly news wouldn't be on for another hour. He popped another beer, wishing he just had someone to talk to.

He put down *The New York Times* Sunday magazine and glanced over at her, admiring the full, sensuous curve of her hip and buttock. She lay on her side, propped up on a pillow, engrossed again in the entertainment section. She was as beautiful as she had been when he'd first seen her on the Broadway stage. The years had been kind, and the fresh blush of youth had been replaced by the more sensual enchantment of a robust and mature woman.

The beginnings of desire stirred as he looked at her smooth nakedness. They'd already made love several times, pleasurably long contests so enthusiastically energetic that both of them had ended up bathed in perspiration. Between bouts they had devoured the *Times* and the Detroit Sunday newspapers. He was amazed at his ability to experience a reawakening of even quiet desire. He would have touched her, but his fingers bore the usual newsprint smudges from the pages of the *Times*.

"Do you miss it?" he asked.

"What?" She turned, her blonde hair falling away from her handsome face.

"The stage."

She turned to lie on her back, exhibiting the legendary breasts that had caused so much publicity when she'd exposed them in *Summer Nights*, the play that had made her a star.

"Oh, once in a while I do. Especially when I read of a part that I think might be perfect for me."

"Why not go back?"

She laughed. "Why? I've had it all. I don't want to be one of those aging New York actresses who haunt revivals and draw nostalgic reviews more suited to ancient museum pieces than flesh and blood artists. I have a full and satisfying life. I'm married to a successful man; I'm still a celebrity of sorts, especially here in Detroit. There is absolutely nothing to gain by a triumphant return."

"Sir Alec—"

"My dear, that's quite different. Nature and playwrights have always been more kind to the male species. Men age better, get juicer parts. Women, God help us, wrinkle badly, then get only walk-ons as screeching caricatures of themselves. Better to quit at the top like Garbo than to play the city of Peoria, pitifully seeking that one last dismal round of applause."

He laughed. "You have the most marvelous voice. It should be bottled and sold like good wine."

"What a pretty image." She smiled and reached down, gently taking his flaccid penis in her fingers.

"You'll get the *Times* all over it," he said, chuckling.

Her eyes narrowed playfully. "If I do, darling, I'll lick it off."

"So much for protest."

"Are you exhausted?"

"Merely resting. Would you care to watch the news before you have your way with me?"

She pretended annoyance. "It'll only put off the inevitable."

"I have a few wagers on the football games. I'd like to see the scores." He reached and retrieved the remote control device from the night table, flickering on the television built high in the bedroom's far wall.

They watched through a commercial, then the local anchorwoman came on, looking grimly intent. "A new disarmament proposal, some tips on beating old man winter, a surprising outcome for our Lions, and a prominent Michigan man is dead. These and more stories to follow on your eleven o'clock Dateline News."

She lit a cigarette while the station ran commercials for a detergent and then a soft drink.

"If the Lions won today," he said, "I'll lose a bundle."

"I thought you were a loyal fan."

He smiled as a national news reporter told of possible developments on disarmament. "I am a fan, but not when money's concerned."

"You have all the money you could possibly use, why bet?"

"I like the excitement, the challenge. I like beating the guy I'm betting against."

"Harvey says you live for competition."

"A harsh judgment, but probably right."

The anchorwoman reappeared. Now she affected a sad, almost melancholy expression.

"One of the state's leading financiers has died," she said. "Today, Augustus J. Daren died at his northern estate in Eagle County. Daren, the chairman of the board of Hanover Square Bank, is credited with bringing a small merchant bank started by his father into national and international prominence. Under his steady hand, Detroit's Hanover Square has gained recognition as one of the world's leading financial institutions."

As she spoke old film clips rolled, showing Gus Daren meeting with the superpowers of the past, including President Eisenhower, under whom he had served as an advisor. Augustus Daren, as a young man, was thickly muscular and his granite features, even when smiling, appeared challenging.

"Daren's life was marked with controversy as well as success." Film clips of his marriages were run in quick succession, as the anchorwoman rattled on with some of the incidents of Daren's life. She spoke about some of the scandals that had been public as old clips showed his son and daughter; some happy clips, and some in connection with those scandals. "Mr. Daren's wife was with him today when he passed away." A still photograph of the lovely Elizabeth Daren came on the screen, followed by an early photo of Daren taken at the peak of his powers.

"Augustus J. Daren, dead today from the residuals of a stroke, at age sixty-eight. Funeral preparations are incomplete."

He flicked off the television.

"Well, that is news, isn't it?" she said. "How will that affect you?"

He seemed lost in thought; then he spoke. "It's odd she didn't call me." Staring at the now empty screen he spoke quietly, as if thinking aloud. "I've been president of Hanover Square in name only. Gus Daren still ran the bank even after his first stroke. I have plans, big plans, but he would never let me off his leash. Even after the second stroke that turned him into a vegetable, I was still powerless. Elizabeth ran the place in his name." He paused, looked over at her, then said softly. "Things will be different now."

He swung his short muscular legs over the side of the bed and stood up. As he stretched she looked on in admiration. His hair had silvered elegantly, and with age his features had taken on a becoming ruggedness. Fully clothed he had the kind of thick physique that made him appear rotund, but naked his surprisingly athletic body was still that of a younger man.

"Some brandy?" he asked.

"Celebration or commiseration?"

He walked to the sideboard and poured healthy portions of Rémy into Baccarat glasses. The liquid reminded him of red-tinted gold. He returned and handed her a glass.

"My French ancestors began as soldiers," he said, holding up the glass and examining it in the light from one of his lamps. "As was the custom in those days, when faced with the enemy the officers on both sides came forward and drank a toast to each other before the battle began."

"How civilized."

"You bet." He grinned, raising his glass in an exaggerated salute. "I am Claude Louis deSalle, of noble French ancestry, and, thanks to my own celebrated and devious talent, president and chief executive officer of Hanover Square Bank."

"I think we've met."

He raised an eyebrow. "Don't disturb me. I'm in the process of making a toast."

"Please go on."

"Elizabeth Daren, now widow of Augustus Daren, up until this moment has held, by a mere whisker, the effective control of Hanover Square."

"Harvey calls her the Spider Woman."

"We all do. Now, to those of us who know and love her, she'll be the Black Widow. And it is to her that I raise my glass."

"A battle toast?"

He took the brandy in one swift gulp. "Absolutely."

She giggled. "God, look at you, Claude, you're as hard as a rock. Harvey was right. Competition is the thing that turns you on."

"Speaking of Harvey, when does he get back?"

"Tonight. He drops off his horrid children with their horrid mother in horrid Palm Springs and flies back. In the company jet, of course, thanks to you."

He smiled. "He is my vice president and one of my dearest friends. I always look out for his welfare."

"Such kindness." She sat up. "Well, you obviously have a lot on your mind and I know better than to get between a boy and his toy, so I'm going to leave. Besides, I think I'd better be there when Harvey gets home. I'll leave you to your thoughts, Claude, no matter how Machiavellian they might be."

Claude Louis deSalle was grateful she was leaving. Augustus Daren was dead, and there was much to do. Often, the battle belonged to the swift.

2

"**W**hat the hell do you want, Gussie? Do you realize what time it is here in London?" His voice was thick with sleep and his tone was angry.

She spoke with exaggerated sweetness. "Oh dear. Did I wake you, Chip?"

"Jesus! I haven't heard from you in years and you call in the goddamn middle of the goddamned night. Are you drunk?"

"Getting there. It's not even midnight here in Florida. As they say, the night's still young."

"You are drunk."

"Not yet, Chip, but I'm working on it. I just got a call from DeDe Williams. You remember DeDe."

She was answered by a disgusted sigh. "I haven't seen that pretentious bitch in twenty years. She was your friend, not mine. What could I possibly care about DeDe Williams? Gussie, if you're not drunk you must have gone around the bend. I always said the booze would finally pickle your brain."

She chuckled. "Is that what you always said? How charming, Chip. How supportive. Have you forgotten, my darling half-brother, that it was you who introduced me to demon rum, among other things?"

"You never needed a guide to any kind of depravity, Gussie, you could always find your own way very nicely. Now tell me what you want or I'm going to hang up."

"Father is dead."

"What!"

"That's why DeDe called me. It's on television back in Michigan. She said they had film clips and everything. They showed you and me, as well as good old Wife Number Four."

"When did he die?" His tone now was sharp with interest.

"Today, apparently. He's really been dead for a year, but I suppose even the machines finally got tired of circulating what blood he had left. Anyway, he's gone."

"Has anyone besides DeDe called?"

"Like who? The grieving widow? No. I suppose I should hear something from her or her lawyers tomorrow, as should you."

"Was there anything said about funeral arrangements?"

"DeDe said they were incomplete. Considering the new widow knew this was coming for a year, you'd think old Number Four would have had something planned."

"She has something planned, you can count on it. Why don't you call her?"

She snorted. "Me? I can't abide the woman. She knows it. I stopped by a year ago to visit dear old Dad, right after the big stroke. God, he looked terrible then, like a wizened old doll. The only things working were the machines they had him hooked to. Quite repulsive, really. Chillingly polite, that was how she was, but I thought she might suddenly hiss at me the way cats do. If I don't hear, I'll have my lawyers telephone father's lawyers in the morning."

"Call me when you find out."

"Call you? What am I, your social secretary? Call yourself, Chip."

"I'll make arrangements to fly in tomorrow."

"What for? A memorial service? You couldn't stand him, Chip. Nor could I. So why should we be hypocrites now?"

"Is that why you're drinking?"

She paused. "Whatever happened, he was my father, and yours."

"This is no time to get maudlin, Gussie. As far as I'm concerned this is strictly a business matter."

"We're both rich now; he saw to that. So we become a bit richer, so what?"

"Before you get too sentimental, Gussie, let me remind you that he set up those trust funds for us because he had to. It was all part of the divorce settlements with your mother and with mine. Paternal love didn't have a damn thing to do with it."

"But the will? If that was true, why would he leave us anything at all?"

He snorted. "Who the hell knows? I never could figure him out. Maybe he did it so he'd look good publicly, or maybe it was his way of ensuring we wouldn't contest his will. It doesn't matter."

"I don't know, Chip. Maybe he loved us after all?"

He laughed. "If he did, he had a funny way of showing it. I don't think he could stand us. Remember how if either of us had a problem or got into a scrape he'd throw an army of lawyers and gobs of money at us, but that was all. He never got involved personally.

He was only interested in keeping the family name out of the muck. Anyway, his money's not important. The big thing is that between the two of us we'll have a good chunk of the bank's stock. We can easily end up controlling Hanover Square."

"So what?"

His tone was suddenly sharp. "If we got control of the bank, Gussie, we might end up ruling the financial world, just as father tried to do."

"Well, well, well. Despite everything, you're Daddy's boy after all, aren't you?"

"Get off it, Gussie; you like power as much as anyone. Hell, if we had control of the bank, you could dominate that Palm Beach crowd of yours like a goddamned empress. Everyone bows to the person who wears the crown. You'd love it."

"And what about the grieving widow?"

"According to the will, she gets a third of everything, but that's it. We could use our stock to control the bank. After that, I don't give a damn what she does."

She paused again, then spoke. "Chip, suppose he changed the will?"

"What?"

"He's been in that woman's control for years. He might have changed it."

"How could he? Jesus, he's been on machines for a year. Before that, the first stroke left him gaga. If he changed it, the damn thing would never stand up in a court of law. She wouldn't have the guts to try and convince anyone the old fart was able to handle his own affairs. No, there's no chance of that."

"It was just a thought."

"I'll fly back to New York. We should set up a meeting, you and me and our lawyers. We have to be together on this, Gussie, or it won't work."

"I don't know, Chip. We've never been able to tolerate each other for long. We might as well be realists."

"There is far too much at stake here to let personal feelings get in the way."

"Chip, don't you feel anything about him?"

He paused, then spoke in a quieter tone. "What's to feel? He was a stranger to me. I have no memories of joyous outings or fishing trips, or anything like that. Do you?"

"He was busy, Chip."

"That's the booze talking, Gussie. If you want to weave some drunken fantasy, that's up to you. I prefer to deal in reality. I'll contact you when I get to New York," he said, breaking the overseas connection.

She replaced the telephone receiver and picked up her drink.

17

Chip was probably right. But perhaps, in his own way, their father might have loved them a little. She hoped he had.

She was surprised as involuntary tears suddenly began to slide silently down her cheeks.

Marie was wrong about Jake's big break.

Donald Bellows had also invited Craig Dow and Cora Simpson to the early morning meeting. The three rivals for the partnership vacancy were each equally surprised, but somehow they managed to conceal it, and greeted one another with a confidence and ease that none actually felt.

Bellows, in shirt sleeves, conducted the meeting in a casual manner, but it was a manner that left no doubt as to who was in charge. Bellows would supervise everything, but Jake Martin was designated to run the day-to-day efforts of the legal team assembled to probate Augustus Daren's will.

While the rivals paid strict attention to Bellows, they were painfully aware of each other.

Craig Dow, as always, looked as if he had just stepped out of a Brooks Brothers ad—immaculately dressed, every dark brown hair in place, with a jutting cleft chin more suited to a male model than to a trial lawyer. Only a nervous pumping of one Gucci-clad foot gave a clue that Dow might not be quite as supremely confident as he otherwise appeared.

Cora Simpson took notes as Bellows spoke. A slender, intense girl, Cora was one of the firm's tax specialists. She always demonstrated a quick intelligence but seemed interested only in legal matters. She was blonde and quite pretty, but her abrupt manner and sometimes sharp tongue chilled any thoughts the male members of the firm might have entertained about a possible romance. Cora was all business.

Jake hoped his rising anxiety wasn't apparent. Teaming the three candidates together seemed to him like an echo of the Roman arena when poor slaves were given weapons and then pushed out to fight for the amusement of the crowd. Like the slaves, each of the three would now be forced to excel, to be, when the contest ended, the champion. Before, he had weighed the merits of his two opponents in an abstract way, since each of them performed different tasks in different departments. Now he would have to measure their strengths and weaknesses in relationship to his own. Both of his opponents seemed suddenly much more formidable. Jake would be forced to think of ways to defeat them. He knew they would be thinking the same thing.

Whoever thought up the idea of putting them together certainly had a Roman's sense of cruelty.

Bellows, surprisingly, assigned to Jake the duty of interviewing potential witnesses, usually the work of a litigation lawyer. Craig

Dow began a mild protest, then quickly abandoned the effort under Bellows' stern gaze. Dow was assigned the task of preparing everything necessary to filing the will and to developing tactical eventuality plans in case of legal attack by Daren's grown children, or by anyone else. Cora was to review the tax consequences of a will contest and to prepare case law research to establish the legality of Daren's will. As Bellows described what he wanted done she took notes fast and furiously.

The tray piled with doughnuts and rolls went uneaten except by Bellows, who munched casually on a jelly roll. None of the other three had much of an appetite. Even the coffee went untouched. Each of them realized that the estate of Augustus J. Daren had been selected as some sort of testing ground. It was clear that they would be measured against each other, that each individual performance would be scrutinized, then judged. And all three were painfully aware there could only be one winner.

Bellows told them they could recruit extra help within the firm if needed, but all "press gang" selections had to be cleared through him first. Section heads were sensitive about incursions into their territory and staff.

Bellows dismissed them but asked Jake to remain.

"Well," Bellows asked after the other two left, "what do you think?"

Jake was cautious, taking time in framing an answer, knowing that now even a casual question might be a subtle test of his partnership potential. A petty response or an unfair denigration could even be a fatal mark against him.

"Cora's a good choice. She knows tax law. She has a quick mind and she works as though the future of the world depended on each case assigned to her."

Bellows nodded. "Perhaps somewhat too intense. I know her family: fine people, quite wealthy. Cora doesn't have to work, you know, but I've always thought she's been trying to prove something. Interesting girl. What do you think of Craig Dow?"

"I only know him casually. We've never really worked together before. He has a good reputation in litigation, so I'm told. Seems capable."

Bellows chuckled. "That's putting it mildly. He's burning up the track in litigation. Born to the courtroom. Eventually I think he'll head up that section. Very promising young man, indeed. If this does end up in court, Craig's skills as a trial lawyer will come in very handy."

Jake wondered if Donald Bellows knew Dow's family too, or what other connections his rivals might have. He wondered if he really had any chance at all. He was beginning to feel even more like an outsider.

Bellows got up and walked Jake to the door.

19

Jake was surprised when Bellows put his arm around his shoulders, like a coach sending a favorite player into the big game.

"This is a good beginning, Jake. No matter what happens, this should prove to be an interesting little adventure. By the way, I called Elizabeth Daren. You can start with her. She expects you up at Raven's Nest this afternoon. I hope that's not inconvenient?"

Jake was surprised, but he had nothing pressing scheduled. "It's no problem."

As usual, Bellows' ready smile was there.

"Good. Thanks for your help."

Jake Martin thought that he saw genuine interest in the respected senior partner's eyes—eyes that had always seemed cold and distant in the past.

Jake decided to take another look at the tape before he headed up north.

He hadn't seen it for over a year and he decided to make sure it was as he'd remembered it. He picked up the telephone and dialed the in-house number for the communications center.

"This is Jake Martin. I'd like to look at a tape made in connection with the execution of the will of Augustus Daren. It was filmed on June 18, 1989. Will that be a problem?" He was assured that the tape would be located and ready in five minutes. "Fine. I'll be right down."

Jake vividly recalled his only trip to Daren's palatial northern estate. He had drawn the new provisions in the will on instructions from Donald Bellows. When the will had been ready for execution Bellows was in Europe, and he had designated Jake to do the job. Jake had felt the assignment to be a significant indication of his growing importance in the firm; he had been thrilled at the prospect of meeting one of the world's most influential bankers.

He remembered he had wanted to make a good impression. Afterwards he wasn't sure that he had. The taping session had been brief and businesslike. Augustus Daren, despite his physical problems, had been a powerful presence, and his wife, so startlingly beautiful, had been cool and regal. Jake had felt awkward and inept and he wondered at the time if it had showed.

Jake made his way to the firm's fully equipped television room. The technician who awaited him was a new hire, replacing Roger Johnson, an outgoing young man who'd originally set up the communications center. Jake had heard Roger had been fired for using the firm's equipment to copy and sell pornographic tapes. But things like that were kept extremely quiet in the halls of Sperling Beekman, so no one knew if the gossip was true or not.

The new man was also very young, had a bad case of acne and seemed nervous.

Videotape depositions of witnesses—especially experts such as

20

doctors and engineers—with both sides firing questions, had become standard evidence in court. They were often offered in place of flesh-and-blood testimony as lawyers and judges strove to find methods to hurry the cumbersome litigation process.

These innovations had proved surprisingly effective. It was a television age and juries seemed perhaps even more fascinated by witnesses up on the screen than by those who appeared in person. Firms specializing in negligence cases produced documentary films showing a day in the life of their crippled or maimed client. Lawyers were discovering new uses for video presentations almost daily. Private companies offered such filming services, but most large firms had created a video section for filming and preserving testimony. And Sperling Beekman had one of the best.

A huge video screen crackled with electronic static as Jake took a seat in the screening room.

"Find it?" Jake asked.

The young man nodded. "Have it ready in a minute."

Jake remembered that Bellows had arranged for a local firm in the north to do the taping, since their own staff was busy at something else. Although the tape wasn't of the usual Sperling Beekman quality, it did the trick.

"Go ahead," he said to the technician.

Jake was amused when the tape began. He had almost forgotten how inept it had been. It opened like a porno movie, complete with pulsating jazz music and a rather voluptuous drawing of a statue of Justice. The video company's name and address appeared in garish red letters directly across Justice's stomach. It occurred to Jake that maybe the company had begun producing X-rated work and had then perhaps branched out into serving the needs of northern lawyers.

Then the logo dissolved and the camera fixed on the imposing face of Augustus J. Daren. Instantly recognizable, he was seated behind a desk in his large library. Daren, a six-footer, was heavy, but there was a sense of muscular power beneath the puffy body. His craggy face was drawn, but he glared at the camera as if staring down an unwanted intruder. His thick, dark hair was beginning to turn a dusty grey, but his belligerent eyes burned with an alert youthfulness.

Daren had been a powerful, dominating presence, and Jake recalled how impressed he had been. Jake's recorded, off-camera voice crackled just a little too loudly on the tape.

"We are here to witness the signing by Mr. Augustus J. Daren of his last will and testament. This tape is being made at Mr. Daren's home known as Raven's Nest, Eagle County, Michigan, this eighteenth day of June 1989. Present are Mr. Daren, his doctor, Milo Faraday, his secretary, Miss Rhonda Janus, and his wife, Elizabeth

21

Daren. I am D. Jacob Martin, of the law firm of Sperling, Beekman, Howe, Woods and Simon."

As Jake made his brief introduction, Daren had continued to glare at the camera with increased and ill-disguised irritation.

Still off camera, Jake asked, "You are Augustus J. Daren?"

The look of disdain became even more pronounced.

"I am." His voice was strong, but the words were spoken somewhat awkwardly.

"And what is today's date, Mr. Daren?"

Daren's hawk eyes narrowed. "You just got through saying it, Mr. Martin." Daren snapped out the words, a particle of spittle flying from the left side of his mouth. "It's June 18th, 1989."

"And what is the purpose of our being here?"

Daren's left arm dangled loosely and was held in his lap. His right hand rested upon a document on the desk before him, his fingers beating an erratic staccato upon its pages.

"We are here so I can sign my new will and have it witnessed." He spoke slowly and distinctly, although there was a slight slurring at the ending of some of his words.

"The will was drafted at your direction, is that correct?"

Daren nodded, then spoke. "Yes."

Jake vividly recalled the room, the lights and the people.

"Briefly, Mr. Daren, can you describe the changes you have directed be made?"

August Daren nodded. The irritation seemed to fade from his bulldog features. He spoke very slowly. It was evident that the left side of his mouth was failing to function properly, but his voice remained surprisingly strong.

"This will is almost the same as my previous one. Everyone gets exactly the same shares." He seemed slightly embarrassed by a bit of spittle, but continued. "The main change is in the control of my shares in Hanover Square Bank." He looked directly into the camera, and added, "My bank."

He continued. "I have vested effective voting control of the bank stock in my wife, Elizabeth. I have determined that to split that voting power could have a disastrous effect on the bank. This change ensures that after my death Elizabeth will have sole control. After she dies, the power to vote the stock will pass to the trustee set out in the will. My main concern is to preserve the bank. And that is the purpose of the changes in my new will."

He looked back at the document. "I've added a few small gifts to individuals," he said, and then proceeded to read them. When he was through he wiped the back of his right hand quickly across the wetness that had formed at the left side of his mouth.

Now it was Jake's turn. "You are left-handed, is that correct?"

Daren nodded. "Yes."

"Can you sign with your left hand?"

Daren slowly shook his head. His eyes were defiant. "I suffered a stroke a few months ago. I have no effective use of the left side of my body. Since the stroke, I have signed everything with my right hand."

"Is your signature different?"

Daren tried to smile, but only the right side of his mouth responded. "Yes. Quite different. It's awkward to do, and it looks just as awkward."

"Whom have you selected as witnesses to this, your last will and testament?"

Daren smirked. "I didn't select them, Mr. Martin, your firm did. My witnesses will be my personal physician, Dr. Milo Faraday, and my secretary, Ronny Janus."

"By Ronny Janus, you mean your personal secretary, Rhonda Janus?"

"Of course," Daren snapped.

"Have you read the will, the document in front of you?"

Daren attempted another smile. "Of course. I didn't get to where I am by blind trust in people, especially lawyers."

Jake remembered that he'd been flustered by that reply, but he had managed to regain himself quickly. His voice continued on the tape. "Do the provisions in the will reflect your desires?"

Daren nodded. "They do."

"Are you doing this of your own free will?"

Daren's eyes narrowed just slightly. "Yes. And it's the obvious purpose of this tape to demonstrate visually that this is exactly my intention." Once again he tried a smile. "And that I'm still in possession of all my marbles."

"Will the witnesses please move up to the desk?" Jake's voice sounded unsure, as though there were a question as to whether or not he'd be obeyed. He wished now that he could have been more assertive.

The camera operator rather clumsily opened the telephoto lens to give the illusion that the camera moved back. At bachelor parties for Sperling Beekman lawyers it had become a tradition to show the absolutely worst stag films obtainable, the cruder the better. Jake recognized a similar amateurish technique in the tape he was watching.

Dr. Faraday, a stout, sandy-haired man, moved into the picture, taking a place directly to Daren's left. Jake remembered that Faraday had seemed nervous that day, although he didn't come across that way on camera.

Rhonda Janus stepped to Daren's other side.

Unlike the doctor, she had been completely relaxed. She was a curvaceous redhead in her mid-forties, and flirtatious too. Jake remembered a certain air of cheerful toughness about her, more like a barmaid than the personal secretary to a very powerful and very rich man. On the tape she looked completely at ease.

"All right," Jake spoke on the tape, "please sign the will where indicated, Mr. Daren."

With some effort, Daren took the pen from the desk with his right hand and laboriously signed the document. He looked up when he had finished.

"Do you publish and declare this to be your last will and testament?" Jake's voice asked.

Daren nodded. "Yes, I do."

"Doctor, would you please sign as a witness, where it's indicated."

Dr. Faraday slid the will toward him and quickly signed.

"Now, Miss Janus."

She smiled, patted Daren's shoulder affectionately, then took the document from the doctor. She signed with a flourish, then looked up, smiling.

"Thank you," Jake said on the tape, again sounding overly loud. "This concludes the signing of the last will and testament of Augustus J. Daren." He repeated the date.

Daren glowered at the camera, then his austere image was dissolved and replaced by the video company's suggestive logo and the canned music. Jake turned to the technician as the tape was rewound and politely thanked him, then sat back in front of the empty screen.

Despite the primitive taping, it was dynamite.

No one who viewed this tape could ever doubt Daren's competency. Although Jake was now self-critical about his indeciveness on the tape, getting Daren to snap out clear, concise reasons as to why his signature would look different had worked out more than effectively. Augustus J. Daren had been lucid and clear and obviously in possession of his faculties.

"Are there copies of that tape?" Jake asked.

"You know the policy of Sperling Beekman," the technician said, his tone reflecting his unspoken disagreement with that policy. "The firm makes a copy of everything."

"Thanks," Jake said, getting up.

"Anytime, Mr. Martin. That's what I'm here for."

Jake was elated. If there was going to be a contest, that little tape would win it. It was having four aces in the hole.

For the first time in a long time, he began to feel just a little bit better.

Other banks in Detroit had raised magnificent modern office towers as tangible monuments to their wealth and power.

Hanover Square Bank, like its competitors, had also built a mirrored glass and steel skyscraper, but the enormous structure

24

served merely as an adjunct to the bank's original and ancient headquarters, a faithful reproduction of a Greek temple that nestled at the base of the newer building.

Gleaming white and carefully preserved like a museum piece, it no longer served as a place where customers could deposit and withdraw funds—that function had long ago been transferred to the new building. Now the splendid Greek copy served solely as the offices for the bank's top-echelon executives.

Located at the heart of a few busy and prosperous blocks in the center of the city's otherwise depressed downtown area, Detroit's financial district controlled enormous fortunes that touched lives and businesses all over the world.

But Detroit, perhaps more than any other American city, was a study in contrasts. The financial district, crowded and lively during the day, was starkly deserted at night; its empty streets were darkly desolate and threatening. During the work day, though, the area pulsated with business and busy people, and Hanover Square's Greek temple served as its hub.

Claude deSalle had been given the huge and elegant president's office in the equally elegant building when he'd been promoted to that position. But despite the ornate trappings of office, the real power had remained in the hands of Augustus Daren, even though he had given up the title of president. He had continued to set policy and make every major decision that would affect Hanover Square.

Daren had retained the title of chairman of the board, and his ownership of fifty-one percent had insured that he maintain control over who sat on the board. Claude deSalle had the salary and the office, but the real authority had remained in the steel grip of Augustus Daren. After the first stroke Daren had designated his wife to serve as his unofficial representative. And after the second, she had continued to exercise the power of his office.

But all that would soon change.

As he entered the bank, Claude deSalle feigned sadness. The truth was that he had to keep from whistling.

The interior of the bank's headquarters was a showplace, a symphony of white marble often pictured in architectural magazines. It had been beautiful when it served as a bank and, with the help of skilled decorators and stonemasons, it was even more impressive as an open, lofty office building, the kind of place where people automatically talked in whispers.

The huge oil painting of Augustus Daren that hung at the entrance had been draped in black silk. It was the only tangible mark of mourning and deSalle thought it appropriately tasteful. He had always considered it an ugly painting and, as soon as it seemed reasonable, he planned to have it removed.

His secretary made some pious murmurings about Daren's death and deSalle responded in kind, despite his inner elation.

As he surveyed his office he felt, for the first time, a real sense of ownership.

"Get me Mrs. Daren," he said to his secretary. "She's at Raven's Nest, I believe."

Claude deSalle sat behind the big mahogany desk. Like the other furniture, it had been Daren's. The office had been outfitted in the mode of a Victorian men's club, with velvet drapes, Persian rugs and Tiffany lamps. It clashed with the clean Greek lines of the building, but Daren had been overtly proud of his choices in decorating.

On that basis, deSalle had not dared change anything, even after Daren's crippling stroke. Patience was a habit he had mastered early in life; it had always served him well. He could wait a little longer and then redo it entirely. Just as he would refashion the bank's plans and policies. His idea for future expansion had been thwarted before. But now everything was possible. He felt wonderful.

He could hear his secretary working her way through Elizabeth Daren's telephone defenses. After Daren's second stroke, Elizabeth had assumed her husband's power, although legally she had had no right to do so. But the majority of the board's members were Daren loyalists, and any challenge to her illegal seizure of control could have cost someone his job if unsuccessful.

So Claude deSalle had smiled and had gone along without protest. It had only been a matter of time, and now that time had come.

For the sake of appearances, he would go easy on her for a while. Daren's fifty-one percent of ownership would now be split up into three parts. Daren had once told him what the will provided. Elizabeth would get a third, the two Daren children a third, and Daren's charitable foundation the remaining third.

The two children were usually at odds, and he had heard both of them speak of Elizabeth in terms that left no doubt as to their disdain for Daren's fourth wife. The fifty-one percent would be fragmented, and he planned to weld together a majority quickly and take the power that had so long been denied him.

Hanover Square, originally instituted as an ethnic bank for Detroit's German settlers, had quietly grown into a worldwide force and its horizons were unlimited. As were the horizons of the man who would direct its destiny.

Claude deSalle's hour had come.

His secretary told him Elizabeth Daren was on the line.

"Good morning, Elizabeth," he said quietly. "I'm so sorry to hear about Augustus. All of us here at the bank feel a sense of profound loss."

For a moment he wondered if she were actually on the line. There was no immediate reply, then she spoke.

26

"Claude, he's been dead for all practical purposes for a year. If anything, it was the machines that died." Her tone was brisk, direct. "I appreciate the thought, but under the circumstances, I think we can dispense with the usual condolences."

"Still, it has to be saddening for you. What have you decided about a funeral?"

"Gus didn't want anything like that," she replied. "I've followed his instructions to the letter. He wanted instant cremation so that his children couldn't use a funeral as a vehicle to make trouble. That's done. But I suppose if we don't hold some kind of memorial it wouldn't look right."

"Perhaps Christ Church?"

"That would be sheer hypocrisy, given how Gus felt about religion. Anyway, his body's been cremated and the ashes scattered, so there's no call for a formal ceremony."

"I could set up something at Ford Auditorium, a noontime memorial with eulogies. The bank people, ours and the rest of the banking community, would fill the place."

She paused again, then spoke in a softer tone. "Fine, Claude; I think that would work. Nothing fancy, just a few politicians to say nice things, and perhaps you."

"Of course."

"Set it up in a week or two."

"Certainly, Elizabeth. Anything I can do to help, I will."

"You might as well set up a meeting of the board of directors too."

"Well, the next meeting is scheduled in November. I think whatever needs to be done can wait until then."

"No."

The single word was spoken with complete authority. "I want it scheduled as soon as possible, by this Friday at the very latest."

He was about to snap out an answer, but he refrained. Sharp answers could wait until he had the votes. "Why would you want a meeting?" he asked.

"To fill Gus's vacancy as chairman of the board."

"Elizabeth, that sort of thing will keep."

"Not this time."

He wondered if she meant that he should assume the office. If she did, he would be more than happy to cooperate. It would mean his plan to take over would be hurried along.

"Who did you have in mind for chairman?"

"Me," she said.

This time he had to pause. Then he composed himself and spoke with a calmness he didn't feel. "Elizabeth, this is a very trying time for you, of course, but these things shouldn't be rushed. Let's put that on the back burner for a while."

"No. I want this done, and I want it done now."

He had hoped to avoid a confrontation, and he sought now to soften what he was about to say. "My dear, this has been a hell of a year for us all. Gus, God rest him, was in a kind of limbo and we all made do, as it were, until things were resolved. But to be frank, Elizabeth, you have no legal standing in the affairs of the bank. I know you were acting for Gus, and that you've attended all the board meetings and the executive committee meetings, but you're not even a member of the board. You've certainly acquired the knowledge and experience to serve as a board member, and I think that can be arranged in time, of course, but not until everything is probated. It's really up to the lawyers, Elizabeth."

"Oh?"

He sighed audibly to indicate his distress at having to tell her the facts of her situation.

"Gus owned fifty-one percent of the bank, Elizabeth, but I understand that's divided among you, his children and his foundation. When it's all probated you will be one of our largest stockholders, and a most valued one, but you will have only a seventeen percent interest. That's not quite enough to name a chairman, as I'm sure you'll agree."

"Where did you get your information?" she asked without any noticeable hostility.

"To be candid, Gus told me what was in his will—in a general way, of course. It's none of my business personally, Elizabeth, but obviously the bank's future would be affected by how he divided up ownership. We had that discussion—oh, what?—two years ago. Anyway, the last time he was here."

"He changed that will," she said simply, matter-of-factly.

He managed to control his breathing and the tone of his voice. "Oh? When?"

"It will be a matter of record in a day or two, so there's no reason you shouldn't know. Gus made the change after the first stroke. He was afraid of what might happen to the bank if the voting power was divided."

"What was changed?" He swallowed. "That is, if you don't mind telling me."

"The division remains as before," she said, "but the stock is vested in a trust and I have been given all voting rights."

"In other words, Elizabeth, as a practical matter, you own fifty-one per cent of Hanover Square?"

"Precisely. It's important to me that I be named chairman as soon as possible. And, as you say, I now have the experience and knowledge to handle the job. Do you have any questions?"

Claude deSalle rubbed his forehead with his free hand. It was as though he had been plunged into a waking nightmare. But somehow he concealed his distress.

"I'll do what I can, Elizabeth, but we will need a quorum. The

28

board members are scattered around, and some of them are traveling. I'll do what I can."

"If there's a problem, call me at once."

He inhaled. "Of course."

"I do appreciate your help, Claude. It won't be forgotten." She was finished, the conversation was over.

He got up, and immediately noticed that his legs felt rubbery. He walked to his windows that looked out on Detroit's narrow Shelby Street. People hurried by below and everything looked so completely normal. But he couldn't shake the intense feeling that he was in a frightening dream.

Claude deSalle couldn't remember when he had last cried; it surely had been some time in childhood. But now he felt on the verge of tears. It seemed so cruel. For a brief moment he had had a tantalizing smell of the power he lusted for, but now it appeared that the dream had been suddenly and summarily jerked away.

Elizabeth Daren had no right to take the prize away from him now. He had earned everything he had. Some of it had come hard, some had come easy, but he had made all of it happen.

He wiped his eyes and felt a surge of grim determination. He would not be denied, not when he had come so close. He would do something, he would make something happen.

Jake returned from viewing the video. Mr. Bellows had scheduled him to drive up north and talk to Mrs. Daren as part of the case preparation. Knowing it was a long drive, he was anxious to get started.

His secretary, taking a message as he approached, looked up. "It's your wife, Mr. Martin," she said.

"Put her through."

Marie seldom telephoned him at work anymore, at least not for something as simple as mere conversation.

Jake went into his office and picked up his phone. He waited until he heard the electronic click.

"Hi, Marie," he said. "What's up?"

"Do you have plans for dinner tonight?"

Her tone wasn't cold, but it wasn't warm either. Just professional.

"I was going to call you," he said. "I have to drive up north and talk to Mrs. Daren. But I can always call and make another appointment."

"That won't be necessary. When will you get back?"

"Late tonight, or tomorrow if I have to stay over. It's quite a hike."

"We can have dinner tomorrow night then. Could you meet me tomorrow at Joe Muer's, about seven?"

"Sure. What's up?"

"I think we need to talk." This time he detected a definite coolness. "Will seven tomorrow be convenient?"

"No problem. What's the subject up for discussion?"

"I'd prefer to tell you that when I see you." She paused, then continued. "What happened this morning?"

"You mean about the Daren estate?"

"Of course."

He looked out at the river as he spoke. "The meeting was just a general thing. Bellows picked a team to handle the estate. I think he really anticipates trouble."

"And you don't?"

"Maybe. But whatever happens we can handle it."

"Who's in charge of the team?" Now she sounded genuinely interested.

"Bellows, but I'm sort of second in command."

"There," she said with enthusiasm, "I told you you'd have no trouble making partner. He wouldn't have done that, Jake, unless the choice had already been decided."

He chuckled. "Not quite. The two other members of the team are also candidates for the vacancy. I think we're all about to be tested. The one who looks best wins."

"You've always been a pessimist," she snapped.

"Maybe. Now, so I won't conjure up all kinds of imagined problems, tell me what this dinner is all about."

"We'll talk tomorrow," she said, and then abruptly hung up.

He replaced the telephone receiver and absently watched an old ore freighter on the river glide beneath the Ambassador Bridge.

At first he had thought their problems had arisen because they were both consumed with advancing their careers. But even as busy as they both were, he now detected a distancing beyond the pressures of work. It was something that eventually would have to be faced. Maybe the time was now. Maybe talking it out would help.

3

It was a long drive. Gladding, near the tip of Michigan's lower peninsula where the inland sea of Lake Michigan emptied into the equally awesome Lake Huron, was almost three hundred miles north of Detroit.

The sparse traffic going north on I-75 flowed swiftly. Huge freight-carrying trucks set the pace for lesser vehicles, roaring along at racetrack speeds.

Jake, a native of Manhattan where a car was more a nuisance than a necessity, had learned to drive late in life, and still looked upon it as a pleasurable adventure, although, like most Detroiters, he now relied on his car for almost all transportation.

The purchase of his sleek white Corvette had been his only real extravagance since coming to Michigan. He justified it to himself as a kind of business expense, a tangible statement that he was achieving status in his profession. He pretended indifference, but the sleek machine had become his secret pet. He liked to touch it, to sit in it, and sometimes just to think about it.

But the Corvette also served as his private escape capsule. He enjoyed driving, and the racy sports car had become his refuge from the tensions of his work and his world. The drive to Gladding was for him more a source of enjoyment than a burden.

Traffic moving north had been more congested as the interstate highway skirted the cities of Pontiac and Flint, then thinned again as those population centers were left behind.

In summer, I-75, which stretched from Florida's tropic swamps all the way to Michigan's northernmost border with Canada, was swollen with vacation-bound vehicles. But in the autumn there were far fewer cars, and in contrast the highway seemed almost deserted in the north, imparting to a lone driver a sense of vast space and quiet remoteness.

Autumn, with its special bonus of color, was Jake's favorite time to drive.

Michigan's north country, the real north, began after Bay City. Long flat farming fields that had stretched for miles suddenly disappeared, replaced by scrub pine forests. Since I-75 had been cut through the center of Michigan's northern forest, the trees got thicker the farther north he drove. The air almost immediately seemed more crisp and clear. Here life seemed ruled more by nature's seasons than by any man-made clock.

He had passed the turnoffs for Grayling and Gaylord, old lumber towns that had been given new life as resort centers, thanks to their proximity to the interstate highway and its moving cargo of monied vacationers.

Gladding's problem was its location. It was too far away from the bountiful corridor of the interstate. From I-75 the only route to Gladding lay over a narrow two-lane road that twisted like a drunken snake through twenty miles of forest. There were many other places that could match or surpass anything Gladding had to offer, places that were much more conveniently located.

Jake took the turnoff for the Gladding road and then eased back on the accelerator. There were no fender-bender accidents up north. Speed and narrow country roads made any collision among the pines a funeral director's dream.

The road was deserted. Metal signs along the way that warned of deer crossings all bore clusters of bullet holes from drunken marksmen trying their aim at the painted black deer outline. He saw only one other vehicle, a pickup truck, during the twenty-mile drive.

The first evidence of the existence of the town was a speed limit sign, shot through with bullet holes. Gladding had been cut from the heart of the forest, and his car passed instantly from thick trees into its main street.

A blinking signal light was suspended over the main crossroad. Virtually nothing had changed since he'd seen it last. It looked like a northwoods version of Dodge City. Everything seemed worn and faded like a frontier town, but one that was slowly dying.

He drove slowly, not out of concern for traffic, because there wasn't any, but out of curiosity. He passed a drug store, a variety store and an IGA grocery. A few cars and small trucks and vans were angle-parked along the curb. There were two gas stations and a hardware. An old movie house had been boarded up, as had an abandoned train station. Most of the stores had wooden falsefronts, although a few turn-of-the–century red brick buildings were clustered around the main intersection. Small frame homes dotted the dirt roads near the center of the town.

A sagging banner hung over the paved main street. Old, torn in several places, its faded lettering proclaimed this to be GLADDING—THE HEART OF THE NORTH.

A single-story building made from logs near the end of the business district housed a saloon. A faulty neon sign saying NORTHWAY had the R missing. Beyond the saloon was a post office, a typical WPA no-frills Depression model. Next to the post office was a much larger red brick Victorian structure that apparently housed the local government offices. A low-built modern school building at the far edge of the town looked miserably out of place.

Then Gladding was gone, and the road once again was bordered by thick clusters of trees.

There was something about the small town that seemed vaguely ominous to Jake. He was glad to leave it behind. Alone once again on the deserted road in his private escape capsule, Jake Martin sped along the few remaining miles to Raven's Nest, the Daren estate.

"How many rooms are there?"

"Sixty," Elizabeth Daren replied. "This was the estate of Robert Floyd, the lumber man. He called it his summer cottage. My husband bought it from Floyd's estate and renamed it Raven's Nest. That was many years ago, and long before I married him."

"It's really quite breathtaking."

Jake's voice echoed slightly in the huge great room. He toyed with the drink he had been given. When he had come up for the signing of the will, he had been quickly ushered in and out and he hadn't really had time to look around.

She was even more beautiful than he remembered. Almost too perfect. Jet-black hair tied back, dark emerald eyes, a Mona Lisa smile. Her figure, while concealed by a woolen sweater and designer jeans, was too full for a high-fashion model, but lean and trim by all other standards.

Jake had seen everything in the firm's thick files on the Daren family. He had read everything about her. She was thirty-nine, one year older than himself, although she looked much younger. She seemed as regal as a queen, although she hadn't been born to wealth. That too had been in the files.

"You're a busy man, Mr. Martin, and you've driven a long way, so suppose we get right to the business at hand."

"That suits me, Mrs. Daren. But you've just lost your husband, so if this is too much for you we can always put it off until . . ."

Her emerald eyes narrowed into emerald shards. "This cannot be put off." Her tone indicated she was no stranger to giving orders.

"Mr. Bellows tells me you feel that a contest is likely over the admission of the will," Jake said. "Perhaps you can tell me why?"

Her cool green eyes appraised him, as if deciding his possible ability and loyalty. She paused, then, having come to a silent decision, spoke again, this time in a much softer tone. "It's a complicated situation," she said. "My husband was inordinately rich. He was also the majority shareholder in his bank, holding fifty-one percent of the voting stock. What do you know about Hanover Square?"

Jake gestured with his hands. "Not much, I suppose. It's an old Detroit bank. I've always considered it like a dignified matriarch, at least in relation to the other banks in the city."

"It's the largest bank in Detroit," she said.

"I don't like to disagree, but the successor to Detroit Bank And Trust—"

"My husband rather artfully concealed the extent of his bank's holdings here and especially abroad. When the total of all assets and allied interests are added up, Hanover Square is just a point or two below the biggest New York banks."

"Are you sure?"

"Absolutely sure." The Mona Lisa smile slipped like a ghost across her full and sensuous lips. "Hanover Square has quietly become one of the most powerful financial institutions in the entire world. The bank's publicity department is employed to mask the extent of the bank's importance and international influence."

"Why?"

"Augustus, like his father, believed more could be accomplished in competition if the opposition didn't realize the strength of the challenger. Augustus wasn't interested in self-aggrandizement, just power. Before he became ill he planned to make Hanover Square the largest and most powerful bank in America and, perhaps, the world."

"Well, like the baseball manager said, we didn't lose, we just ran out of innings. Your husband just ran out of time, I guess."

"Perhaps the game isn't over," she said evenly. "What do you know about me?"

"You mean, did I look you up?"

She nodded.

He hesitated, then decided to be frank.

"When I was assigned to this matter I went over all the firm's files on your husband and his bank. Your husband's files are as thick as encyclopedias, and complete with newspaper clippings. Obviously, there was a lot about you. Some of it, to be straight with you, is not too flattering, Mrs. Daren."

She showed no emotion. "Go on."

"Maybe I could use another brandy."

She signaled and a maid appeared as if by magic. His glass was instantly filled.

Jake sipped and then continued. "How frank do you want this?"

"Just get on with it."

He nodded. "As you well know, your husband's divorce from his third wife was a blood bath, at least according to the clippings in the files."

"She used everything she could think of to get leverage for a better settlement."

"Did it work?" Jake asked. "The dollar figures in the files seemed a bit ambiguous."

"It worked," she said sharply. "Go on."

"Well, according to your predecessor, you were being kept in a pretty fancy apartment by Augustus Daren. She claimed you were his mistress."

"I was."

34

Jake felt extremely uncomfortable under her gaze. "Is this too painful?"

"No."

He tried to choose the right words so as not to offend her. "Everybody loves that kind of stuff, Mrs. Daren, especially if it concerns the rich and the powerful. Sex and money, it sells a lot of products, including newspapers. She claimed you had hypnotized Augustus Daren, using sex, kinky sex, as your choice of weapon. She hinted that you did more than merely model in your career in New York."

"She claimed I was a prostitute."

He nodded nervously, took a sip of brandy, then continued.

"Your husband's two children obviously weren't pleased when you married him. They refused to show up. The newspapers made quite a thing out of their nonappearance at the time. Taken from a total point of view, a number of people have tried very hard to paint you as an adventurous gold digger."

"You're a lawyer, Mr. Martin: did they succeed?"

Slowly he put his glass down.

"Regrettably, I think perhaps they did. Oh, you've done some charity things since your marriage, but not enough really to alter public opinion. You're a beautiful woman, Mrs. Daren. Frankly, beautiful women can be very sexy, and your photographs do emphasize that quality."

She would make an excellent poker player, Jake thought. She exhibited no reaction, none whatsoever.

Her half-smile flickered back into place. "In your opinion then, the public perceives me as something of a bimbo. To use a highly overworked term."

"Well, celebrity can be an odd thing, Mrs. Daren. It can go either way. A publicity man once said that a squirrel is just a rat with good public relations. A public image often has little relation to reality."

Jake smiled nervously, wondering why she didn't react. "You're wealthy, beautiful, young. Why should you even care what the great unwashed might think?"

"I would if they were to sit on a jury."

"Do you think it will come to that?"

"I do anticipate a civil suit concerning my husband's will. I'm afraid some people won't like the provisions giving me control of Hanover Square Bank."

"Who?"

For the first time her smile was without restraint. Then she laughed. Jake found it an altogether pleasant sound.

"Needless to say, as you saw from those old clippings, my husband's two children by previous marriages are not what anyone would call my greatest fans."

"If they contest the will, there's a forfeiture clause. They'd risk

35

everything they're meant to receive under the will," Jake said. "Would they do that?"

"They would if they thought they could win."

"Why?"

Her eyes were fixed on him "Whoever controls the bank has enormous power, here and abroad. Under the will, I will have control but only by a whisker. I anticipate a number of people will use Gus's children to try to take that power away from me."

"And therefore you're worried about how you might look, if there is a trial."

"It could be important."

Jake frowned. "May I ask you some personal questions? If all this should come down to a trial we should know what we might be up against."

"My strengths and weaknesses?"

"Exactly, if you don't mind."

"Where should we start?"

"The beginning, I suppose. Where were you born? Your family, the works."

She nodded. "All of it is pretty standard stuff. I was born in a small Pennsylvania town. My father owned a men's clothing store. My mother worked at the store."

"Are they living?"

She shook her head. "My father died when I was fifteen. A heart attack. My mother ran the store after that, but she got cancer and died three years later. I sold the store, but I didn't get much."

"Any brothers or sisters?"

"No. I got married when I was nineteen. Not many people knew about that."

"Did Mr. Daren?"

"Yes."

"Any children from that first marriage?"

"Shouldn't you take notes?"

He smiled. "I'll remember. What about children?"

"I did get pregnant, but I miscarried."

"Abortion?"

She paused for a fraction of a moment. "No, although I was thinking about it at the time. The marriage wasn't working out. He was just a kid, too. The miscarriage saved me from having to make the decision. After that, we got a divorce."

"Is he alive?"

"As far as I know. I haven't been back since I left."

"Where did you go?"

"New York."

"College?"

"Not then. I did go for a year, but much later. City College. I went nights. I'm afraid I wasn't much of a student."

36

"Flunk out?"

She nodded. "I was more interested then in having a good time."

"Did you work?"

She laughed softly. "What money I had ran out rather quickly. I took a number of jobs: secretary, sales clerk, that sort of thing."

He looked at her. "The clips said you were a model. Is that true?"

"What are you saying? Do you mean did I hook?"

He knew he was blushing. "It's happened before, and not just in New York."

"It never got quite that bad."

"What kind of modeling?"

She looked away. "I never did hit the big time. You can find me in some editions of some old Sears catalogues. I'm too full-figured to do high fashion, but I was okay for ski and swim layouts for JCPenny, among others."

"Mrs. Daren, I'm not exactly looking for titillation. But we don't want to run into any jolting surprises later. Did you ever do any nude stuff, racy layouts, anything like that?"

"I did nude modeling."

Jake waited for a more complete answer.

"I modeled for artists, not photographers. There are no glossies of my bare backside floating around, if that's what you mean."

Jake felt inadequate. He wished the firm had assigned Dow or an experienced trial lawyer to do the questioning. "This is a complicated world, Mrs. Daren," he said. "You have to realize I had to ask. You just never know what might be out there."

"There are no skeletons in my closet."

Jake looked around the gigantic room. One wall, housing a fireplace large enough to roast a cow, was built entirely of huge boulders. It was definitely a man's place.

"How old were you when you met Augustus Daren?"

"Twenty-eight."

"Where did you meet him?"

"In New York."

"The clips are a little vague about the beginning."

"Well, it was simple enough. A computer company was exhibiting a new banking system. Like me, a number of models were hired to grace the proceedings as a kind of living window-dressing. That's not unusual in New York, by the way. It's done all the time with new products and at conventions."

"What did you do? Pose with a computer?"

"I was a hostess. We all were."

"Were you supposed to leave with the customers, if they asked you?"

Anger flashed in her startling green eyes for only a moment, then she looked at him and answered with perfect calm.

37

"We weren't whores, Mr. Martin, and we weren't hired with anything like that in mind. I'm not saying some girls didn't leave with the men they met at those things. We were all young, adventurous, and I suppose all looking for the one great romance. Some girls viewed those shows as an opportunity to look for a rich husband."

"Did you?"

She paused. "Is all this really necessary?"

"I think it is. But it's up to you, obviously."

"I was living with someone at the time, a young musician. I wasn't looking the night I met Augustus."

"Did you leave with him?"

"We went to dinner."

She looked away, but when she smiled, it was a gentle smile. "He was something, Augustus. I didn't even know who he was. But there was an aura of power about him. That can be an immense aphrodisiac for women, you know."

"So I hear."

"Somehow I never thought of him as an older man, although he was almost thirty years my senior. He was charming, mature and completely in charge. I fell in love. My musician was suddenly a thing of the past."

"But Daren was married then?"

"Yes, that's true, but I didn't break that up. The marriage was all through before he ever met me. They lived under the same roof, but that was all." She smiled. "He called the arrangement they had an Irish divorce. She was Catholic, but not a very good one."

"Did he bring you to Detroit and set you up in the apartment as the clips say?"

"Sounds scandalous, doesn't it? I suppose it was. But I was content to be his mistress."

"You didn't want him to marry you?"

"I fantasized about it," she said with a wistful smile, "but I never expected it."

"And then you married him after he got the divorce?"

"That's right."

"Was it a happy marriage?"

"What do you mean by that?"

He was embarrassed. "Did you take any lovers? Or did he?"

This time, the anger lingered in her emerald eyes. "No. And I want you to know I consider that question insulting."

"I'm sorry, Mrs. Daren, but you tell me you think you may end up on the witness stand before a jury. I doubt if the people attacking the will are going to avoid asking that kind of thing. Lawsuits can get nasty. If we are to be of any help, we really have to know what we can expect."

"I'll say this exactly once, Mr. Martin, so listen carefully. We had a wonderful marriage. We were compatible in every way, especially sexually, until his first stroke. Sex was the only thing affected by that. He was my husband, my lover, my friend, and most importantly, my teacher."

"I didn't mean—"

"The second stroke left him in a permanent coma. After the first stroke I ran the bank on his instructions. After the second stroke, I ran the bank by myself."

"That's quite a feat, isn't it? I mean, you have no education in banking, or, for that matter, any previous experience in banking."

She shook her head emphatically. "You're quite wrong, Mr. Martin. Augustus gave me a better economics education than I could have gotten at any university in the world. And he trained me to take over for him. He trained me, Mr. Martin, to be an extension of himself. In the past year I've proved that I can run the bank."

"The will gives you that power, Mrs. Daren," Jake sipped again at the brandy. "Can you tell me why your husband changed it?"

"Shortly after our wedding," she said quietly, "my husband drew up a will providing that I get a third of his estate, and that his two children share another third, and the rest is to go to the charitable foundation he created."

Jake nodded. "I know."

"Later, after his first stroke and after I had demonstrated my abilities and my interest in the bank, Augustus decided to make the change giving me effective control. He felt his children were weak and would be used by people who would come after the bank like wolves after red meat. You must understand that the bank was his life. He was determined that it continue, and that's why he trained me to take over."

"Do you think you can?" Jake asked, wondering how she would react.

The emerald eyes grew narrow, and seemed to change to an even deeper shade of green. "I not only can, I have. Gus and I made great plans. I am determined to carry them out, Mr. Martin."

"Is there anything else I should know?"

"About me?"

Jake nodded.

"I think we've covered it. Is your firm prepared if we do face a legal challenge?"

Jake smiled. "Mr. Bellows has already put together a team of lawyers, just in case."

She seemed satisfied. "Oh, one more thing. I've hired a public relations firm to handle this matter."

"Outsiders? You said you have public relations people working for the bank."

She nodded. "The bank's staff is large, but their expertise is limited to the banking field. I decided I'd need someone with somewhat wider experience. The firm is Stevens and Casey. Lee Stevens will take personal charge. I'll have him contact you."

"You've used these people before?"

She shook her head. "No. But they come highly recommended."

"I'll probably think of a dozen things I should have asked, Mrs. Daren. Would it be an imposition if I called you?"

"Not in the least. Will you stay for dinner?"

She was probably the most beautiful woman Jake had ever seen. He was both intimidated and attracted. "I really have to get back," he said.

"You can stay the night. It's a long drive back." There seemed to be a different tone in her voice, more feminine, more personal. He wondered if that might only be his imagination.

He stood up. "Thank you, but I can't. There's too much to do. I'm grateful for your help."

Her eyes seemed to penetrate his. The personal tone was suddenly gone, and she was in command once more. "Mr. Martin, be assured that I will do whatever I have to do to keep control of my bank."

Jake did not fail to notice that it was the first time Elizabeth Daren had referred to Hanover Square as her bank.

Claude deSalle continued making arrangements for the public memorial service for Augustus J. Daren. Everything would be exactly as he had promised Elizabeth Daren. In that, he had kept his word.

But he hadn't kept his promise to call the individual members of the bank's board of directors to have her named as chairman. He knew he'd have to do it eventually. Word of his neglect might get back to Elizabeth from friendly board members, and then the battle would be joined before he was ready. He would make the calls to the board, but first he planned to contact the children of Augustus Daren. The memorial service provided the perfect excuse.

Augustus Daren Jr., called Chip since birth, was forty-four, and the product of his father's second marriage. Chip's mother, a Detroit socialite, had died shortly after her divorce from Daren.

Augusta Daren, the old man's daughter, was now thirty-nine, conceived before marriage, but born in wedlock, thanks to a hasty divorce from Chip's mother, and an even hastier wedding ceremony only days before Augusta, called Gussie, made her appearance.

Her mother, Dorothy, the third Mrs. Daren, had originally been a British showgirl and had proved to be surprisingly popular with the auto executive wives.

It was these wives, without question the center of social power in Detroit, who took Dorothy into their inner circle where, by the time Daren had demanded a divorce, she had firmly established herself as one of Detroit's reigning society mavens—those powerful women who dictated who was in and who was out. Dorothy, who had raised Chip along with Gussie as brother and sister, had been an indifferent mother and wife, but she had become a legend as Detroit's most prominent hostess.

Augustus Daren had little interest in social affairs—and even less in raising children—and so he allowed Dorothy free reign. She took care of every detail of her famous parties, but in matters familial, she hired others to manage the two children.

Given this lack of love, the later exploits of both Daren children were easily explainable. But both Chip and Gussie were growing older, and their public escapades less frequent and much more restrained.

When it finally happened, Dorothy and Augustus Daren's divorce had been like a public fight to the death between two rabid panthers. The people of the city of Detroit feasted on every word printed about the scandalous charges.

Elizabeth, the young New York model, was front-page stuff. Circulation of both of Detroit's newspapers dropped markedly when a settlement agreement was reached. For many it was like having the World Series called off after the third game.

The marriage between Daren and Elizabeth, because of all that had preceded it, also made headlines.

Over the years, Claude deSalle had taken special pains to remain in contact with both Chip and his half-sister. He wasn't particularly fond of either, but he gambled that one day his extra effort might pay off. Now he felt that special day had come.

He traced Chip's progress from London to New York and tracked him down at the Sherry Netherland Hotel.

"Claude deSalle here," he said smoothly into the telephone. "I had a devil's own time finding you, Chip."

"I just got off the damn plane from London," Chip Daren replied testily. "They had some kid howling his lungs out all the way across the Atlantic. I couldn't sleep."

Chip, Claude deSalle recalled, had always been something of a whiner.

"Let me express my condolences, Chip. As you know, your father and I were quite close."

"Yeah, yeah. Look, deSalle, I appreciate the sentiment, but I got to get some sleep. We'll talk some other time."

"A public memorial service has been arranged for your father," deSalle said. "I thought you'd want to know the details."

Chip sighed with evident disgust. "All right, go on."

Quickly, deSalle gave him the details.

"Very good, deSalle," Chip said, as though he were addressing a servant, "I'll be there. And when I get there, I'll take over the bank. I'll use my father's old office."

Claude deSalle smiled, but said nothing, letting the pause arouse curiosity on the other end of the line.

"I said I'll be taking over the bank, deSalle. Didn't you hear me?"

"I heard you, Chip. But that may be a problem."

The answer was almost a growl. "There'll be no problem. I talked to my sister and she's with me in this. We can use our combined interest to put together a coalition, at least enough to gain effective control."

Claude deSalle made no reply.

"If you're worried about the widow, forget it. I'll run her right out of town. She's be no problem."

"I'm afraid she will be, Chip," deSalle replied evenly.

"What do you mean?"

"Under your father's last will, he did leave you and your sister a third of his estate, but he left control of the bank to your stepmother."

"She's not my goddamned stepmother! And what the hell do you mean, control?"

"Just that. As I understand it, that's what the new will provides. I'm told it's about to be filed for probate. Elizabeth, your . . . er . . . father's widow is demanding to be made chairman of the bank's board."

"What!"

"I'm sorry to be the one to break the news, Chip. I thought you knew."

"We'll sue!" Chip bellowed.

Claude deSalle held the receiver away from his ear.

"When was this so-called will executed?" Chip demanded.

"Between strokes, so to speak," deSalle replied. "The firm of Sperling Beekman is handling it."

"I didn't see him then," Chip was still bellowing, "but everyone knows he was a fruitcake, a drooler. He couldn't wipe himself, let along make out a will. Don't you worry, we'll get that thrown out in short order. I'll fly into Detroit immediately."

"As you wish."

"And I want my father's office set up for me."

"I can't do that, Chip, as much as I might like to."

"Why not?"

"Your step—your father's widow is taking it."

"Goddamn! She won't get away with this. I'll call Sperling Beekman and have a stop put to this business."

DeSalle smiled, then spoke quietly. "I'm afraid they can't represent you, Chip. They drew the will and they're handling the probate. You can always check that with Donald Bellows, but I think it would be a conflict of interest for them to take you on as a client."

"Screw them, then. I don't need them. If I have to, I'll get the best lawyer in town and stop her dead in her fucking tracks."

Suddenly he stopped, although deSalle could hear his excited breathing. Then Chip Daren spoke again. "Look, Claude, I haven't been to Detroit in years. The only lawyers I know there are the Sperling Beekman people; they handled all the family business. Clearly I can't use them. I'll need somebody else fast. Who would you suggest?"

"I don't know if it would be ethical for me to recommend someone, Chip."

"We're friends, goddamn it, Claude." Chip's imperious tone had changed suddenly. "I'm asking as a friend."

"Well, there's the bluestocking firms, of course."

"I don't want them. The sons of bitches are incestuous. They don't fight, they deal. I want a fighter, Jack."

"The number one trial lawyer around here at the moment is a fellow named T. G. Sage. He's been quite successful. Although there's no doubt he's controversial. The newspapers have taken to calling him Tiger Sage."

"Harvard?"

"I have no idea."

Chip paused. "Good though, huh? Tough, really tough?"

"From what I read."

"Fine. I'll get in tonight. Would you give him a call for me?"

"I don't think that would be such a good idea, Chip."

He heard an irritated snort. "Okay, I'll call him myself when I get there."

"Let me know where you're staying, Chip?"

"I'll stay at the Book Cadillac."

"It's closed, and has been for years."

"Jesus! You're kidding. The Book?"

"You could try the Westin, or the Omni. They're new."

"Okay. I'll be in touch."

Claude deSalle hung up the telephone and grinned.

T. G. Sage was just the man for the job. If hell was to be raised, he was the ideal man to do it.

Things were beginning to work out very nicely.

Joe Muer's, located on Gratiot Avenue near the core of the city but not part of it, had survived depressions, riots and urban rot. The restaurant, one of the few in Detroit still served by waiters and waitresses in tuxedos, was rated as one of the nation's outstanding seafood emporiums and a Detroit landmark.

Jake arrived on time and was mildly annoyed that Marie was late. But she had made a dinner reservation in her name, and he was shown to a table in one of the large rooms off the main hallway.

He ordered a Manhattan. On the long drive back from Gladding Jake had stopped for the night at a motel outside Flint so he had not been home, nor had he found time in the busy day to call Marie. He wished she would come.

When she entered the crowded dining room, heads turned. Marie had developed a presence. She moved regally through the tables, coolly regarding the diners as a queen might casually inspect her subjects.

"I'm sorry," she said as she sat down across from him. "I got held up at the last moment." She looked up at the waiter. "We'll order now."

"Are you in any special hurry?" Jake asked.

She ignored him and told the waiter what she wanted. Jake ordered pickerel.

"What's this all about, Marie?" he asked, as soon as the waiter left their table.

She didn't reply at once. But when she did speak, she looked away. "Things haven't been great between us."

He sipped his drink. "Things are a little strained, I'll admit, but we're both busy people under a lot of stress. Everything will work out."

"I don't think it will."

He finished the drink, and still she avoided his eyes.

"Marie, what are you really trying to say?"

"I'm saying that I think we should get a divorce, Jake."

Stunned, he signaled the waiter for another drink to give himself time to think.

"All this is pretty sudden, isn't it?"

"I've been thinking about it for a long time. I decided to put it off until you were made partner. And I think that's a certainty for you now, so there's no reason to wait any longer."

"Goddamn it, Marie! What the hell has my making partner got to do with whether we stay married or not?"

This time she did look directly at him.

"Please keep your voice down," she said coolly, then continued. "Law firms are basically conservative. A divorce in progress could affect a lawyer's chances for promotion. We'll hold off filing until your partnership becomes official."

He didn't quite know if what he was beginning to feel was anger or fear.

"Why, Marie? Are you that unhappy? We have more than five years invested together. That's half a decade. It would be foolish to walk away without at least trying to save things. We could try marriage counseling. I know it's worked for other people."

"I've made up my mind, Jake."

He fought hard to control himself. In the beginning everything had been so wonderful. There was no one he had ever loved more than he'd loved Marie. He had come to Detroit because of her. He had abandoned all that was familiar to him to start a new life with

44

the woman who had defined his universe. Now she was saying it was over, finished, done. None of it made any sense.

He knew there'd been problems recently, but he always thought problems could be solved. Now he was being told over a dinner that looked for all intents and purposes like a business meting, that it was all over.

"It is as simple as that—you've made up your mind? I can't believe anything's quite that simple."

"Michigan is a no-fault-divorce state. If you agree, we'll split everything down the middle."

"Like your two-hundred-thousand debt?"

She shook her head. "No. Obviously that's my obligation."

He took the fresh drink from the waiter. "Well, here's how it goes. I don't want a divorce."

"I'm reminding you, Jake, this is a no-fault state," she said rather sharply. "What you want has little to do with it. I want out, and that's my right."

"Jesus Christ."

As the waiter returned with their food, they both fell silent.

"Enjoy your meal," he said cheerfully once he had served them.

Jake's laugh was hollow as he thought of the irony.

"We have separate pension accounts," she went on, toying with her food. "We'll each keep our own. The joint accounts, savings and checking, and the stock can be split down the middle."

"Marie—"

She ignored him completely and continued briskly. "We each have our own car. The lease on the apartment has another year to go. If you want it, you can have it, or we can sublease it to someone else."

Jake pushed his plate away untouched.

"This is ridiculous."

"We can work out something on the furniture."

He attempted to reach across the table and take her hand, but she drew away. "We need some time together, Marie. This isn't something that can be disposed of over a restaurant table. Let's go home and talk this out."

She shook her head. "I've already moved my things," she said. "Emily Johnson is spending the winter in Florida and she's letting me use her condo in Grosse Pointe."

"You're saying you've already moved?"

Once again, she looked away. "My personal things, my clothes. It's much better this way, Jake. We've been living in an armed camp anyway. We'll both feel better."

Again there was an uncomfortable and long silence.

"So that's it? Five years down the drain, just like that? What the hell for, Marie? All I need from you is a reason. I think you owe me at least that."

"We've grown apart," she said quietly. "It happens, Jake."

"What kind of fucking answer is that? This isn't some kind of daytime soap opera. What the hell's going on here? Does it matter to you in the slightest that I still love you?"

"Keep your voice down," she snapped. "There's no point in fighting about this."

"No? I'm still waiting to hear a reason."

"I'm not saying it's all your fault, Jake. But you've made no real attempt to fit in here. You have no friends, no outside interests, at least none that relate to your life here. It's like living with an exile."

"Marie," he said, trying to keep from sounding hostile, "it must be apparent to you that I work damn near all the time. What in hell do you mean, fit in? I barely have time for sleep. Jesus, we both know what it takes to make partner in a large firm. Look, let's not make one hell of a mistake here. You want to live away for a while, okay. But let's get some counseling. This is just too important to walk away from. At least it is for me."

"No, Jake. It's over."

He sat back, shook his head, then looked directly at her. And then he got it.

"There's someone else, right?"

She met his eyes straight on and with defiance.

"That's totally irrelevant, isn't it?"

"I deserve an answer," he said. "So answer me. Is there someone else?"

There was a moment's hesitation, but when she quickly said, "No." She immediately looked away.

He felt physically sick. He suspected she was lying.

"Well," he said slowly. "Maybe things will change. Maybe it will still work out somehow."

She shook her head without looking at him. "No, Jake. I'm sorry. I really don't think things will change."

Marie got up and quickly left the restaurant. He was going to follow her, but then thought better of it.

"Is everything all right, sir?" The waiter asked, smiling.

"That depends on your point of view," Jake said. "Bring me the check, please."

And even though he wasn't a big drinker, he desperately wanted to keep drinking, to ease the shock and the overwhelming sense of loss and hurt. But getting drunk was a fool's response. He needed to think, not to dull his mind. He felt an urgent need to talk to someone, but there was no one.

Jake Martin had never felt so alone in his life. All his concerns about his career, all the strategies that had seemed so important, were now suddenly reduced to nothing. They were meaningless. Tomorrow another meeting was scheduled on the Daren estate, but now it seemed completely irrelevant. He just didn't care.

He tipped the car porter who delivered his Corvette.

"Have a good one," the young man said, grinning.

Jake decided to go for a drive. This was, after all, the car capital of the world, and he hoped the mechanical act of driving might somehow help him sort out the turbulent thoughts and emotions that were overwhelming him.

4

Donald Bellows provided no coffee for this morning's meeting. This time his manner was much more brisk and businesslike.

"Well, let's see what we've accomplished thus far. Cora?"

Cora Simpson, like Jake and Craig Dow, knew the partnership might be on the line with her every answer. But Jake thought she managed to hide it coolly, if she did feel any nervousness.

"The basic law is with us, of course," she said. "The will is presumed valid. But we all knew that."

"Indeed," Bellows said rather abruptly.

"However, when we file the will I believe we must do so in Eagle County."

"What?" Bellows' question was more like an accusation.

Cora maintained an unperturbed front, and she spoke with quiet authority.

"When Mr. Daren experienced his first stroke he moved his home and operations up north. I talked to his widow. She said he was ashamed of his impairment, and that was the reason. He didn't want to be around people. He had everything transferred there, his voting registration, even his driver's license was renewed there, although physically he could no longer drive. Apparently, things like that are winked at in Eagle County."

"That's opinion, Cora," Bellows said curtly. "Just stick to facts, if you will."

Craig Dow tried to conceal a smug smile. Jake Martin, although a rival, felt a kinship with her. But at the moment, he had a difficult time trying to concentrate on the Daren estate. His mind was still in turmoil over his personal problems.

"Facts it shall be," Cora replied to Bellows, just as curtly. "Estates are usually decided wherever the deceased was officially domiciled at death. Eagle County is where Augustus Daren lived. Eagle County is where he died. And like it or not, Eagle County is where his estate has to be probated."

Bellows swore. It was an uncharacteristic reaction.

47

"Cora, are you certain? We have established some very good connections over the years with the probate judges and the staff here in Wayne County. Especially the staff, since they run things anyway. It would put us at a distinct disadvantage to try this in some godforsaken northern court." He made it sound as if somehow she was at fault.

She colored slightly but showed no other apparent reaction. "We could file anywhere," she said evenly. "And if no one objected, we could try the matter here or in Timbuktu, I suppose. But legally the jurisdiction is in Eagle County, whether we like it to not."

"Would that give you any problems, Craig?" Bellows asked.

Craig Dow smiled easily. It was a confident smile which somehow implied that this was his meeting.

"Not really. Cora told me what she had discovered. We are fully prepared to file in Eagle County. If there is a legal challenge to the will, it might be even better if brought there."

Jake, although he had been designated as team leader, wondered why no one had told him of such an important development. He felt even more like an outsider.

Donald Bellows allowed a small smile. "What advantage could we possibly find in a wilderness like Eagle County, Craig?"

"Speed," Dow answered. "The Wayne County probate docket is jammed. Even with connections, we might have to wait a year or more before we could try the matter. In Eagle County it would be instantaneous."

"How so?" Bellows enquired.

"Outside of Augustus J. Daren, nobody up there has two nickels to rub together. They live penniless, and they die penniless. The probate docket it open. We can get immediate action."

"You're certain about this?" Bellows asked.

"I checked," Dow replied evenly. "The probate judge up there is an old woman. She's more a notary than a judge."

"A lawyer?" Cora asked.

Dow nodded. "Yes. Her docket is open and we can be first in line."

"Well, at least that's a plus." Bellows glanced at Jake. "You've interviewed Elizabeth, Jake. Anything startling we should know?"

"I don't think so," Jake replied. "Perhaps this would be a good time to view the videotape."

"What tape?" Craig Dow asked.

Donald Bellows beamed. "Jake had our late client execute his will in front of the camera. He tells me it's dynamite. But we're all busy today and the tape will keep. We can look at it some other time." He raised his hands to signal that the meeting was over. "I think everything is developing quite well. Thank you all." He again turned to Jake. "Can I have a minute of your time, Jake?"

Jake nodded. As if he had a choice, he thought to himself as Cora and Dow departed.

"Chip Daren is waiting in the partners' conference room." Bellows was no longer smiling. "He wants to discuss the will. To put it mildly, he's upset. I wonder if you might attend this little meeting with me? Sometimes people misinterpret what's said and I think it might be wise to have another lawyer along."

"As a witness?"

Bellows nodded. "Precisely. Shall we go?"

The partners' conference room was far more elaborate than the one used by the associates. Chip Daren sat in one of the large leather chairs at the long polished table. He glared up at them as they entered.

Chip Daren was a younger model of his dead father. The same set jaw, the same piercing eyes.

Bellows' greeting was cordial, ignoring Daren's patent hostility. He introduced Jake. Daren ignored Jake's offered hand.

"It really is nice to see you after all these years, Chip," Bellows said.

"Cut the bullshit, Donald," Chip snapped. "Do you have a copy of this so-called will?"

Bellows handed him a copy.

"We're going to have this thrown out. I hope you realize that," Chip said, holding the document as if it were diseased.

"I can understand how you feel, Chip," Bellows replied evenly as he sat down across from Daren. "But it was your father's wishes."

"The fuck it was," Chip snapped. "It was that bitch's doing, I know that. She'll be goddamned sorry when we drag her into court."

"Chip, we've been friends for a long time, and the firm has served your father for longer than that. Obviously we can't represent you, but allow me to give you some advice."

"Like what?"

"There's a forfeiture provision in that will," Bellows said.

Jake watched as Chip's expression went from anger to suspicion.

"What's a forfeiture provision?" Chip demanded.

"It states that if a beneficiary contests the will in court, that person loses everything he or she would have received in the will."

"What?"

"You and Gussie are to receive one third of your father's bank stock under this will, although not the power to vote that stock. If you unsuccessfully contest the will, you'll lose your share. That's called the forfeiture clause."

"That won't hold up in court," Chip said, but without as much bluster.

"I'm afraid it will, Chip. The courts have upheld forfeiture in all similar cases."

"So if Gussie and I contest this we don't get a penny?"

Bellows nodded. "Yes. Of course, if Gussie didn't join in an action, she'd still get her share."

Chip's eyes narrowed with interest. "Oh?"

"One third of the bank, as I figure it, is worth about two hundred million dollars. So you would be risking one half of that if you brought the action. All of it, if both you and Gussie sued."

Chip pursed his lips as he seemed to digest what he had been told. "Suppose I made a separate deal with Gussie. I'd bring the action and she'd split her share with me if I lost, what then?"

Bellows shrugged. "It wouldn't be illegal, I suppose, so long as Gussie didn't join formally with your suit. Still, Chip, you would be gambling an enormous amount of money. Even with your wealth you'd have to view a hundred million as a substantial sum."

"That's my business, isn't it? And Gussie's," he added.

"I would be saddened if you felt you had to take action, Chip."

Daren stood up. "Then get your crying towel ready, Donald. Like the old saying goes," he smiled without humor, "I'll see you in court."

Daren slammed the door as he stalked from the conference room.

"You may wonder why I told him about the possibility of contesting the will without losing everything," Bellows said, looking at Jake. "As lawyers we must always be fair. Chip could get that information from any attorney he might consult." Bellows stood up and placed a hand on Jake's shoulder. "We must always be fair, Jake, in everything we do."

Bellows smiled. "By the way, Jake, if we must file the will in Eagle County someone has to do it. I know you just returned from there, but would you mind? I'd rather one of our team handled it. You might be able to sound out this woman judge up there and let us know what we might expect."

Jake desperately wanted to talk to Marie. It was an imposition to be asked, but a refusal would be a black mark against him when the new partner was selected.

"I'll go, Donald."

"Good. You can get an early start tomorrow and be up there in plenty of time to file. You must stop by and see Elizabeth again. Not an unpleasant task, eh? And I know she'll be interested in Chip's threat."

He beamed at Jake. "It's nice to have someone around you can depend on, Jake."

Chip Daren was escorted to T. G. Sage's table at the Detroit Athletic Club.

T. G. Sage was not what he expected. A stout man in his fifties with overlong grey hair, he was reading *The Wall Street Journal* through a pair of reading glasses perched on the tip of his fleshy nose. He looked up at Daren, his clear blue eyes making a quick appraisal.

Sage's suit was rumpled, his tie slightly askew and his shirt looked a size too large. He made no effort to rise. "Please sit down," he said in a surprisingly soft voice. "Can I order something for you? I consider lunch perhaps the most important meal of the day."

"Just coffee," Daren said.

Sage nodded to the waiter, who scurried away.

"I hope meeting here isn't too inconvenient," he said. "I have just completed a closing argument to a circuit court jury and this afternoon I must begin another case in Recorder's Court. "It's a busy day, but that's the way I like it. Lunch, quick as it is, will be my only free time today, I'm afraid."

Sage seemed more like a kindly old uncle than a courtroom terror. Daren wondered if Claude deSalle knew what he was talking about. The lawyer didn't resemble a tiger in any aspect.

"I wanted to talk about the possibility of hiring you to bring an action at law for me and my sister. Well, for me, anyway. My sister is backing me but she won't be a formal part of the case. I've talked to her and we've worked out everything between us."

Sage grinned, exhibiting uneven teeth. "A family that sues together, stays together, eh? By the way, retain is the proper word to use with lawyers, Mr. Daren. We like to perpetuate the illusion that we aren't for hire." He chuckled. "It stems from a day when our profession was a bit more noble, perhaps. Today if you drop a twenty-dollar bill, you're liable to be crushed to death by a stampede of greedy advocates."

He picked up a roll and tore it in half. "What's this all about?" he asked as he munched on the unbuttered roll.

Chip Daren proceeded to describe the problem.

"Do you have a copy of this will?" Sage asked.

Daren gave him the copy he had received from Donald Bellows. "I got this just this morning from the people at Sperling Beekman."

As he gulped his coffee, Sage made a slurping sound. "From what you tell me it sounds more like a job for a large firm, to be frank. These probate things can drag on for years. I'm a trial lawyer, and that sort of thing just isn't my cup of tea."

Daren was shocked. "You mean you're turning me down?"

Sage laughed. "Most of my cases are referred to me by other lawyers and firms. I suppose I'm something akin to a British barrister. I have little to do with the clients as such. Most of the preparation is done by others. I merely try the case."

"If it's a question of your fee . . ."

"Money makes the world go round," Sage said, his eyes twinkling, "but I do rather well as it is and, happily, I'm able to pick the cases I try. That wasn't always true." He chuckled. "A prolonged and dry proceeding over an old man's mental state sounds terribly dull. As I say, not my cup of tea at all."

"It would hardly be dull," Chip protested. "Whoever wins will control one of the most powerful banks in the world. The eyes of the world will be on this case."

"And who represents the widow?"

"Sperling Beekman."

"Did they draw this will?"

Chip nodded yes.

Sage noisily finished his coffee. "You must realize that the law creates a presumption that a will is valid."

"I don't understand."

"If wills were easily overturned, every family with money would be in a battle royal before the coffin was lowered into the waiting grave. Overturning a will is uphill, to say the very least. You start in these matters, to use a sports analogy, trailing badly with two men out in the ninth inning. The odds for success are not very good. It's what lawyers call a rebuttable presumption. It takes a hell of a lot of solid evidence to overcome the presumption of validity.

"The law presumes that your father was competent and that the will he signed was valid. You must show by an extraordinary degree of proof that this was not the case if that will is to be discredited."

"In other words, we can't win?"

Sage took up a battered leather briefcase and put the copy of the will in it. "I didn't say that. It would be a most difficult task; I didn't say impossible." He smiled. "I come from the school that teaches nothing is ever impossible."

"Please take the case." Chip was surprised at his own fervor. There was something about this round, rumpled man that automatically made you want him on your side.

T. G. Sage stood up. He was short and stubby.

"I have quite a full schedule, Mr. Daren," he said. "I try to set things up so that I stay busy." He grinned. "Sperling Beekman is one of our better law firms, perhaps our best. They breathe rather rarified air over there and tend to think extremely well of themselves." He chuckled. "It might be fun to prick that balloon of elite pomposity. Sometimes the quality of the opponent can make an otherwise dull matter interesting."

"So then you'll take the case?"

"I'll think about it. As I say, I do have a rather hectic schedule. I am a one-man operation, and that's sometimes a difficulty."

He looked at Daren over the rim of his half-glasses.

"If you do decide to pursue the matter, I would require a retainer of one hundred thousand dollars."

"Then you will take the case?"

He smiled. "We'll see. You may not wish to proceed, but if you do and I later find I can't work your case into my schedule, the money, less any expenses, will be returned to you. Frankly, I wouldn't agree to that if I were you. Much too chancy."

"I'm willing to take that risk."

"We're all gamblers in our own way, aren't we?" He glanced at his watch. "I have to go."

"Can I give you a lift?"

"My chauffeur is outside with my car, but thanks."

T. G. Sage hurried toward the door, then stopped and looked back.

"Where are you staying?"

"The Westin."

He nodded. "I'll read the will, then I'll be in touch."

"Claude. How nice to see you again." The words were spoken with only a slight hint of a German accent as the big man smiled and stepped forward. He embraced Claude deSalle in an unrestrained bear hug. "How long has it been, dear friend?"

DeSalle managed a smile as he was released. "Last year," he replied. "The world monetary conference in Vienna."

Paul Schiller, who had the thick body of a weightlifter and the enthusiasm of a born salesman, was extroverted and boisterous, an odd combination for the head of one of Germany's largest banks.

"I hope it's not too much of a bother, meeting me here in Windsor," Schiller said.

"No problem, Paul. Detroit is only five minutes away by tunnel, as you know."

"I would have gone across to see you, Claude, but my entry into your country from Canada would have been recorded by your customs officials. Some people might have become curious why I would feel the need to make a quick visit to Detroit."

"You haven't gone into smuggling, have you, Paul?"

The German peered at him for a moment, then laughed. "Ah, you and your jokes! No, but the international financial picture is very volatile now. Some of my competitors watch my every move. Right now I am officially at a conference in Toronto. No one knows I've driven down here."

Schiller had taken a Windsor hotel room that looked out on the Detroit River. Two other men were in the room, but Schiller didn't introduce them, and that neglect indicated to deSalle that they were both minor employees.

Paul Schiller, only forty, had already built a reputation as the architect of Germany's surging manufacturing economy. The son of the world famous economist, Helmut Schiller, he had earned fame beyond even that of his father, mixing politics and banking with remarkable skill.

"I need to talk to you, Claude," Schiller said.

53

DeSalle glanced at the other two men. "It's a nice day, Paul. Let's take a walk. Just the two of us."

Schiller laughed. "Always careful, aren't you? That's one of the many things I like about you, Claude."

They put on coats although it was a beautiful Indian summer's day. DeSalle led Schiller to Windsor's downtown riverside park.

"What a view!" Schiller said, pointing at the Detroit skyline directly across the river. "You have a magnificent city, Claude. It's hard to believe all the stories about murder and crime looking at it from this distance. Very like a woman, eh? So gorgeous, but so dangerous."

"Why did you want to see me, Paul?"

Schiller leaned against the metal railing near the water. He watched admiringly as two young women strolled by, then spoke quietly. "You own offshore banks."

"No." DeSalle leaned next to him as they both gazed out at the water.

"Oh, not officially, of course, but you do. So do we. You control a large Swiss financial house. We have one almost across the street from yours. You have a Tokyo branch. We have a Tokyo branch."

"So?"

"Many in Europe are concerned over the growing influence of your bank, Claude. Did you know that?"

"This is a competitive world, Paul. That comes as no surprise."

"We, my bank, fear Hanover Square."

DeSalle shrugged. "You are as big, perhaps bigger. I don't see that you should."

"Hypothetically—is that how you say it?—suppose we were to offer a plan to merge our banks. How would you feel about that?"

"It probably couldn't be done, not legally."

"Suppose it could? Using some innovative techniques, of course." Schiller continued, "It would make the combined bank one of the largest and most powerful in the world. Does that concept appeal to you?"

"It depends."

Schiller grinned. "Suppose you were made head of it, with bonus options equal to your rank?"

DeSalle watched a flight of ducks skimming over the river. "That sounds very much like a bribe. Usually, a person must do something to earn such . . . ah . . . consideration."

Schiller chuckled. "We approached Elizabeth Daren several months ago with the same proposition. Did you know that?"

"No."

"She turned us down. She is a woman to be feared, Claude. My bank wishes to avoid a competitive war, so to speak, between our institutions. We might win, but there's always the chance we might lose. She seemed quite determined, even eager, to enter into a

54

contest for supremacy. But that's all in the past. Now that her husband is dead, she loses her effective hold on the bank. You could, we think, influence Daren's children and enough other stockholders to agree to what we propose."

"You didn't waste much time, Paul. The old man just died."

The German nodded. "What we propose would make you a very powerful world figure, Claude, and a very rich one."

"There's going to be a will contest, did you know that?

"What do you mean?"

"Elizabeth Daren claims the old man left a will giving her voting control in the bank, fifty-one percent to be exact."

"Verdammen!"

"How do I know you'll deliver on your promises if I am able to get the board to agree to some kind of merger?"

"But she controls the bank," Schiller protested. "You just said so."

"I said there would be a will contest."

The German turned and studied him. "This will is no good?"

"I think that's how it will turn out."

"We can't operate on guesses, Claude, there's far too much involved. We have political upheaval in our own country. Our law may be changed with a new administration. We have to act now, within four months at the most, otherwise it can't be done."

DeSalle nodded in agreement. "I can understand that. But you still haven't told me what assurances I can expect. The kind of deal you propose is hardly the type to be enforced in the courts."

"You know something, about this will thing?"

"Maybe."

Schiller pursed his lips, then spoke. "You will propose the merger. We will agree and ask that you head up the combined bank. If that isn't done you can back out. That's fair."

"What about the options?"

"That's also part of the transaction. It would all be done up front."

"And your part of this deal, Paul, or are you just doing this for the general good?"

Schiller smiled. "I will get the same bonus provisions as yourself."

"What else?"

"If this comes off, Claude, I expect to be named to an especially high governmental post, one with great potential, perhaps even leading to the highest Germany can offer." He looked off across the water. "We will both profit very nicely, believe me, if it can be done."

"It can be done."

"How can you be so sure?" Schiller's concerned expression slowly changed to admiration. "You've—how do you say it—fixed it!"

Claude deSalle merely chuckled.

5

Jake's secretary ushered Lee Stevens into his office. In his mind's eye, Jake had envisioned a public relations man to be sharp-eyed, plump and flashily garbed, a walking ad for polyester, like a basketball coach or a racetrack gambler.

But Lee Stevens was impeccably dressed in a Paul Stuart suit and carried an expensive topcoat. He was younger than Jake, looking no more than thirty-five, if that. Rail thin, he had a thatch of reddish hair, and his large brown eyes seemed slightly protuberant. His movements were unnaturally quick, so filled was he with barely contained nervous energy.

They shook hands and Stevens sat down across the desk from Jake.

"I understand you talked to Elizabeth," Stevens said.

"Mrs. Daren. Yes, I did."

Stevens' toothy smile was slightly lopsided. "I prefer informality. Did she tell you I'd be running everything connected with this will business?"

"We were under the impression that Sperling Beekman would be handling the legal work," Jake said, restraining a smile.

Stevens chuckled. "You know what I mean. I'll take care of everything and anything that has to do with the media. At the moment, it's more defense than offense, but I'm hoping to talk her into launching a campaign to establish a new public image. You know, grieving widow makes large contributions to good causes, that sort of thing. A few photographs with crippled children can go a long way in influencing the great unwashed."

"Maybe she doesn't want to be a hypocrite," Jake said.

Stevens slowly raised one eyebrow as if appraising Jake. "A little hypocrisy sometimes can go a long way. Anyway, that's all in the future. I'm here to set up a procedure with your firm for handling press relations while this will business is going on. Are you in charge of the case?"

"I'm one of a team of lawyers assigned," Jake said.

"Okay, you'll be my contact over here. First thing, I want everybody to understand that no one talks to the press unless they talk to me first. You can see to that."

"Mr. Stevens, this is a law—"

He held up a hand and smiled. "I know what you're about to say. It's always the same, doctors, lawyers, whatever, you all think you

56

can handle public relations. Then one day you see yourself looking like a bumbling idiot on the six o'clock news and you come running to someone like me to repair the damage. If you people do it my way from the start, you won't have to look like incompetent imbeciles."

Jake frowned. "I don't think—"

Stevens again held up a restraining hand. "Ever hear of David Royal?"

"The rock star?"

"The same. What do you know about him?"

Jake shrugged. "He was in some trouble—drugs and teenagers, as I remember. But he got himself straight and is back on top, as far as I know."

Stevens' smile was icy. "He was our client. David makes more money than General Motors. David hasn't changed one damn bit. You've formed the opinion of a star reformed by the magic of public relations. After his front page arrest—you'll probably recall the garish headlines—we managed to have him sent to a rehabilitation center in lieu of jail. From the stories we've planted, you, like everyone else, thought he'd become a cross between Mother Teresa and St. Francis."

"But—"

"No buts. We were able to pull off a major miracle. However, David's no longer a client. He wouldn't follow our guidelines. One of these days they'll catch him with a nose full of candy and an arm full of prepubescent girls, and then that beautiful bubble we've built so skillfully will burst."

"This is quite different," Jake began.

Stevens shook his head. "Not really. As a matter of fact, our handling of David Royal is why Elizabeth hired us. She heard about what we did."

"We?"

"Stevens and Casey. We're a small public relations firm. Basically, it's a two-man operation, just me and my partner Jerry Casey, plus a couple of secretaries. Casey and I are both former newspapermen. I worked at the *Miami Herald*, the *New York Post* and the *Detroit Free Press*, plus a few years in advertising along the way. Casey's about the same. He was at *The Detroit News* when we met. At the time we were both investigative reporters, swimming in the murky depths of criminals and crooked cops."

Stevens, without asking permission, lit a cigarette, then continued. "We were drinking in the Anchor Bar one night, crying the blues about newspapering, when we decided to chuck it all and go into business for ourselves. Something nice and clean. That was almost five years ago. We're not millionaires, but we get by."

"And you handle people like David Royal?"

Stevens' smile seemed almost sardonic. "We specialize in everything. We have a few solid business accounts. They pay the rent. But our main claim to fame comes from show folks. It's kinda fun."

Jake found Stevens both pushy and at the same time engaging. "If we have to get out a press release, Mr. Stevens, we'll call you, of course."

Stevens shook his head. "That's part of my job, true, but you'll need more than that. I can be a very handy fellow to have around, Jake." He grinned. "Sometimes I can be a nuisance, but overall I think you'll be glad I'm on your side."

Jake stood up to indicate the interview was at an end. "We'll be in touch." He offered his hand.

Stevens stood and shook hands. "Legally, what happens next?"

"I'm going up to Eagle County tomorrow to file the will."

Stevens frowned. "You should always let me know if you're going to do anything like that. I can call my contacts at the papers and get you some good ink."

"That won't be necessary," Jake said. "There's a possible legal challenge brewing. We don't want to excite anyone. Sometimes it's best to let sleeping dogs lie."

"Sleeping dogs can bite. Keep that in mind." Stevens cocked his head slightly, his expression suddenly grim. "You have a job to do," he said quietly, "but I do, too. I intend to do mine, no matter what. I hope you fully understand that." He paused, smiled coldly, and added, "Jake."

T. G. Sage listened to the young prosecutor's impassioned speech of protest. Sage's client, a young man of patrician bearing, sat impassively next to him, his cool eyes showing no emotion whatsoever.

The prosecutor was making a novice's mistake. The only requirement was a pro forma objection to the request for bail reduction. Everyone, including the prosecutor, knew it was a fait accompli. But the young man, apparently trying to make an impression, was making a fiery speech more suited to the stage than the courtroom. Judge John Harvard Hathaway's eyes were slowly narrowing into dangerous slits, although that was his only discernible change of expression. Everyone called him John Harvard Hathaway to distinguish him from his cousin, John University of Chicago Hathaway, who sat on the circuit bench. Lawyers never said Judge Hathaway, but always identified each by using his school of origin as a middle name. John Harvard Hathaway, a Recorder's Court judge, was known to have a nasty temper.

Bored with the harangue, Sage shifted around and looked back at the spectators' section. His client's father, an almost identical older model, sat as impassively as his son. A lawyer waited with his client. Otherwise, the court's seats were empty. Sage was surprised when Chip Daren entered, almost on tiptoe, and took a seat at the back. Sage caught his eye and nodded an acknowledgement of his presence, then turned back to the business of the court.

"This man," the prosecutor pointed at Sage's client, "has battered a young woman almost to the point of death. If he hadn't been stopped, he would have killed her, and we wouldn't be here on a charge of assault, but murder!"

The judge's eyes had narrowed so much that Sage wondered if he could actually see out of them.

"If what you say is true," the judge's voice was low and deceptively gentle, "then why didn't your office charge him with attempted murder? That charge is still on the books, isn't it? I mean, the legislature hasn't changed that too?"

"It's on the books," the young man said, misreading the judge's tone as an endorsement. "And I'll concede that should have been the charge. But I wasn't the one who decided on the degree. Our office is overworked, and this may have slipped through. It happens."

"Well, I'm here to do justice," the judge said quietly. "Do you wish to upgrade the charge at this time?"

"Your honor, that's not my job. Bail has been set on the charge brought at two hundred thousand. I don't think that's enough, under the circumstances, but it certainly shouldn't be lowered, as Mr. Sage suggests."

John Harvard Hathaway's voice was barely audible. "Mr. Sage didn't suggest, he made a formal request for reduction of bail, as is his right." He glared at the prosecutor. "From what you've said here today, I don't think you've got a case at all. It sounds more fiction than fact to me, based on what you've just told me. I might entertain a motion to dismiss."

"You can't!" The young man's shout of protest was more out of surprise than anger.

"Oh, can't I?"

"What I mean is, this case, this man . . ." the prosecutor's voice trailed off.

Sage sighed and got to his feet. "If the court please," he began slowly, "we believe that eventually this charge will indeed be thrown out. However, all we wish today is to have the exorbitant bond reduced to a reasonable amount."

The judge had indicated in chambers that he would reduce the bond to fifty thousand, a sum easily handled by the client's family. Sage's client had picked up a young waitress, a girl who had been impressed by the Mercedes he drove and his expensive clothes, but not impressed enough to have sexual relations in an alley. She had paid for this reluctance with a broken nose and some lost teeth. The defendant alleged self-defense, that he was the one in danger of rape. That unique defense had worked for him in two previous cases.

"Judging from your little speech," the judge said, his voice

59

rising in anger, "you have a lot of nerve even bringing a case. I'm going to release the defendant on his own recognizance."

"What?" The young man spoke, then colored, knowing he had gone one step too far.

John Harvard Hathaway smiled, but there was no warmth in the expression. "Did I hear you correctly?"

"I'm sorry, your honor," the young man said quickly. "I apologize. I got carried away."

"Next time you get carried away to jail." The judge nodded to Sage. "The previous bond is canceled. Your client is free on his own recognizance."

Sage nodded solemnly. "Thank you, your honor."

"Can I go now?" his client asked.

Sage nodded yes. He was far too experienced to expect gratitude.

Father and son left the courtroom together.

Sage gathered up his papers and followed. Chip Daren pursued him into the hallway.

"Ah, Mr. Daren," Sage said. "I've been meaning to call you."

"Oh?"

"I'm afraid I won't be able to handle your case after all. I've been retained to defend Mr. Jeffrey Arkman, the chap who caused the collapse of the Bookman brokerage firm. I'm sure you've read about it in the papers. Trial is set to begin in mid-January. So, as I cautioned you, I can't get myself tied up in the will contest."

"Our case will be all over before then."

Sage shook his head. "I'm afraid not. These things have a way of dragging out. I have to depose witnesses, as does the other side. It's called discovery in the law, and it can take time. You'd be well advised to get a firm that specializes in these matters."

Chip Daren became visibly agitated. "It won't take any time at all."

"Unfortunately, these things do," Sage said. "It is the nature of the beast."

"Not this beast," Daren said. "This can be brought on for immediate hearing."

Sage raised a quizzical eyebrow. "Oh?"

"They're going to file the will in Eagle County. There's nothing on the docket up there. It can be heard immediately."

Sage shrugged. "Perhaps. But I still have to know what the witnesses will say."

"I can tell you that."

"Oh?"

Chip Daren nodded confidently. "They're family friends. I know what they'll say."

Sage smiled. "You never know what people will say on the stand, even if you have interviewed them. Of course, you can get a pretty good idea, and get them on the record in case they change their minds. That's the real purpose of discovery."

"We won't need it in this case."

Sage began to walk slowly. "Why this sudden hurry?"

"The bank. There's a number of things happening in the banking world. We must get control before the end of the year or a great opportunity for expansion will be lost."

"The other side will sniff that out, believe me. That'll use every delaying tactic in the book. I'm pretty good, Mr. Daren, but they have well-defined rights by court rule. Without any kind of artifice they can delay a hearing for months, at the very least."

"They'll want the case heard quickly for the same reason," Chip Daren said. "Win or lose, both sides will want this decided quickly."

"How can you be so sure?"

"I'm sure."

Sage stopped. "It sounds as if you have a source within the enemy camp?"

"I can't say."

"I won't ask the logical question, Mr. Daren. Just allow me to state my position. I'm often accused of unethical conduct, but the accusations are without foundation. My clients, sometimes murderers, sometimes manufacturers, may act unethically, but I don't endorse such conduct nor have I ever become party to such a thing. I don't care what my clients might do so long as I'm not involved, or informed. If I should find a conspiracy exists that violates the law, I will withdraw from the case. Is that understood?"

"So, you'd rather not know where my information comes from?"

Sage chuckled. "If you tell me you can't say, I'll abide by that. But if I proceed, let's understand each other. If what you've been told turns out to be wrong, you must be ready to take the full consequences."

"I don't understand."

"I'll accept as true what you choose to tell me. If it turns out wrong, then it's on your head, not mine. It's your case, and your risk. If you want to do things that way, all right, but let me warn you, such information is sometimes put out by opponents with the purpose to lead one astray."

"That's not the case here."

"If I try this matter I will be flying blind, so to speak. I will be relying on the information you provide. As I say, the risk is entirely yours."

"I'll take that gamble."

Now Sage's chuckle was without humor. "I shall want that in writing. Client's memories are sometimes lacking or inaccurate."

"Whatever you say."

Sage pushed through the doors to the street. It was the beginning of Detroit's rush hour and traffic was already heavy on St.

Antoine Street. The air was thick with exhaust and noise. Sage stopped at the top of the courthouse steps. He thought perhaps a week or two up in uncrowded, clean northern Michigan might provide a pleasant interlude.

"I can devote October and November to this matter. But if it continues beyond that, you'll have to get a substitute attorney. I shall want that understanding put in writing also."

"Agreed," Daren said.

"How do you know the will is to be filed in Eagle County?"

"Let's just say that I know."

Sage nodded. "I won't ask your source, at least not at the moment. I have some serious reservations about all this, my friend, but I also have an annoying sense of adventure."

T. G. Sage hurried down the steps, then stopped and turned. "Be in my office tomorrow at noon. If I decide to go ahead with this, I'll have the necessary papers ready for your signature."

Jake was frustrated.

Marie would not return his calls. He desperately wanted to talk to her, but she was making herself completely unavailable. The drive to Gladding added to his frustration. The problem with Marie had to be put aside until he got back. This time he found the long drive a burden. Filing the will was a job that could have been done by a first-year associate or even a clerk, and Jake resented being sent.

Gladding was just as it was. It seemed to Jake that the very same cars and trucks were still parked in exactly the same spaces against the curb. The town appeared frozen in time.

A police car and a county truck were parked in front of the large red brick Victorian building he had identified as Gladding's governmental headquarters. Jake presumed it also housed the Eagle County offices. He pulled up and parked at an angle near the police car. A pine board suspended between two rustic posts had the words EAGLE COUNTY carved deeply into its wood. A wooden flagpole was planted just behind the sign and to the right of an old artillery piece, apparently the county's war memorial.

Climbing out of the Corvette, Jake stretched for a moment to ease the cramping from the long drive. He was surprised how chilly the air had become. A brisk breeze whipped the small pines bordering the walkway into a frenzied dance.

Somewhere among the small wooden houses built at the back of the main street a dog barked lazily, as if for no purpose except to relieve its boredom.

A small car moved along the avenue and pulled into a spot in front of the drug store. Dressed in jeans and a work jacket, a woman got out and disappeared into the store. He saw no one else.

Jake took out his briefcase and walked up the cracked walk to the entrance. He could not shake the feeling that somehow he had been transported back in time. Gladding seemed like a tired, worn little town, a place more suited to the early fifties. So different from Detroit, it could just as well have been on the moon. The building's old concrete stairs were in need of repair. He climbed up and opened a huge, ancient oak door.

Inside, a narrow, high-ceilinged hallway ran the length of the building. A large iron stairway led to the second floor. Small lettered signs hung above the office doors that dotted the hallway. Everything was constructed of unpainted, varnished wood that looked so old as to be original. The hardwood floor had been so worn down it felt uneven underfoot.

Jake peered around the open door marked SHERIFF as he walked past. The room looked deserted. A man worked in the office marked CLERK, but he didn't even bother to look up.

The door under the PROBATE COURT sign was open and Jake found himself in a small cluttered office. Seated at a desk was a woman busily typing in a two-fingered style on an old Underwood typewriter. She held her head erect, at an awkward angle as she squinted through the bottom half of her bifocal glasses at the typewriter keys. A cigarette bobbled between her thin lips as she worked. Her skin, stretched tight on prominent facial bones, had the weathered consistency of old leather. She wore a man's checkered lumberjack shirt over worn denim jeans. Jake noticed she wore heavy boots. Her hair, dark but streaked with gray, looked more chopped than cut. She wore an old-fashioned green eyeshade.

"Whaddya want?"

He was surprised she knew he was there, she hadn't even glanced up or acknowledged his presence. The cigarette jerked up and down as she spoke.

"I'm here to file a will for probate," Jake said.

She struck a few more keys on the typewriter, studied her work for a moment, then stood up.

She was a small woman, and apparently thin, although her body was concealed by the oversized shirt. Jake guessed she might be around sixty, although she could have been older or younger. She had the look of a person who spent most of her life outdoors.

She cleared some papers from a wooden counter. "Let's see it," she said.

He put his briefcase on the counter and snapped it open.

She stroked the leather. "What does something like that cost?"

He smiled. "It was a gift from my wife."

"I figure this little baby," she patted it, "would run around five hundred, maybe more. Must be nice to have a spouse with money." She smiled, still keeping the cigarette clamped at one end of her mouth. Her teeth were discolored by tobacco stains. "Or maybe she bought it with your dough. That would mean she's not rich, but she's smart."

Jake shrugged. He found even the mention of his wife was painful, so he ignored her. "I have everything here," he said, taking out the file. "The petition, the will, affidavits. Everything's in order."

"Maybe. Maybe not." She took the petition and studied it carefully. "I take it you're from Sperling Beekman?"

"Yes."

She looked up from the papers and appraised him with surprisingly clear blue eyes, enlarged slightly by the refraction of her glasses. "You're a little old to be a messenger, so I presume you're an attorney?"

"Yes, ma'am. I'm one of the firm's lawyers. My name's Martin. Jake Martin."

She returned to the documents. "I thought this case might end up here."

"Did you know Mr. Daren?"

She flipped through the pages of the will. "Met him a few times. You expecting a fight on this thing?"

He felt she was stepping beyond the boundaries of a court clerk. "You never know," he said.

"This town could use a little excitement," she said, still examining the will. "We're dying on the vine up here. If we could generate a little publicity, it might help our tourist business, such as it is." She took the butt of the cigarette from her lips and stubbed it into a cracked dish that served as an ashtray and was already filled with crushed stubs.

"Where do you keep the wills once they're filed?" Jake asked, looking around at the piles of papers and general clutter.

She popped a fresh cigarette into her mouth and lit it with a kitchen match that she ignited by scratching the tip across the top of the rough wooden counter. "Depends. That pile over there is closed cases; the ones on the desk are in progress. We'll find room somewhere."

"Look, this is a very important document. A fortune is involved here. I must insist—"

She laughed, which at first he mistook for a wheezing cough. "Relax, I was pulling your leg. We put these things in a special vault over at the bank. The whole damn town could burn to the ground, but that safe would still be standing with everything in it preserved." She took out a hand stamp and began to rap the stamp into an ink pad and then on the pages of the documents he had presented.

"I wonder if I could talk to the judge," he asked.

"To put the fix in?"

He laughed. "No. But we'd like to schedule this as soon as possible."

She continued stamping the pages. "I'm sure I don't have to tell a hotshot from the city like you, but we have to notify everyone mentioned in the will, plus the heirs at law."

64

"We can do that almost immediately."

"Oh yeah? They passed some kind of new law that makes big firms the court now?"

"I didn't mean it that way," he said. "The heirs at law are all in the will, that's all. They can be notified directly. We've included their names and addresses in the documents submitted."

"In a hurry, huh?"

He nodded. "No use waiting."

"I wonder if the other side will see it the same way?"

"Other side?"

"I saw that clause about the bank's voting stock," she said. "Do you think those kids of Daren's will sit still for that?"

He was surprised. She had picked out the problem, although it had been deeply buried in pages of legal language.

"Is there any way I can have a minute with the judge?"

She grinned. "What do you want with that fierce old bitch?"

"I don't want to discuss the merits of the case. I just want to talk about scheduling."

"What about scheduling?"

"I'd rather talk," he grinned, "to—what did you call her? That fierce old bitch."

Her blue eyes narrowed only slightly.

"I'm the fierce old bitch, sonny. Now, what did you say you wanted to talk about?"

6

Jake had driven from the Eagle County offices to Raven's Nest. He had called Marie once more from the Daren estate, and once more he had gotten the same answer from her secretary. Marie was unbelievable.

He then joined Elizabeth Daren in a small room facing the lake. The room, a kind of breakfast room off the kitchen, was almost all windows and provided an unobstructed view of Lake Bradford. The heavy clouds had moved off and now the water and the distant shore were bathed in the late afternoon sun.

Elizabeth Daren was dressed casually, wearing a deep green sweater over dark slacks. The green tended to accentuate her unusual emerald eyes. She seemed more at ease with him, but he wondered if it might be only his imagination.

"Well, what did you think of Lila Vinson?" she asked as she finished pouring tea.

"The judge appears to be quite a character."

Elizabeth Daren sipped from her delicate china cup and nodded. "Did you have a problem?"

Jake had been asking himself the same question since leaving the offices of Eagle County. "I'm not sure. I don't know what to make of her. She seems rather fiercely independent."

"You have to realize that the people up here are different," she said. "Most of them live very close to the bone, economically speaking. Perhaps that's what makes them so independent, Mr. Martin; they have very little to lose. Whatever it is, there's a quality about them that you won't find elsewhere. At least, I haven't."

"Do you know her?"

Elizabeth Daren put down her tea and nodded. "Before he had the stroke Gus used to like to have the local officials here at least once during the summer. He wanted to stay on good terms with the local people. My contact with Judge Vinson has been strictly on the handshake level. Are you worried about how she might feel about me?"

"Some people resent wealth."

She nodded. "Very true. But if Gus's children do dispute the will, both sides should be even on that score. Gus set up trust funds for them years ago that have made them both very rich."

The sun was causing long shadows to fall across the lawn, and Jake realized it would soon be dark. At night, the five-hour drive back to the city would be very long. He quickly finished his tea.

"By the way, is Rhonda Janus still your secretary?"

"She was my husband's secretary." Her quick reply carried a hint of disapproval.

"I thought maybe you might have kept her on."

Elizabeth Daren shook her head. "No. After the second stroke there was nothing for her to do."

"So you let her go?"

He was answered by a frosty smile. "She was no longer needed." She paused. "I did give her a year's salary as severance pay."

"Where is she now, if you know?"

"I understand she's moved to someplace in Florida."

"She's a witness to the will, Mrs. Daren. We'll have to contact her." He studied her for a moment. "I don't mean to be out of line, but do I detect a note of hostility when you speak of her?"

Elizabeth Daren frowned, then slowly smiled. "How perceptive you are. To be frank, I always thought she might have once been my husband's lover, or possibly they might have had an affair. Oh, this all happened before I arrived on the scene, I admit, but I found it galling that Gus kept her on."

"Did you ask him to let her go?"

"Several times. Gus always denied there had been anything

between them. She lived up here, with us, even after Gus's first stroke. Do you know much about women, Mr. Martin?"

Marie immediately came to his mind. "I thought I did. But now I'm not too sure."

"Well, it wouldn't take a genius to know having a former lover of one's husband in the house isn't exactly a young girl's dream."

"I suppose not. Were you jealous?"

"It makes no difference now, does it?"

"I suppose not."

She smiled. "I'm sure we have her address around here somewhere. I'll have Ronald get it for you before you leave."

"Thank you. How about Dr. Faraday? Has he gone too?"

"Milo's taken a position with Gilbert Hospital in Detroit. More tea?" she asked.

He shook his head.

"Milo was wasted here. He has rather splendid credentials. My husband paid him a king's ransom to stay here and be his personal physician. At the time he said he wanted to get away from the pressures of medical practice. He was worried about burning out. Toward the end, I think life up here began to wear a little thin for him."

"When did he move to Detroit?"

"When Gus finally died."

"Just days ago then?"

She nodded.

"Did you have any problem with him? Please be frank."

"How frank?"

Jake shrugged. "He'll be a key witness to your husband's capacity to make a will. If there was any difficulty, even a hint, I should know about it."

Her eyes were fixed on the lake beyond. "Milo came with us after a rather upsetting divorce. I suppose such things make a person vulnerable." She smiled. "He developed a schoolboy crush on me. I was flattered, of course, but it soon became a nuisance."

"Nothing more than a crush?"

"Do you mean, did I go to bed with him?"

Jake felt her close scrutiny. "Mrs. Daren, this is serious business. If I wanted titillation, I wouldn't have to drive three hundred miles for it. This is strictly lawyer-client. What was your relationship?"

She laughed, which surprised him. "Everything was quite unilateral. He had the crush, I didn't." Her eyes appraised him for a moment, a very long moment. "Does that disappoint you?"

"Mrs. Daren, none of this is personal. I'm just trying to anticipate possible problems." He glanced at his watch. "Well, I had better be going."

"Stay for dinner," she said.

"I'd like to, but it's a five-hour drive back to the city. If I leave now—"

"Stay the night," she said. "God knows, we have plenty of room."

"Thanks, but—"

"Your wife will worry, is that it?"

"I'm separated," he said, then instantly regretted it.

"Is there a girlfriend waiting?"

"No."

"Then stay the night." She paused as she studied him. "I'd appreciate the company, to be frank. Of course, if you have something you really need to do . . ."

Jake wondered if he was afraid of her. Certainly no one was waiting for him back in Detroit.

"They'll expect me back at the firm tomorrow morning," he said, without much conviction.

"I can fill you in on the latest gossip up here. Maybe even talk about some things that might make a difference to the case. The firm couldn't object to that, could they?"

He laughed. "You make it hard to refuse, Mrs. Daren."

"Please call me Elizabeth," she said with a knowing smile.

"Everyone calls me Jake."

"Jake it shall be," she said. "I'll have someone show you to your room." She stood up. "Make yourself at home. Take a walk by the lake, if you like. Dinner's at seven."

He smiled. He liked her. He could fully understand Dr. Faraday's crush. He would have to be careful, he thought. It would be a mistake to like her too much.

Jake's room was actually a suite. All the furniture was constructed of pine and made to appear rough and rustic, although the quality was obvious. A large fireplace took up most of one wall in his sitting room. But he noticed that modern heating vents had been unobtrusively built into the log walls.

His bedroom, as large as a sitting room, contained a high canopied bed. The down-filled mattress looked enormous. There was enough closet space for a platoon, and a thoroughly modern bath.

All the suite's windows faced Lake Bradford. The lake's surface was gunmetal blue broken by occasional whitecaps.

Jake had brought along no casual clothes, only a change of linen and a fresh shirt in case he couldn't drive straight back to Detroit. In that event he had planned to stop as before at some convenient motel. A night at Raven's Nest was completely unexpected.

For a fleeting moment he was going to call Marie to tell her he wouldn't be home, but then he remembered. Marie was no longer there. No one waited for his call. The realization made Jake feel empty and very alone. He needed to get out for a while. Lying in an empty room would only give him time for painful thoughts and memories. He put on the topcoat he had brought along and left his room.

He went down the wide curving staircase to the main room, larger than most hotel lobbies.

"Can I help you, sir?"

A young woman, dressed in a maid's uniform, smiled uncertainly.

"I thought I'd take a walk down by the lake."

"Take that hallway," she indicated. "You'll find a door there."

Outside, Jake was surprised at how chilly it had become. He pulled his collar up, and walked down the sloping lawn toward the water's edge. A huge log boathouse had been constructed there. Two long rock piers extended from the boathouse out into the deep water of the lake, providing safe access for larger boats.

Lake Bradford, he remembered from the map, was almost ten miles long and at points perhaps three miles wide. He stood on the shore. He could see no other houses or cottages on the far side or anywhere else. He watched a flight of ducks wing erratically just above the choppy surface of the lake, which seemed untouched by man or time, as pristine as when first seen by human eyes.

Jake turned and looked up at Raven's Nest.

When seen from the lake, Raven's Nest was even more impressive. Night came quickly in the north, and the estate's lights had been turned on, giving the hotel-sized building a warm, inviting look, like an illustration on a tourist's postcard.

Jake's thin topcoat failed to keep out the chill. He was about to go back when he saw a man striding down the slope from the main house.

"Mr. Martin?"

The man was middle-aged and stocky, attired in a corduroy jacket and turtleneck sweater. He approached Jake, walking with purposeful, military gait.

"I'm Jake Martin."

"My name is Ronald, sir. I'm in charge of this place. I understand you have some questions?"

"Well, Mr. Ronald, I—"

The man's fleshy face split into an amused smile. "It's not Mr. Ronald, sir, just Ronald. I'm Mrs. Daren's butler." He chuckled. "Up here they refer to me as the administrative assistant, since butler has a rather foreign sound to the locals. My proper name is James T. Ronald. I prefer, at least here, to be called Ronald."

"You sound British?"

"I am. Transplanted here to your country about twenty years ago. I have since become a citizen. Now, Mr. Martin, how may I help you?" Ronald was almost as tall as Jake. His salt-and-pepper hair was closely cut and brushed. His manner was dignified but friendly. In his carefully tailored clothing he looked out of place in the primitive setting of Lake Bradford.

"How long have you been employed by the Darens?" Jake asked.

"Almost a year. Before being hired here I worked for Mr. Henry Baylor, the financier."

"The one who was sent to prison?"

The butler smiled. "The very same. Fortunately for me, the federal bureau of prisons won't allow prisoners to bring their butlers along. Mr. Baylor, before he left on his . . . ah . . . enforced vacation, was kind enough to recommend me to Mrs. Daren."

"Who held the job before you?"

"A venerable old gentleman who had been with Mr. Daren for years. Seagraves is his name. Almost eighty now, I think. He's retired and lives in Florida."

"Did you know Mr. Daren before he had the stroke that crippled him?"

Ronald shook his head. "No. When I came here, he was already comatose and on the life support."

"Let me explain my purpose in asking." Jake said. "I may need testimony from the staff as to his competency, prior to the final stroke, of course."

Ronald nodded. "Ah, that may be a bit of a problem, sir."

"Why?"

"Outside of a few people, groundskeepers and the like, I let most of the others go after I took over."

"Why?"

Ronald seemed to possess only one expression, that of pleasant interest. "Two reasons, actually," he answered. "Old Seagraves was getting a bit dotty toward the end, and some of the people were stealing the place blind. Those who weren't tended to think of the job as a godgiven right. Service around here wasn't quite up to snuff. Those who were either lazy or incompetent were let go on that basis." He paused only for a moment, then continued. "The others were let go, you might say, for political reasons."

"What do you mean?"

"Most of the people who were employed here were Gladding natives. We, the Darens, that is, were having a small dispute with the townspeople. Anyone whom I felt might have sided against the Daren family was let go. With severance pay, of course."

"What kind of dispute?"

"It's been going on for years, I've been told."

Ronald gestured toward the darkening lake. "Most of this side of Lake Bradford is owned by the Darens. Almost all of the other side of the lake belongs to a lumber company. The local people believe, correctly I'm told, that Mr. Daren's bank controls that company."

"So?"

70

"You must understand this area, sir. Except for tourism, there is absolutely no commerce up here. The local people wanted some of the land along the lake made available for development: condos, golf courses, resorts, all that sort of thing."

"They wanted to buy it?"

Ronald chuckled. "No. Our neighbors up here have no money. They wanted the land put on the market to interest outside developers. They hoped to see the construction of a new recreational area and the creation of the jobs it would bring. Mr. Daren, as I understand it, refused to consider selling any of his land. The townspeople tried to get the state government interested, but with no success. Local politicians have used the issue to whip up votes for themselves and things, I'm told, sometimes got a little hot. After Mr. Daren's stroke, the townspeople hoped for a change, but Mrs. Daren said nothing would change. There was grumbling, as you might imagine."

"And?"

"I arrived about that time. Some members of the staff seemed to echo that grumbling. I got rid of them at once."

"How about Seagraves, your predecessor? Maybe he could testify to Daren's competency?"

Ronald shrugged. "I said he was retired in Florida, and that's true enough. But it's at a very nice rest-home. I'm informed Seagraves has carried being dotty to its ultimate extreme. He'll be of no help to you on that score, I'm afraid."

"How about the people you let go? Do you think they would be hostile?"

Ronald chuckled. "Would you?"

"Oh, great."

"It may not be quite as bad as it sounds, sir. The lumber company employs a number of locals to harvest trees at various times, and most of the groundskeeping staff are Gladding people. The town is not without some economic reliance on the Daren family. The locals may jump around a bit, but never too high."

"Do they hate the Darens?"

Ronald shook his head. "I doubt it. These are a very practical bunch up here. They live off the land, most of them, and it's a hard scrabble, believe me. Hate takes far too much energy. They need all they have just to survive." He smiled. "However, like the rest of us, they're not above looking out for their own self-interest."

"What kind of jurors do you think they might make?"

Ronald thought for a moment. "You have to remember these are independent people. They would look out for themselves, but beyond that I think they'd be fair."

"But you're not sure?"

His smile was just a trifle wider. "Is anything ever really sure, sir?"

71

Elizabeth Daren had changed for dinner. She wore a clinging floor-length dress of black silk. To Jake it looked as though the fabric had been buttered on and the effect seemed more provocative than if she had chosen to come to the dinner table naked.

Jake felt like a character in a *New Yorker* cartoon. Dinner was being served for just the two of them at a very long table in a huge baronial dining room. Elizabeth sat at the head of the table and Jake sat to her right. He wondered if she dined alone here every night.

The food was exquisite, and each excellent course was accompanied by a different wine. Jake had once tried to become an expert on wines. He had neither the time nor the motivation to develop a truly discerning palate, but he had gained enough experience to know that the wines being offered at this table were very rare and expensive.

After the meal they were served coffee, and then brandy.

"Your butler tells me there's a dispute going on with the townspeople," Jake said.

"I wouldn't call it a dispute," she said. "The people from town would like us to throw open our land to developers. Gus was opposed to that, and so am I. I suppose they thought that after Gus's death I might change my mind. But I won't."

"Why not sell some of it off just to keep everyone happy?"

"We own almost all of the northern shore of Lake Bradford," she said. "Our land extends back several miles to a federal wildlife reserve. The south shore of the lake—thousands of acres—is owned by a lumber company. Our bank controls that company.

"Years ago, during the lumbering days up here, someone managed to get the title to a few hundred feet of Lake Bradford frontage at the far eastern end of the lake. There's a small marina there now plus some run-down rental cottages and a combination dancehall and bar, the Lake Bradford Lounge. It's a dive, the kind of place that draws troublemakers like flies. The whole place looks like a gypsy camp."

She sipped her brandy. "If we put part of the property up for sale, that kind of blight would spread. Then this lovely, pristine part of the north would become nothing more than a jumble of honky-tonk motels, trailer parks, and saloons. Just the thought is unbearable."

"If the people up here feel strongly, it could affect our case, should someone challenge the will. It might make getting an impartial jury a little dicey."

"How could that affect anything? This property was held jointly. I became sole owner on Gus's death. Whatever happens under the will couldn't make any difference. I own it, period."

"But what about the south shore? Apparently, that really belongs to the bank, right?"

"As a practical matter, yes."

"The locals might think they'd have a better chance of opening up the south shore if you lost control of the bank. That's the sort of thing that might affect a jury's verdict."

"Perhaps. But Lee Stevens is already looking into ways to change public opinion up here on that issue, if possible—as you know."

"Oh?"

"Weren't you informed? I told Don Bellows that Stevens had some ideas on the problem."

"He must have forgotten to tell me." Jake thought this weak answer made it appear as if Bellows regarded him as nothing more than an unimportant functionary, or worse, as someone not to be trusted. He felt embarrassed.

For a moment they sat together in painful silence.

"Tell me about yourself, Jake," she said. It was the kind of question people ask to end embarrassing breaks in conversation.

"Nothing much to tell," he replied. "I'm just a normal run-of-the-mill guy."

She smiled. "No one is run-of-the-mill, not when you really get to know them. Do I hear an echo of New York when you talk?"

He laughed. "I thought I had no accent at all, but I guess that's not quite true, is it? I was born and raised in Manhattan."

"Born there? I always had the impression that everyone in Manhattan came there from some other place."

"Most do, I suppose. My father had a restaurant supply business in the city. My mother was managing a restaurant when they met."

"What are they doing now?"

Jake thought about his father. It was sometimes difficult even to recall what he had looked like. "My father died when I was fifteen. A heart attack."

"He must have been very young."

Jake shrugged. "Fifty-five. I came along rather late in their lives."

"How about your mother?"

"She died three years ago. A lung problem. She got pneumonia and couldn't shake it. She smoked three packs of cigarettes a day. That didn't help. I tried to get her to quit, or at least cut down, but she went back to running restaurants and she said she was too busy to try."

"You and I have similar backgrounds," she said. "Both orphans. Any brothers or sisters?"

"No. I'm the last of the Martins, Manhattan branch."

"Where did you live in the city?"

"An apartment on the West side in the eighties."

Elizabeth Daren smiled. "You must have been close to Zabar's."

"Practically around the corner. You really do know the city," Jake said.

"Where did you go to school?"

"Columbia, undergrad and law school."

"Would you like some more brandy?"

Jake shook his head. "No, thanks. I wouldn't mind a little more coffee, though."

She signaled the maid, then once more turned her unusual eyes to him. "So, tell me, how did a nice New York boy like you end up in Detroit?"

He laughed. "Your question reminds me of that old joke, the one the brothel customer asks the prostitute: How did a nice girl like you end up in a place like this? And she answers: Just lucky, I guess."

Elizabeth merely smiled. "Well, was that how it happened, just luck?"

"No, not exactly. My wife-to-be was a fellow student, but a year or so behind me. I passed the New York Bar and put in a couple of years with a Manhattan firm, a big one, in their litigation department. Mostly, I carried books and there didn't seem like much of a future there for me. My wife was a Michigan girl. She got a good job offer, so I sort of followed her back to Detroit when she graduated."

"She's a lawyer then?"

"Yes. With the firm of Brosner Whitney."

She nodded, as if assimilating the information. "You said, I recall, that you're separated."

He sipped his coffee before replying. "That just happened. My wife is the one who wants the divorce."

"And you don't?"

Since he found answering painful and embarrassing, he merely shook his head and again sipped the coffee.

Elizabeth's emerald eyes seemed to become mischievous. "You weren't caught playing around, were you, Jake?"

"No. It's nothing like that."

She eyed him speculatively. "You're an attractive man. It's a logical assumption. What's the trouble, if I'm not being too nosy?"

He shrugged. "I don't know, to be frank. I think the main problem is that our careers have been just too demanding. We have never had much time for each other."

"Perhaps marriage counseling might help?"

"I suggested that. At the moment, my wife doesn't seem inclined toward anything like that."

She gazed at him but didn't speak. Her tranquil expression gave no clue to her thoughts, which made him even more uncomfortable.

She looked away from him and then spoke softly. "I lived in New York, in several places," she said. "As a matter of fact, at one time several girls and I shared an apartment not far from yours. I moved around quite a bit—you could in those days. There were places still

74

to be had then for reasonable rents. I lived on Riverside Drive for a while, Murray Hill, and also near Gramercy Park."

"When you were a model?"

"That, and a hundred other jobs. Then I met Gus. I followed him to Michigan, just as you did your wife." She laughed softly. "So that's how I ended up in a place like this; like you, just lucky." She stood up. "Let's move into the main room. It's more comfortable."

Jake followed her to a large leather sofa facing the gigantic fireplace. Flames crackled all around the stacked logs, occasionally sending up cascades of sparks that looked like miniature firework displays.

Night had fallen and everything beyond the windows was pitch-black. It was as if the huge lake didn't even exist. Elizabeth patted a place on the sofa near her. Jake sat, sinking down into the soft warm leather.

"Have you ever heard of a lumberman's knee?" she asked.

"What is it?"

"A drink. As far as I know, it's strictly local. Great for cold evenings. Would you like to try one?"

"Well, I don't know . . ."

She rang for a maid. "Have the kitchen prepare the makings for two lumberman's knees."

The maid went to the fireplace and carefully laid the tips of two metal pokers into the flames, then scurried away.

"Do you ever get homesick for New York, Jake?"

He shrugged. "At first I did. Now, occasionally I still do, but I'm really too busy to think about it."

"No other family there? Aunts, uncles, anyone like that?"

Jake sighed. "Nope, I'm afraid not."

She studied the fire for a moment. "That's basically my situation, too." She paused, then spoke again. "It can get lonely."

"Sometimes," he said.

The maid brought a tray containing two quart-sized pewter mugs which she set down on a low table in front of them.

"I'll do it myself, Catherine," Elizabeth said.

The maid nodded, then left.

Elizabeth smiled. "I rather like doing this." She took one of the mugs and carried it to the fireplace. Moving with the easy grace of a dancer, she extracted one of the pokers the maid had placed in the fire. The tip glowed fiery red.

Elizabeth Daren was a truly beautiful woman, but beyond that there was a sensual quality about her, rigidly contained but nevertheless potentially explosive. Jake watched, realizing he hadn't made love for a long time. He felt the stirrings of desire. She was a client, and his career depended upon her case. Desire, especially dangerous desire, was something he couldn't afford. Still, he could not take his eyes away from her.

Elizabeth moved the glowing poker tip like a sword point, bringing it up and then plunging it expertly into the mouth of the mug. A blue flame erupted from the mug with a loud sizzle, filling the air with the pungent aroma of nutmeg and ginger. She lay the poker aside and brought the steaming mug to him, holding it carefully.

"This is hot." Her face carried the glow from the fire. "Be careful. Just sip."

She repeated the process with the other mug, then joined him, sitting just a bit closer than before.

"Let it cool for a moment, then try it," she said.

He could feel the heat as he brought the cup to his lips. The steam from the mug was like an intoxicating incense. Carefully, he sipped. It tasted like nothing he had ever had before, being both sweet and tart, powerful but smooth. He felt as if the warmth from the drink was spreading all the way down into his fingers and toes.

Elizabeth was watching him, smiling. "Do you like it?"

"What's in it?"

She pursed her lips and blew gently on her own drink before sipping. "Whiskey, rum, some gin and enough spices to supply every Cajun cook in the country."

She studied her drink, then looked at Jake. "They use this for everything up here. It takes the place of champagne for weddings. They make a batch for funerals. And when they're sick, they take it in place of tranquilizers and pain medications. It might not help, but it's guaranteed to make you feel much better about whatever ails you."

Jake drank again. "When this is all settled," he asked, "will you continue to live here?"

She looked at the fire as though the flames might supply an answer. Finally, she spoke. "I'm not sure." Her tone softened slightly. "When Gus was alive," she paused, "and was functioning, this was as near to heaven as I ever expected to get. But that's all changed."

Jake sipped again. The drink was cooling and he could drink it without fear of being burned. "Did you ever think about going back to New York?"

"Going back to New York is always a possibility. A lot depends on what happens with the bank."

"Don't worry about that," he said, surprised at his own new sense of confidence. "You'll have no trouble."

"I'm in your capable hands, is that it?"

He smiled. "Elizabeth, I'm just one insignificant cog in a mighty legal machine. You have the harnessed power of Sperling Beekman at your command. How can you miss?"

"How about you, Jake? If your divorce should go through, will that mean major change for you?"

It was his turn to study the dancing flames. For a moment he was tempted to confide in her, to tell her about his quest for

76

partnership, and how fragile his career seemed, but he thought that might make him appear insecure and weak. He didn't want to appear weak to those penetrating emerald eyes.

"Everything is sort of up in the air," he said, trying to sound breezy. He held up the mug. "What do they call this drink again?"

She smiled. "They call it a lumberman's knee, because of the kick." Her face was close to his. "Would you like me to make you another?"

He shook his head. "You're right about the kick. I think not, thank you."

Elizabeth stood up. "It's been a delightful evening, Jake. I appreciate the company. Very much." She touched his arm. "Can you find your room all right?"

Jake wondered what her reaction might be if he asked her for a date. He hadn't asked anyone out in years, not since Marie. He was almost tempted to ask now, but he checked himself. She was one of the richest women in the country and he was a struggling associate lawyer. She might laugh. He looked at her. "I'm fine," he said, then added. "We'll do everything possible to help you, Elizabeth."

She studied him, the flickering light from the fire seemed to bring a new, more intense quality to her eyes. The green became deeper, darker. "I've met many lawyers, Jake, but you're by far the sweetest." She bent down and kissed him gently on the lips. "Good night."

Long after she was gone, and long after he had gone to bed, he was still conscious of the warm silky touch of her lips.

7

"We are but fragile creatures and our time on this earth is brief. Most of us are born, live out that allotted span and die, affecting only the lives of our own immediate families and perhaps a few close friends."

The bishop cocked his head slightly and smiled. "However, some of us, whether by design or by fate, are destined to touch the lives of many others during that earthly sojourn. Such a one was my friend, Augustus Daren."

Bored, Jake only half listened. The bishop was the last in a parade of speakers at the noontime memorial service for Gus Daren. Each speaker, including the clergy, Jake was told, had been asked to restrict his remarks to only a few minutes. But some had stretched their eulogies well beyond that. A few of them even strayed beyond the obvious subject matter. The mayor, making only a passing reference to Daren, had launched a stinging attack upon press and media reporters whom he claimed were being unfair to him in reporting the latest city hall scandal. The memorial service provided his honor with the rare opportunity to scold the reporters without having to answer any potentially embarrassing questions.

At least the mayor had been entertaining, but the bishop's monotone was like the droning voice of a hypnotist. To keep awake, Jake turned and looked over the crowd. Ford Auditorium, built at the edge of the Detroit River, was filled to capacity. Jake guessed that the overflow crowd numbered nearly two thousand. Most were well-dressed clerks and other bank employees turned out in force from Hanover Square and its neighboring banking institutions in the city's central business district. They were augmented by government workers and elected officials.

But sprinkled among the bankers and politicians were ragged street people who seemed unlikely mourners for an international banker, especially one who was not particularly known for his charitable acts. But the big auditorium was a haven from the wind and the speakers provided a kind of free entertainment. Under the stern eye of an army of uniformed policemen stationed throughout the auditorium, the bag ladies and panhandlers were well behaved.

The power structure of the city had turned out in force, and the audience was sprinkled with political power brokers from every segment of the community. Each major bank was represented by its top officers. Every financier of note in Detroit was also present. Jake smiled. If the power of money had an odor, the aroma in Ford Auditorium would have been completely overwhelming.

Elizabeth Daren sat in the front row facing the auditorium's stage. Dressed in black, she was surrounded by men and women Jake presumed to be officers and directors from the Hanover Square Bank. Donald Bellows, looking like a protecting angel, sat directly next to her. Seated a few rows back, Jake had wanted to say hello to Elizabeth, but the opportunity hadn't presented itself. It had been only days since he'd spent the night at her estate, but to Jake it seemed much longer.

Daren's two children were also in the front row, but on the opposite side of the auditorium.

Chip Daren had the look of an offended bulldog. He glowered at the bishop, silently trying to will him to shut up and sit down. Hostility seemed to emanate from Chip Daren like body heat.

The daughter, Gussie, was a surprise. Jake recognized her from pictures in the files. Also dressed in black, she was tall for a woman. Unlike her brother she held herself with elegant bearing and betrayed no emotion. Thin as a reed, she had Daren features, with high cheekbones and a wide nose. She was pretty but not beautiful. Gussie at thirty-nine was the same age as Elizabeth Daren, but she seemed older. The old newspaper clippings in the firm's file reported Gussie's youthful wild escapades, but today she looked the picture of dignity.

Jake, several rows from the front, was still close enough to study the man seated between the Daren children. It was the first time he had seen him in the flesh, although his picture was often in the newspapers and Jake had seen him on the news giving impromptu interviews on courthouse steps.

Lawyers feared him, but to Jake he looked like a dowdy old uncle. While everyone else in the auditorium appeared to be suitably solemn and stonefaced, T. G. Sage appeared to be sincerely enjoying himself. He had laughed with genuine amusement at some of the mayor's bitter jokes and actually seemed interested in the remarks of the other speakers, studying each of them over the rim of the half-glasses that perched on the end of his nose. Short and stocky, to Jake he looked very unlike any kind of "Tiger." They would soon have a chance to find out how Sage had achieved that name.

T. G. Sage had filed objections to the will on behalf of Chip Daren, serving Sperling Beekman with a copy. The lawsuit was now a reality. Jake had reviewed Sage's pleadings, which were short and to the point, but which also contained mostly unsupported charges of incompetency. Tiger Sage gave no hint of what evidence he might offer at trial to prove his allegations.

Cora Simpson had not come to the memorial. She was back at Sperling Beekman preparing the firm's formal answer to Sage's charges.

Jake was surprised that Sage's action had been met with such equanimity at Sperling Beekman, almost arrogance. Donald Bellows, sounding like a football coach, had assured his Daren Estate team that they had nothing to worry about. The law was with them, Bellows had said, and Sage would have overcome almost impossible odds to upset the Daren will. Jake wondered at Bellows' breezy confidence. T. G. Sage had the reputation of never taking foolish cases, and when he did take a case he usually won it.

Jake wondered if Donald Bellows' cool assurance came from having nothing at stake personally. If the Daren case was lost, someone would get the blame. And, as team leader, Jake was the logical candidate. If the case was lost, Jake's career at Sperling Beekman would be lost right along with it.

". . . And I say to his lovely widow and his two wonderful children," the bishop was finally coming to a conclusion, "think not of your loss. Rather, think of how the life of Augustus Daren illuminated his world and everyone in it."

A few of the street people began to applaud, but they were quickly silenced by ominous glares from the scowling policemen.

The bishop took his seat next to Detroit's other leading

clergymen, looking extremely pleased with his own performance, like an actor who thought he had done especially well.

Claude deSalle, the president of Hanover Square, who had been serving as a de facto master of ceremonies, stood up. Jake had set up an appointment to interview deSalle as a possible witness to Gus Daren's mental capacity. The memorial gave Jake a chance to assess what kind of a witness he might make.

Claude deSalle, short, with his fireplug body encased in a very expensive suit, moved with surprisingly fluid grace. His personality—quick, charming and slightly challenging—was the kind Jake thought women might find attractive. He wasn't handsome, not in a classical sense, but he had an interesting face, crowned by a flowing mane of silver hair. To Jake, he looked much more like a bishop than the real men of the cloth seated behind him on the platform.

Turning from the lectern, deSalle thanked the clergy in order of appearance, then the governor, the mayor, and the other speakers. His voice, smooth but commanding, possessed a quiet authority. Jake thought he would make a very persuasive witness.

". . . And we wish to thank each and every one of you for sharing with us these few moments in memory of a great man and a good friend," deSalle said to the audience. "We were greatly blessed by his presence and we shall all deeply feel his loss."

For the first time, he smiled. "Augustus Daren loved his bank. In order to ensure that the Daren name not be lost in that association with his beloved institution, I take pleasure in announcing that this morning the directors of Hanover Square Bank met and elected Elizabeth Daren as chairman of our board, to fill the position left vacant by her husband's death."

Jake happened to be looking at Chip Daren as deSalle spoke. Chip's face flushed angry red and he started to rise, but was restrained by the hand of T. G. Sage. Sage merely smiled and whispered something that kept Daren in his seat. His sister Gussie showed no reaction whatsoever.

"The officers and employees of Hanover Square, the friends and family of Augustus Daren thank all of you for coming."

It was over. The auditorium buzzed with activity as people moved toward the exits. DeSalle formally shook hands with each of the speakers.

Chip Daren, still red, was talking excitedly at Sage, who seemed slightly amused by the whole thing.

Donald Bellows quickly escorted Elizabeth away from any possible encounter with Daren's children. Elizabeth moved regally through the throng of the powerful clustering about her, shaking hands and looking as if she had done nothing else all in her life.

"Jake!"

Jake turned and saw Lee Stevens pushing through the crowd of people to get to him.

"Well, what did you think?" Stevens asked when he reached him.

"About the memorial?"

"I thought it worked out well. We had the press covering it like a blanket. There should be some swell shots of Elizabeth on tonight's news."

"Did you put this whole thing together?"

Stevens shook his head, almost reluctantly. "That fellow deSalle put the strong arm on the banking community to get the troops out. But I took care of the rest. Not bad, eh?"

Jake nodded his agreement.

"You know, if she was interested, I could probably put Elizabeth into the state house, maybe even the senate. She's a knockout, but she always looks as if she knows exactly what has to be done."

"Regal," Jake said.

Stevens' smile widened. "That catches it nicely. She's regal, no doubt about it." He lit a cigarette, despite all the signs in the auditorium prohibiting smoking. People were continuing to crowd toward the exits. "Have you had lunch?"

"No," Jake replied. "I have to get back to the office."

"With this mob on the street, the restaurants around here will be jammed. Let's walk up to Lafayette and grab a couple of Coney Islands."

"I really do have to get back to the—"

"Jake, you're busy, I'm busy, everybody's busy. But this is work, and we have to talk. You may not have to eat, but I do. C'mon, I'll buy."

"Well, it's a matter of time. I have to—"

"This is all billable time," Stevens said. "You can charge it against the Daren Estate. And it could be important. Okay?"

"Okay."

They walked with the exiting crowd up Woodward Avenue, the city's main thoroughfare, passing Detroit's City-County Building, the hub of city power, and the imposing statue of the "Spirit of Detroit," a green metal giant who looked as though he was about to use a spiked universe held in his left hand to impale some metal people held in the palm of his right hand. He looked, to Jake, indecisive about what to do.

They walked up toward Kennedy Square. A concrete space lay where the old city hall once stood; the park was now the roof of an underground garage.

"I hear you've been up north in Gladding," Stevens said. "Have you ever lived in the northland?"

Jake shook his head.

"I did once," Stevens said. "Those people up there are different. I don't know if it's good different, or bad different, but they are different. They're polite, but they don't take easily to strangers. You never really know what any of them is thinking. Of course, the whole bunch up in Gladding are hungry to grab the Daren land, or at least open it up, if they can. A local politician running for the state legislature is doing his best to stir things up."

"I heard about the problem, but not the politician," Jake said.

Stevens snorted. "Down here, if a politician's raising a fuss, you just find out what church he goes to, slide into the pew next to him and slip him a nice fat envelope. He might not become your friend, but he isn't your enemy anymore. Up there, it's different."

Jake laughed. "They don't go to church?"

"It's not that, exactly. It's just there are wheels within wheels up there. It's as full of secrets and intrigues as an Istanbul café. They should have named the place Enigma. I prefer doing business in the city."

"Do you pass envelopes often?"

Stevens laughed. "Never, as a matter of fact. If I find an envelope is necessary, I let the client know and leave it up to him. It's what you might call situational ethics."

They turned into Lafayette Street. Two Coney Island restaurants, almost identical, operated next door to each other. Stevens chose the older establishment, which turned out to be jammed, but they found two empty stools at the counter. The heady, pungent aroma of onions and chili awakened Jake's hunger.

Stevens ordered for both of them: two Coney Islands each, which in Detroit meant two long hot dogs on buns, each smothered in diced onions and hot chili. The waiter, who could manage only a few words in English, set two steaming mugs of coffee in front of them.

Stevens sipped gingerly at the scalding coffee. "The people up in Gladding want Lake Bradford opened to tourists and the money they'd bring in. They think it's a matter of survival. Anyone opposing them could get hurt."

"Do you think Elizabeth Daren is in danger?"

The waiter slammed the Coney Islands down in front of them as he continued a loud argument in Greek with another waiter.

"I don't think they'd shoot her. Anyway, she's got plenty of protection. But I doubt they'd be particularly friendly on a jury, if you take my meaning."

"She said you were taking care of that."

Stevens munched on his Coney Island, expertly avoiding spilling any of the chili and onions. "Did she now? I'm trying. If she'd agree to open up a mile or two of the lake for development, that'd change things; but she won't. I'm good at forming public opinion," he said, taking another bite, "but I'm not a magician."

Jake tried to eat with dignity but gave it up. Unlike Stevens, he followed each bite with napkin damage control. It was sloppy, but it was good, very good.

"Aren't you worried about the case?" Stevens asked.

"We have a videotape of Daren describing his will. He's absolutely lucid and in control. No jury, even one in Gladding, would have any question about his competency after seeing that tape."

"I'd like to take a look," Stevens said.

"One of these days when we aren't quite so busy, I'll have it set up for you."

"Has anyone in your office talked to Rhonda Janus?"

"The witness to the will? We will, of course, but I don't think we have as yet. Why?"

Stevens again wiped away some chili. "As part of maybe getting a feel for opinion up in Gladding, I tried to contact Rhonda Janus in Florida. I thought as the old man's former personal secretary she might know something useful." Stevens chewed, then washed it down with a gulp of coffee. "She's gone."

"Dead?"

He chuckled. "Perhaps, given everything, that might be better. No, she's taken off. Her condo's being looked after by a friend, some retired guy from Cleveland. I got the idea they might be more than just friends. He says he doesn't know when she'll be back."

"So?"

"I talked to the gentleman. I used to be an investigative reporter and even over the phone I'm pretty good at getting people to talk. Anyway, our Rhonda took off just a couple of days after they turned off Gus's machines."

"So?"

Stevens looked at him. "Elizabeth said you seemed intelligent. Think about it, Jake. One of your two main witnesses is gone. I think someone has her under wraps. You and I can't talk to her; we can't find out what she might say. My guess is she'll surface on the day she's scheduled to testify, and what she has to say won't be good."

"That's only a guess."

He nodded. "That's right. But conjure on this. You'll have a jury selected from a bunch of people who think they might see a profit if the case goes against Elizabeth. That tape of yours might be good, but if Rhonda, a witness to the will, shows up and turns on you, that might be just the point a jury would need to nail Elizabeth with an unfavorable verdict." Stevens finished his coffee. "In other words, to be a bit vulgar, Jake, there's a possibility that you boys might be stepping into one very deep tub of shit."

He wiped his mouth with a paper napkin. "My, those were good. How about another?"

After the crowds at the memorial, Claude deSalle took Elizabeth Daren back to his ornate office in Hanover Square's headquarters. It was the first time they had been alone during the hectic day that had begun with the special board meeting to elect her chairman and had been followed by the memorial service.

The temple-like building that was the Hanover Square Bank always seemed to deSalle to be a sanctuary in the middle of Detroit's busy business district. It seemed especially so now.

He smiled at her. "There's a small office down the hall. I'll move over there when you move in here."

She was lovely to look at as she sat so confidently on his long leather couch. Claude deSalle regretted that the beautiful Elizabeth Daren was out of bounds, but much more was at stake than his personal pleasure or male ego, much more.

"I won't need this office, Claude. Not at the moment, anyway. For the time being, I'll continue to work from Raven's Nest. As before, I'll come down for the executive meetings."

He nodded. She sounded as though she had a definite timetable. He wondered what it might be.

"May I offer you a drink?"

"Vodka, straight up," she said.

"No problem." He went to the huge chart of the federal reserve system and hit the secret button. "Gus loved this," he said as the chart rolled back revealing a small but complete bar. "Ice?"

"Please."

He fixed the vodka for her, and a water and bourbon for himself. He handed her the vodka and sat on the other side of the sofa.

"To Gus."

She smiled and sipped, her eyes fixed on him.

"You did an excellent job today, Claude. Gus would have appreciated it."

"It was nothing."

"You're an able executive," she said.

"Thank you."

She studied her glass. "I imagine you're curious why I wanted to be named chairman."

"Well, as I said, it's none of my business, but I think—"

"I'm negotiating with some foreign banks," she said easily. "I needed the title to provide myself with a little more credibility."

"Negotiating?"

She stirred the ice in her drink with her finger. "Gus said that no one can afford to stand still in this business. You are either going up, or coming down." She smiled. "He said the banking business is like a bouncing ball."

Claude deSalle forced himself to appear indifferent. "Perhaps. With all due respect to Gus, I like to think it's somewhat more stable than that." He smiled casually, but his senses were on full alert.

She shifted. Ordinarily, he would have been fascinated by her long legs, but not today.

"I've been approached by several German banks," she said.

"They propose a kind of confederation between their houses and Hanover Square. They want to take advantage of laws they think might soon be changed."

"Oh?" He thought of Paul Schiller. The German had told him she had refused his offer of consolidation.

"It's crucial that we expand internationally. Gus thought so, and so do I. Someone has to be in a position to finance the Russians. It's a whole new financial frontier." She spoke with quiet authority. "The Germans offer one possibility," she said, finishing her drink. "But an alliance with the Japanese may be a much more profitable proposition."

He forced himself to smile. "My, you really have been busy, haven't you?"

"Gus said the Germans and the Japanese, because they didn't have to invest in their own defense after the war, have had a tremendous advantage. All their money has gone into their own commerce."

"We protected them," deSalle said, wishing he had made his drink stronger. "Now they seem to have all the chips."

"No matter," she smiled. "Both Germany and Japan have financial institutions that are giants compared to even our biggest banks. Especially the Japanese."

"They do have a lot of money."

"They do indeed," she answered. "And they're looking for influential partners. But the situation is volatile. We must be in a position to act fast. We have to beat any other American banks with the same idea. Combining our assets with a foreign giant could make Hanover Square the most influential bank in America."

"There are laws against that sort of thing, Elizabeth," he said quietly.

"Yes. But I think both the Germans and the Japanese have come up with legal solutions."

"Oh?"

"Nothing's firm, but I think it can be done." She put her glass down on the coffee table. "Being named chairman is just the first step. I'll keep you informed on the negotiations."

"Our lawyers should be at your elbow, so to speak, during discussions. So should I," he said, somewhat too passionately, which he regretted immediately. Quickly he sought to soften his words. "Well, I suppose both the lawyers and myself can get into it later when things start to firm up." He wondered if he sounded as insincere to her as he did to himself. "Of course, this nuisance about Gus's will could delay things."

She stood up. "I doubt it. Whether the probate case goes quickly or not, the negotiations will continue. I think the Japanese are amused by our legal system. Over there, apparently, this sort of thing never happens."

"Well, let's hope it's all settled shortly," he said.

"It will be. I'm chairman of the board now, and that's what counts. With a little luck, we could end up making financial history."

He took her hand and lightly kissed her cheek. "Whatever happens, I'm your firmest supporter, Elizabeth."

She returned the perfunctory kiss.

"Are you staying in the city?"

She shook her head. "No, I'm flying directly back. Thanks again, Claude. You handled things expertly."

He walked her through the bank to her waiting limousine, waving to her as it pulled away from the curb. Then he hurried to his office.

This time he poured the bourbon straight and gulped it down. Elizabeth Daren might not care if the probate case was delayed, but he did. If she won the case or even if it was delayed, he would lose his chance to become head of the bank, and he would have to kiss his deal with the Germans good-bye.

Claude deSalle wasn't prepared to let that happen. He finished the whiskey and then dialed Chip Daren's number. It was time to heat up the battle.

As he returned to the office, Jake's mouth felt like a flame-thrower, the aftereffect from the hot chili and onions of his Coney Island lunch. His breath felt like it could buckle paint. For that reason he kept his face turned away from his secretary, merely nodding as he accepted the telephone messages she handed him. He retreated into his office, and then glanced through the messages. Most were routine, but one was from Marie.

He dialed her number with a rising sense of excitement. Marie's secretary seemed unnecessarily formal as she put him through.

"Hello, Jake." Marie was brisk, all business.

"I'm glad you called," he said. "I've been leaving messages for you everywhere."

"I'm sorry about that, but things have been really hectic around here."

"Marie, we have to talk this thing out. How about dinner?"

"I'm afraid not."

"Okay. How about lunch tomorrow? Anywhere, Marie. You pick the place and I'll be there. It doesn't have to be lunch. I could come to your office, if you like. But we have to talk."

"Jake, it won't help."

He felt his pulse race. She had to listen. "Look, let's go for counseling. We're not the first couple who've had trouble in their marriage. You choose the counselor if you like. Then, if that doesn't work—"

"You're making this very difficult."

"I'm not making anything difficult," he said. "I'm trying to stop this before it gets out of hand."

"It already has."

"What do you mean?"

"I'm filing for divorce tomorrow. I called as a matter of courtesy."

"Courtesy! Jesus, this isn't some two-bit negligence case we're settling here, Marie; this is our marriage, remember. Our lives. My life. If you're interested in courtesy, don't file anything, just give me a chance to talk to you first."

She continued in a softer tone. "Roger Bartlett is representing me. He said he'd call you and arrange for service. Roger thought you probably wouldn't want to be served with the papers at your office."

"Well, isn't that sweet of Roger? How fucking civilized! Don't do this, Marie. I'll come over to your office right now. Talk to me, Marie. I'm not going to bite. At least hear me out."

"Roger will do my talking for me," she said quietly.

He swung around in his chair and looked out the window. Dark rain clouds were forming over Canada.

He paused, trying to control his rising anger. "I thought you weren't going to file until I was made partner? That's what you told me."

"You'll make partner," she said. "I've thought it over. Divorce no longer carries the stigma it once did."

He was clutching at straws. "Look, hold off until the partnership question is decided. All I'm asking for is a month, maybe two."

"No, I can't. I'm sorry, Jake."

"What's the fucking hurry?"

"There's no need to shout."

"Oh, no? You don't seem to be listening. We're living apart. There's no question about a property settlement. Why the hurry, Marie? Answer me that."

For a moment he wondered if she had hung up, then she spoke, her tone icy. "I don't have to answer to you for anything."

He took a deep breath to calm himself. "Marie, we have five years of our lives invested here. I'm not asking much, just a good-faith effort to try and save our marriage."

"Roger will contact you."

"I'll oppose this, Marie. Tooth and fucking nail!"

He heard fury in her clipped tone. "I keep telling you, this is a no-fault state. There's no question of money or children. What are you going to fight, Jake? I want out. Period. That's all the courts require here."

"Look, I apologize for being angry. I'll come over and we'll talk this over like adults."

"Absolutely not. If you have anything to say, say it to Roger Bartlett."

"Fuck Roger Bartlett! This is between you and me. I don't need any—" He realized this time she had hung up.

Jake's heart was pounding. He saw the reflection in his window. Someone was standing in his open doorway.

He swung around and glared at Cora Simpson.

"I'm sorry, Jake," she said. "I just came over. I didn't realize you were making a private call."

"You heard?"

She held a large office case file, clasping it to her with crossed arms. "Well, I didn't hear much, except you intend to do something nasty to a Roger Bartlett."

Jake stood up and slammed the receiver down as he hung up the dead phone. "He's my wife's divorce lawyer." He started to come around the desk.

"Where are you going?" Cora asked.

"Over to Marie's office."

She blocked his way. "I wouldn't, Jake."

"Get out of the way, Cora."

She shook her head. "You'll make a complete and utter fool of yourself. Of course, that might mean one less candidate for the coveted partnership, but even I don't want to win that way."

"Come on, Cora; this is none of your business. Let me pass."

She held up the file. "I was planning to talk to you about the Daren estate. Suppose we go out somewhere and grab a beer? We can talk about the Daren case, or your problems. You can pick the topic."

"Cora—"

"Take a few minutes out to cool down, Jake. If, after that, you still want to go over and wring your wife's neck, I won't stop you."

He was about to shove her out of the way. "I have to go. I have to know why she's doing this. There has to be a reason, and I want to know what it is."

"You might not like it."

"I have to find out."

Her expression was suddenly grim. "I know why," she said softly.

"I'm not kidding, Cora."

"Nor am I."

"What do you mean?"

She stepped around him and lay the file on his desk. "Close the door, Jake."

She studied him for a moment, then she spoke, "God, I hate being the one who has to tell you."

"Tell me what?"

"First, close the door."

He did and then turned to her. "Well?"

"It's common gossip. But obviously no one has told you. Jake, you know the big downtown firms: everyone knows everyone else. It's like a little country village sometimes, everyone knows everyone else's business."

"So?"

"Your wife is involved with one of the partners at her firm."

"That's bullshit!"

She shrugged. "Maybe, but I don't think so. As the saying goes, the two of them are an item. He's just gone through a divorce so I suspect remarriage may be looming in the not-too-distant future."

He felt ill, as if he had just received a killing blow. "And who is this guy supposed to be?"

"Harvey Kellerman."

"Kellerman! Christ, he's old enough to be Marie's father. No way, Cora."

She sat on the edge of the desk. "That's the word, Jake. Kellerman is good-looking, he's one of the most powerful lawyers in the state, and he's rich to boot."

Jake walked to the window and looked down at the river without really seeing it. "The son of a bitch."

She said nothing.

His throat was tight. "If you're right," he said, "that would account for all those late nights, and the overnight trips." He swallowed. "Boy, talk about being a rube."

"I'm sorry, Jake."

He looked up at the clouds darkening the autumn sky. "I love her, Cora. I don't want this to happen."

"Jake, honest to God I didn't want to tell you, but I was afraid you'd go over there and make a complete mess of things." She sighed. "Maybe it would have been better if I'd kept my mouth shut."

Jake turned from the window. "Jesus, I can't even stand to think about it, but I had to know." He slowly shook his head. "God, it never entered my mind but, given everything, it's probably true." He looked at her. "You were right to tell me, Cora. Otherwise, I would have played the fool as well as the cuckold. Jerks are not made, they're born."

"You're not a jerk," she said. "If I were in your shoes I'd get damn good and mad. As far as I'm concerned, your wife's a thoughtless, heartless little bitch. If she marries Kellerman it'll serve her right. Harvey's a player who can't keep that thing of his in his pants. She'll get everything back in spades."

He heard the sound of rain against the window.

"Do you want to be alone, Jake?"

He shook his head. "I don't know what I want. All this has a real nightmare quality to it."

"I'll buy you a drink."

He tried to smile but his face felt stiff. "Is that your prescription for everything?"

"No. But in this case, it might help."

"It just might."

8

Jake's first conscious feeling was the throbbing pain. Reluctantly he opened his eyes and found himself staring up at an unfamiliar ceiling. The main source of pain seemed localized behind his eyes. For a moment he lay still, then he risked looking around.

He found that he was clad only in shorts and socks and lying on top of the covers in the middle of a large bed. The bedroom was lived in, with cosmetics and personal items strewn on every available furniture top. He was definitely not in a hotel. Beige drapes had been drawn across what he surmised was a window. Jake tried to sit up but fell back as a wave of dizziness assaulted his senses.

Moving by inches, he slowly rolled to the edge of the bed and carefully pushed himself up. He squinted at a clock radio on the night stand. It was 8:10 A.M. He carefully lifted his legs over the side of the bed.

"I thought I might have to call an undertaker, but it looks like you're alive. " It was Cora's voice coming from another room.

"Where am I?"

She walked in, smiling and dressed for the office.

"My place," she said.

"Oh God, Cora, what happened? I feel like I've been run over."

"You're not much of a drinker are you, Jake?"

He sighed. "Obviously not. Did I make an ass of myself?"

She shook her head. "You weren't a problem, really. I listened and you drank. But you went fast, Jake. One minute you were slightly tight and the next you were completely zonked. There was nothing in between. You wanted to drive home, but I persuaded you to come up here."

He realized he was almost naked. He ran a hand through his matted hair. "Did we . . ."

"I think I'm pregnant, Jake."

"What!"

"I'm joking. I tried to get some food and coffee down you but you threw up. That's not a terrific way to begin a romance."

"Oh my God."

"I walked you in here to get you out of your clothes so I could clean them up, but you passed out." She smiled wryly. "I got you out of your shirt and sponged it off, but I think the shirt and tie are goners. Everything's hanging up in my bathroom."

"I'm sorry, Cora, I truly am. I don't know what . . ."

Her smile faded. "Do you remember how this all started, Jake?"

"We were at the office." He stopped as it all came back like the force of a bad dream. "Kellerman," he said. "You told me about Marie and Kellerman."

"Yes."

He nodded carefully so as not to increase the pain in his head. "Mine was not a very adult way to react, I'm afraid."

"Human, though." She looked as if she was going to pat his shoulder, then stopped. "Jake, I have to be at the office for an eight-thirty conference. There's fresh coffee in the kitchen. If I were you I'd try a little toast, but only that for a while."

"Where are we, Cora? I don't know where you live."

"This cozy little place is on the fifth floor of the Riverfront Apartments. I can walk to the office from here or grab the People Mover."

"My car?"

"It's parked wherever you usually park it. I took your keys away before you could get to it. They're on the kitchen counter, by the way." She glanced at the little clock. "I have to go, Jake. Will you be all right?"

"Yeah." He pulled a sheet around his naked legs.

"Cora," he said, "where did you sleep?"

"Would it make you feel guilty if I said the couch?"

"Yes."

She smiled. "Well, don't worry. I have a guest bedroom. I slept in there."

"I really am very sorry about all this. And ashamed."

"Forget it, Jake."

"I won't. I owe you."

She shook her head but said nothing, and then she was gone. He heard a door close softly somewhere in the apartment.

For a moment he fought the impulse just to lie back and seek the refuge of sleep. But he knew he had to find the energy to get moving. It was essential that he pull himself together, go home for fresh clothes and then get to the office.

Dr. Milo Faraday was scheduled for a pretrial interview at two o'clock. Jake knew he couldn't even think of calling in sick. It was too important. Bellows would expect a briefing on what the doctor could be expected to say on the stand. Another spasm of dizziness swept over him as he tried to stand. Jake sat back on the bed and decided to wait a few minutes.

He sat quietly, and then he thought about Marie. And about Harvey Kellerman.

91

Much to his surprise, hot tears began to slide silently from his eyes.

Cora Simpson didn't have time to walk and decided the People Mover would be quicker. She tossed the two quarters into the slot and pushed through the turnstile, taking the escalator up to the station platform. Detroit's People Mover was really only an elevated train system despite its fancy name. The system had a short span of track circling the downtown area of the city. Two automatic cars appeared every few minutes, looking like unspoiled steel subway trains.

The cars arrived and the doors opened. Cora stepped aboard. It wasn't crowded but she decided to stand since the journey would only take a few minutes.

She thought about Jake Martin, wishing they weren't rivals. She liked Jake. He seemed genuinely honest and upright. Men like that were rare and Cora found herself resenting Jake's wife, a woman who was tossing away something other women dreamed about.

Jake was an attractive man, but a relationship of any kind was out of the question. Especially now.

Cora had spent a lifetime proving she didn't have to rely on her family's wealth or power. She had earned honors in college and had done equally well in law school. Despite that, everyone still seemed to dismiss her efforts as mere fluff, just something she chose to do while waiting to inherit.

Getting the partnership would change that. Nothing could be allowed to stand in the way. Not even a man as interesting and attractive as Jake Martin.

Claude deSalle drove down Jefferson Avenue, his big gray Mercedes moving like a monarch among lesser vehicles. The sparse midmorning traffic moved east in a relaxed flow.

He smiled to himself as he passed workmen razing a strip of decaying store buildings, preparing the site for development. Hanover Square had provided the mortgage money. Soon, a new complex of glistening high-priced apartments would rise on that site. The money had been hard to come by, but deSalle had put the financing package together. The developers knew they owed him more than mere gratitude. Eventually he would find a way they could return the favor.

Easing his big sedan into the right-hand lane, he then took the cutoff to the Belle Isle Bridge.

Belle Isle, a city park designed by Frederick Law Olmstead, the same man who had masterminded New York City's Central Park, was a true island situated in the middle of the Detroit River. The island, three miles long and one mile wide, had once been the city's chief source of recreation. But time and social change had eroded the island's universal popularity. Like New York's famous park it was beautiful, and also, at times, extremely dangerous. But midmorning on a crisp, autumn workday, the island was safe enough.

DeSalle drove over the nearly half-mile of bridge, then followed the river drive around the rim of the island. The skyline of Detroit's business section glittered only a few miles down the river. Almost alone on the island, his only companions were a few other cars and an occasional jogger.

He circled Scott Fountain and looked over at Canada. The tree-lined Canadian shore, like the island, was a picture of flaming autumnal colour.

Driving past the Marine Museum, deSalle headed toward the far eastern tip of the island. He passed a parked car here and there. The island was a magnet for both lovers and the lonely. Some cars had two people, others just one. The white BMW that had been described to him was parked near the old Coast Guard station, as instructed. DeSalle pulled in and motioned the driver to join him.

"I was about to leave," Chip Daren said as he climbed into the passenger seat. "Why do we have to meet out here? This is like something out of a cheap movie. We're not spies."

DeSalle merely smiled. "It's risky if we're seen together, Chip. I'm supposed to be neutral in this family dispute. I'm not, of course; we both know that. But if anyone suspected otherwise I would lose my ability to help you, at least in any effective way."

Chip sneered. "This is just ludicrous. What's wrong with using the telephone?"

"Nothing, I suppose. But it's frighteningly easy to tap a phone nowadays, Chip. You can buy the tiny equipment needed in any radio supply store."

A loaded ore carrier, one of the old lake vessels, very long and low in the water, glided down the river. The old boat's bow cut the water, forcing a huge white wave before it. It seemed almost close enough to touch.

Chip glowered in the direction of the passing boat. "Well, what did you get me out here for?"

"Sage, I understand, has filed your opposition to the admission of your father's will?"

"Yes."

"You told him, I take it, that time is of the essence?"

Chip nodded. "I don't think he likes doing it that way. He wants to do—what do the lawyers call it?—discovery. I really didn't understand what he meant."

DeSalle watched the boat. "Discovery is the term lawyers use to describe a process of finding out what the other side expects to prove. Our lawyers at the bank use it all the time. They go to court and get private documents held by the other side. They interview and question opposition witnesses. If it was a card game, it would be like getting to see what the other player is holding. Lawyers love it, but it takes time. You told Sage that discovery in this case is out of the question, I presume?"

"Yes, but he didn't like it." Chip managed a rueful smile. "He really wants to know what's going on, but he's afraid it might be unethical, so he doesn't ask. He dances all around the issue, hoping I'll give him a hint without compromising him."

"You didn't tell him about me?"

"Of course not. But he's not stupid. He suspects we have someone in the enemy camp. As you asked, I'm keeping you completely out of it."

DeSalle nodded.

"Sage doesn't like me much," Chip said. "I think he's only taking this case so he can kick the crap out of Sperling Beekman. He's an odd character. I don't think money is his first priority. It's competition that turns him on. If it wasn't for the chance to go up against Sperling Beekman, I don't think he'd have taken the case."

"I trust he's taking it seriously, that this isn't just some Don Quixote adventure for him?"

"He's serious enough. He's hired a private investigator to go up north and dig up whatever he can find."

"I'll have some names of people up there to contact. You can pass them on to Sage."

"He won't like getting just names without knowing where they came from. He's warned me that unless I'm completely open with him, I take the consequences of any concealment."

"That's fair enough," deSalle said. "Will he press for an early trial, do you think?"

"He said he has another case scheduled in January. If the case runs beyond Christmas, he'll withdraw. He made me sign a paper agreeing to that."

"Well, then it's in everyone's interest to get this over and done with, isn't it?"

"Suppose Number Four tries to delay things?"

DeSalle smiled. "That, Chip, would be most unlikely. Let me take care of Elizabeth."

"You're a good friend, Claude. I won't forget what you're doing, nor will Gussie."

"You told Gussie?"

"She is my sister, well, half-sister. Besides, she wouldn't have agreed to split her share if we lost without knowing you were working behind the scenes. That's a lot of money to risk, even for her. She had to know, Claude."

Now it was deSalle's turn to nod in agreement. Anyone challenging the will forfeited his share if he lost. It had been deSalle's idea that only one of the Daren children bring suit, with the other agreeing to split the remaining share if the case was lost. Chip had successfully sold the idea to Gussie, but deSalle didn't know she knew about his role in the plot.

DeSalle pursed his lips, then spoke. "Well, it's spilt milk, isn't it? Just don't tell Gussie anything more unless you first check with me. And make sure she keeps what she already knows to herself."

"I'll try. We aren't exactly . . . ah . . . close, as you know."

"I'll talk to Gussie," deSalle said quietly. "Anything else I should know? Otherwise—"

"Anything else? Is that all you dragged me out here for, to make sure things move along?"

DeSalle disregarded Chip's whining. "Just keep after Sage. It's absolutely essential that this case gets heard right away."

"And if it doesn't?"

"In that case, you will end up losing. Does that make it essential enough for you, Chip?"

Jake had managed to change and get to his office. Thankfully most of the effects of the hangover were ebbing, but he felt a sense of overpowering fatigue. He checked himself in his office's mirror. He was pale, but that seemed to be the only outward sign of his excesses.

Dr. Milo Faraday was precisely on time. He was ushered into Jake's office. Faraday, a man in his late fifties, seemed to have aged a bit in the year since Jake had seen him witness Augustus Daren's will. The doctor's sandy hair was beginning to show streaks of gray. Stout to begin with, Faraday appeared to have put on even more weight. The fabric of his expensive suit strained against the bulge of the doctor's ample stomach.

They shook hands and Jake indicated a chair in front of his desk.

"How have you been, Doctor?"

"Fine, thank you."

Jake, struggling with the hangover, knew he had to assess Faraday's potential as a witness, and also discover if any bitterness existed because of his dismissal by Elizabeth Daren. Jake tried to marshal some enthusiasm for the task.

"What are you doing now?"

Faraday's face was round and unexpressive. "I'm working with a group of doctors in Oakland County," he said. "It's a temporary arrangement. Their neurologist passed away and they needed someone to fill in until they get a replacement."

"Would you consider making it permanent?"

"No." Faraday snapped the answer, then continued in a softer tone. "I'm through with active practice as such. It's become more like a business than a profession. You work long hours and when the malpractice insurance people and the IRS get through, you have comparatively little left to show for your effort."

Faraday took out an open roll of mints and offered them to Jake, who shook his head. The doctor popped one into his mouth. "It's a smoking substitute," he said, replacing the roll in his pocket.

"How did you come to be Mr. Daren's personal physician?"

"I had a practice here in Detroit and Gus Daren was referred to my care after his first CVA."

"What precisely is a CVA?"

Faraday munched on the mint. "Cerebral vascular accident. You lawyers have your language, we have ours. Translated, it means stroke."

The doctor shifted in the chair. "The Darens made a rather handsome offer to me at the time if I would relocate up north and become his sole treating physician. It came at a good time," Faraday continued. "I had begun to limit my practice anyway. Also, I was in the middle of a rather upsetting divorce. So the offer from the Darens was like being offered a sabbatical, an escape. It was a chance to climb off the wheel, so to speak."

Jake thought Faraday was a little too young to think about retirement. "So, what are your plans?"

Faraday seemed to look beyond Jake, as if slipping into a pleasant dream. "Teaching," he said simply. "I'm extremely well qualified for that. I taught at Wayne State, part time, for years. Adjunct faculty. I'm published, and with all due modesty, I think I'm what one might call a nationally known neurologist." He smiled a cold smile. "Of course, the money isn't what one could earn in practice, but the right offer might compensate for that loss very nicely."

"Any prospects?"

Faraday's smile kept flickering on and off like a mechanical afterthought and never quite seemed genuine. "I have one or two local possibilities but I'm most interested in one in Florida. Frankly, I'm looking for a university in a nice warm climate. I've had it with our Michigan winters."

"That's understandable."

He nodded. "I'm fifty-eight," he said. "I've lived here all my life. I'm thoroughly tired of the hassle of winter, the snow here, the ice. Last year up in Gladding finally did it for me. It was like living in the Yukon. If I never see snow again, it will be too soon." He smiled again. "Hopefully, I'll find a small medical school in Florida soon. No patients, no malpractice worries, no medical insurance forms, just a nice, quiet, warm life."

"When will you know?" Jake asked.

The smile once more flickered out. "Soon," Faraday said. "Now, what can I do for you, Mr. Martin?"

"Augustus Daren's will has been filed for probate," Jake said. "Mr. Daren's son is contesting the will, claiming his father was not mentally competent when the will was signed."

The doctor merely nodded.

"As one of the subscribing witnesses, you'll be called to testify."

"Oh?"

"Ordinarily it's just a formality. The witnesses testify they saw the will signed by the deceased in their presence."

"So?"

Jake leaned back in his chair. "This time your testimony may be more than just a formality."

Faraday said nothing.

"As Mr. Daren's personal physician, I'm sure you'll be asked to describe his mental condition at the time of the making of the will."

"I see," the doctor said, popping another mint.

"Would you mind, Doctor, if I taped our conversation?"

"To what purpose?" Faraday asked.

"Mostly for my own recollection. Memory can play tricks. I'd like to record this for that purpose only. This is all quite informal. You're not under oath."

Faraday seemed to be thinking. "Would you be offended if I refused?"

"No," Jake said, surprised.

"I think we should just do this, as you say, on an informal basis."

"But—"

Faraday's cold smile returned. "I've appeared a number of times as a witness in court, Mr. Martin. Doctors are sued or have to take the stand for or against other doctors. It's part of life, I suppose, but it's all quite distasteful to me. I would prefer just to talk. Unless you have some other reason than memory reinforcement to tape our conversation?"

Jake sighed. It wasn't worth alienating the man. "Whatever you say."

Faraday nodded. "Good."

Jake took out a yellow pad to make notes. "When did you first meet Augustus Daren?" he asked.

"He had suffered the first . . . stroke," he said. "I was called in to consult."

"You never knew him before that?"

Faraday shrugged. "I knew of him by reputation, of course. He was a public figure. But I had never met him personally before seeing him at St. John's Hospital."

"And thereafter you agreed to become his personal physician?"

"Yes. It was a very good offer, given all the circumstances."

"What was the agreement?" Jake asked.

"Is this necessary?"

Jake nodded. "It may come up. I have to know." Jake wanted to see if Faraday's account would differ with what he had learned from Elizabeth.

The hint of a frown played over the doctor's expressionless

97

features. "I was to get a yearly salary, plus a place to live, of course."

"How much was the salary?"

"I don't see—"

"It may come up," Jake said, forcing a smile.

"Three hundred thousand."

"Anything in addition to the salary?"

Faraday hesitated.

"Please, Doctor, it's important."

"I was to receive a bonus at the end of each year of three hundred thousand dollars."

"A bonus? For what?"

"To keep me happy in my work, I suppose." The smile flickered back on.

Jake knew Faraday was being evasive, avoiding telling the truth. "Wasn't there something about your divorce involved?"

Another mint was popped. Faraday's eyes seemed to be appraising Jake before he spoke. "If you must know, the bonus arrangement was a way of defeating the outrageous claims of my wife. I declared only the salary, not the bonus, since that would be paid after the divorce went through." Faraday frowned. "Your courts are very severe with doctors, it seems. I was ordered to give my wife, now ex-wife, half of everything—home, investments, private retirement plan and regular income."

"So you used the bonus as a device to . . . ah . . . restore some economic justice, so to speak?"

Faraday nodded vigorously. "Yes. But don't think ill of me. She didn't put me through medical school or anything like that. I was well established when I met and married her. She had been married before, I had not." He sighed. "I must say her experience in divorce courts stood her in good stead. For the brief time she spent as my wife she got more than a star quarterback or a twenty-game winning pitcher."

"That's too bad."

"So much for your system of justice, eh? Anyway, as you can see, the Daren offer came like a life preserver to a drowning man."

"Your arrangement terminated, I take it, upon Mr. Daren's death?"

"Yes. I suppose that's one of the reasons Daren proposed my employment on that basis. If he lived, I got paid. It became in my very best financial interests to keep him alive." Faraday's smile was cool. "Daren was, of course, a genius in matters of business."

Jake nodded.

"You see, he was interested in getting the very best medical care after the first CVA. But he was determined to run things his way; that applied to doctors too. Augustus Daren was a difficult patient, to be frank. If he agreed with my instructions, he followed them, otherwise they were ignored."

"What about after the second stroke?"

Faraday paused, then spoke quietly. "I could have let him slip away, you know. But the widow wanted maximum effort made to keep him alive. And, as I said, that was to my benefit also. So I did just that. Finally, there was nothing anyone could do, and that was that."

"What about this year's bonus?" Jake asked. "Do you still get it?"

"I suppose, technically, I'm not entitled to it since I didn't keep him alive through the end of the year, but that matter has been resolved."

"How?"

"Is this really necessary?"

"I'm afraid it is. The other side may bring it up."

Faraday shrugged. "Mrs. Daren paid me the bonus and my full salary to the end of the year. She gave me the check the day Mr. Daren died."

"That was generous."

The doctor's cold eyes seemed to become even colder. "Do you think that's what it was?"

"Don't you?"

"Perhaps."

Despite the doctor's calm manner, Jake detected a certain hostility. "What else could it be, do you think?"

"I was a loose end. She got rid of me. The money merely ensured that I would go quietly."

"Was there trouble between you?"

For the first time, the doctor looked away. "I lived there, you know, for almost two years. It's quite isolated up there. There's nothing much to do. Until Daren's second stroke, we all had dinner together every night. We played cards, that sort of thing."

"So?"

"When the second stroke put Daren down, there were just the two of us. I thought we, Elizabeth and myself, were growing, well, rather close, after that."

"A romance?"

His face became a mask. "I was very vulnerable, of course, just having gone through the divorce. Apparently I misinterpreted the relationship."

Jake tried to smile. "You made a pass?"

He was answered by a frown. "Hardly that; I'm not the type. However, I did propose what I thought was a logical relationship under the circumstances."

"And?"

"I no longer ate dinner with the lady of the house. We existed, after that, on a very formal basis." The humorless smile appeared again. "She was glad to pay me off and see me off, as they say." He looked beyond Jake. "I was glad to go, frankly."

Jake took out a copy of Daren's will. He turned to the last page and handed it to the doctor. "This is a photocopy, of course. I trust you remember signing as a witness."

He studied it for a minute, then handed it back. "Yes."

"And you recall that everything was videotaped?"

Faraday nodded. "I do recall that, yes." His smile now oddly turned into a chuckle.

Jake was puzzled but didn't pursue it. "Tell me a little bit about Augustus Daren's physical problems," Jake asked.

"You mean after the first CVA?"

Jake nodded.

Faraday pursed his lips as if searching for the right words. "I'll try to keep this as simple as possible, without boring you with complex medical terms. Cerebrovascular accidents are a neurological disorder due to a pathological process in a blood vessel of the brain. It usually occurs due to one of three primary processes: thrombosis, embolism or hemorrhage."

Jake was making notes. "That's certainly keeping it simple."

Faraday's smile carried a hint of a sneer. "Thrombosis is the formation of a blood clot in the vessel. An embolism is also a clot, but it is formed elsewhere and travels up to the vessel like a cork, effectively blocking it. Hemorrhage is merely bleeding from a leaking vessel. The result is usually the same, no matter what the cause."

"And that is?"

"A portion of the brain is deprived of blood and the result is brain damage," Faraday answered. "Some cerebrovas—strokes—do little lasting damage. If the patient survives, with active rehabilitation much or all normal function can be restored. In other instances, like the first stroke Augustus Daren suffered, the brain damage is more extensive. Daren lost the use of the left side of his body." Faraday shrugged. "Of course, the second and last stroke was far more massive, profound and irreversible. Without the machines he wouldn't even have been able to breathe. He lost all sensory ability. He was, as they say, a vegetable."

"What caused Daren's strokes?"

Faraday sighed. "I wanted to do an autopsy, but Elizabeth wouldn't hear of it. It would have served no purpose, I suppose, except to satisfy my own curiosity. It's my opinion that both times it was an embolism. He had a history of minor circulatory problems in the legs and I think that was probably the source of the clots. The brain is a most mysterious organ; we are just beginning to understand how it functions. Even with an autopsy I might not have been able to pinpoint a cause, not after such a long period of deterioration."

"Prior to the second stroke, he was all right mentally, I take it?"

Faraday shook his head. "That depends on your definition."

"But you said only one side of his body was affected," Jake protested.

"Brain damage is a tricky thing," Faraday answered. "Daren's memory was affected at times. That's common in such circumstances."

"He was perfectly all right the day I was up there," Jake said.

Faraday raised an eyebrow. "You were with him for only a few minutes. Gus became very good at concealing his problems. He covered up many deficiencies with his usual bluster."

Jake stared at Faraday. "He was competent when he signed that will."

"Perhaps. Again, it depends on your definition."

"What is your definition?"

Faraday smiled. "He occasionally had problems with memory and concentration. His emotions, too, were unstable at times. That's not uncommon with stroke victims. The inability to sometimes think straight, frustration, the resulting anger: all that can be quite upsetting."

Jake could feel his heart beating at a triphammer beat. "Doctor, are you trying to tell me that Augustus Daren was incompetent when he signed this will?"

Faraday's smile flickered on once more. "I'm not trying to tell you anything, Mr. Martin. You asked my professional opinion relative to his condition, and you asked my personal observations. I'm merely replying to your questions."

Jake tried to control himself. It would be counterproductive to let Faraday see how upset he was. "You said you played cards with him, right?"

Faraday nodded. "Yes."

"He was competent enough to do that, wasn't he?"

"Sometimes. Daren liked poker better than bridge. But some days he couldn't seem to remember the cards, let alone the winning sequence. It was most embarrassing for him. He often tried to cover up by throwing a tantrum. It didn't work." Faraday sighed. "I felt sorry for him."

"Did he always know who you were?"

Faraday nodded. "Yes, although sometimes he couldn't remember the names of the people who worked up there."

"Could he read?"

Faraday nodded. "Oh yes, although sometimes he complained that he kept reading the same thing over and over again."

"He ran his business all during that time, did he not?"

Faraday pursed his lips. "That's a bit difficult to answer."

"Why?"

"Elizabeth, in my opinion, seemed to do most of the work. She consulted with him, but I think she was the person who really made the decisions."

"Are you telling me she exerted undue influence over him?"

Faraday shrugged. "I wouldn't go that far."

"Did he suffer delusions?"

"Not as far as I know."

"But you're saying he was incompetent?"

"At times he might have been, in my judgment. Other times he was clearly capable."

Jake glared at him. "When you acted as witness to the will, you didn't express any reservations."

"I wasn't asked."

"Would you have, if I had asked you?"

Faraday shrugged. "I don't know, really. I'm a doctor, not a lawyer. I really can't say who is competent and who isn't, at least not in the legal sense."

"If not a doctor, then who?"

Dr. Milo Faraday's smile seemed suddenly sinister. "A jury," he quietly answered.

9

He followed the directions he'd been given and found the two-rut road. Worried that his transmission might be ripped out by the high ground between the deep and sandy ruts, he gingerly guided the car into the tracks of sand, carefully inching his way down a twisting, pine-covered slope.

The trees had been cleared away at the bottom to make room for a house, which wasn't much more than an elongated tarpaper shack, its sides constructed from mismatched lumber, its slightly swayback roof patched haphazardly with tin and old scrap shingles. A small black dog raced from the house, yapping with excitement. He drove very carefully to avoid running it over.

Parked in front of the place was an old battered van. Next to it lay the remains of what had once been a Chrysler sedan, reduced now to a rusted steel skeleton.

Circling his car, the black dog barked with feverish menace.

A man stuck his head out from the front door, then motioned him to come in. "Don't worry about Lucy," the man called. "She won't bite. She's just real happy to have some company."

He opened the car door slowly, prepared to slam it shut if Lucy attacked. But the dog, her tail now wagging as she continued to bark, merely followed him to the front door where the man waited.

"I take it you're Mr. Linden?" the man said.

He nodded.

The man, gray-haired with a thin and weathered face, could have been fifty or eighty. He was one of those outdoor people whose facial skin has been mummified by weather to the point that they seem ageless.

"C'mon in."

The windows were small and curtained. It took a minute for him to become accustomed to the dimness of the musty interior. The furniture, like the roof, had been patched often. Nothing matched. A television set showing a snowy picture lit the room with a flickering illumination.

"Sit down, Mr. Linden. Can I get you anything?"

"No, thanks." He sat in an old overstuffed chair, its springs long since surrendered to age, and almost sank to the floor.

The man switched off the television, then pulled up a kitchen chair and sat opposite him. "What can I do for you, Mr. Linden? Your telephone call sounded mysterious."

"I understand you once worked for Augustus Daren. I'd like to ask you some questions about that employment, if you don't mind."

"You a lawyer?"

"No, I work for one. His name is T. G. Sage."

The old man grinned. "Are you a private investigator?"

He took out his identification, flipped it open and handed it to the old man.

"I'll be goddamned," he said. "Oliver Linden," reading the name from the license. "You're one of 'em all right." He handed back the identification. "I thought folks like you only existed in movies and on the TV."

Linden smiled. "I'm real enough."

The old man seemed to be enjoying himself. "So you are, but you don't look like the kind you see in the movies. No offense, but you look like you just got out of college. Nice suit, you drive a nice car: I'd take you for an insurance salesman, if I had to guess."

"Not Humphrey Bogart?"

"Nope. Old Bogie was as thin as a dipstick. You look like you're carrying a little more weight than you should."

Linden was annoyed at the man's editorializing, but took care not to show it. "Would you mind if I tape record our conversation?"

"No skin off my nose. Go on."

Linden took out a small recorder and placed it on the arm of his chair. He switched it on.

"Okay, so you're Philip Hunt, right?"

"So they tell me."

"You once worked for Augustus Daren?"

"Yeah, for almost forty years."

"Did you quit?"

Hunt shook his head. "Nope. I was fired, you might say."

103

"By whom?"

"Mrs. Daren."

"Why?" Linden asked.

Hunt shrugged. "She said they didn't need my services anymore. I got a nice check—she called it severance pay. I put that in the bank. Between that money and the social security, I manage to get by."

"What kind of work did you do for the Darens?"

Hunt smiled. "In England I would have been called the gamekeeper, but up here we don't go for fancy titles. Mr. Daren called me his guide. I think on the books I was listed as a gardener, but my job was to take Mr. Daren, and anyone else he brought along, out hunting or fishing."

"Sounds like an easy job."

"That's one way of looking at it. But there was a lot more to it than taking rich folks out for sport. I had to see our deer herd was maintained. And I had to ensure that game birds were in good supply. I even had to make sure that damn lake was stocked with fish from time to time."

"Where did you keep the deer?"

"In the woods, Daren's woods. We didn't have 'em penned up or anything like that. They were wild. It was my job to see they were fed and cared for, without scaring them into the next county. When Mr. Daren felt like hunting, there was plenty of game, game of all kinds. We even had some black bears, but they became a nuisance so we had a bear hunt and got rid of them. If you ever go to Raven's Nest you'll see 'em. There's bearskins all over the place. Those are the hides of the ones we shot. It was one hell of a hunt. We had senators, ambassadors, and bigwigs of every stripe up here for the bear shoot."

Hunt stood up. "I'll make us some coffee." He continued talking as he filled the battered coffee pot from the spigot in the kitchen sink. "I got to meet a lot of people over the years. We used to have some big hunts up here in the old days. Mr. Daren would bring up important and famous people and it would usually turn into one hell of a party. Everybody was half-loaded most of the time. I was always afraid someone would get shot. We had a few close calls, but that was all." He reached up and took a whiskey bottle from a battered cupboard. "I use this in place of cream. You want some?"

Linden shook his head. "Did you get to know any of the Darens?"

The old man poured a healthy jot into a chipped cup, gulped it, then poured some more. "I knew all of them, all of his wives and both his kids. I taught those kids to hunt and fish."

"What about the present wife?"

He put the coffee on the old stove, turned up the flame and then sat down again.

"She isn't much for hunting or fishing. She'd go out with Mr. Daren when he did, but she only went as an observer, if you know what I mean. She's the kind that likes to walk in the woods and muse. That kind."

"Did they get along?"

"I guess. The other wives and Mr. Daren didn't. But this one seemed to be much quieter. If they fought I didn't hear about it." He grinned. "You know how it is when you got a houseful of serving people, you damn near drown in the gossip. As far as I know, everything was all right between them."

"Did you see Augustus Daren after he had the first stroke?"

Hunt nodded. "Sure. Lots of times."

"How was he?"

The coffee pot began to emit an asthmatic wheeze. Hunt got up and poured out two cups.

"You sure you don't want any whiskey?"

Linden shook his head.

Hunt handed a cup to Linden and sat down again. "That stroke really took the wind out of his sails. Did you know him?"

Linden sipped the strong coffee. "No."

"Augustus Daren was a no-nonsense man. Very strong, very commanding. Like a general. Were you ever in the army?"

"No."

Hunt looked at Linden as if he had just revealed a sad little secret from his past, then continued. "Generals are different from everyone else," he said. "They strut around like they own the whole damn world, glaring and snorting and ready to make trouble. That's a little like how Augustus Daren was before the stroke. A real man's man, you know what I mean?"

"And after?"

Hunt sipped the whiskey-laced coffee. He paused, then spoke. "Pathetic is the word I'd use. I really felt sorry for him."

"Tell me about it."

"His left side was paralyzed. He couldn't use either his left arm or leg much. Even his mouth didn't work right. He could talk and you could understand him, but he sort of slurred his words. And he drooled, too. He couldn't help it and it embarrassed him."

Linden nodded. "Did you see him often during that time?"

"In the beginning, almost every day. Both the doctor and his wife thought it would be good for him if he could get out and do some hunting and fishing."

"But you said he was partially paralyzed."

"Sure was," Hunt said. "He couldn't walk without help. I rigged up some fishing tackle so it could be handled with one hand, and I fixed a sling for a rifle so that if I put it to his right shoulder he could sight and shoot just using his right hand." Hunt paused and looked down at his cup. "He tried, you know, but his heart just wasn't in it.

105

I'd take him out in the boat, but it didn't seem to interest him anymore. We'd only stay out a short time, even if we were catching fish."

"How about hunting?"

"That was even worse. He couldn't walk through the woods anymore, so I'd set up a blind where he could sit and be comfortable. It would frustrate the hell out of him. Sometimes he'd just ask to shoot at random. He used an automatic rifle, so I just fed the clips until he got tired of doing that. We went out shooting only a few times. Mostly we just fished."

Linden finished the strong coffee. "Did you get along with him?"

Hunt shrugged. "Well, he was irritable, but you had to expect that, seeing as what happened to him."

"How was he with other people?"

"He didn't see many people. Want some more coffee?"

"No, thanks."

Hunt stood up and walked to the kitchen table, poured some more whiskey into his cup, but nothing else, then returned to his chair. "Mr. Daren didn't want people to see him after the stroke. Even the ones who worked in the main house didn't see him that much. He was like a—what's the word?"

"Recluse?"

Hunt smiled. "Yeah, yeah, that's it, a recluse. He spent most of his time in his bedroom, which is large enough to play tennis in, by the way."

"Who saw him on a regular basis then?"

"Well, there was his wife, of course. His butler talked to him. That was the old butler, not the fella that's there now. Mr. Daren's secretary, Ronny Janus, was close to him. She saw him every day. He had his own doctor living right there, so he saw him daily too. Outside of those people, I guess I must of been the person who saw him most."

"Every day?"

He slurped some whiskey, then continued to speak. "In the beginning, right after they got him out of the hospital and brought him up here to live, I saw him every day. Like I said, everyone thought getting him outside and doing things would be good for him. But it didn't work like they thought it would, and things sort of slowed down. After a couple of months we cut down the activity and I probably saw him only two or three days a week. Some days we'd go out, some days we wouldn't."

The investigator glanced over at the tape recorder to make sure it was still working and that the tape hadn't run out.

"How would you say he was mentally?" he asked.

Hunt finished the whiskey in his cup. "Not too good. He was real depressed. Everyone was worried he might shoot himself. That was another reason we stopped hunting."

"Did he say anything about suicide?"

Hunt shook his head. "Not in so many words. But the doctor was worried. At one point I was told to take every weapon out of the house and lock them away. Mr. Daren just couldn't adjust to what had happened to him. It was sad."

"But otherwise he was all right?"

"Nope."

"What was wrong?"

"The man's dead," Hunt said. "What's the point?"

Linden pretended that it wasn't vital information. "I suppose there's no point. But I'm curious."

"Sometimes he was goofy."

"How do you mean, goofy?" Oliver Linden asked.

"He'd mistake who you were and think you were someone else. He sometimes thought I was the old gamekeeper, the man who had the job before I did. It was kind of weird when he did that."

"Happen often?"

"Often enough. And his memory was shot, too. That bothered him a lot. He couldn't think of names and places, and he'd get confused. Sometimes he'd forget and call for a wife he'd divorced years before. He tried to put on a good front, but it really didn't work."

"But he ran his business from up here."

Hunt laughed out loud. "The hell he did! It was his wife who ran everything. She always told people she was acting under his direction, but she wasn't. She did everything: wrote letters under his name, did all the telephoning, the works. Ronny Janus used to get pissed because she had to do what Mrs. Daren told her to do. They didn't like each other, but even with that the two women worked together pretty well. Between them they did a decent job of covering up for him."

"So you don't think Augustus Daren could handle his own affairs?"

"Maybe, some days. But I doubt it. That stroke had messed up his mind, too, just like it did his body."

"Perhaps his doctor didn't think so?"

"Faraday?" Hunt laughed. "I didn't think that stuck-up ass was much of a doctor. I wouldn't let him lance a boil on my butt, frankly. Besides, he had a hell of a case on Mrs. Daren. He followed her around like a slobbering hound. Can't blame him, of course. Ever see her?"

"No."

Hunt shook his head. "Mr. Daren sure had an eye for the ladies, but this last one was the best."

"Do you think she was having an affair with the doctor?"

"Maybe. I'd have no way of knowing. Pretty woman, but sort of cold, if you know what I mean? I don't think she'd have anything to do with anyone if it wasn't to her advantage."

"You don't like her?"

"I don't dislike her. She never did anything to me, but she isn't what you'd call a charming person."

"She fired you."

"Sure did. But, like I told you, she was generous. And to be honest, there's no point in keeping someone like me around if no one is going to hunt or fish. When Mr. Daren had that second stroke, he was just like a vegetable. There wasn't anything more for me to do."

"You don't hold a grudge then?"

Hunt chuckled. "No reason to."

"Would you testify to what you've just told me?"

"Why not? It's the truth." Hunt smiled. "By the way, what's the name again of the lawyer you work for? I forgot."

"T. G. Sage."

Philip Hunt frowned. "I think I've heard that name. Is he from around here?"

Linden pocketed the recorder as he stood up. "No. He's from Detroit. He represents Daren's son."

Hunt nodded.

"Mr. Hunt, is there anyone up here who you think might be able to help me find out how Mr. Daren was after the first stroke?"

"Ronny Janus could. I hear she's moved to Florida. As far as anyone living up here, I'll give it some thought. If I come up with a name or two, I'll give you a call."

"Thanks for the coffee. I'll be in touch." Linden handed Hunt a business card, then walked to the door. "If you think of anyone I should talk to, or anything else you think I should know, call me. Reverse the charges."

"Will do."

Hunt watched from the door as Linden got in his car, turned around, and then slowly made his way up the gutted drive. Lucy barked furiously as she chased the moving car. Hunt could hear her even after the car had disappeared beyond the trees. He waited until she came trotting happily back.

After he'd let her back in, he closed the door quietly behind him. He filled his chipped cup half full with whiskey before sitting down to dial the number.

"This is Phil Hunt," he said into the receiver, when the secretary answered. "Is the man in?"

He was put through immediately.

"Well, just like you said, he was up here," Hunt said. "I told him what he wanted to hear. Just the way we discussed it." He chuckled. "He wants me to find witnesses just like you said he would. I will, of course, but that's going to cost money. These people won't do it for

108

free, not if we want them to testify our way. How much can I spend?"

He smiled at the reply. "An open checkbook, eh? God, I like the sound of that. Don't worry, I'll pay only what I think I have to. Tell me, is this detective or the lawyer he works for in on all this?"

Hunt nodded at the reply. "Yeah, I didn't think they were. All that detective knew was my name and that I had worked for Daren." He sipped from his cup, then snorted. "Some detective he is! You know, that damn fool thinks he found me."

"I'll be down at the lake for a while," Elizabeth Daren said to her butler as she slipped into her fur-lined jacket.

An east wind had come up, whipping the tops of the tall pines back and forth in a frenzied dance. Above the trees, low gray clouds scudded across the sky so fast the effect resembled the illusion produced by time-lapse photography.

The local people always said an east wind was bad luck, that it never brought anything good. The saying, like much of the local wisdom, had its source with the Ojibway Indians who had passed along their taboos and beliefs to the lumbermen and trappers who had come north looking for wealth in the then virgin Michigan forests. Such tribal folklore had been true often enough to earn a certain credibility, and only foolish people dismissed it out of hand. More often than not, an east wind had been the harbinger of danger.

Elizabeth inhaled deeply, enjoying the crisp, clear air as she walked toward the lake.

Lake Bradford, four hundred feet deep in some places, had been gouged out of the rock by a passing prehistoric glacier. That great depth usually provided a kind of steadying tranquility to the surface, but the powerful east wind was causing battalions of whitecapped waves to march in increasing fury across its now turbulent waters.

A bench at the side of the log boathouse had become her favorite place. Alone and shielded from the wind, she often felt as if she had become one with nature, a feeling that brought a comforting sense of peace. Elizabeth had come out to the bench often during the past year to watch the lake and to think.

It had been a year of torment. She had followed Gus's instructions, keeping him on the machines, buying precious time so she could solidify her power and position. It had been his plan, but several times she had almost wavered and abandoned it. She had mourned him, despite the machines that had provided the illusion of life. She had begun the necessary grief work even while the respirator whispered and the electronic screens were filled with the neverending waves and blips.

Intellectually, she had accepted the fact that he was dead, but emotionally it had sometimes been another matter. It had been a time of secret tears.

Except on rare occasions, she no longer cried.

Elizabeth had been surprised by how much she still missed him. They had gone far beyond the usual husband/wife relationship. He had become her teacher, and she his apt and adoring pupil. He had discovered and tapped an aptitude for business in her that had surprised them both and had given joy and richness to their union. They had become master and disciple long before he had been so bitterly crippled by the first stroke.

A southbound flight of ducks flew in formation just below the swirling clouds. She watched until they disappeared.

Gus had known, after being cruelly twisted by the first stroke, that time was running out. He had brought the bank along to a crucial point. But he sensed he would never live to see the victory he so desperately wanted. So her lessons had quickly progressed from the theoretical to the practical. He made her run the bank. He told her what to do and how, and she did it. Mistakes were corrected without rancor. There were no problems between them. She, too, knew she had a limited time to get ready.

He had drilled her on what to expect, what to do, whom to watch, and the tactics to be used in the event of his death. The future of the bank became the main interest in life for both of them, an obsession. Augustus Daren was ensuring his life's work would not be wasted, that his ambitious plans for his bank would be carried out. Having discovered her newfound and surprising ability, Elizabeth was determined to use this talent to achieve the result they both now wanted. But time was their enemy. He had told her that she must play for time until she was ready and strong enough to fight for control.

The second stroke came much too soon. He had foreseen just such an event. He had told her what must be done if it happened and she did it.

Sometimes, especially when she had sat next to him in that awful room with the machines making their dreadful whispering sounds, she wondered if she had done the right thing. Sometimes she had talked to him, knowing he couldn't hear. It had just seemed to make everything worse.

The flight of ducks had disappeared into the distance. While she watched the clouds rolling above, her mood seemed to reflect the turbulence above her.

If only she had had the luxury of time, just a few months more. But she hadn't. Elizabeth wondered if anyone was ever really ready to face the ultimate challenge in their lives when it came.

International banking frontiers were suddenly open and unique opportunities existed, but not for long. Like a gold rush, it would soon be over. Gus had predicted everything with amazing accuracy. The Russians needed billions of dollars to finance their new economy. That need wouldn't go on forever; Gus had predicted that, too. Whoever got the Russian business would dominate the financial world.

Gus had given her the knowledge and the skill. Now, with a touch of luck, she was ready to forge an international alliance that would propel Hanover Square into that world leadership. The horizon was unlimited, but the time to do it was now.

She had promised Gus. It had become a covenant between them. It was a covenant she had every intention of keeping. But first her control of the bank had to be established. Everything depended on the will contest. If the will failed, everything failed.

Elizabeth tried to put that prospect out of her mind, although it was the kind of dark thought that seemed natural enough when an east wind was blowing.

The lunch had been chatty and convivial, exactly the kind of informal meeting Claude deSalle had in mind. Most of the other diners at the Detroit Club had returned to their offices, but deSalle lingered at a corner table with Wilson M. E. Hoff, Ph.D.

Dr. Hoff, who looked like a stork and was almost seven feet tall, was also entirely bald, and a scraggly chin beard gave his bony face an Oriental cast. Dr. Hoff moved and gestured with an awkwardness which suggested that, despite his seventy years, he still hadn't quite mastered coordinating such an elongated body.

Chairman of the Daren Foundation, he was the leader of the trustees who were the absolute dictators as to how the immense fortune Augustus Daren had set aside for charitable and artistic purpose was to be spent.

Hoff, a former professor of economics at the University of Michigan, had been selected for the powerful post as head of the Foundation by Augustus Daren himself. Daren thought Hoff would prove a valuable spokesman for the Foundation, lending an aura of academia to its efforts. Also, it was Daren's firm belief that Hoff was honest. As usual, Augustus Daren's instincts had proven true on both counts.

"Another brandy, Wilson?" DeSalle was one of the few people on earth who called Wilson Hoff by his first name. Doctor or professor were the titles he demanded from all but his academic colleagues and a select handful of others.

Hoff's Mandarin face split into a wide grin. "Another brandy, Claude, and I wouldn't be able to drive back to Ann Arbor. After my cataract surgeries I'm danger enough on the roads, without adding too much alcohol to the mix."

"How is your vision?"

"Just fine. Well, almost. I wouldn't want to cut a diamond or perform brain surgery, but putting that aside, the old eyes are quite serviceable."

Their waiter, moving like a shadow, refilled their coffee cups and was gone.

As the Foundation chairman, Wilson Hoff was an important man. But to deSalle he was not only important, he was absolutely vital to his plan, for Wilson Hoff also sat on the board of the directors of the Hanover Square Bank.

"What do you think of this fuss over Gus Daren's will?" deSalle asked.

"A family squabble," Hoff answered, sipping his coffee. "It's too bad, isn't it? The way money can tear a family apart."

DeSalle merely nodded. "Obviously, they weren't a family in the usual sense. Or perhaps they were. Families are a complicated business, no matter what the circumstances."

"How true. Of course, I have to look at all this from the position of the Foundation. As you know, Claude, the Foundation gets one third of the estate, regardless of what happens. Since we have no real stake in who wins or loses, we're really fence-sitters in this whole affair."

"I'm afraid that's not true."

Hoff's eyebrows shot up in silent question.

"The will contest is rather pivotal to the future of the bank," deSalle said. "The third of Gus's estate that the Foundation gets is in Hanover Square stock. If the bank gets hurt, obviously the stock gets hurt."

"I don't follow . . ."

"Suppose Elizabeth Daren loses the will contest?"

"Oh, I rather doubt that."

"But suppose she did? What would happen?"

Hoff took another sip. "She wouldn't have control of the bank, that's all."

"She would have just seventeen per cent ownership."

"As would the Foundation," Hoff said.

"So, even if the Foundation threw in with Elizabeth, if that happened, it would still provide a voting block of only thirty-four per cent."

Hoff chuckled. "A pretty hefty chunk, you'll agree."

"Ordinarily, yes."

Hoff sat back in his chair. His long fingers drummed a tattoo on the linen tablecloth. "You're trying to tell me something, Claude," he said. "Why not come to the point? We're old friends."

DeSalle nodded in agreement. "All right. If Elizabeth loses, I believe Chip Daren and his sister, Gussie, are going to try to take control of the bank."

Wilson Hoff's laugh was hearty. "Why, that's ridiculous. The two of them combined couldn't keep a checkbook, let alone run a bank. I don't care what they might want, such a thing just couldn't happen. They could never pull it off."

"I think they are being used."

"By whom?"

DeSalle shook his head as the waiter started to the table. The waiter retreated out of earshot.

"Wilson, there are a number of stockholders who don't believe Elizabeth is qualified or competent to run Hanover Square."

"Oh, I've heard that, but—"

DeSalle held up his hand. "I'm not saying I agree with them, I'm just reporting on their attitude. They believe Elizabeth is too young, far too inexperienced, and completely without the background necessary to lead the bank."

"Gus trained her," Hoff said defensively.

"I'm her most ardent supporter, Wilson, believe me. But there are many who aren't her fans. I think someone is working behind the scenes as we speak to line up their votes for a takeover. They'll use Chip as their front man."

"That would be a disaster!"

"Exactly," deSalle said quietly.

"Who are these people? I'm sure you know."

"So far I have only suspicions."

Hoff frowned. "Don't beat around the bush, Claude. Who do you think's behind this?"

"The Japanese."

"What?"

"I've been approached by several Tokyo banks. They want to buy Hanover Square."

"Well, that might not be so bad, Claude. God knows they have the money. If the price were right, everyone would profit."

"I agree, if it was as simple as that."

"Isn't it?"

DeSalle smiled smugly. "I'm afraid not. They're ruthless. I think they'll come in with some kind of merger deal, chew up the valuable assets and spit out the bones, so to speak. We, the stockholders, would be left with those very bare bones. In other words, if all this should take place, Wilson, the value of the Foundation's share might be very seriously diminished."

Hoff stared as if in thought for a moment, then directed his attention once again to deSalle. "Well, what do you propose?"

"At this point, nothing. If Elizabeth prevails in the will contest, you and I both agree the bank would be in good hands. The depositors and stockholders, including the Foundation, would be quite safe."

"And if Elizabeth should lose?"

"Then we must move heaven and earth to stop Chip Daren and the people behind him."

"And put Elizabeth in?"

"That would be wonderful, but I doubt we could do it."

Wilson Hoff scowled. "But why not?"

"The combined thirty-four percent, as you say, would be formidable, but even with that as a base, I don't believe we could marshal a majority. There are just too many people opposed to Elizabeth. We'd have to find someone else if we managed to stop Chip."

Hoff shifted in his chair and leaned back. "What about you, Claude?"

"No, no. I think I'm too closely allied with Elizabeth."

"Oh, I think you'd be perfect," Hoff protested. "If we have to come up with a compromise candidate, you'd be ideal. I'm sure Elizabeth would agree."

"Well, all this is academic at this point anyway, isn't it?"

"Not at all. If Elizabeth should lose in court, we'd have to be in a position to move quickly. Getting Chip Daren in would be like getting a ticket on the *Titanic*. We have to start preparing contingency plans. I should discuss this with Elizabeth."

"I wouldn't, at least not now," deSalle said evenly. "She has so many burdens. It might destroy her resolve if she had this to worry about too. These are perilous times for her, Wilson. We—all her friends—should do everything we can to protect her."

Hoff nodded. "I agree, but you and I should become a committee of two so we can organize effective action should it be needed."

"That's sensible."

"Good. Obviously, I have to place the Foundation's interest above all else, that's my obligation. But that aside, I think you and I can prepare a defense of the bank, should that become necessary."

DeSalle walked Hoff down the stairs to the canopied entrance of the club. The uniformed valet brought up Hoff's old but well-kept Lincoln. Hoff folded his long form awkwardly into the car, his knees nearly touching the steering wheel.

"I think it would be wise if we keep everything to ourselves for now, Wilson," deSalle said in parting. "We don't want to panic anyone."

The tall man nodded conspiratorily as the valet closed the Lincoln's door. DeSalle watched Hoff drive away.

"It's a gorgeous day, Mr. deSalle," the valet said. "A little windy maybe, but we won't see too many more sunny days like this."

Distracted, deSalle nodded his agreement and turned toward Fort Street. It was indeed a beautiful autumn day. Brisk and clear, the weather matched his mood.

It had gone even better than he had hoped. Without realizing it, Wilson Hoff had just put the Foundation's voting power in Claude deSalle's pocket. Even if Hoff should decide to tell Elizabeth Daren about their conversation, Hoff would report that deSalle was absolutely loyal and acting solely to protect her best interests.

114

Claude deSalle allowed himself a small smile.

The cool breeze whipped up scraps of paper as it blew down busy Fort Street. He lowered his head to avoid the dust and debris being swirled about by the freshening east wind.

10

"**W**ell, battle is joined, as they say." Donald Bellows grinned. Jake, Dow and Cora had been summoned to his office. Bellows was the picture of confidence.

"We've received notice of a pretrial hearing from the Eagle County Probate Court," Bellows said. "It's set for this Monday. That's what I'd call fast action. Unless this fellow Sage throws a monkey wrench into things, we might even be able to dispose of this case by Thanksgiving."

"You still don't want discovery, Donald?" Craig Dow asked.

"What's to discover? The only testimony available to them would be from disgruntled former employees. It doesn't take much imagination to predict what they might say. We don't need discovery for that. And if they want to introduce expert medical testimony as to competency, they'd have to bring in doctors who never examined Gus Daren. Faraday was his only physician. We can probably keep anyone else off the stand, but even if we didn't, the testimony would be mere speculation and wouldn't carry much weight. We know what we can expect. This is the rare case where discovery isn't needed."

Bellows held up a typed report. He nodded at Cora Simpson. "This is superb. You've done an excellent job in gathering case law, Cora. It's very complete. No matter what the other side might try to throw at us, we are ready. I am quite pleased, really."

"Thanks, Donald," she said, trying to conceal her obvious pleasure at the compliment.

Bellows turned to Jake. "Did you talk to Milo Faraday?"

"Yesterday."

"Milo lived up there at Raven's Nest," Bellows said to the others. "He was Gus's treating physician. He's a very impressive fellow, as I remember. I don't care how good this Sage is supposed to be, he won't shake a man like Faraday."

"Faraday might hurt us," Jake interjected.

"How?"

"He says Daren's mind was affected by the first stroke. According to him, Daren was sometimes incompetent."

115

"Does he say Daren was incompetent when the will was signed?" Bellows asked sharply.

"No," Jake said.

Bellows smiled. "Well, there you are! The law only cares that the decedent be of sound mind as far as his testamentary affairs are concerned. He can howl at the moon otherwise and it makes no difference legally, at least not in Michigan."

"I got the impression Faraday might hedge if the going got a little rough. He seemed hesitant about Daren's state of mind. If he's like that on the stand, it could hurt."

Now Bellows frowned. "Faraday probably didn't realize just how important his testimony is to the case. Doctors can be somewhat dense sometimes. Talk to him, Jake. You don't have to tell him what to say, just let him know that this is not the time for uncertainty."

"What kind of witness do you think he'll make?" Craig Dow directed his question at Jake.

"If he doesn't crawfish on competency, as Donald says, he'll be impressive."

"Speaking of problems," Bellows said, "this fellow—this Lee Stevens—Elizabeth Daren has hired to handle public relations is proving to be a nuisance. I think he may have even frightened Rhonda Janus into hiding."

"She's the other witness to the will?" Dow asked.

"Yes," Bellows nodded. "Apparently, this Stevens tried to contact her. God only knows why, but he did. I know Ronny Janus and I suspect she doesn't want to get caught in the middle of a family feud. I think he panicked her. We've been unable to reach her. I'm sure she'll show up eventually. Ronny's a good scout."

"Stevens thinks she may testify against us," Jake said. "He thinks she's disappeared for that reason."

Bellows chuckled humorlessly. "How would he know? He never even met her. I think he's just trying to build up his fees. We'll see. Just watch out for Stevens. I don't like his type."

"Why do you want to go up to Gladding for the pretrial?" Jake asked.

"It's just a formality, really," Bellows said. He looked at Craig Dow. "Are you free to go, Craig?"

"I'm in the middle of a series of depositions on another matter, Donald. But I can have them assigned to someone else if you wish."

Bellows shook his head. "That's not necessary. Jake, how about you? After all, you're the only one of us who has met the judge."

"Sure," Jake said. "I'll go."

"Should I go too, Donald?" Cora asked.

"That won't be necessary. One lawyer from here should do quite nicely. Otherwise it might look to the locals as if we were ganging up on T. G. Sage."

Bellows turned to Jake. "We could fly you up there on a charter.

116

The Darens have a landing strip long enough to accommodate jets. But for now I think it would be more politic if you drove. Private jets might cause adverse reaction up there. We don't want to turn T. G. Sage into a David fighting the big city Goliath. I hope that doesn't inconvenience you?"

"No problem," Jake said.

"Press for the earliest trial date possible, Jake. Don't let this fellow Sage stall things."

"Right."

Bellows stood up, signaling the meeting was over. "This is all going along very nicely."

"Shouldn't we hire someone to try to find Rhonda Janus?" Jake asked.

Bellows shook his head. "She'll be here. You worry too much, Jake. You must learn to relax." He was smiling, but his tone seemed to Jake to suggest real disapproval.

The sheriff's car drove slowly up the crushed stone drive and parked in front of the attached garage.

She opened the kitchen door. It was dark, and the light coming from the door illuminated him like a soft searchlight.

He locked the car and walked toward her.

"I thought you weren't coming," she said.

"I would have called." He climbed the two stairs, kissing her on the lips as he passed by her into the kitchen. "Iggy Hanson got himself tanked again. I drove him home."

"Iggy'll kill himself one of these nights."

He laughed. "I'm not worried about Iggy. Hell, he's eighty-four. It's the rest of the world I'm concerned about. Drunk or sober, Iggy only knows one speed—wide open. Sometimes I think about getting the old coot's license revoked."

"You're the sheriff, you can do it. You should."

He sniffed at some soup steaming on the stove, then took off his jacket. "Hell, Iggy's old but he still enjoys life. I think if I took his car away he might shrivel up and die. That car is his lifeline."

"You're a wimp."

He grinned. "You never noticed before?"

"I take it you haven't eaten?"

"You take it right."

She busied herself fixing him a bowl of soup. He watched her, appraising her as with a stranger's eyes. She was small, almost bird-like. He remembered how beautiful she had been. To him, she still was, but a stranger would notice only how aged and tough her weathered skin had become. A stranger would see the bifocal lenses that magnified her eyes. He saw only the eyes. She dyed her hair, he knew that. It was as jet-black as it had been in her youth. Beneath

117

the worn jeans and the oversize checkered shirt she still had the body of a young girl, or so it seemed to him.

She set the bowl of soup before him and then followed it with a plate of sliced beef and the thick crusted French bread that was his favorite.

"Aren't you eating, Lila?" he asked, blowing on the first spoonful of soup.

"I already did. I didn't know if you were coming."

"It's Thursday."

She sat down at the table and lit a cigarette. "Tuesdays, Thursdays and Sundays, if you can get away. Tell me, Russ, do you have anyone else on the route? I've often wondered about Mondays and Wednesdays?"

He tore off a portion of the bread and buttered it. "How come you don't worry about Fridays and Saturdays?"

"Those are your busy days, Russ. People drink and get in trouble on weekends. It's the other days that tend to arouse my curiosity."

"Well, Monday used to be devoted to a lady over at Crumley, but she moved. I save Wednesday for emergencies."

They both laughed. The "schedule" was more than a standing joke between them, it was her way of telling him she missed him, without having to speak the words.

"How's Martha?" she asked.

He took another spoonful, then answered. "Oh, fine. This afternoon at a quarter after three she remembered who she was, found her teeth, took a bath and drove to town."

"No need to joke."

"She's the same, maybe worse. I awoke this morning and found her out by the woodpile. Marcie didn't hear her get up. She was out there, just sitting on a stump and staring at the woods. She was stark naked. It was freezing, but she didn't seem to notice."

She shook her head. "You had better think about getting her into a nursing home, Russ."

He nodded. "Marcie won't hear of it. She insists she can take care of her."

"Well, Martha's her mother. It's natural, I suppose. But Marcie should start thinking of living her own life."

He chewed some bread, then spoke. "Those nursing homes aren't cheap, Lila. I couldn't afford to pay for very long."

She shrugged. "I told you how to do that, Russ. You could get a divorce. You'd have to pay something, of course, but the state would have to pick up most of the nursing home cost. Martha would be indigent and she'd qualify for help."

He put the spoon down. "You know I could never do that, Lila. I couldn't. I remember Martha like she was."

"Yes," she said softly. "So do I." She inhaled deeply on her cigarette. "I suppose I was just being selfish."

He made a sandwich of the beef slices. "You wouldn't want me as a husband. I'm fine as a three-day-a-week lover, but you'd tire of me if I was around for any longer than that."

She looked at him and laughed. "You know, Russ, you're probably right. Maybe it's the sneaking around that really appeals to me."

"You'd hardly call this sneaking around," he said. "Christ, the whole county knows about you and me."

"It's not even hot gossip anymore, is it? Two old farts playing grab-ass."

"I'm an old fart," he said, munching the sandwich. "You are still a hot young thing."

"If you think fifty-five is young, Russ. I really don't have to worry much about the other nights of the week. People probably think we play Scrabble here at night."

"Little do they know."

"Want some pie?"

"Did you make it?"

"Store-bought."

"Then I might have a slice."

"Louse!"

She got up and prepared the pie. "We'll have some visitors up here this Monday."

"Oh?"

She sliced some cheese and placed it on the plate with the pie, then brought it to him.

"I'm holding a pretrial on the Daren will."

"This Monday?"

She sat down. "We'll be up to our ass in big city lawyers."

"You worried?"

She grinned. "I've been a lawyer for over thirty years, and a judge for almost ten of those. Are you kidding?"

"You're used to local shitkickers like old Charley Callaghan. Charley hasn't cracked a law book in fifty years. Real lawyers might run you up a tree."

"Want to bet?"

He laughed. "No way. Hell, I'm scared of you, so I think you'd probably terrorize strangers."

She ground out the cigarette in an ashtray. "At least it will be interesting."

He worked on the pie. "Mind how you decide things, Lila. Some of the county folks are getting pretty riled up about the Darens owning half the world. You're up for another term next year. You don't want to piss everybody off a few months before you ask them to vote for you again."

119

"I'll do what's right."

"You might be opposed this time. There's a young lawyer over in Crumley who is starving to death. He'd love to have a nice steady judicial income. Don't give him anything he can run on."

"Are you talking about that Casper kid? The one with the thin little wife and the two sick-looking kids?"

"A couple of sick-looking kids can win elections for their father. I'm not telling you what to do, Lila, merely suggesting you look out for yourself. I'm all for a little enlightened self-interest in the courts."

"Fuck you, Russ."

He pushed the empty pie dish away and grinned.

"I thought you'd never ask."

Jake dialed the familiar number. Marie hadn't returned any of the calls he'd made. Her secretary answered, and as soon as she heard his voice her measured tones turned icy. Marie was eternally unavailable.

"Did you give her my messages?" Jake asked, trying to control his rising anger.

"Ms. Chandler suggests you call her lawyer, Roger Bartlett." Marie's secretary read him Bartlett's telephone number, then repeated it slowly, as though she were speaking to someone who might have difficulty with numbers, or even long words.

Jake sighed. "Tell Ms. Chandler that I said hello."

He paused for a moment. Bartlett was one of Detroit's leading divorce attorneys. Jake dialed and was put through as soon as he identified himself.

"Jake, how are you? I'm so glad you called. I have the complaint right here." Bartlett's voice was deep and satin smooth. "I can send it over there, or perhaps you'd prefer to drop by my office."

"I'm trying to reach my wife," Jake snapped. He always resented people like Bartlett who called him by his first name without ever having met him. "I want to talk to Marie, Mr. Bartlett, before this goes any further."

"Call me Roger," Bartlett said easily. "I'm sure that can be arranged, but not at the moment, I'm afraid."

"Why not now?"

"Have you done much divorce work, Jake?"

"None."

Bartlett chuckled. "Like everything else in life, divorce cases seem to follow a pattern. At least most of them. Things are a little sticky in the beginning. Feelings run high for a while, then they simmer down. That's the time to talk things over, Jake, not now."

"Marie won't see me, is that it?"

"More or less. That's probably best for everyone at this point. There are no children, and apparently no money problems, so there's really no necessity to meet with her now. Perhaps you and I could get together. I've drawn a proposed settlement agreement."

"Look, I want to talk to my wife."

"Let's meet for a drink after work today, Jake. I'll bring along the papers and we can chat."

"I don't want to talk to you, damn it! I don't want this divorce."

He was answered by a deep sigh. "Isn't it always the case: doctors make the worst patients, and lawyers make the worst litigants." He paused and continued in even smoother tones. "Jake, there's nothing you can do here, not a thing. As a lawyer you know that. Let's be civilized about this."

"You can be as civilized as you like, I—"

"Jake." It came out almost as a whisper. "You're angry, and I don't blame you. But trust me, I always do my best to effectuate a reconciliation in every divorce case I handle."

"Your success rate must be pretty rotten—you seem to handle more divorces in this city than anyone else."

Bartlett chuckled. "Well, let's say I try my very best. Now, how about that drink?"

"No."

"How would you like service handled? I'll do it any way you prefer."

"I prefer the hard way. If you want to serve me, find me."

Now Bartlett's chuckle reflected genuine amusement. "Jake, that's no problem. I can have you served at your office, although I don't like to do that to a brother lawyer unless I have to. Marie tells me you're involved in the Daren litigation. You really can't hide, can you? My man can lay the paper on you in court if necessary, but I'd rather spare you that embarrassment."

Jake looked out of the window at the river. Bartlett was right, service was inevitable. There was no point in trying to avoid it. "You can have me served here at my office," he snapped.

"Are you sure you wouldn't rather just meet me for a drink?"

"I am absolutely positive."

"Jake, I've been divorced four times. I can understand how you feel, but the rage passes quickly enough. The best thing is to avoid embarrassing yourself." He paused. "My man can be over there in twenty minutes or less. Will you be there?"

"Yeah."

"We'll have that drink another time. I look forward to meeting you, Jake." Bartlett hung up.

Jake slammed the receiver down with great force. As if in protest, the phone rang immediately.

"I have a Mr. Lee Stevens on the line," his secretary said. "He insisted on waiting. He says it's important. Do you want to talk to him or should I get rid of him?"

121

Jake didn't feel like talking to anyone. He decided to get rid of Stevens as quickly as possible. "Put him on," he said.

"What's up?" Jake asked.

"Elizabeth tells me we're scheduled for a pretrial hearing up north next Monday."

"That's right."

"What's that all about?"

Jake regretted taking the call. "The judge will talk to the lawyers to see if a settlement's possible, and if not, to set up a trial date and the ground rules."

"There's to be no settlement," Stevens said brusquely.

"I know that," Jake snapped.

"Who's going to be there?" Stevens asked.

"Just the lawyers."

"I'll have Elizabeth there," Stevens said.

"But there's no need for that," Jake protested.

"Sure there is," Stevens said. "I'll set up something with the press people. We'll get a gang of them up there. I'll prepare something Elizabeth can read them. It'll make a terrific photo opportunity. That old courthouse up there will make a great background. We can steal a publicity march on the other side."

Jake was becoming furious, but he realized it was merely referred rage, the direct result of not being able to see or talk to Marie. He took a deep breath and tried to calm himself.

"If you turn this into a publicity circus, it could backfire. The judge could get sore," he said evenly. "It's going to be a quiet little meeting in the judge's office, that's all."

Stevens snorted. "Do you think that's how T. G. Sage is going to treat it? As just a quiet little meeting? This case is going to be tried in the press as well as in the court, pal, and you might as well get used to it. You may not intend to win, but I do."

"What the hell are you talking about?"

Stevens paused, then spoke, his tone much sharper. "Are you sure you're up to something like this?"

"What do you mean by that?"

"Can't Sperling Beekman send someone with a little more experience with this sort of thing? No offense, Jake, I like you, but this case isn't going to be some legal tea dance, this is total war."

Although he was angry, Jake had to acknowledge that there was some justification for Steven's comment. He had not asked for the assignment, but he wasn't about to admit to Stevens his own doubts about his ability to handle it.

"Get this, and get it straight," Jake snapped. "I don't want any publicity whatsoever connected with this hearing. It could damage the case."

"That's your opinion. I—"

"Are you paying the legal fees?"

"Elizabeth is, but I have a job to do—"

Jake snarled. "Who the hell do you think you are? You aren't a lawyer. You aren't running this case."

"Neither are you. Bellows is. You had better clear this no publicity foolishness with him."

Jake's hand trembled with rage. Again, he fought to control his anger. "I'll say this one more time: no publicity. Is that clear?"

"If Sage pops out a press release and cleans your fucking clock up there on Monday, your ass, my friend, will be grass."

"I'll take that risk," Jake growled, slamming down the receiver for the second time.

Jake sat quietly for a moment. He wondered if he detected a hint of real displeasure from Bellows or had he only imagined it. Whatever, Stevens' anger was real. Jake's world seemed to have turned strangely hostile. Jake wondered if it just seemed that way because of his personal problems and the depression those problems were causing.

Jake's secretary opened the door and looked in. "There's a man here from Roger Bartlett's office. He says he has something for you. He refused to give it to me. He said he has to hand it to you. Do you want to see him?"

Hostile wasn't even catching it.

Gussie Daren let the hot sun burn away the residual pain and malaise. She lay in her briefest bikini next to her pool. Beyond, the Atlantic drummed along the long seawall of her estate, producing a hypnotic beat she usually found soothing but, on this Saturday, was more annoying than comforting. She had finally forced herself to get out of bed, gulped down two Bloody Marys and some Bayer. Now she lay quietly and hoped the vodka and aspirin, plus the sun, would help cure what was surely a world-class hangover.

She remembered the dinner party, and some of the evening after, but most of the rest of the night was blank. She remembered laughing a lot, but she had no idea what time she had gotten home or what she might have said or done. As was her custom when she was in the throes of a hangover, she considered giving up drinking altogether. She had made at least a dozen half-hearted attempts, but temperance usually lasted only until the next party.

Her mouth felt thick and dry as she signaled her maid, who always stayed close by, to bring another drink; then she sank back. She was thirty-nine years old. She still looked good, she knew that. Long legs and a trim body were genetic gifts from her mother. But eventually the years of abuse would show up in the horrible way women she knew tended to grow old. Skin became thickened and wrinkled, and what had been slender became bony. Down in Florida the plastic surgeons loved rich women. They wielded their scalpels, snipping and scraping away at the aging flesh like white-coated miners digging into rich veins of gold. But there was only so much even the most talented doctors could do.

Like her dead father, Gussie Daren had been married four times. But unlike him she had had no children. The decision not to have children had been deliberately made long ago. She knew she would be a dreadful parent, like her own mother and father. The marriages, except for the last one, had been disasters.

Gussie still missed Paolo, her last husband, even if they were beginning to have problems just before he died.

Paolo, the Brazilian polo player. He had been almost as rich as herself, and nearly as wild. He was good at many things, including swimming, but not when he was drunk. He had taken his last intoxicated swim off the sea wall after one of their legendary parties. What was left of his drowned body, after the fish got through with it, had washed up several miles down from the sea wall where the waves now beat their steady tattoo.

For a while, Palm Beach had been abuzz with dark rumors about Paolo's death. At the time, murder was "in" and Gussie found she unexpectedly enjoyed her status as a notorious widow and possible suspect. But the hint of scandal had been short-lived. Everyone, including Gussie, got bored with the whole business and Palm Beach life went back to normal.

"Gussie!"

She recognized the high-pitched shriek, but she turned her head and raised her sunglasses as though she were examining a stranger.

"God, Gussie, how wonderful you look! If I were a man or a follower of Sappho, I'd have a go at you myself."

Gussie lay back.

"How are you, Hildy?"

Hilda Parkinson, always referred to as Mrs. Parkinson Pharmaceutical Company, sat down near Gussie's feet. She whipped off her beach coat. Tall, even taller than Gussie, she was so thin that each of her ribs stuck out like an illustration in a medical school anatomy chart. Her bikini top was as sparse as that which it was designed to cover. Like Gussie, her skin had been tanned to a deep chocolate.

"Well?" Hildy said.

"Well, what?"

Hildy had often been compared to Katherine Hepburn. She had the same high cheekbones, the same expressive eyes, the same prominent teeth. Her husband, the ancient George Parkinson, apparently had had a crush on the actress and had subsequently chosen Hildy as an acceptable, and younger, substitute.

The maid brought another Bloody Mary.

"God, that looks good. Bring me one too."

Hildy turned to Gussie. "Well, what was he like?"

Gussie knew she'd have to admit to an alcoholic blackout, but her curiosity had to be salved.

"Who?"

Hildy laughed. "Gussie, I don't know how you do it! You never look drunk. You don't remember?"

"Would I ask if I did?"

"The writer. You left with the writer."

"The little skinny one? What was his name? Charles Fox?"

Hilda giggled. "He had a wide mouth. I think that's what attracted you. He's probably hung like a horse. The size of the mouth is usually a giveaway. Was he?"

Gussie tried to call up a memory, any memory, of the night before, but nothing appeared in answer to her summons. "Jesus, I don't know. Maybe nothing happened."

"You insisted on taking him back here." Hilda's cackling laugh drowned out the sound of the Atlantic. "Did you look in your bed? Hell, he might still be there. He isn't very big. You might have tucked him under a pillow, or something."

Gussie's maid brought the drink for Hildy.

"When did Mr. Fox leave?" Gussie asked in a bored, I-don't-really-care tone.

"About ten this morning," the maid replied, her face expressionless. "Cook fixed him breakfast. He said he had a plane to catch."

Hildy chuckled, but remained silent until the maid moved away. "Well, there you are. He might have been the greatest fuck in the world, and now you'll never know."

"Or the worst," Gussie replied glumly.

"You better take it easy with the old demon rum, Gussie. The season's just beginning. You might end up in the sack with Warren Beatty and never remember it. Wouldn't that be awful?"

"The season can start without me," Gussie replied. "I have to go up north."

"Why?"

"So I can lend family support to Chip's scheme to get my father's will tossed out."

Hildy became serious. "Will you have to testify?"

"I don't think so. Why?"

"Well, those things can get dicey. You know, like that Johnson and Johnson thing, all the soiled family linen run out on the line for all the world to see."

"The lawyer doubts it will come to that."

Hildy sipped her drink, leaving a red tomato juice line above her glossy upper lip. "I wouldn't go if I were you. Detroit's a dreadful city."

"The trial won't be in Detroit. It's going to be up in northern Michigan."

Hildy made a face. "That's even worse. My God, you'll freeze."

Gussie smiled. "I spent my summers up there as a kid. In a way,

125

I almost look forward to going back. I'd like to see if things are still the way I remember them."

"They never are. Why go? Tell Chip to fuck off."

Gussie was feeling better. The headache was almost gone. "Nothing's ever that simple, Hildy. This thing's quite complicated. If we win, we can take control of my father's bank."

"Why in the world bother? You're already rich enough."

Gussie raised her sunglasses and squinted at her. "No one is ever rich enough. You should know that. Especially around here. Chip says we can double, maybe triple, our holdings if we can get the bank."

"Has Chip changed? You saw him at the funeral."

"He's older, a little heavier, but he's still the prime asshole he always was."

"Then why get involved with any scheme of his?"

"Blood is thicker than water, Hildy." She finished the drink and lay the glass down on the tile. "And money is thicker than blood. I couldn't care less about my dear half-brother, but I owe it to my bank account. We have a kind of partnership in this thing."

"Partnership?"

"Chip sues and takes the risk of losing his share. I agreed to split mine if he loses. But if he wins, we'll make a fortune."

"Another fortune, you mean." Hildy frowned. "You know, Gussie, if a smart lawyer got you on the stand, well . . ."

"Well, what?"

"He could fire up some old embers. You haven't exactly been a cloistered nun, have you?"

"So?"

Hildy shrugged. "As I say, it could get sticky."

Gussie scowled. "If it does, my beloved stepmother will regret it far more than I will. Compared to her, I do look like a nun."

"Sticky, sticky, sticky!"

Gussie started to get up.

"What's the matter?" Hildy asked.

"That writer! You don't suppose that skinny little son-of-a-bitch might have AIDS? He's from New York."

Hildy shrugged. "Everybody's from New York. Besides, he probably used a condom. It's the thing to do nowadays."

"What if he didn't?"

Hildy patted Gussie's leg. "Perhaps you might become a mommy. Ever think about that? You might just need that second fortune after all."

11

It had rained for a while around Saginaw, but otherwise the roads had been dry and the autumn traffic predictably sparse. Jake made good time and arrived in Gladding with time to spare.

He was hungry and there was still an hour until the scheduled two o'clock hearing. In Gladding, for some reason everyone parked at an angle. Jake pulled into a space between two almost identical mud-splattered pickup trucks and parked in front of the town's only hotel, the Eagle Inn.

The Eagle Inn, an ancient three-story red brick building, was located next to the railroad tracks, rusty and unused. Jake walked up the three worn stone steps to the hotel's entrance, went through the door and found himself in a narrow hallway. On his right was a small, untended registration desk. The hotel's restaurant was on his left.

In order to get to the restaurant, Jake had to walk through a small, dimly lit taproom. Two men, dressed in faded work clothes and seated at stools at the end of the bar, were engaged in animated conversation with the chubby blonde barmaid.

The restaurant was separated from the taproom by a narrow doorway. Bright in contrast to the bar, the restaurant was pleasant but plain. The tables were covered by immaculate white tablecloths. Some of the chairs didn't match. The carpeting was threadbare, and a baked goods display was located near the cash register counter.

An elderly couple lingered silently over coffee. Jake was the only other customer. He took a table near the large front windows. A plastic-covered menu card was propped up between the salt and pepper shakers and a sturdy sugar bowl. Jake extracted the menu and was surprised by the selection offered.

"Hi."

He looked up. Blonde and stocky, she was almost a twin of the girl behind the bar. Jake guessed her age as early twenties. She wore a loose-fitting blouse over jeans and held an order pad in her hand.

"Can I get you something from the bar?" she asked.

Jake shook his head. "No, thanks. Just coffee and a ham sandwich."

"You got it."

She walked to a slot where the kitchen was located and put in his order, returned with a glass coffee pot, turned up his cup and filled it.

"That your car out there?" she asked, nodding toward the window. "The Corvette?"

"Yes."

"Nice. What brings you here?"

Jake smiled. "I've got some business in town."

She leaned against the table, almost uncomfortably close. A plain girl, she was still attractive, her best feature being her soft brown eyes.

"Are you one of the lawyers up for the Daren case?"

He nodded. "How do you know about that?"

Her grin, which revealed uneven teeth, was warm and infectious. She laughed. "That case is big news up here. In case you haven't noticed, this isn't exactly New York or Los Angeles. Since they closed the movie show, the courthouse is our prime source of entertainment."

"Is Gladding your hometown?"

"Yup. No one ever moves here, they just move away. Whose side are you on?"

"Pardon me?"

"Are you a lawyer for Mrs. Daren, or for the old man's children?"

"Is that important?"

She nodded. "Up here it is."

"Why?"

Her expression was guarded, as though she were deciding whether the question merited a frank answer, then she spoke. "The Darens own damn near the whole county. The rest of us sort of live off the crumbs that fall from their table and handouts from the government. We could support ourselves if we could open up this area for tourist business, but the Darens have always refused to sell or lease any of their land."

She laughed, but there was no humor in it. "For example, just look at this place. This was a railroad hotel in the old days when lumber was our main business, but now everything is harvested and the trains haven't run by here in years. If it wasn't for the hunting season and adultery, the owner here couldn't even pay the taxes on this dump. This town needs help."

Jake sipped his coffee. "Why would the Daren case make a difference?"

"Wait a minute." She went to the kitchen slot and returned with his sandwich. The ham was thick and the bread looked homemade.

She pulled up a chair and sat next to him. "We thought maybe Mrs. Daren might change her mind after her husband died. But she says this is her home and she likes things the way they are."

"She does own the land," Jake said, finding the sandwich delicious.

"Sure. But from what we hear, if the Daren kids, if you can call them that, can break the last will the old man made out, they might open things up. They couldn't care less what happens up here, so I'm told anyway. With them we might have a chance."

"But you're not sure?"

"All life's a gamble, isn't it?" She studied him. "So? What side are you on?"

He looked at his coffee, then answered. "My firm represents the widow," he said.

She raised one eyebrow, then laughed. "Well, if we had known that before, we could have put something in the sandwich."

"Are feelings around here that strong?"

She patted his hand. "Some are, some aren't. Anyway, none of this is your fault, you're just doing a job." She paused. "You might try talking to the widow though. Like I said, we could use some help."

"I don't know if it'll do any good, but I promise I'll talk to her."

At that, she brightened. "Appreciate it. Will you be coming up here again?"

"There's going to be a trial. I'll be up for that."

"Where are you going to stay?" she asked.

"I haven't thought about it."

She grinned. "You don't have much choice. If you don't like this place, you could try my cousin's motel. It's just outside of town. They call it a fleabag, but it's not so bad really. He'd appreciate your business. Tell him his cousin Marie sent you over."

"Marie?"

"Marie Neilsen. What's wrong with Marie?"

"Nothing. That's my wife's name."

She looked out at his Corvette. "See, if we start fooling around, you won't have to worry about talking in your sleep."

Jake laughed. "I suppose not."

"You want some dessert? We have some homemade apple pie."

"I have to get going."

She walked with him to the counter. He paid the bill and then left a tip at the table.

"Don't forget about my cousin's place," she called after him.

"I'll keep it in mind."

Still in deep conversation, the same two men were with the barmaid in the taproom as he retraced his route.

The sun had come out and it had turned into a beautiful and bright northern day. The air was so brisk and crystal clear it was a pleasure to breathe. Jake decided to leave the Corvette where it was and walk the short distance to the courthouse. He retrieved his briefcase from the car.

Gladding wasn't very large. He walked past a hardware store and a small drugstore. Both carried placards in their windows advertising an autumn pageant in Crumley and a bingo night at the local Catholic church. In the distance, a dog barked, sounding to Jake like the same one he had heard the first time he had come up.

He looked for a fancy car parked at the courthouse, but saw none. Apparently T. G. Sage had not yet arrived.

It was only a few minutes before two o'clock. Jake opened the heavy door and walked down the hall. For the first time, he noticed a small sign in the form of an arrow pointing up the wide staircase. It read, simply, COURTROOM. He passed the staircase and walked to the end of the hall and the probate office.

Judge Lila Vinson sat behind her desk. The green eyeshade and outdoor clothing had been replaced by a dress and makeup. Jake thought the judge looked out of place in such dainty apparel.

"I was beginning to wonder if anyone was going to show up," she said. "Are you here alone?"

Jake nodded.

"I thought I'd have to put up with a platoon of Harvard men from Sperling Beekman. I'm disappointed."

Jake laughed. "You know the old story about the Texas town that had a riot and wired the governor for help? The train came and one Texas Ranger stepped off. The town's mayor asked him why the governor had sent only one ranger, and the ranger replied, 'There's only one riot, isn't there?' Well, here I am."

Her expression didn't change. "I suppose if you're the only thing Sperling Beekman could find to send up, they must feel pretty confident. Is your client coming?"

"No."

"Just as well. I wouldn't let her say anything anyway. Have you eaten?"

"At the Eagle Inn."

"Food's pretty good there. Henry Labarge is the cook. Sober, there's not a better chef this side of New York. Drunk, Henry's worse than one of the Borgias. Where did you go to school, Martin?"

"Columbia."

"That figures." She sighed. "Well, this isn't Ivy League country up here, sonny."

Jake laughed out loud. "One riot, one ranger; that's how I look at it."

A ghost of a smile on her thin lips was the only indication that the judge was amused.

"You haven't changed a bit, Lila."

They both turned.

T. G. Sage stood in the doorway.

The judge looked him over slowly. "You have. You look like a sausage with gray hair," she said to Sage. "I remember you as a skinny redhead."

He chuckled. "Being rotund is my own fault. God's responsible for the gray hair. How have you been, Lila?"

"Pretty good. I'm a tough old broad, Theodore."

Lila Vinson looked at Jake. "Theodore and I went to law school

130

together. Nothing quite as fancy as Columbia, just the old University of Detroit Law School. You were a year behind me, right?"

Sage shook his head. "A year ahead."

Suddenly, Jake experienced a sinking feeling.

"I take it this young man is the opposition?" Sage stuck out his hand. "T. G. Sage."

"Jake Martin." Jake found Sage's grip firm and sure. "I'm from Sperling Beekman."

"No offense, Jake—may I call you Jake?—but I expected someone more senior. Maybe one of your legendary top partners."

"This is just the pretrial hearing," Jake said weakly.

For the first time, Lila Vinson smiled. "Tell Theodore your one riot, one ranger theory."

Sage chuckled. "I know the story. I'm impressed."

"Let's get to business," the judge said briskly. "Would you like to see our courtroom? It's one of the last real gems in this business."

"Delighted," Saga said. "Lead the way."

The judge guided them up the stairway, and Jake noticed that she had good, strong legs, even though she was walking as though she were unaccustomed to high heels.

"How long have you been with Sperling Beekman?" Sage asked as they climbed the long staircase.

"Almost five years."

"Are you a partner?"

Jake looked at him, but he could read nothing in Sage's pleasant expression.

"I hope to be."

Sage merely nodded.

The judge stopped before a huge oak double door at the head of the stairs. "Take a look at this," she said, pushing the doors open.

The second-floor courtroom was as large as the building itself, an arena dominated by a high, domed ceiling. The judge's bench, all polished mahogany, was carved in rising tiers so that it looked more like an altar. All the walls were paneled, and the spectator seats, also made of mahogany, gleamed like church pews.

"Inspiring," Sage said, his voice reflecting the awe that Jake also felt.

"This was built when Eagle County was the center of the lumbering industry. There was plenty of wood and plenty of money then. Judge Hammerly, the local district judge, sits in Crumley, but he hears his Eagle County cases here. We share a circuit judge—O'Dowd—with an adjoining county. He loves to preside here too." She walked to a far wall and flipped a light switch so that the courtroom was flooded with light from the large crystal chandeliers above. The highly polished wood caught the light like mirrors and the reflection made the total effect even more impressive.

"There's no reason why we shouldn't do our business right

here." She walked to the doors and shouted down the stairs. "Mildred! Come up here a minute. Bring your pad."

"Mildred is the deputy court clerk," the judge said as she came back. "She's a certified court reporter. She can do it all, shorthand, stenotype or recording machine. She'll do this in shorthand, if that's agreeable."

Sage nodded. Jake did too.

Mildred, a stout woman in a tight dress, smiled nervously as she lumbered through the courtroom door, her breathing labored from climbing the stairs.

"Let's all sit at the counsel table," the judge said. "This will get formal soon enough."

The judge moved a chair to the head of the table. Jake sat on one side, Sage on the other. Mildred took a position at the far end, her pad and pencil at the ready.

"I'll give you all the legal stuff off the case file later, Mildred. This is in the matter of the petition for the admission of the will of the late Augustus Daren." She looked at Jake. "Who represents his estate?"

Jake recited his name and the name of his firm as Mildred's pencil bobbed along with the cadence of his words.

Sage spoke in a surprisingly soft voice. "I am T. G. Sage, the attorney representing Augustus Daren, Jr., the son of the late Augustus Daren." He looked down the table at Mildred's busy pencil as he spoke. "As my pleading filed with the court indicates, we assert the will offered to the court is not valid in that the testator, Augustus Daren, was without testamentary capacity at the time the challenged document was signed."

"In other words, he didn't know what he was doing?" the judge asked.

"We are prepared to prove that he didn't even know who he was, let alone what he was doing."

"I object," Jake said.

They both looked at him.

"To what do you object, Mr. Martin?" the judge asked.

"To Mr. Sage's characterization of Mr. Daren's capacity."

The judge sighed. "He's just stating his position, Mr. Martin. He has an absolute right to do that. This is simply a pretrial conference. Let's not get silly. Objection overruled."

She turned to Sage. "Is this a nuisance suit, or is it for real? You've got a hell of a burden of proof here, Theodore."

"I wouldn't waste my time, Lila, if this was just a family squabble."

"We'll see." She turned to Jake. "Do you want a jury trial? You're entitled under the law, as you know."

Jake thought about the waitress and the difficulty of finding jurors who weren't already prejudiced against Elizabeth Daren. But balanced against that concern was his discovery that Sage and the judge were old friends. He wondered if she could be trusted to be fair, given the circumstance. Either choice was risky. It was the kind of decision that Donald Bellows should make. But if Jake asked for time to consult his office, the judge might think it an indication of a basic uncertainty about the strength of the case.

"We'll waive trial by jury," he said. As he spoke the words he wondered if Donald Bellows would approve. If not, Jake knew he could be in for serious trouble.

Lila Vinson turned to T. G. Sage. "Theodore?"

Sage sat back, slowly surveying the elegant courtroom as he spoke. "Lila, no offense, but I generally prefer a jury. This case is no exception. We ask trial by jury."

"Don't you trust me, Theodore?"

He laughed. "With my life. But perhaps not with my clients' lives. Judges see too much. They tend to become cynical after a while and, in my opinion, tend to look at things with an eye far too cold. A jury, I believe, generally takes a softer approach." He smiled at the judge. "Anyway, over the years, I seem to do better with juries."

"Less work for me," the judge said.

Jake was glad that Sage had demanded a jury. It relieved him of the consequences of his decision. Even Bellows couldn't complain now. The decision had been taken out of Jake's hands.

"How long will you fellows need for discovery? Make it reasonable. I want to get this thing heard and over with as soon as possible."

"We will require no discovery," Sage said evenly. "We're ready for trial now."

Jake was surprised. He hoped his expression didn't show it.

The judge turned to him. "Well, ranger, it's up to you. How long do you think you'll need?"

Jake remembered Bellows' insistence that discovery be waived. "We're ready to go, as is."

She sat back and studied each of them for a moment. "Well, just as soon as I think I've heard everything, I find out I haven't. You must be the first two lawyers in history who are anxious to proceed on time. Is there something going on here that I should know?"

"The issue is simple. This should be quick," Sage said.

She looked at him skeptically, then turned to Jake. "How many days will the trial take, do you think?"

Jake, who had never tried a lawsuit, now felt the crushing weight of that inexperience. "Two days," he said, hoping he sounded more assured than he felt.

The judge turned to Sage. "And your estimate?"

Sage pursed his lips, studied the ceiling for a moment, then spoke. "I think maybe a half-day to select the jury, if we're lucky. The rest of that day for opening statements." He paused, thinking, then continued. "I'm not as optimistic as my opponent. I see the trial lasting a week, perhaps less. It depends on the witnesses, of course. Some may take longer than others."

The judge nodded. "Nothing's ever sure." She squinted at a calendar hanging on a wall near the elaborately carved jury box. "We're getting close to deer-hunting season. Up here that's important economically. I'd have to adjourn the trial for those two weeks if we were in progress then. Deer hunting is sacred in these parts. How about setting a date in December?"

Sage frowned. "That might cause some scheduling problems. Could we possibly try it earlier?"

Bellows had emphasized speed. "I'd prefer that, too," Jake said.

"The courtroom has to be available and I have to make sure we can get a jury. But we could start Monday, November 6th," she said. "That's only two weeks away, but it gives us a full week before the hunting season starts. Would that be too soon?"

"That's agreeable," Sage said.

Jake wondered if Craig Dow would have sufficient time to prepare. But as Sage had said, the issues were simple enough. "That would be fine with us," Jake said.

"Are you both sure?" the judge asked sharply. "I don't want to be chasing this thing all over the calendar. I only grant adjournments for certifiable severe illness, like a heart attack. Flu won't do it for you. And if your grandma cools while we're working, that's just too bad. You can send flowers, but you can't leave. I'm known as a tough judge when it comes to running my docket. Am I making myself clear?"

Sage smiled. "I shall be ready."

Jake nodded in agreement.

"Good. We go to work promptly at nine o'clock, November 6th. Now, any other business?"

Sage opened his battered briefcase and extracted some papers. He handed one to the judge and the other to Jake.

"I know we agreed on no discovery, but I thought I'd let everyone know the people I anticipate calling as witnesses."

Jake examined the list. There were eight names, each with an address listed. The first four names were local people whom Jake had never heard of. Two of the witnesses were medical doctors, one from New York, the other from Cleveland. Milo Faraday and Rhonda Janus were also listed.

"What is this?" Jake protested. "These last two are our witnesses!"

Sage shrugged. "This is just insurance. You might decide not to call one of them. I shall want the opportunity to question both."

"But they are witnesses to the will itself. They have to be called."

134

"Not both," Sage said. "Just one. In this case, given the circumstances, I would prefer to have testimony from each of them."

Jake felt rising panic. He wasn't a trial lawyer, but he sensed that the inclusion of the two witnesses meant much more than Sage said it did. He didn't know exactly what he should do or say. But he felt he should do something.

"These doctors on your list," Jake said, trying to buy a little time to think, "did they examine Daren?"

Sage shook his head. "No."

"Then I'll object to them as witnesses."

The judge snorted. "He's only telling you whom he expects to call. Don't yell before you're hurt. You can object when and if he does call them."

"But—"

She held up her hand, silencing Jake. "Sonny, I'm not going to try the case here and now."

Jake wondered if an experienced lawyer like Sage would list someone as a witness without first finding out what he could expect. Milo Faraday said he had talked to no one about the case, but Jake began to suspect that wasn't true. And Lee Stevens had warned him Rhonda Janus might testify for the other side. Now that suspicion also seemed to have ominous substance.

Sage had listed both addresses correctly, even including the zip codes. Both addresses, especially Faraday's, who had just moved, would be difficult to obtain, unless someone had access to the files of Sperling Beekman. It seemed paranoid, but Jake wondered if Sage might have a source within the firm.

"Are you planning to call anyone besides the witnesses to the will?" the judge asked, breaking Jake's train of thought.

"We have a videotape of Augustus Daren executing the will," Jake said. "We plan to introduce that."

"I will probably object," Sage said, "but I would like the opportunity to view the video before trial."

"We can set that up," Jake said. "Pick a time when it's convenient."

"Anything else?" the judge asked Jake.

Jake wished Dow or someone who knew evidence and procedure had come along. "I'm not sure," he said, slowly. "We may have rebuttal testimony. We may call Donald Bellows. He was Mr. Daren's legal adviser."

Sage chuckled. "Since he's a partner in Sperling Beekman, the firm trying this case, I think his testimony would be an obvious violation of the canon of ethics. But, as the judge says, I'll hold off any objection until the proper time."

Jake knew he should make some reply, but he couldn't think of a single thing to say. All he could do was to feel embarrassed.

The judge rescued him. "Well, Mr. Martin, the burden of proof at this point isn't yours. It's up to Mr. Sage to overcome the presumption that the will is valid. Since both parties have uncharacteristically eschewed discovery, the whole question of what's admissible and what's not is really up in the air until we start the trial." She stood up. "Now, unless there's anything more, we'll see each other right here two weeks from today."

Jake and Sage followed the judge and the clerk down the wide staircase.

"Will you be trying this case, Jake?" Sage asked.

Jake shook his head. "I'm in the firm's estate planning section. One of our litigators will take over from here."

"Any candidates at this point?"

"Probably Craig Dow."

"I don't believe I know him." Sage emitted a small laugh. "I presume he's the firm's young courtroom lion of the moment?"

"More or less."

The judge stopped at the bottom of the stairs. "Theodore, do you still drink?"

Sage nodded. "On occasion."

"Would you and the ranger here want to step into my office? I have some rather good bourbon hidden away in my desk."

"I have time for one, Lila, but then I have to get back. It's a long drive back to Detroit."

"How about you, ranger?" she asked.

"I have to see my client, then I have to get back, too. I'll pass, if you don't mind."

She smiled. "Are you sure you can trust me and Theodore alone?"

"Legally or sexually?" Jake instantly regretted his all-too-flippant remark, but it was too late.

The judge's eyes narrowed, and then the sound of her wheezing laughter echoed down the narrow hallway. "You know, ranger, you might not be such a horse's ass after all."

Jake pulled into the vast parking area at Raven's Nest. The sun glinted off the rippled surface of Lake Bradford. Once he'd gotten out of the car he paused for a moment just to enjoy the beautiful day and then proceeded to the house. Jake was surprised when Elizabeth Daren herself opened the door for him.

"I didn't expect you so early. Is the pretrial hearing over already?" she asked.

He nodded. "Trial is set for November 6th. The judge wants to try the case before hunting season starts up here. The other side has demanded a jury."

"Are you alone?" she asked, looking past him.

"It's just me."

"Come in." She led him into the enormous main room. "I had

presumed Donald Bellows would come up, or one of your firm's main trial lawyers."

Despite the mild autumn weather, a fire was crackling in the huge fireplace.

"This was just the pretrial," Jake said. "Bellows didn't think anyone else was needed. It was basically just a meeting to set a date and iron out some procedural ground rules." Jake hoped he sounded more confident than he felt.

"Sit down and tell me everything, Jake. Would you care for a drink?"

"Please. Scotch and water would be great."

Elizabeth nodded to a maid. "For me too," she said. Then she turned to Jake. "Did you get along with Judge Vinson?"

"I met her before, as you know. She was dressed up today."

Elizabeth smiled. "My, that is different. She must consider this really important."

"She's blunt, but she seems to know what she's doing. There is one alarming thing, though."

"Oh?"

"She and T. G. Sage went to law school together."

"Will that influence her?"

Jake shrugged. "It could. But we'll have a jury, so it's not fatal, even if she is partial. We'll just have to be alert. If she favors the other side, we'll put it on the record, to preserve it for appeal."

The maid returned with the drinks.

Jake sipped the scotch. It was a very strong drink.

"You mentioned appeal. Do you think we'll lose?"

"No. Certainly not," Jake said. "But if the judge did something to cause us to lose, we'd appeal and we'd make it stick."

"And the other side," she asked. "If they lose, won't they appeal too?"

"Probably not. They have a tremendous burden of proof. If they can't get that over at trial, they wouldn't have much of a chance on appeal. If they did bring an appeal, it would only be for nuisance value and we could probably get it dismissed quickly."

She hadn't touched her drink. "Time is very important."

"So it seems. Sage could have demanded time to interview potential witnesses. Since he didn't I presume he's acting under instructions to hurry things along."

"Chip, or whoever's behind him, knows that time is of the essence."

Jake reached into his briefcase and took out Sage's list. "I have a list of witnesses Sage plans to call. He's named some medical experts, but since they never examined your husband we may be able to block their testimony. He's listed four local people. Do you know who they are?" He handed her the list.

She studied it for a moment. "Philip Hunt worked for us. He was

137

my husband's fishing and hunting guide. He was on the payroll as a groundskeeper."

"Did you fire him?"

"I wouldn't call it that. After Gus's second stroke there was no point in keeping the man on, there was no work for him. He was old enough to qualify for social security anyway. I gave him several years' salary as severance pay."

"That was generous."

"Gus was very fond of him."

"Why do you think they might call him as a witness? It doesn't sound as if he should have a grievance against you."

"I didn't share Gus's fondness," she said. "I found Hunt somewhat troublesome. After the first stroke he tried to run Gus's life. At first, I went along with it because I thought it might help in Gus's rehabilitation. But Hunt kept pushing Gus beyond his physical capabilities and that just made him feel worse. I put a stop to that. I suppose Hunt resented it."

"How about the others on the list?"

Elizabeth shrugged. "The other three are women who worked here. They were here before Gus and I were married. When I came here for the first time, the three of them seemed to be running things pretty much to suit themselves." She smiled. "I think the old butler might have had affairs with all of them. They didn't seem to worry much about him. Anyway, whatever the reason, they weren't doing their jobs, so I got rid of them."

"Before or after Mr. Daren had the first stroke?"

She looked up. "Oh, I see what you mean. Unfortunately, all three were let go after Gus's first stroke. They were angry, to put it mildly."

"When they worked here, did they have much contact with your husband after the first stroke?"

"Not much. He kept to our rooms. As I told you, he was ashamed of what the stroke had done to him. I told him it was foolish, but he was a very proud man."

"But they would have seen him then?"

"Probably, but only occasionally at best." She looked at the list. "I notice Milo Faraday and Rhonda Janus are listed as witnesses. For them?"

"Evidently, although Sage says he's named them only for procedural reasons."

She handed back the list. "Rhonda I can understand. She had visions of becoming the next Mrs. Augustus Daren until I came on the scene. But Milo surprises me."

Jake finished his drink. "I interviewed him last week. I think his testimony might hurt us."

"Why?"

"Faraday said your husband was mentally incompetent much of the time."

Her emerald eyes narrowed. "That's a total lie," she snapped. "Gus's mind was as sharp as it ever was."

"Not according to Faraday."

She frowned. "May I be frank, Jake?"

"Please."

"Milo, to put it crudely, was in heat up here. I already told you, I turned him down." She shook her head. "A man like Milo must be accustomed to that. He has the personality of a turnip and he's not exactly dashing, is he? But I honestly don't think he'd lie out of spite."

"Then why would he say that?"

She paused, then spoke. "Money. He pretends to be interested in only medicine, but it's money that really excites his passion. I presume someone has paid him or has promised to pay him."

"That would be hard to prove."

Elizabeth watched the fire for a moment, then looked again at Jake. "Will you be trying the case, Jake?"

He shook his head. "I'm not a trial lawyer. Craig Dow is the firm's top litigator. He'll probably conduct the trial. Of course, Donald Bellows may decide to do it himself."

"Shouldn't this Dow have been up here to handle things today?"

Jake shrugged. "We have a team of lawyers assigned to your case and I'm the nominal head. I suppose that's why they sent me."

She studied him. "Do you think you could do it if you had to?"

Jake shook his head. "I did have about two years as an associate in litigation in a New York law firm but I've never actually tried a lawsuit. I'm a probate and trust expert, at least that's what they pay me for. A jury trial would scare me to death, though in this area of law, it's usually cut-and-dried. And I *am* a specialist at the firm in the area."

"You don't look like the kind of man who would scare easily."

He grinned. "If I were to try it, Elizabeth, you'd be the one who should be scared."

"Will you stay for dinner, Jake?"

"It's a long drive back; I really should get started."

"You could stay over again and go back in the morning."

"I'd like to, of course, but—"

"Stay as a favor to me, Jake." She looked beyond him, out at the lake. "It sounds childish, but I'm a little worried about all this and I'd feel better if I had someone to talk to. Besides, to be frank, I'm lonesome. Do you ever feel like that?"

She was regal and beautiful, but somehow, to him, she looked genuinely vulnerable. And now especially, he knew exactly how it felt to be lonely. There was no real reason for him to go back. It was painfully obvious that no one was waiting for him anymore.

"I'd have to leave very early tomorrow morning," he said.

She seemed to study him for several moments, then she smiled. "I'll personally guarantee that you're awakened early."

Awake, Jake lay listening to the gathering wind. The warm autumn air, pushed south by a weather front from chilly Canada, had been replaced by turbulent cold air. The muffled sound of Lake Bradford's waves rushing against the shore produced a steady primal beat. The effect was soothing, but he was still unable to sleep.

Even in his bedroom, the same room he had had before, a trace of the pungent smoke from the main room's fireplace hung in the crisp air like a lingering perfume. Snuggled warmly beneath the enormous down comforter, listening to the wind, he should have slept easily, but Jake found his mind racing from one disturbing thought to another.

He tried not to think of Marie. Memories evoked whirlpools of torturing emotions: fear, anger, confusion, but most of all, pain.

Jake realized he had made a mistake by not calling Donald Bellows as soon as the pretrial hearing was over. Elizabeth Daren had been diverting, and when he had remembered to call, Bellows had left the office and was not at home. Jake left a number of messages, but Bellows had not called back.

Lately, it seemed that Bellows was becoming cool toward Jake, not a good sign for his partnership aspirations, if, that was, Jake's perceptions weren't being colored by the events of his troubled personal life.

Bellows would be delighted with the speedy trial date, but Jake decided to put off discussing his suspicions that a leak might exist within the firm. He would wait until he had more than mere suspicion.

The wind howled outside, whistling against the window. Jake listened as he replayed the events of the day.

Craig Dow would have a tough time finding an impartial jury among the people of Gladding. And despite T. G. Sage's benign manner, Jake sensed the older lawyer would easily live up to his fierce reputation. And Sage knew the judge, which might make things much worse.

Even though they were in competition for partner, Jake felt sorry for Craig.

It would all be up to Dow from now on. Since he had little practical courtroom experience, it had been unfair to assign the pretrial to Jake, but he had survived and it would be a great relief now just to watch the action from the sidelines.

Everyone of significance in his life danced across his thoughts in a jumbled array: Marie, Bellows, Cora Simpson, Sage, and especially Elizabeth Daren, whom he found so disturbingly attractive. Given the circumstances, it was foolish to engage even in a fantasy about her.

A cold bright moon shone through the window near his bed. Wind-whipped clouds occasionally scudded across the moon, riding the sky like Halloween witches. Jake listened to the distant sound of the waves and tried to divert his thoughts.

Elizabeth Daren also watched the moon from her bedroom. She had thought about nothing but the bank for months now, every moment spent reviewing what Gus had told her, endlessly planning the counters for moves he had said were to come.

But tonight was different.

She found Jake Martin attractive. He had an innocent quality about him that she seldom found in men. He was honest, she sensed that, and intent on doing whatever was asked of him. She smiled. He always seemed a bit awkward, but it was appealing, not unlike those old roles Jimmy Stewart played, the gangly good-hearted hero, always intent on doing the right thing.

She had never even looked at another man after meeting Augustus Daren. He had completely filled her life in every way possible. Elizabeth wondered if she would ever feel about anyone the way she had felt about Gus. She doubted that she would. But there was more to life, she knew, than banking.

Someday, when the smoke of the corporate battle cleared, she would need companionship. And if she never found anything as intense as her feeling for Gus, she suspected she would find someone who would ease the terrible loneliness she was just now beginning to feel.

But that someday was still far off. She had pledged herself to completing what she and Gus had begun. And she would do it.

The moon seemed especially cold in the clear night air. She tried to think of something else besides the awakened need she was just beginning to acknowledge. She tried to put out of her mind the memory of being held, the intense feeling of physical comfort that it brought with it. She reminded herself that this was no time to begin an affair.

Elizabeth closed her eyes and listened to the wind and the soothing sound of the lake.

12

Sherman Murphy's newspaper column, like an old cruise ship, had metamorphosed through a succession of names. When he had first come from Houston to *The Detroit News,* the column had been named "Sherman's March" by a committee of news editors. He had been hired to bring to the paper a light-hearted feature, a fey, satirical view of the old Motor City, something the editors felt was needed to offset the more strident and crusading veteran news columnists.

But reader surveys quickly showed Detroiters shunned "Sherman's March." Fey was not a particularly hot style in a tough industrial city. Sherman Murphy started making discreet job inquiries to big newspapers in other cities, but itinerant columnists were not in great demand, especially those indulging in light whimsy.

He had a year's contract, and rather than pay off the remaining term the tight-fisted news editors tried a new name for his offering. "Murphy's Law," they figured, would fly. He was sternly advised to get more acerbic, and damn quickly.

Like a timid swimmer dipping a tentative toe in unknown waters, he wrote a piece about a tough one-legged Hungarian barmaid who worked in a Detroit downriver bar. She was called Peg Leg Peg. Murphy's prose reshaped the original, a foul-mouthed, disgusting woman, until she emerged as a clear-eyed populist philosopher spewing forth hard truths for a tough town.

Sherman Murphy had unwittingly hit the mother lode. Within months, with columns about Peg and other Detroit characters whom he managed to turn into legends, he became the hottest ticket at the paper. The column was quickly renamed "Murphy's Turf," and he was king of the city. He had a new contract for more money than he had ever expected to see. He was no longer Sherman Murphy, or even Murphy—he was Murph.

Murph was forty, but his fleshy, blotchy face made him look ten years older. He had never before had a Texas drawl, but he quickly developed one. He started wearing cowboy clothes for the first time in his life. A river of cheap whiskey consumed in his search for suitable characters for his column had burned his vocal cords until his voice was beginning to sound like rusty truck brakes.

He was better known than the mayor, and for a while he became almost as powerful. When Peg Leg Peg died—she had drunk herself unconscious, slipped behind the bar and suffocated on her own vomit—Murphy attributed her death to a broken heart over the declining social values of her native city. Two thousand people turned out for the funeral of the dead downriver philosopher.

But Peg Leg Pegs were hard to come by and over the years Murphy had been forced to invent similar characters. But his inventions never quite brought to the printed page the lurid vitality of the flesh-and-blood lunatics he found, reshaped and immortalized. Like a cannibal, he needed human meat for his literary diet. The readership response surveys showed he was slipping. His contract was coming up for renewal and the bottom-line news editors were suggesting he should consider taking less, a lot less. Murph was beginning to panic.

Murph had established a saloon route so that sources could know where to find him. Monday nights he was at the Money Bush, the trendy bar frequented by bank people and lawyers. Murph had invented Herbie the Stockbroker while sitting at the Money Bush's curved bar. Herbie had done well for a while and then people lost interest. Stockbrokers, unless they were crooked, just weren't very exciting.

The bartender slapped the telephone down before Murph.

"You got a call," he snapped. The bartender disliked being forced to act as Murph's private secretary, especially since Murph never tipped.

"Murph here," he said, speaking loudly to be heard over the talk and laughter of the crowded bar.

"This is T. G. Sage."

"Who? There's a lot of noise here."

"T. G. Sage."

Murph grinned. "Hey, Tiger! How you doing?"

"I might have something for you, Murph."

"What?"

"I said I might have an item for you," Sage repeated.

"Can I call you back, Tiger? This place is too goddamn loud. Where are you?"

Sage gave him the number for the Eagle Inn in Gladding.

Murph knew the lawyer wouldn't have gone to the trouble of finding him unless he really had something.

"I'll go over to the paper and call you from there, okay? Ten minutes, tops. Don't leave."

T. G. Sage hadn't planned to spend the night at the Eagle Inn, but the drinks and then dinner with Lila Vinson had lasted longer than he had anticipated, and it was far too late to make the drive back.

Once an old railroad hotel, the Eagle Inn housed only twenty rooms. As far as Sage could determine, he was the only guest. There were no private baths in the Eagle Inn, but a common bathroom was

143

located at the end of the hall, marked by one forty-watt bulb burning above the rickety and slightly warped door.

Sage sat on the bed as he awaited Murph's call. It was an old-fashioned brass bed, its metal discolored by age and use, but it seemed comfortable enough. A braided rug, badly worn, covered part of the bare wood floor. The room, long and narrow, had one window set above a decrepit radiator.

Outside, the wind had picked up almost to gale force, but the old radiator kept everything warm as steam thumped through its metal coils. The steam heat seemed to accentuate the aroma in the high-ceilinged room, a slightly sour mix of mustiness, old cigars and whiskey.

Sage opened his battered briefcase and extracted his cigar case. He still allowed himself the luxury of one cigar at night. With practiced ritual he sniffed it, snipped the tip, moistened both ends and then, with great relish, lit it.

The ashtray had once been a jar cover. Next to it on the pine night table was a brass lamp with a fake birch-bark shade. The telephone, crowding the lamp, was the most modern thing in the room. Sage puffed on the cigar and waited.

He lay back on the bed and looked up at the ceiling. It was lined with scrolled tin plating that had been painted over a multitude of times. He thought about the men and women who had used this room during the days when the rail line carried the laborers and adventurers north to the mineral and lumber riches of Michigan.

He had studied their history. They had come like an international army, Swedes, Irish, Finns, Cornishmen, battalions of all kinds of new Americans intent upon finding their own place in their adopted country, moving to wherever the dream led them. The wood they cut had built enormous cities. The ore they mined had produced the raw product for America's manufacturing miracles.

Those loggers and miners were gone now, leaving behind only memories, traditions and a few hardy descendents who, like scrub pines, clung to a chancy existence in the lonely, poor but exquisitely beautiful north.

When the phone rang, he got it on the first ring.

"Tiger?"

"Where are you, Murph?"

"At the office. I'm up here on the fourth floor. The feature people here at the *News* don't work at night so it's quiet and I have access to the computer terminals. The city room is a zoo tonight. Two cops shot each other in a drug raid and the paper's covering it like the invasion of Europe. How you doing, Tiger? You getting laid up there?"

Sage smiled. "I'm in an ancient, dilapidated hotel room with the bath conveniently located just down the hall. This, however, is

144

considered the zenith of luxury in Gladding. I shudder to think what a hooker might look like up here, even if such a creature existed."

"Whatcha got for me, Tiger? This rag is already laid out for tomorrow, but if something's hot, I still have time to send it to the Troy plant and squeeze it in."

Over the years Sage had carefully cultivated newspaper people whom he considered savvy, trustworthy or influential. He offered a fair exchange. He provided inside information when he could, information that sometimes led to front-page stories and an appreciative writer. In return, he was often able to plant items in the papers or on television that served the interests of his clients. "Murph's Turf" had seen a number of good items provided by Sage, who considered Murph to be part of his personal and private communications network.

"A trial date in the Daren matter has been set for November 6th," Sage said. "We had a pretrial hearing here in Gladding today."

"Is that date for real, or is that one of those convenient maybes you lawyers seem to love so much?"

Sage puffed on the cigar. "This one is a go."

"November 6th," Murphy repeated. "Where?"

"Here in Gladding," Sage smiled, "the heart of the north. That's how the local people like to refer to the place. It looks more like a misplaced crossroads, but if that's how they feel about it, who am I to argue?"

"Probate Court, right? You saw the little item the paper carried when you filed the lawsuit?"

Sage nodded. "I was surprised, frankly, that it didn't get more play."

Murph laughed. "It was a long, sexy piece when our reporter wrote it, but around here the editors weren't too excited about the case, so they sliced the shit out of it. A baseball score would have gotten bigger play."

"So it seems," Sage said. "The judge who will hear the case is Lila Vinson." Sage slowly spelled her name. "She's the probate judge for Eagle County. I gave her and the other side a list of the witnesses we expect to call."

"None of this is real sexy, Tiger. It's just a minor squabble between rich folks as far as my editors are concerned. Even if you get this will kicked out, everybody comes away with the same amount of loot, don't they?"

"In money, yes. But power is another thing entirely."

"Sure, it is, but if it doesn't sell newspapers, who cares?" Murphy said.

"This might interest you, Murphy. I have reason to believe Doctor Faraday—the physician who lived with the Darens—may testify that he went along with signing the will because he was bribed by the soon-to-be widow."

145

"How much?"

"It wasn't money."

Murph said, "What then?"

"Sex, or so I understand."

"Jesus Henry Christ! Can I quote you?"

Sage laughed. "Not yet, Murph, at least not on that point. I do expect to unearth similar revelations as the trial progresses. Do you think that might then sell a few newspapers?"

"Tiger, you have to give me something now. If I call this Faraday, will he talk to me?"

"No."

"Then how the hell am I supposed to get even a hint of this into the paper?"

"All our conversations with the judge today were recorded by a court reporter. You could say, as if you had been there, that a heated exchange took place between the attorneys and that T. G. Sage promised revelations about what went on during the last few years of Augustus Daren's life, revelations that will show improper and shameful means were used to hold a sick old man captive."

"Did you say that?"

"No, but I referred at the hearing to my pleadings filed in the case. And I do say it there. Maybe the legal language isn't quite so colorful, but it's there essentially."

"My bosses are gunshy about libel suits, especially after that chiropractor took the paper for two million bucks."

"He settled that for half a million."

"Doesn't make any difference to my editors. Even one dollar is too much. They want every reporter to stick their hands in the wounds, so to speak. Inferences are out at this newspaper."

Sage laughed. "By the way, the firm on the other side—Sperling Beekman—was represented up here by a young man, D. Jacob Martin. Everyone calls him Jake, apparently."

"So?"

"You can say he objected to everything. He did, but he didn't get very far."

"Tiger, can I at least tell my editors about the sex stuff? If I don't, the case won't create enough interest around here to get it off the business page."

"You can tell them, just don't use it yet. I'll set it up so you can use it in your column when the times comes. I promise you that."

"You're not just setting this up so you boys can meet in the back room before trial and settle the damn thing, like you lawyers usually do? You're not using me just to get leverage, are you?"

"Murph, have I ever?"

"No."

"And I'm not now. This won't be settled. This will be unconditional surrender only. There's too much at stake here."

"It's just over who gets to run the bank, isn't it?"

Sage chuckled. "Whoever wins will have the power of billions of dollars and the position to make billions more. What would you do for that kind of power?"

"Kill."

"Exactly."

"If I do stick something in the column, the rest of the media will be all over you like flies on horsehit, Tiger. I'll get lost in the rush."

"Murph, I'll tell you everything I'm going to do just before I do it. Just you, nobody else. This is going to be a big national story. And if it breaks wide open, as I expect it will, you could end up with a national reputation. What would you do for something like that?"

"Kill."

"I like you, Murph. No matter how complicated the question, you always manage to come up with a reasonable answer."

Murph cranked up the computer, called the Troy plant, and pulled the item about the drunken television anchorman that had been the lead for his Tuesday column. He substituted what T. G. Sage had told him, leading the reader to believe that old Murph had been right there, sitting at the right hand of the judge herself. As promised, Murph left out the sex stuff, but alluded to it, he thought, rather cleverly. It was dynamite. After tomorrow, the Daren case would no longer be a page-three item.

The call from T. G. Sage had carried with it an almost mystical quality. Had he been a religious man, Murph would have thought it divine intervention, but he settled for just great good luck.

He needed something to increase his lagging readership, something that would skyrocket those survey numbers before his contract came up for renewal. That something was at hand, and he knew it.

His readers wanted exotic characters who were real people. He would give them that, and more. The Daren case opened up the entire north country to him like a land grant. Michigan's north was untapped, virgin territory. He had taken his vacations there and had found it inhabited by characters who made Peg Leg Peg look like a debutante. Murph had ignored the area and its denizens because his column required a definite Detroit connection.

But the Darens were definitely Detroit, and the case would provide the city hook he needed.

The young Hemingway had mined the human riches of northern Michigan's sandy loam, finding exotic people and dramatic stories there that were equal to or better than the best of the darkest and deepest veins of the vaunted Southern writers.

Robert Penn Warren and William Faulkner and the rest of them could shove all the stifling heat, the swamps and the Southern Spanish moss up their collective Dixie asses. Sherman Murphy would go north, where only the toughest plants, men and animals survived.

Murph would make the people of Gladding and Eagle County famous. He would be their Boswell, their Dickens. There might even be a book in it. Jimmy Breslin wrote books, so did Carl Hiaasen. Why shouldn't he?

Murph smiled to himself. He didn't need anyone's approval to head north and cover the Daren trial. His contract allowed him to be his own boss, giving the paper only the right to refuse to run a column if they determined it to be in bad taste or actionable.

T. G. Sage might be right on the money. With just a little bit of luck. "Murph's Turf" could even go national. Look at Mike Royko at the *Chicago Trib.*

The possibilities provided by the Augustus J. Daren trial, Murph thought to himself, were wonderfully boundless.

Craig Dow picked up a *Detroit News* on his way to the office. His secretary provided the usual coffee, and as he drank it, he scanned the paper's pages. Usually he ignored "Murph's Turf," considering it superficial and foolish, but the Daren name caught his eye. The lead item wasn't lengthy, and he read it quickly.

Dow presumed from the way it was written that the columnist, Murph, whose fat face beamed from atop the column logo, had been at the Eagle County pretrial hearing.

Trial, according to the article, had been set for November 6th, and there would be a jury.

Murph broadly hinted that dark Daren family secrets might be revealed under cross-examination, but he offered no foundation of fact for the innuendo.

Jake Martin and T. G. Sage had engaged in a heated verbal battle, according to the story, with Sage coming out on top. Dow smiled. Jake would have been no match for the experienced Tiger Sage.

That there would be a jury was disturbing. Craig Dow didn't like juries. Juries were unpredictable. He preferred to go to trial before judges, men and women whose preferences and prejudices were well known, and whose reactions could be reasonably foreseen.

T. G. Sage had built his substantial reputation by winning jury cases. It was unlikely that the veteran trial lawyer would take on such a public case unless he thought he had an excellent chance for another success.

Dow pushed the paper aside. The Daren case had the potential of turning into a career-destroying trap.

If Sperling Beekman lost the case, the firm would also lose millions of dollars in annual legal fees from the Daren bank. If that happened, someone would pay dearly. Donald Bellows, secure in his lofty position with the firm, had nothing to worry about, even if the case were lost. He was nearing the mandatory retirement age anyway. If anything went wrong, it would be the man or woman who handled the courtwork who would hang.

And Craig Dow knew the firm expected him to try the case.

He finished his coffee, and then, unexpectedly, he smiled. If there was going to be a sacrificial lamb, it wouldn't be Craig Dow. There was no way he could refuse to try the case, at least not outright, but he could find a way to escape, or failing that, find a way to insulate himself from any blame if things did go wrong.

Slowly, an idea began to form at the back of his mind about just how he might accomplish that.

All that was needed was a dash of cleverness.

13

Tired from the long drive, and still confused by his own unresolved inner conflicts, Jake got off the elevator, opened the glass doors and walked down the hallway toward his own office.

He had been unable to shake off the lingering sense of unreality since awakening. Breakfast at Raven's Nest was served to him, but Elizabeth failed to appear, and the servants had seemed almost overly polite, like bit actors who were worried they might forget their lines.

When he had inquired, he had been told that Mrs. Daren was still asleep. But the answer had come out just a little bit too quickly, too well rehearsed. Jake wondered if there was some reason she didn't wish to see him. Perhaps she realized how attracted to her he was and resented it. Still, it had seemed a pleasant evening. It was just one more puzzle to be added to the others in his life and career.

"Mr. Bellows wants to see you," his secretary said. "Right away." The girl looked worried. "I think he's angry."

"About what?"

She shrugged. "He didn't say. But you'd better hop right up there."

He glanced at his watch. It was almost one o'clock. "He's probably at lunch."

"No, he's not. He said he would be waiting."

Jake heaved a resigned sigh. He tossed his briefcase on the secretary's desk.

The next floor, the partners' floor, could be reached by elevator or by a circular stairway in the law office's private hall. The associates in the firm called it the stairway to paradise. Although technically speaking, only the partners were supposed to use it, Jake took the stairs.

Bellows was waiting. He looked up as Jake walked into his office.

"Where the hell have you been?" His usually smooth voice crackled with irritation.

"In Gladding," Jake replied. "I spent the night at Raven's Nest after the court hearing. It was too late to try to drive back last night."

Bellows' eyes narrowed. "You should have called immediately and reported what happened up there."

"I did call," Jake said. "I left messages here and at your home."

"That was late. You should have called at once." Bellows tossed a copy of *The Detroit News* at him. "Have you read this?"

"No. I drove straight here."

Bellows didn't invite Jake to sit down, but he did anyway. The paper had been folded to the "Murph's Turf" column.

"That jackass wrote about what he saw and heard at the hearing," Bellows said.

Jake shook his head. "But there were no newspaper people there," he said, as he quickly read the column item.

"This sort of thing," Bellows said, gesturing toward the newspaper, "doesn't make things look at all good for our client, Jake, or for this firm."

"Murphy wasn't there. I don't know where he got this stuff."

"Is it true, what he says?"

"I suppose the basic facts are correct, but they're twisted. It was nothing like what he intimates."

Bellows' expression was grim. "The media people have been calling since this damn thing came out this morning. I've fended them off, of course, but I don't like to be caught by surprise. You should have let me know what to expect. I don't want anything like this to happen ever again. Do I make myself clear?"

Jake nodded. "I had no idea this would happen. As I said, the hearing was just an informal meeting. There was no one there except the judge, the court reporter, Sage and myself."

"The judge seems to have ruled against you on every point."

"That's how Murphy makes it sound. I did object to some of Sage's proposed witnesses, but all the judge said was that it wasn't the time to make the objections. She didn't rule on anything."

Bellows did not appear to be appeased. "I see we have a jury trial. How did that happen?"

"Sage demanded it. Under the law, he's entitled to one."

There was no purpose in pointing out that Jake had been without instructions in the matter. Bellows seemed irate enough without risking provoking him further.

Donald Bellows arched one eyebrow. "One of the people who has called is that Lee Stevens, the public relations man Elizabeth

Daren hired. He accused you of completely mishandling this entire matter."

"Legally?"

"He said you refused to accept his guidance on how the hearing should be handled for public relations purposes."

"Stevens wanted to turn it into a circus."

"It seems someone did," Bellows snapped.

"But nothing happened," Jake protested. "That story makes it sound as if it did, I admit, but I did everything by the book. We have a trial date; we have a list of the witnesses Sage will call; we went over some of the normal ground rules. That hardly merited an emergency phone call to you."

"This newspaper thing, Jake, it shouldn't have happened." Bellows pursed his lips and put his fingertips together as if in prayer. "Well, it's water under the bridge, in any event. We just have to make sure things like this don't happen again."

Jake knew the question he was about to ask might spell the end of his career with the firm. But he needed the answer.

"Have you lost confidence in me?"

Bellows studied him for what seemed an unnecessarily long time. Then he said, "No, Jake. If I had, you'd be off this case. But we all learn by our mistakes, if we're wise. This wasn't handled in the usual efficient Sperling Beekman manner, but it wasn't fatal."

"I did what had to be done. I—"

Bellows held up a restraining hand. "Of course you did, Jake. But perhaps this Stevens fellow does have a point. From now on we had better consider the media as another opponent. Sage has begun to try the case in the newspapers. If we can't stop that, then we'll have to meet him in battle in the media as well as in the courts."

"Perhaps Craig Dow should take over—"

Bellows shook his head. "Craig is extremely busy at the moment, Jake, on other important matters. I haven't lost confidence in you, you're still the man in charge and you know the applicable law as well as anyone here. The preparation will be entirely up to you." Bellows' strained smile held little warmth. "This chap Stevens is a nuisance, he's so damned pushy, but I think it's essential that we work with him. Please put in a call to him."

"I will of course, but—"

Bellows stood up. "Very good, Jake. Now, if you'll excuse me, I have another meeting."

Jake used the partners' winding stairway again, wondering now if he would ever earn the right to use it as a partner.

At the moment, he thought, it didn't look good.

Rhonda Janus was bored, which surprised her. She didn't believe anyone could be bored in a place that charged four hundred dollars a day, a price that didn't even include meals. Even the tiny liquor bottles stocked daily in her room's refrigerator weren't included in the four hundred. It shouldn't have concerned her, since they were paying for everything, but a life spent watching pennies had developed and honed habits that would not be discarded easily, even when someone else was picking up the tab.

They had flown her out to Hawaii first class, and initially she had been thrilled at being a pampered guest in one of America's most exclusive—and expensive—resorts. She had traveled and registered under the assumed name they had given her, which had added a spicy tang of adventure to the trip. She was now Mrs. Rita Hoover, a rich widow from Florida. That was the name she was registered under and that was the name everyone at the resort called her. Hoover, like the vacuum cleaner. That had seemed to amuse them when they had given her the name.

At first it had all been exciting, like being a spy. She was instructed never to call home, never to call Ed. They had given her a mainland number, but it was to be used only in an emergency.

After a few days spent in Hawaii, the initial sense of adventure had soon paled, and the excitement had worn off quickly.

Rhonda appraised herself in her room's mirrored wall before struggling into the spandex bathing suit. Gravity, after forty-two years, was beginning to exact a toll. The breasts, which had been her pride since high school, were beginning to droop. Her bottom, too. Between cellulite and gravity, she was being slowly robbed of her major calling cards.

She sucked in her stomach and tucked in her buttocks, deciding there were still a few good miles left on the old body. Anyway, Ed seemed to like what he saw.

Her red hair continued to be full and flaming. Forty-two years old or not, she knew she could still turn a few heads. At least for a while.

She struggled into the bathing suit, considering the effort worthwhile, since the spandex helped smooth a few bulges here and there. Then she slipped into the short silk robe and the expensive beach clogs she had bought in the resort's elegant boutique. Like everything else, she had charged them to the room.

When she had first arrived in Hawaii, the air—filled with the fragrance of lush and exotic flowers—had felt as soothing as a warm balm, but now she found it almost irritating. There was something extremely dull about consistently good weather. She left her room and walked down the winding path toward the pool.

Rhonda had done everything when she first arrived in Maui: the volcano trip, whale watching, and shopping in tourist-choked Lahaina. And she had done everything at least twice. There was nothing left to do now except luxuriate by the pool.

By now, the waiters who attended the pool had come to know her by name, and as she passed they called their greetings.

She was feeling so alone. Her one fling at the resort had been with an aging cardiologist from Boston. Slim and charming, he resembled a gray-haired Jack Kennedy. But the romance had been disappointing. His Irish Catholic guilt—he had a wife back in Boston—kept him from an erection until a sufficient amount of liquor washed away his sense of sin. Afterwards, he became tearfully maudlin. When he had completed his three-day seminar, she was glad to see him go.

She took a pool chair near the bar and made herself comfortable. Rhonda Janus had never been much of a reader, but lately it had become her chief source of entertainment. She had worked her way through almost every paperback novel in the resort's newsstand.

Around her she saw a sea of charring flesh, and she could sense acres of hangovers. The guests occupying the poolside deck chairs were either older people who had banked enough throughout a long life to afford the place, or cow-eyed honeymoon couples who would start their life together deeply in debt in order to buy a romantic and hopeful beginning.

Since she saw no one who looked interesting enough to talk to, she ordered a Bloody Mary from the young Polynesian waiter and tried to lose herself in her latest book.

But she couldn't concentrate.

She thought about the curves and turns that her life had taken. By rights, she should have been the fourth Mrs. Augustus J. Daren. If she had been, she could not only afford to stay in a place like this, she could buy it outright, if she so desired.

She had taken it as a personal insult when Gus Daren had picked up with the slut from New York. She thought it would be just another of Gus's passing romances, but that slinky green-eyed witch had walked away with the ultimate prize.

Rhonda Janus should have been the widow Daren, but she wasn't. Instead of inheriting a fortune, she had been sent packing by that green-eyed bitch, with a paltry pittance the widow Daren called severance pay.

It was so unfair.

Rhonda was lonely and she was beginning to loathe both Maui and the damn resort. The only thing that prevented her from catching the next plane out was hate.

She hated Elizabeth Daren.

But soon she would get her chance to even the score. No matter how bored or how lonely she might become, that thrilling prospect alone kept her there, reading, by the pool.

The maid served tea and then withdrew.

"It was good of you to see me, Mrs. Daren."

153

She smiled at the two of them. "You're a very long way from home, Mr. Yamashita."

I. K. Yamashita, one of the world's most powerful men, was small, almost delicate. Although he was in his sixties, his smooth skin made him appear to be much younger. What hair he still had was combed straight back, and his brown eyes, slightly enlarged by thick lenses, seemed mournful. About him there was a calmness, a sense of serenity found only in ancient priests or very wise men.

His young associate, Mr. Icura, who insisted on being called Sam, exhibited no apparent nervousness at being in the presence of his legendary boss. Sam Icura was American-born and a product of the best schools. He was tall, whippet-thin, and his almond eyes reflected an alarming hardness. In contrast to the serene Yamashita, Icura seemed about to explode with barely contained energy.

Yamashita sipped at the tea he had been given. "I am making a tour of some of our overseas ventures," he said softly. "We have branch banks in California, and, of course, our new Chicago operation, which Sam heads. I thought it would be nice to meet you in person, since I've heard so much about you."

"So you just popped in from Chicago?"

He smiled, but without warmth. "In a way. I'm traveling from here to New York and then on to London."

"Gladding, Michigan, is hardly in that league. I'm flattered."

"As you know, Mrs. Daren, we are interested in Hanover Square Bank."

She nodded, but said nothing.

"I've been informed of your legal difficulty," Yamashita said, glancing over at Icura. "Your country is so interesting. You settle everything in court. As you know, we do things a bit differently, but then we spring from a far different tradition. Japan has only a handful of lawyers. America seems to have armies of them." He paused to take another delicate sip at his tea, his eyes peering at her over the cup. He continued, "We would like to acquire your bank."

"It's not for sale," she said evenly. "We might, however, consider a partnership of some sort."

"A merger?"

Elizabeth shook her head. She could remember exactly what Gus had told her about the Japanese ambitions. He had predicted precisely what they would try to do. "No merger," she said softly. "We wish to keep our autonomy."

"You know how large we are," Yamashita said softly.

"I know."

He smiled wistfully. "We could grab you up, you know, like a large dog might grab up a small bone."

"A buyout? You might like to do that, but I control the majority interest in the bank."

"Unless you lose the lawsuit," he said gently.

154

"I will still own a large block of stock, even then," she replied evenly.

Yamashita sighed. "Ah, but not enough to stop us, obviously, since your stepchildren own an identical amount. We will buy what stock we need to take the bank. Through, ah, certain parties, we already own a considerable block."

"If that's your plan, why tell me?"

Yamashita's expression, almost bland to begin with, now became etched in stone. "What we propose is a form of risk insurance. For both of us."

"Oh?"

"We will agree to buy your one-third interest in the bank now. We will give you four times what the stock is worth. Then, we will buy what little additional stock we need to obtain control for considerably less. If you agree, no matter what happens, you will make a fortune." He smiled shyly. "You see, this way, you have nothing to lose, Mrs. Daren, no matter what happens in your courts."

"But if I win the lawsuit, it's my bank then, so what you propose wouldn't be especially smart on my part, would it?"

He shrugged. "Oh, I think it would, given all the circumstances. Win or lose, if you sell now, you gain enormous profit. If not, your stock's value might be seriously diminished. If you sell, but wish to retain a title," he smiled, "do not forget that, after all, we invented the concept of saving face. We will work out something very nice for you. Deputy Chairman of International Operations, something like that."

"For show?"

"We are a Japanese company, Mrs. Daren. Our executives are Japanese. We have our own traditions. Women in our country are . . . ah . . . influential, but not in your Western manner. They are like shadows, seldom seen. That is changing, but I'm afraid a title is all we could provide now. Admittedly, primarily for show. Still, with the money we offer, you could buy out most American businesses, if being an executive is really important to you."

"Another bank?"

He slowly shook his head. "No. We would demand that as a condition of sale, but you would be free to own and operate any other kind of business."

Elizabeth said, "Unfortunately, banking is all I know, or really care about."

Yamashita sighed. "Fate is often decided for us. If I were you, I would take our offer, Mrs. Daren. When I leave here the offer goes with me. There will be no second chance. We don't operate that way."

"I'll take my chances," she replied.

Sam Icura spoke, his tone much harsher than Yamashita's.

"There are other banks, Mrs. Daren. I'm sure we'd receive a warmer reception elsewhere."

"I know you would, Mr. Icura. But it's Hanover Square you want. We have the international contacts and reputation you will need for expansion. And our assets are not inconsiderable."

"Compared to us," Icura said, his smile sliding into a sneer, "your bank is but a midget."

"Is that why you two have flown all the way up here in your private jet? Are you particularly fond of midgets in Japan?"

What sounded like an asthmatic cough turned out to be laughter from I. K. Yamashita. "She has you there, Icura," he said softly.

"If I win, gentlemen, I will then make a counterproposal. We will be working partners, your bank and mine. Between what you have in assets and what we have in contacts, it could be a tremendously exciting and profitable venture."

"Never," Icura snorted.

As though she hadn't heard him, Elizabeth continued. "Russia is opening up, gentlemen. The face and fortune of Europe is changing. In a way, it's like the gold rush, isn't it? Together, as equal partners, we can seize the moment. The German banks are poised and ready. Together, we could beat them at their own game."

Icura was about to reply, but Yamashita raised a hand to silence him. The soft eyes seemed to appraise her anew. "You are very shrewd, Mrs. Daren. Perhaps we might be able to do business on such a basis. Of course, as things stand, it would depend."

"On what?"

He smiled sadly. "You must first win your lawsuit. If you do, we might consider such an arrangement."

"And if I lose?"

All expression left his face. His mournful eyes suddenly turned hard. "Then, we will buy your bank, and carry out what you propose for ourselves. And unless you accept our offer now, you could possibly end up ruined, Mrs. Daren. Are you sure you really want to take such a gamble?"

"Getting up in the morning is a risk, Mr. Yamashita."

He nodded slowly. "I seldom gamble," he said, quietly, getting up. "But, I must confess, I often admire those who do. If it wasn't against our interests, I would wish you good fortune."

"You'll regret this, Mrs. Daren," Icura snapped.

Elizabeth smiled her most dazzling smile, hoping to show more confidence than she felt. "Perhaps. We shall see."

Elizabeth was thinking about the implications of the visit by the Japanese bankers when the maid told her Lee Stevens was on the telephone. She took the call in the library.

156

"Have you seen today's *Detroit News?*" Lee asked as soon as she came on the line.

"No."

"Well, that fellow Murphy's column is devoted to what happened up there yesterday. A little bird named Sage apparently whispered in his ear. Anyway, we didn't come off very well."

"What did he say?" she asked.

"It's not so much what he said, it's the way he said it. I warned your lawyers about something like this happening but they ignored me."

"I'll have someone run into Gladding and get the paper."

"Elizabeth, I'm not very pleased at the way this case is being handled, to be frank."

"Sperling Beekman is the best in the business."

Stevens merely grunted. "That may be, but they seem to be very cavalier about this matter."

"In what way?"

"The lawyer assigned, this Jake Martin, has never been in court before, yet they sent him up there to take care of things. That doesn't seem entirely wise to me."

"It was just a procedural matter," she said. "The firm has assigned a team of lawyers to handle all aspects of the case. Mr. Martin is one of their probate experts, and this does happen to be a probate matter. I think things are being handled properly."

"Perhaps legally, but these people have to start thinking about the impact publicity can have in something like this. I called Donald Bellows and complained about how this was botched."

"And what did he say?" she asked.

"Bellows didn't come right out and admit they dropped the ball but he had agree to consult with me from this point on." Stevens paused, then continued. "Look, Elizabeth, I'm not trying to make myself appear important here, but law cases are affected by public opinion. You can tell a jury not to read the papers or discuss the case, but they do. They're human. They see something in print, or watch something on television and that becomes the truth, whether it is or it isn't. That's as true up there in Gladding as it is in New York. Murphy's column today wasn't fatal, but if you get enough negative press you can pretty much forget about winning anything. Image-making, spin control, however you want to characterize it, has become a fact of life."

"So what do you suggest?"

"I'd get rid of this Martin. I'm sure he means well but he just doesn't realize what's going on. Have Bellows take over, or one of the other veteran lawyers in the firm."

"Jake Martin impresses me as totally honest and this is an area of the law in which he is an expert."

Stevens sighed. "Maybe, but drawing up a trust agreement and butting heads with someone like Tiger Sage are two different things. I think Martin is out of his depth, probate expert or not."

"I don't agree," Elizabeth said quietly, and her firm tone indicated the matter was no longer open for discussion.

"If that's the way you feel . . ."

"It is," she said. "However, I do agree that more attention has to be paid to presenting our side of the story before the public. Did Donald Bellows have any specific suggestions?"

"He said to work it out with Martin."

"Does that give you any problems?"

Stevens chuckled, but without humor. "A few, but none that can't be managed. That's presuming that Martin and I can work out something reasonable."

"I'm sure you will."

He paused for a moment before continuing. When he did, she heard a more somber tone in his voice. "I hope you understand my position here, Elizabeth. You're my client and I want to use whatever skill I possess to serve your best interests. If I see something I think may be harmful to you I have a duty to speak up."

"I appreciate that."

"Maybe you do, and maybe you don't, but that's part of what public relations people do. We're supposed to provide a fresh eye, among other things, even if what we see makes the client uncomfortable. Does that give you any problems?"

Elizabeth smiled but kept her voice cool. "If it does, I'll let you know. Is there anything else?"

"I'll talk to Martin," he said, hanging up.

Elizabeth sat quietly for a moment. In her mind, this was always Gus's library, the one room that had been exclusively his. She still felt like a trespasser. Everything in the library was just as it had been when he was alive. All the trinkets and gadgets he had collected in his many travels were left just where he had put them.

She swiveled around in Gus's great leather chair and looked out of the windows. The weather that had prompted Icura and Yamashita to hurry away was now upon them. Dark clouds rolled above the slate gray water.

Gus had said they would come, the Japanese. He had even foreseen the pretty words and then the threats. Even the offers of money, almost to the penny. Gus had been like a great chess master who was able to predict what series of moves a prospective opponent might make.

It was as if he had written the script. Everything was exactly as he said it would be; the only thing left was the ending. Gus had taken every precaution to ensure she would end up with control of the bank.

Sperling Beekman had been his selection. She wondered how

Gus might have reacted to Lee Stevens' misgivings. That was something they had never discussed.

For a moment her confident sense of purpose seemed to desert her. Elizabeth wondered if she were really up to the battle that lay ahead. If Gus had been wrong about her abilities, then all would be lost.

Lee Stevens thought Jake Martin was operating out of his depth. She wondered if that might also be true of herself.

She tried to put such frightening thoughts out of her mind. Soon enough, she would find out what was true.

14

Jake escorted T. G. Sage down the halls of Sperling Beekman toward the communications center.

"Jake, have you ever been in the executive offices of General Motors?" Sage asked.

"No."

"It looks just like this, businesslike but sterile."

"I take it you don't approve."

The older lawyer chuckled. "This office arrangement, I'm sure, is quite efficient, but it strikes me as rather impersonal. I prefer a more flesh-and-blood approach to the law, and surroundings that reflect it. Of course, I deal primarily in flesh-and-blood people. You folks handle corporations, clients who have no blood, heart or soul. Robot lawyers for robot clients, I suppose."

"It isn't quite that mechanical around here," Jake laughed. "Here we are," he said, opening the door to the communications center.

"My God, a screening room," Sage said. "I thought these things existed only in Hollywood."

"We probably have better state-of-the-art equipment," Jake said. "We're equipped to handle anything that needs to be filmed or recorded."

Sage sighed as he selected a seat facing the big screen. "Single practitioners like myself soon won't stand a chance."

"From what I hear, you do pretty well."

The pimply-faced technician appeared. Jake decided the young man's anxious expression was congenital.

"We'd like to see that videotape you ran for me the other day," Jake said. "The Augustus J. Daren will."

The young man nodded. "Okay. Just be a minute."

Jake took a seat next to Sage.

"I appreciate your cooperation, Jake, in letting me see this tape," Sage said. "Perhaps I've become cynical, but I wondered why you agreed so easily. I expected some resistance."

"I do have a reason," Jake said. "This thing is pretty powerful stuff. I think that after you see it you may want to talk your client into withdrawing the objections to the will."

Sage smiled. "Ah, cynicism rewarded. I thought I detected a motive."

The technician reappeared, now looking even more anxious. "I can't find the tape."

It's that one you ran for me," Jake said.

"I know, I know," the young man protested quickly. "But it's not where I put it."

"You might have misplaced it."

"No, sir, no I didn't."

"There's a copy," Jake said. "Run downstairs and get it."

The technician nodded and hurried out.

Sage chuckled. "It seems nothing is ever as well organized as it appears."

"We make copies of everything," Jake said. "It's the firm's policy."

Sage merely nodded. "By the way," he said. "Judge Vinson and I had dinner after you left. To put your mind at ease, there was no discussion of the case. Lila Vinson isn't that kind."

"Are you?" Jake asked, smiling.

"That's called "backdooring"—whispering in a friendly judge's ear, poisoning the judicial mind with a little unilateral evidence." Sage grinned. "I've been guilty of that a time or two, I confess, but this wasn't one of them."

"Still, it must be nice to have a friend as the trial judge."

"It can also work against you," Sage said. "That's also happened a time or two. The judge bends over backwards to favor the opposition, to show impartiality." He sighed. "Fortunately, Lila Vinson won't favor either side. I believe we can count on a good fair trial, something I'm finding to be more and more rare."

The technician returned. He was obviously flustered and looked first at Sage and then at Jake before speaking.

"I can't find it; it's not there," he said, simply.

"What do you mean, you can't find it?" Jake demanded.

"I don't know," he said, helplessly. "It's just gone. We have all these things cataloged. The original is gone, and so is the copy."

"Who signed them out?" Jake snapped.

"Nobody."

"What do you mean, nobody?"

The technician looked like he was about to cry. "I don't know. Nobody signed them out. They're just gone. The original and the copy."

160

"Are you sure you looked for the right one? You were with me. You watched it."

"I ran it for you, that's true, but I didn't really watch it. All these legal things are kind of boring. No offense. But I looked for the right one: the Daren will video. It's gone."

Jake, trying to control anxiety as well as anger, spoke evenly. "Well, just keep looking. Those tapes have to be around here somewhere."

He turned to Sage. "I'm sorry about this."

Sage studied Jake for a moment before speaking. When he did, his voice was no longer friendly.

"There are two possible constructions here," he said. "First, this whole thing may have been an elaborate little playlet staged for my benefit. You've made a good faith offer to show the tape, which is found missing so that I can't see and prepare a defense, and then, magically, the tape is 'rediscovered' during the trial, putting me at a distinct disadvantage."

"That's absolutely not true," Jake protested.

Sage shrugged. "We shall see. If such a trick is attempted, you'll quickly find out why they call me Tiger; let me assure you of that."

His expression softened only a bit. "Frankly, you don't impress me as someone who'd attempt such a shabby maneuver. If that is the case, this incident has a far more ominous import for you than it does for me."

"What do you mean?"

"If the young man hasn't misplaced the tape, then someone has taken it." He cocked an eyebrow. "It wasn't me. And, by the way, it wasn't anyone connected with me. What that means is that someone within your firm seems to be working against you, Jake."

T. G. Sage stood up in preparation to leave. "Apparently, you are, as the Bible puts it, in the presence of enemies."

Donald Bellows listened impassively as Jake told him about the missing tape.

When he had finished, Bellows slowly shook his head. "You should have made arrangements to safeguard that video, Jake."

"But we have a copy—"

Surprisingly, Bellows smiled. "Yes. And I'm sure it's around here somewhere. That new technician hasn't impressed me as being terribly sharp. I don't think he'll last long here. I'll have some of our clerical people go through everything. They'll turn it up."

"And if they don't?" Jake asked.

"It's not a major disaster," Bellows said. "You still have the flesh-and-blood witnesses. The video would have been helpful, obviously, but nothing can beat good old direct testimony from real breathing people."

Bellows again smiled. "How did Sage react?"

161

"He thinks we might have staged the whole thing, to keep him from seeing it before trial."

"He's clutching at straws. We're still in the driver's seat, Jake. Sage has an almost overwhelming burden to show Gus Daren was goofy. Frankly, I don't know why he took the case. He can't win."

"Do you remember the tape?" Jake asked. "You viewed it just after it was made, when you got back from Europe."

"Probably, but I don't recall it. There's so many of these testamentary videos and damn living-will tapes, they all seem to run together in my mind."

Bellows stood up. "I'll get some people hunting right away. But let's not panic, Jake. We have a sure winner here, tape or no tape."

He walked Jake to his office door. "Let's not panic," Bellows reiterated, "but let's not be careless, either. Enough said. Right, Jake?"

Jake found it difficult to adjust his eyes to the dim light in the bar, then he saw Lee Stevens sitting at a booth in the back. There was no wave of recognition, just a cold stare.

The place, on Woodward, was almost empty.

He had called Stevens as Bellows had requested. Stevens, anger in his voice, had insisted they meet in the bar. Jake walked toward the far booth where Stevens sat.

Lee Stevens' thin face didn't hold a clue.

"Okay, I'm here," Jake said, sliding into the worn leather seat of the banquette. "What's this all about?"

"Do you want a drink?"

"No thanks."

Stevens sipped his beer. "I warned you about the publicity business, didn't I?" It was more a statement than a challenge. "And you saw what happened? Sage got to that idiot Murphy and beat your rear end off."

"That's a matter of opinion."

"When I read that piece planted in the *News* today I went a little berserk," Stevens said. "I tried to get you fired."

"What?"

Stevens nodded. "I demanded Donald Bellows fire you. I was enraged, to put it mildly." The words were spoken softly, more in sadness than in anger. "I demanded he assign an experienced trial lawyer to the case, someone who wasn't so disgustingly naïve."

"You've got a damned nerve."

Stevens looked at him. "This isn't exactly a nickel-and-dime matter, is it? I have a client, too. I have to protect her interests. Besides, by not following my advice you made me look very bad."

"I presume Bellows put you in your place?"

Stevens smiled wryly. "No. As a matter of fact, he assured me your firm would give me complete cooperation, but that was all."

162

Stevens signaled for another beer. "I complained to Elizabeth, too. She seems to like you. Something puzzles me," Stevens said, studying him. "You're a probate lawyer, right?"

Jake nodded. Now he was more curious than angry.

"And you've never tried a court case?"

"Most lawyers who do my kind of work never do. I had a few years with a New York firm in their litigation section. I carried books for other lawyers mostly. I did some court work, small cases, motions, that sort of thing."

"Yet you're running the show. The pot up for grabs is in the billion-dollar range and your firm gives the case to a guy who has never set foot in a courtroom. How come?"

"You're wrong," Jake said. "I'm just organizing things. The firm has assigned a litigation team to the case, including the firm's best trial lawyer. What more could you ask than that?"

"And you don't think anything's a little weird in this whole setup?"

"No. We have a missing tape, but other than that, everything is going along just like any other important case."

"Missing tape? What do you mean?"

Jake regretted mentioning it. "It's been misplaced."

"What tape?"

"We had everything videotaped when Augustus Daren signed his will."

Steven's protuberant eyes almost popped from his head. "And that's missing!"

"Misplaced. We're looking for it."

"Jesus! Who did the original taping?"

"A private company from Bay City."

"Did you contact them? They might have a copy."

"I called just before coming over here. The company is out of business, has been for almost a year. Apparently it went bust. There's no forwarding address, they just packed up and left. Anyway, there'd be no reason why they would keep a copy."

"Digging into things used to be my line of work. I'll give it a shot, just to make sure."

The bored bartender delivered a bottle of beer and picked up the empty.

Stevens poured the beer slowly. "Look, I was a little hasty about things today."

"An apology?"

He shrugged. "It would be better if we worked together rather than against each other. It would be better for Elizabeth."

"Agreed."

Stevens nodded slowly. "I have a nice little public relations campaign all worked out. Sage isn't the only hustler who has

163

somebody in his pocket. I'll start going to work on my people. But here's what you need to do."

Stevens began talking, reverting to his usual intense rapid-fire style.

Jake sighed and signaled the bartender for a beer. He didn't feel like it, but it was obvious that Stevens' presentation was going to take a while.

He chalked it up as being a suitable end to a bad day.

When they were in town, Craig Dow had dinner with his parents on the first Thursday of every month. Although he found these evenings a tiresome chore, they limited the contact he was expected to have with either parent and served the purpose of staving off any other parental intrusions into his life.

Tonight, he was determined that the dinner would serve a much more important purpose than fulfilling mere filial obligation. His mother had just turned fifty, although she pretended to be much younger. Laura Dow was originally a Thurston, an old-money Grosse Pointe family, and she proclaimed her blood line as being the American equivalent of royalty. The old Thurston money had mostly trickled away, but the Grosse Pointes were liberally sprinkled with threadbare Thurstons who looked down their genetically long noses at anyone who arrived in the Pointes after the turn of the century as "newcomers."

Laura liked to imply that her husband, Marshall Dow, was distantly related to the Dow Chemical family. He wasn't. He had taken over his father's small factory and had made a huge fortune in plastic manufacture, including toilet seats. And although Laura deplored "new money," she enjoyed spending as much of it as Marshall allowed.

His mother managed to stay bone thin, despite her ability to consume enormous quantities of vodka. Marshall Dow matched her drink for drink, although he was beginning to show the effect with a permanently flushed face and a dour disposition that sometimes turned mean. Craig knew the Grosse Pointe police had been called several times to restore peace when the fighting had escalated beyond the merely verbal.

Drinking seemed to be the only common bond still remaining between his parents. His father, he knew, had several girlfriends and made little effort to conceal the fact. Craig had often wondered about his mother. Other women in her circle flaunted their lovers. Perhaps, like her drinking, she was artful in concealing a secret life.

Because the Dows employed a splendid cook, the dinner was delicious, although the portions, as usual, were more in keeping with the spartan style of a dieting spa. At the Dows, food was always grudgingly doled out as though it were part of the family fortune. Liquor, on the other hand, flowed in abundance.

164

"If something isn't done soon about the damned workmen's compensation laws in this state," his father snarled, after dabbing his mouth with a napkin, "it will drive out the few businesses that remain. It's legalized robbery."

Craig's father had two pet peeves: Michigan's law covering injured workers and income taxes. Those two subjects were the only ones capable of rousing him from his usual near-comatose state.

"One of my people banged his elbow pulling on a towel in the men's room. That's all; no fracture, no bruise. He's off, claiming he can't work. I have to pay the conniving son-of-a-bitch compensation. I'm going to wait till he comes back and then fire the thieving bastard."

Craig half-smiled. "I understand that's illegal."

His father's expression was a sneer. "I'm not entirely defenseless. I'll find a way."

"Are you seeing the Bruning girl?" his mother asked, cutting his father off in the middle of his usual denunciation of state and federal laws.

Craig shook his head. Carol Bruning was the daughter of his mother's lifelong friend. Both women were looking to make a match, to put the two together like brood animals, so that a darling little grandchild could be suitably hatched in time.

But Carol Bruning, although pretty, had earned the local reputation of going down more often than a Trident submarine. Craig found her amusing in a parking lot, but he did not consider her suitable marriage material. Carol's proclivities aside, the Brunings, like the Thurstons, had a good pedigree but little money, and there was no financial advantage in merging with a dwindling bank account.

"I've seen her a few times," Craig answered. "Nice girl, but not my type."

"You should marry," his mother said.

"Don't push him, for Chrissake." His father sipped at his full glass and glared at her.

"It would help his career." His mother returned the glare through narrowing eyes.

"He doesn't need any help." His father turned to him. "Any word on the partnership?"

Craig was pleased the subject had come up without his having to introduce it.

"A bit of trouble there, I think."

"Trouble?" his father snapped. "Jesus, don't I throw your firm enough legal business? What the hell kind of trouble?"

"We represent the Daren widow," Craig said, taking time to sip from his after-dinner brandy. "It's a sticky case and could backfire. I think they want me to try it." Craig decided not to mention the

165

missing videotape, although that circumstance had determined what he planned to do.

"So try the damn case, that's your business," his father growled.

"I've met her, you know," his mother interjected. "You would think Elizabeth Daren was the queen of England, if you didn't know better. She's just a whore who got lucky."

His father glanced at her. "Among others," he said softly.

"What the hell do you mean by that?"

Craig spoke before a full-blown fight erupted. "I could get hurt professionally if I should try the case. It's become more than just complicated. We stand a good chance of losing. The case will be all over the front pages, especially if it's lost. Sperling Beekman doesn't like being associated with losers."

"Who does?" his father said. "Wiggle out of it if you feel that way."

"I don't know if I can."

"Talk to Bellows."

"He doesn't seem to see it as such a danger, but then it's not his career that's at stake, is it?"

"Do you want me to talk to him?"

Craig managed not to smile as he looked at his father. "Well, that might help. It would have to be handled with a certain amount of finesse."

Marshall Dow snorted. "Give me some credit. I'll talk to him," he said belligerently. "Look, your firm is getting rich off me. What the hell good is money if you can't buy anything with it? Leave it to me. I'll take care of things."

Craig now smiled with unfeigned warmth. "I'd appreciate it, Dad."

"I want some clarification," his mother spoke in a rising and quarrelsome voice. Startled, they both looked at her.

She was directing her slightly out-of-focus, boozy glare at her husband. "Were you calling me a whore just now?"

Dinner, Craig knew, was officially over.

"Ah, Jake, may I have a minute?"

Jake looked up, surprised to see Donald Bellows standing in his office door. Bellows seldom came down from the partners' floor.

"What's up?"

Bellows stepped into the office but didn't sit down. "A little glitch has come up, Jake. Craig Dow apparently will be tied up in court when the Daren trial begins."

"Oh? Who will try the case?"

Bellows smiled. "Craig may be free in time to come up and handle the main work, but someone needs to start things off and perhaps even finish, if it comes to that. I've given the matter some thought. "You've had some litigation experience with a top

New York firm. We're mindful of that and your reputation as one of the best estate men in the state. You've got to lose your virginity sometime and handle a big one if you're ever going to make partner, Jake. I think you're the man for the job, Jake."

"But I've never tried a case," Jake protested. "I mean, I'm flattered that you thought of me but I have no experience in that area."

Bellows chuckled. "This isn't the usual contested case, Jake. All the legal issues are quite clear-cut and the law imposes an enormous burden on the other side. A law clerk could handle it, in all honesty. Not that I think of you, Jake, as a mere clerk. You are after all the senior associate in this section and an acknowledged expert in probate matters. You are the man for this job, believe me."

Jake felt a rush of feeling, although he couldn't distinguish whether the emotion he felt was triumph or fear. "I'll do my best, of course, but wouldn't Elizabeth Daren prefer you or one of the main litigation partners to conduct the trial?"

Bellows shook his head. "You've made a favorable impression with our client, as well you should. Don't worry about Elizabeth, Jake, I'll explain everything to her satisfaction. Besides, I'll be up there with you. If anything gets sticky I'll be right at your elbow. And, as I say, Craig may be able to break free and take over, although I really don't think we'll need his expertise in something as simple as this."

"But it's a jury case," Jake said.

"Juries are just people, Jake. There is nothing magic in presenting a set of facts to a jury, especially in a case like this where the law is so strongly on our side. You may find it quite a pleasurable adventure."

Jake tried to smile. "I hope it's only that."

Bellows turned to leave. "You'll do fine. We have every confidence in you. I'll be there, so will Cora. This offers you a chance to shine, Jake." He chuckled. "Considering the opening for partner, it couldn't come at a better time, eh?"

Before he could reply, Bellows was gone.

Jake sat quietly, his thoughts racing. Bellows had mentioned the partnership. Jake wondered if being assigned to conduct an important case like the Daren probate might be an indication that the firm was about to invite him to join as a fully fledged partner.

Or, he wondered, was it the final test? Jake felt confident if he was matched against what he really did, the drawing of probate documents, the world of wills, codicils and trusts; in that arena he would be considered partnership material. He was indeed an expert in that field. But a jury trial? Was he being favored for the partnership or was this a subtle way of letting him fall on his face? His thoughts raced with possible implications.

Cora Simpson came in, her smile a bit tentative. "I just heard," she said. "Is it true?"

Jake shrugged. "Have you ever tried a jury case, Cora?"

She shook her head. "No. We seldom see juries in tax matters."

He nodded. "How would you feel if you had to try the Daren case before a jury?"

"Scared."

"That catches it pretty good. I'm petrified."

"Why isn't Craig Dow handling it?"

"Bellows said Dow is tied up in another case, but that he may come up to take over if he can break clear in time."

"We have an army of litigators. Why not one of them?"

Jake smiled. "Bellows seems to think this is almost no contest, a breeze, as he puts it. I suppose that's the reason."

She seemed to study him for a moment, then spoke. "Perhaps this means they've decided on you for the partnership slot. Did you think of that?"

"It crossed my mind."

She looked away. "I still consider myself in the running, Jake; I'm still your competitor. On that basis, I really can't wish you good luck, can I?"

"Nothing's been said to me, Cora. As far as I know, the partnership contest is still wide open."

She paused, then spoke. "Anything new with your wife?"

"The divorce is going ahead, as far as I know."

"How do you feel about that?"

He shrugged. "I'm not really sure. Emotionally, I feel numb."

Cora started to say something, then checked herself. "Perhaps we can talk about it when we get up to Gladding."

She turned but stopped at the door. "Jake, if I don't get the partnership, I hope you do."

15

"**I** can't stay, Lila. Ken Swanson fractured Lee Maguire's skull in a fight. Maguire's in intensive care in Grayling and Swanson's in my jail. If Maguire dies, it might mean a murder charge." He smiled. "Common drunks can go unattended, but letting a possible murderer run around an unlocked jail wouldn't look so good if anything happened."

"What about dinner?"

"I'll grab something from the hotel later."

"I'll make you a sandwich. It'll only take a minute." She walked to the oven, grabbed some potholders and took out the ham she had prepared. "Swanson and Maguire have been fighting for years, but it's usually just shoving and punching. What happened?"

"Nothing unusual. Both had a snootful and were duking it out back of the Northway saloon as usual. Maguire got knocked down first this time, but his head hit a car bumper. Must have caught him just right. He's in a bad way."

"Sounds like self-defense," she said, slicing into the ham.

"If Maguire lives, he won't press charges. If he dies, well then I suppose the prosecutor will have to do something. We'll see."

"What's the talk in town about the Daren case?" she asked.

"That is the talk of the town. You're going to be a star, Lila."

She smirked. "They want to admit television cameras. The chief justice called me."

"I thought that was forbidden."

"Not anymore. But it still depends on the case, and on the judge. Our beloved chief justice wants to make a few points with the television people. But I said no."

"Why? This isn't just local, Lila. You could be on the national news every night if you play your cards right. Wouldn't you like to see Dan Rather talking about you?"

"That's all I need. What kind of bread would you like, whole wheat or rye?"

"Rye. I'd rethink the cameras. That kind of exposure could lead to important things."

"Bullshit. Do I want to be circuit judge, or be on the court of appeals? Never. I have a nice life here and I like just what I'm doing." She spread butter thickly on the bread. "What's the mood in town?"

He shrugged. "Excitement. Everybody figures to make a little money. Between the lawyers and the newspeople, every available

169

room is booked. People are offering to rent out rooms in their own homes if it becomes necessary." He smiled. "It's like a carnival coming to town."

"How do they feel about Elizabeth Daren? Will she be in any danger?"

He thought before answering. "I doubt it."

"How about her lawyers?"

He grinned. "At least they're all in one place. The lawyers for both sides are booked into the Eagle Inn. The rest of the rooms will be filled with newspaper guys." He laughed. "Going to the bathroom over there will become a media event."

"You don't think anyone might harm her lawyers?"

"You know our people, Lila. They want that land opened up around Lake Bradford, but they're realists. They might hassle the Daren lawyers, but I don't think anyone would actually go beyond that. It wouldn't gain any kind of advantage if they did."

"If you hear anything different, let me know right away."

"Why?"

"Because if feelings get too high, I can always move the trial to another county."

"Aw shit, Lila, you wouldn't do that, would you? I mean, we don't get much entertainment up here. You'll have a couple hundred people packed into the courtroom every day. It's going to be like a state basketball championship or something. Oh God, if you move the show away from here you can forget about running for re-election. People would be so pissed, you'd never win them back."

"I'd rather risk that than have some hothead blow a lawyer or two away."

He laughed. "Hey, they say there's too many lawyers running around now. We might set a precedent. Maybe we could start a hunting season to keep the attorney population in balance, like we do with the deer."

She finished making the sandwich, then wrapped it in plastic. "Keep your eyes and ears open, Russ. I don't want this thing getting out of hand."

"You going to wear your robe?"

She nodded. "Sure. This isn't some two-bit sanity hearing. I'll have to look and sound like a big city judge if I expect any respect from these big city lawyers."

"Are you going to wear anything under it?"

Her eyes narrowed. "You really like those dress-up games, don't you?" Then she laughed. "Well, I'm sorry to disappoint you, but I'm going to be absolutely prim and proper." She looked him up and down. "And I shall insist everyone else act the same. You had better wear your best uniform."

He took the sandwich and grinned. "Damn, it's going to be one hell of a show, Lila. I can hardly wait until Monday."

Elizabeth Daren watched the snowflakes fall silently outside her bedroom window. Lake Bradford looked slate gray in contrast to the white of the fast-falling flakes. The temperature had dropped, and the prediction was for several inches of snow to fall in the north. Watching the falling snow was almost hypnotic.

"Mrs. Daren." Her maid interrupted her serenity. "Mr. deSalle is on the phone. Do you wish to talk with him?"

Elizabeth sighed. Her brief moment of tranquillity was over. She picked up the phone next to her bed.

"Yes, Claude." Her voice was sterner than she had intended.

"Good morning, Elizabeth," he answered cheerfully, despite her tone. "How are you?"

"I'm fine, Claude. What do you want?"

She was answered with a soft chuckle. "Well, nothing really. I just wondered, since the trial starts next Monday, if you might like me to come up? Just for support, show the flag and that sort of thing."

"I don't think that's necessary, Claude, but I do appreciate the offer."

"Sometimes these things can get quite nasty, Elizabeth. I thought you might not want to be alone."

"I'm not likely to be alone, Claude. I have a house full of servants and security people. And Sperling Beekman will be sending up a platoon of lawyers."

"Will the lawyers be staying with you?" he asked.

"No. Donald Bellows thought that might create an unfavorable impression. They've taken rooms at a perfectly dreadful little hotel in town."

"What does Bellows think of the case now?"

"Nothing's changed."

DeSalle paused, weighing carefully what he was about to say. Then his tone became quietly confidential. "Elizabeth, we hear things on the street, so to speak."

"Oh? What things?"

"Rumors, but sometimes they have a way of coming true."

"What rumors?"

She was answered by a sigh. "It's probably just idle gossip, but I've heard that the two witnesses to Gus's will have, well, gone sour."

"What do you mean by that?" she asked.

"Elizabeth, if I could be more specific I would be, but it's just one of those little whispers one hears from time to time. Has Bellows said anything?"

"No," she said, although she had been told by Jake Martin that both Milo Faraday and Rhonda Janus might be a problem. But deSalle had no need to know such information.

"Probably nothing to it," he said. "However, Elizabeth, have you given any thought to trying to settle this matter?"

"There's nothing to settle," she said. "Either Gus's will is valid or it isn't."

Claude deSalle's voice turned into a croon as he talked. "Since the whole thing revolves around control of the bank, I was thinking that it might be profitable to explore some alternatives with the other side."

"Why?"

Again there was a pause before he continued. "To be frank, Elizabeth, if those rumors should have any basis in fact, you could lose. I thought, if you're interested, I might explore with the other side the possibility of shared control, or something like that."

"Are you in contact with the children?" she asked.

He chuckled. "Not the way your tone implies. Chip Daren called me on the phone, but that's all. Still, I do know both of them. I would be happy to serve as your ambassador if you wish."

"What kind of shared power are you talking about?"

"Ah, there are several possibilities. We could create a co-chairmanship or something of that nature."

"There'd be nothing but endless fights."

"Perhaps, but if we made it a troika, the third person would have a tie-breaking vote. That's just one of a number of possibilities, but it is an interesting thought."

"Who would you suggest as the third member?"

"Well, it could be anyone who you people decided upon. It would have to be a person trusted by both sides, obviously. I'm sure that could be ironed out."

She knew he was nominating himself, and she had to smile.

"Claude, I'm afraid that third person would then have the ultimate power. He, or she, could play both ends against the middle and get whatever was wanted. The other two would end up as puppets."

"Oh, I don't know, Elizabeth. We could work out something that would prevent that, I'm sure."

She wondered if the children had put him up to calling, or if he was making one last try for control.

"There will be no settlement, Claude," she said with impeccable reserve. "Win or lose, I'm willing to take my chances in court."

"I was only trying to suggest something to protect your interests. I hope you understand that."

"Of course."

"If you change your mind, Elizabeth, let me know. Many times these things are settled in the smoke of ongoing battle."

"I know that. But this isn't going to be one of them."

"Perhaps I should come up, Elizabeth. As an adviser. It might be advantageous if I were around, just in case something went wrong during the trial."

"It won't, Claude. Thanks for the thought."

"I'm always here, if you need me."

"I appreciate that, Claude," she said. "Thank you."

Elizabeth hung up and turned her attention once more to the falling snow. Gus had predicted everything. She knew exactly what to expect. Everyone was behaving just as Gus said they would. It was almost eerie. Claude deSalle, like a sheet of soft plastic wrap, had many uses, but like the plastic wrap, he was just as transparent.

She wished Monday would come. She was anxious to get started.

One way or the other, it would soon be over.

"Thank you for coming, Mr. Sage." Donald Bellows stood up and extended his hand. "This is indeed an honor. I've read so much about you."

"Only half of it true, Mr. Bellows." Sage noted that Bellows' grip was firm and as enthusiastic as his broad smile. He reminded Sage of a high-powered salesman greeting a promising prospect.

"I'm afraid I don't have much time for lunch," Sage said. "I'm in the middle of a trial in circuit court, so I'll have to eat and run."

They were in the upstairs dining room of the Detroit Club. Sage noted that Bellows had arranged to be seated at a table far away from the other diners. Their conversation would be completely private.

"Since you're at trial, I presume you're not drinking," Bellows remarked.

Sage chuckled. "You presume wrong. My rapier wit will hardly be diminished by one very dry martini."

Bellows smiled, then looked up at the waiter. "One very dry martini, Edward, and Perrier with a twist for me."

"I understand we'll be staying at the same place in Gladding," Bellows said, turning his attention to Sage. "What kind of a place is this hotel? I understand you've stayed there."

Sage found the questioning interesting, since few people knew he had stayed in Gladding.

"Not the Plaza, I'm afraid. It's an old railroad hotel. The rooms are small but reasonably clean. And the bath is conveniently located at the end of each hallway."

Bellows frowned. "Are you, ah, joking?"

Sage's hearty laugh caused several heads to turn. "Not at all. It's on the rustic side, but comfortable enough. Fortunately, the trial should be short. We won't have to accept the town's hospitality, such as it is, for too long."

The waiter returned with the drinks and they ordered.

173

Sage raised the martini in salute, then sipped. "I was surprised you people didn't request discovery."

"Nor did you."

"I had my reasons."

Bellows smiled. "So did we."

"Will you be trying the case?" Sage asked.

"No. And the litigator we had assigned is tied up, so Jake Martin will probably handle the courtwork. You've met, of course, at the pretrial."

Sage nodded. "Nice young man. He told me, I believe, that he has no trial experience."

"That should be no problem, he's a probate expert."

"There is an enormous difference between drawing a will and trying a jury case," Sage said.

"Frankly, I don't think there'll be any difficulties. The issues are simple enough. But if I'm wrong, we have, as you know, some outstanding trial people who can step in if needed." Bellows chuckled. "We protect our clients' interests at all times. Which really brings me to the subject of this lunch."

The waiter returned with their food. Bellows waited until he was gone.

"I think it's incumbent on all lawyers to seek ways to avoid litigation, don't you?"

"A most noble thought," Sage said, tasting his fish and finding it excellent. "What did you have in mind?"

"Nothing specific, really. I thought we might explore the possibilities of settlement, just between us."

Sage looked up. "Without benefit of client, I presume?"

"Not at this point. This is what the doctors would call exploratory. What would it take, do you think, for Chip Daren to drop the case?"

Sage finished the martini. "Not money. Not in this matter. Everybody is filthy rich as it is."

"No one, they say, is ever rich enough."

"This might be said to be a grudge match as far as Chip and his sister are concerned." Sage smiled. "Perhaps if the widow, your lovely client, were reduced to begging in the street, my client might be persuaded to withdraw, but nothing short of that will do, I'm afraid."

"Chip Daren wants control of the bank," Bellows said.

Sage nodded, dabbing his lips with his napkin. "That's really the nub of this matter, isn't it? If the widow Daren could be persuaded to accept the previous will, giving the Darens control equal to their shares, I think we could all save ourselves a trip up north."

"Remember, this is only an exploratory discussion between lawyers."

"Obviously." Sage smiled. "However, if this does go to trial, I

174

plan to wipe the courthouse floor with your client. I think she should be told that. She can choose to save herself a great deal of embarrassment if she agrees to abide by the previous will."

Bellows face was without expression. "Every settlement has to be based in fair give and take. Suppose my client agreed to something less? Something that would assure a kind of shared control."

Sage glanced at his watch. "What kind of share?"

"Something that would give Elizabeth Daren less than fifty-one percent control of the bank."

"She'd do that—give up ultimate control?"

"The matter would be in the hands of all the stockholders at that point. They might decided she should continue running the bank."

"Or they might give it to someone else."

Bellows nodded his head.

"But that might not be my client," Sage said.

"Possibly. The matter would be decided in a kind of democracy."

"Will she go for that?" Sage asked.

Bellows shrugged. "Frankly, I haven't advanced the idea to her. But I might, if you think your people might consider the proposal."

"I won't suggest anything to Chip or his sister until I know your client will agree."

"As I say, I haven't talked to her."

"I would suggest you do so. I deal in negotiation, not fantasy." Sage glanced again at his watch. "I hate to eat and run, especially when the other fellow's paying, but I must." He stood up. "But while we are basking in the delights of Michigan's northland, I shall make it a point to buy you a meal, and drink if it's after sundown."

Bellows smiled. "It's been known to happen that lawyers can be opponents and remain friends."

Sage studied him for a moment. "Sometimes," he said, and then turned and left the dining room.

Donald Bellows was no longer smiling.

Sherman Murphy sipped his second Bloody Mary, and with it he began to experience a welcome lessening of the hangover's horrific grip. His eyes were becoming less light-sensitive and he found he could now read his column without squinting.

Today's "Murph's Turf" was a rehash of an old, proven standby, the dying kid at the baseball game. The dying kid column was always a guaranteed, surefire hit. Sister Céleste picked the dying kid. In return, Murph's plug in the column for her children's hospice brought in a ton of contributions. Sister Céleste, often described as a living saint, nevertheless understood the practical aspects of worldly things, so that when Murph needed a dying kid for the

175

baseball column, Sister Céleste always came through. All over the city salty tears were running down appreciative cheeks as readers choked on Murphy's turgid prose about a dying boy's last wish to see one final Tiger game.

The dying kid and baseball was like money in the bank, but he was careful to space the columns so they didn't lose their punch from overuse.

This year's dying kid had been uppity and hostile, and although he was a baseball fan, he hated the hometown Detroit Tigers with the passion of an opposing manager. Murphy had barely refrained from strangling the bald-headed little nuisance when he had taken the ingrate to the game. But he felt pride at bending some of the kid's surprisingly obscene comments so that they emerged as a suitable and sentimental endorsement of the great American game.

It was hokum, but it sold newspapers.

Since he was fast running out of hokum, he was hopeful the Daren case and the people of the north might be his salvation. His future depended on the Darens.

Sherman Murphy, as noted by each of his former wives, was not a fastidious man. He often went without bathing until he himself noticed what had become disgustingly evident to others, then he washed. However, owing to the importance of the person he was scheduled to interview, he had showered and shaved. He had even clipped the ragged, drooping mustache he affected. His usual cowboy clothes just weren't suitable for the occasion, so he donned an unaccustomed tie and found an old sports jacket he had tossed and forgotten in a closet.

The third Bloody Mary dissipated any remaining anxiety he had about his appearance. He set out for the interview.

A security man, dressed in a sports jacket more expensive and much better fitting than Murphy's own, met him at the reception desk of the Westin Hotel, escorted him into the elevator and up fifty floors to the suite of Augustus Daren's only daughter.

A maid led Murph into a vast, long sitting room overlooking the Detroit River and, apparently, most of Canada. Entering from one of the suite's many doors, Augusta whirled into the room, reminding Murph of the sweeping television entrances made by Loretta Young so many years before.

"Mr. Murphy," she gushed, "how nice to meet you."

"The pleasure's mine," he mumbled. She was dressed in a flowing fuchsia frock, a cross between a dressing gown and something one might wear to a charity ball. It was cut very low. She was tanned and attractive.

"May I offer you some coffee?" she asked, "or perhaps something stronger, although it is quite early."

"Would it shock you if I asked for a Bloody Mary?"

She studied him and then smiled slowly. "Not at all. And being a good hostess, I would be forced to join you, wouldn't I?"

Murph returned the smile, then reverted to his acquired Southern accent. "I'm not often the source of temptation, ma'am, but so be it."

The maid, who always accompanied Gussie whenever she traveled, was dispatched to fetch the drinks.

He sat at the end of a mile-long leather couch; she sat near him. "I read your column," she said. "I cried. Such a sad little boy."

He measured her for a moment, then replied. "Actually, the kid was an enormous pain in the ass. Dying or not."

"Mr. Murphy!"

"I hope I haven't shocked you, ma'am."

She shook her head, but smiled. "I suppose you newspaper people see so many things that you tend to become, well, less than sensitive."

"I may be lacking in many things," he said as the maid came in and handed them the blood-red drinks, "but I try to be honest. That's why people aren't afraid to talk to me."

"My brother said I shouldn't talk to you." She took a healthy gulp of the drink. "He doesn't think we should talk to anyone from the press. At least not until after the case."

Murph was pleasantly surprised to discover his drink contained more vodka than tomato juice. "You don't have to talk to me unless you want to," he said, trying to make his tone as reassuring as possible.

"I'm not concerned." She took another swig, leaving a red mark over the top of her lip. "But if you get into forbidden territory, I'll let you know."

He nodded. He suspected this was not her first drink of the day, and he felt an instant kinship. "Are you going up north for the trial?"

"I wouldn't be here in Detroit if I wasn't."

"Where are you going to stay?"

She studied her drink. "I was raised at Raven's Nest," she replied quietly. "It was my childhood home, at least in the summers. You'd think Number Four would have invited me to stay while the lawyers did their work, wouldn't you?"

"Number Four?"

"My father's last wife." She finished her drink, then nodded to the maid who silently disappeared.

"Is that so strange?" he said, carefully selecting his words. "After all, your brother is bringing this case against her."

"We both are," she said.

"I thought—"

She shook her head. "Oh, you're right, legally. He's the one bringing the lawsuit, but I'm sharing the risk."

"I don't understand."

"The lawyers call it a forfeiture clause. Anyone who opposes the will loses their share. So Chip is the one who is formally opposing . . . her. Since I'm not a party, I can't lose, although I am supporting him in every other way."

"If he loses, what then?"

"He won't, but if he does, I've agreed to split my share with him."

"Is this something the lawyers figured out?"

She shook her head. "No. This is strictly between Chip and me." Her eyes widened. "You're not going to put that in the newspaper, are you?"

"Not if you don't want me to," he said.

"I could tell immediately that you were a nice man."

"If not Raven's Nest, where will you be staying during the trial?"

Gussie shrugged. "We've taken rooms at a Holiday Inn at Montmorci."

"We?"

"My brother made the arrangements." The maid handed both of them fresh drinks. Gussie giggled. "We have separate suites, just in case your jaded journalistic mind conjures up something incestuous."

Murphy grinned. "Where I come from—the deep, deep south—screwing your sister is looked on as a rite of passage."

Gussie whooped, but managed to keep her drink from spilling.

"Montmorci is at least forty miles away from Gladding." Murph said. "Why so far?"

"Where are you staying?" she asked.

"The Eagle Inn in Gladding. It's close to the courthouse."

"It's a dump. Darens don't stay in dumps. It isn't allowed. The Holiday Inn of Montmorci might not be five star, but it will do, at least as long as we have to stay up there. My brother will have a car and driver available."

Murphy realized she might be a possible conquest. It was a contest between lust and a possible column. The column won out.

"So, how do you really feel about your stepmother?"

Suddenly her eyes narrowed warily. "Elizabeth is a very complex person."

He grinned, sipping the drink and finding it stronger than the first. "In other words, you hate her guts."

She didn't reply for a moment, choosing instead to look out the enormous windows at the river and scene below. Then she spoke. "Hate is far too strong a word, Mr. Murphy."

"Call me Murph. Everybody does."

She nodded. "I'm Gussie to my friends." She managed a half-smile. "I'm not fond of Elizabeth," she said. "But this case has nothing to do with personal feelings."

"Oh?"

She sipped her drink, then her eyes met his. "This lawsuit is about power," she said softly. "None of us likes each other, for that matter, but the control of my father's bank is what this is all about."

"Well, since none of this is personal, tell me a little more about Elizabeth. You know, just some background stuff. Your brother, too, if you don't mind? You know, just plain old family gossip."

The wary look in her eyes told him he had gone one step too far.

She shook her head. "No, I think not. At least not now."

"About your brother? Does he feel the same way about things as you do?"

She paused, then spoke in a slightly more distant tone. "We will probably be up north almost a week," she said. "Perhaps you and I could get together up there. It might be a little easier to talk about things then."

He knew the interview was over.

"I'd like that," he said. "When are you leaving for the north?"

"Tonight."

"So am I." He paused. "Look, none of this is going in the paper. You can trust me."

"I appreciate that."

"If you want to talk, you can get me at the Eagle Inn in Gladding."

"It's nice to know I'll have a friend up there." She paused, then added, "Murph."

The maid showed him to the door. Although no dark family secrets had been revealed, Murphy decided it was an excellent beginning to his northern adventure. Eventually, he would get her to talk.

And that might turn out to be a bigger column than the dying kid at the baseball game.

16

Jake wondered what the locals did about laundry in Gladding. He couldn't remember seeing a laundromat or a cleaner. He decided to play it safe and pack sufficient clothing for five days. He selected two of his best suits to take along. As an afterthought, he also added an old ski jacket and some casual clothes, although he knew he probably wouldn't have any leisure time.

The phone rang, an annoying interruption.

"Hello," he snapped.

"Jake?"

He was startled to hear Marie's voice. "Yes."

"You sound angry."

"I'm not. I was busy packing."

"I heard you're going to try the Daren case. Is that true?"

"So it seems." He tried to conceal the excitement he felt at the sound of her voice.

"I called to wish you luck, Jake."

"Thanks. Look, Marie, let's get together. I have some time before I have to leave. I think we should talk."

"There's nothing to talk about, Jake."

"But—"

"This call was probably a mistake," she said.

"Marie, I know about you and—"

"It's over between us, Jake," she said quickly. "I have a chance at happiness and I'm going to take it. I don't know what you may think, but I didn't make this decision lightly." She stopped, then continued in a softer tone. "Eventually you'll thank me, Jake. We would have just made each other miserable."

He was about to protest, but he stopped himself. Perhaps, he realized, she was right. In any event, his feelings too were changing. The hurt was being replaced by a welcome numbness.

"Okay, Marie, whatever you say."

"I don't want us to be enemies," she said.

"I have enough of those as it is."

"Oh?"

"It's nothing. Thanks for the good wishes."

"They'll have to make you a partner now," she said.

He looked around at the apartment. He would have to move, he decided. There were just too many memories.

"We'll see," he replied.

180

"Someday we'll both laugh about this whole situation, Jake."

He shook his head. "Maybe. I can't imagine actually laughing about all this, but I do hope you'll be happy, Marie."

"Thank you, Jake. Good luck up north."

He sat quietly for a moment. He wondered if it always happened like that. Acceptance. Hope had flickered out and for some reason he found he could now accept what had been so obvious all along. She was right. It really was over between them, and had been so for some time. It was, he thought, a little like a death in the family. It came as a shock, unbelievable at first, then, eventually, painfully, it became an accepted fact. Finally, like it or not, life did go on.

The phone rang again. Jake, feeling numbed, wondered if Marie had something more to say.

"Hey, Jake."

He recognized Lee Stevens' voice.

"What's going on? I understand you're going to try the Daren case. I thought Craig Dow was going to do it."

"He was," Jake said. "But he's tied up in another lawsuit. I'm supposed to fill in for him until he can get up there."

"Why doesn't Bellows try the case?"

"It's hardly my place to ask. He said he would help guide me along. I suppose if I screw up too badly he'll step in."

"Jesus, given the size of Sperling Beekman, how come a top litigator isn't being assigned to this case?"

"Good question. Frankly, I don't know the answer. Bellows still believes this will be only a walkover. He's not worried."

"Even with Tiger Sage on the other side?"

"The law of probate practically guarantees a win for us."

"Do you really think so?"

"Yes, if everything goes according to plan. The law is definitely in our favor."

There was a pause, then Stevens spoke again. "I've got a possible lead on the guy who filmed the videotape when Daren made his will."

"Have you talked to him?"

He was answered by a soft chuckle. "He left Bay City by the light of the moon. I understand he was making blue movies and got in some jurisdictional trouble with the local toughs. That and he owed everybody in town; so he took off. I think he's in Chicago."

"Sounds like a dead end," Jake said.

"Who knows? I'm going to follow it up. Can't hurt. My partner, Jerry Casey, will be up in Gladding to handle the public relations stuff until I get there. Please don't talk to the media guys unless he briefs you first."

"I—"

"Please," Stevens said, cutting him off. "Just do this for me, okay? You do your job, and we'll do ours. Casey is smooth as a wet snake. He'll make sure you don't step in any doo doo. Deal?"

Jake sighed with resignation. He had too many other things on his mind to argue. "Okay," he said reluctantly.

"This tape thing is probably a lost cause, so as soon as I check it out I'll see you up there." Stevens paused again. "Jake, don't sound so worried. Maybe Bellows is right, maybe this will be a piece of cake."

"It better be," Jake answered. "It's my first jury trial."

He was answered by a chuckle. "Maybe it's like learning to swim. You're being tossed into the deep end of the pool. Which is okay if you don't drown, Jake. Good luck." Stevens hung up.

Jake was almost packed. But he didn't want to forget the book. He had spent most of the previous night studying its pages as though they offered the key to life itself. It was an old book, one he'd bought at a used-book store when he was in New York and still in law school. It had been out of print even them, although once it had been a standard text for evidence and procedure courses in a number of the nation's law schools. The previous owners had marked up most of the pages, but it was still readable.

It was an excellent, practical volume, detailing the steps in trying a lawsuit, telling how to select a jury, how to question witnesses, and when to make objections. It was the only weapon he would have.

The book would have to serve as his bible and guide, his road map for finding his way.

Jake hoped it would help. He couldn't call on the author for any additional tips, though. The book had been written fifteen years before by T. G. Sage.

"At least David had a slingshot," Jake said aloud as he tossed it on top of the shirts he had packed.

Phil Hunt hated the noise the pine branches made as they scraped along his brand new Blazer's cherry red sides. The Blazer was touted as a rugged back-country vehicle, a luxury van that could go anywhere, but he drove it slowly along the rutted path as if it was made of glass. He had never owned a brand-new vehicle before, and he loved everything about his gleaming Blazer, especially that fresh-from-the-factory smell.

Phil Hunt knew every trail and track in Eagle County. He had been born there and he had gone hunting there with his father almost as soon as he had been able to walk. Hunt had an almost supernatural instinct about forest creatures and was famous locally as a guide, even before Augustus Daren hired him to be the gamekeeper for Raven's Nest.

It had been a job he was born to do, and he had hated to see it end.

The house trailer looked even shabbier than the last time he had visited. A wisp of smoke from the homemade chimney indicated that someone was home.

Hunt pulled the Blazer up to the trailer's door.

She came out as he turned the motor off.

Stella Runyard had become even fatter than before and had to hold the side of the trailer's door in order to manage the two steps to the ground. Her face, resembling a mask painted on an overblown balloon, was still pretty.

"Where'd you steal it, Phil?" She waddled around the Blazer, her eyes wide in admiration.

"I bought it," he said. "Nice, huh?"

"Somebody die and leave you some money?"

He laughed. "Nope. I decided to spend some of my own, since I haven't figured a way to take it with me when I go." He looked around. "Where's Vincent?"

She smirked. "How should I know, I'm only his wife. He said he had some work in Rose City. He should have been home last Tuesday. But knowing him, he's probably drunk and shacked up with some bitch he picked up in a bar." She laughed. "Eventually he'll find his way back here, sober and sorry. Did you want to see him?"

Hunt shook his head. "Nope. It was you I wanted to talk to."

"C'mon in. I can offer you coffee or a beer."

"Beer's fine."

He followed her as she laboriously climbed back up the two homemade steps. Her haunches and thighs were enormous, straining against the worn fabric of her giant jeans. He remembered what a pretty figure she had had when she worked at Raven's Nest. Stella Runyard was only forty, but no one would ever know it. As she wheezed from the exertion of movement, she took two beers out of the small refrigerator.

He sat down on a seat at the back of the trailer. Stella handed him a can of beer, then turned off a small television set. She eased her bulk onto a long bench lining the side of the trailer.

"So what's up, Phil?"

"I might be able to put you onto something so you could make a few bucks."

She sipped her beer and giggled. "On my back, maybe?"

He smiled. "Nope, nothing like that. How long did you work for the Darens?" he asked.

"I don't know; two, maybe three years, why?"

"Did you ever talk much with the old man?"

She looked past him, as if remembering. "Hell, yes. Before he brought his new wife home, I think he was considering getting into my pants. Horny old goat. But he never did anything about it." She sipped the beer. "Too bad. They say screwing the boss is a sure way to get ahead in life."

183

"Were you still working there when he had the first stroke?"

She nodded. "Sure. Well, at least for a couple months anyway. Why?"

"How did he seem to you?"

She shook her head. "It really took the wind out of his sails. He still liked to talk to me, but he didn't have that old fire in his eye anymore."

"You were one of the few who saw him then, as I recall?"

"He was embarrassed about his mouth and all." She smiled. "He liked seeing me, though. I was one of his favorites. I think that's why his wife let me go, she was jealous."

"How did he seem to you after the stroke? Mentally, I mean?"

"I presume all this has come connection with the trial coming up?"

He nodded. "It might."

"You mentioned something about money?"

He merely nodded.

Her eyes betrayed a sharp interest. "Vincent's one of the best carpenters in the north, but he works only when the spirit moves him," she said softly. "And the spirit hasn't moved him much lately. This goddamned trailer is falling apart." Her eyes suddenly seemed moist. "We could use some money."

Hunt spoke quietly. "The lawyers for the Daren children are looking to break the old man's last will."

"I know that."

"They're looking for witnesses who might be in a position to testify that the old man wasn't right in the head when he signed the will."

She said nothing, but her eyes were fixed on his.

Phil finished the beer. "Of course, they can't pay someone for that kind of testimony. That wouldn't be legal. But they might buy something from them."

"Like what?"

He shrugged. "Oh, maybe something like this place."

She laughed. "Jesus, we got eighty acres of scrub pine and sand. You can't even grow weeds. A junk company wouldn't take this wreck of a trailer as a gift. What would they offer, a couple of thousand?"

He shook his head. "Like you say, the trailer isn't very valuable, but they might go five hundred an acre for the land."

"What! That would be forty thousand dollars, Phil. Nobody in their right mind would—"

He held up his hand. "Of course, they'd have to know what kind of testimony they might expect."

She bit her bottom lip. "You know," she said softly. "For that kind of money we could move away from this godforsaken place.

184

Vincent's a master carpenter. We could move south and start our lives all over again."

Phil nodded. "If you were called as a witness, what would you say about Daren's state of mind after the stroke?"

Her eyes narrowed. "What would they want me to say?"

"It has to be in your own words."

She paused, then spoke with surprising authority. "Well, he didn't know what he was doing much of the time." She looked at Hunt. "Is that the kind of thing they want?"

"Go on."

She smiled knowingly. "He was like a baby. He had to be cleaned and wiped and he liked it when you talked baby talk to him." She stopped, thought for a moment, and then continued. "He sometimes didn't know what he was doing or even who he was."

"You saw all this yourself?"

She nodded eagerly.

"You're sure?"

She laughed out loud. "Absolutely."

"Here's what they propose, Stella. They'll draw up an option to purchase your property for forty thousand, and give you a five-thousand-dollar deposit. After the trial, they'll come up with the rest and you can deed this place over. Okay?"

She whooped, tried to stand, then fell back laughing. "Goddamn right it's okay."

"Vincent has to sign too. Any problems there?"

She giggled. "For forty thousand dollars, Vincent would let you hack off his dick. Don't worry, he'll sign."

Hunt nodded. "Everything will be done in a corporation's name, but nothing will be filed until after the trial." He paused. "As I said, this has nothing to do with what you might say on the stand."

She laughed. "Of course not."

"Stella, it might be wise if Vincent didn't know the details of this little transaction. You can make up a story about mineral rights, if you want. You can tell him a research outfit is buying the place."

"Vincent won't even think about anything except the money." She looked out the trailer's small and grimy window. "Forty thousand dollars." She said it slowly, reverently, then she grinned. "How about another beer to celebrate? Or maybe something else?"

He looked at the huge mounds of flesh, ill-concealed beneath her bulky clothes. "I'm too old for anything but beer," he said with a chuckle.

"I remember a time when you didn't have to be asked twice."

"Me too, but that's all I do—remember."

"Pity," she said as she pushed herself erect to get two more beers.

"Is that how you got the new Blazer?" she asked, as she labored to the small refrigerator. "Are you going to be a witness too?"

"Maybe," he said.

Stella was smart. She would make a good witness. The price of her testimony was steep, including his bonus for finding her, but he had been told not to worry about the cost.

There was plenty of money to go around.

"I think it's silly that you're driving up there yourself. Why have a chauffeur if you don't use him?"

T. G. Sage smiled at his secretary. "I want the good people of Gladding to think of me as just a humble, hard-working lawyer trying to fight off the brutal assault of a rich, powerful law firm. Showing up with a chauffeur would ruin my act."

She guffawed. "You can buy and sell every damn lawyer in Sperling Beekman."

"Maybe yes, maybe no. However, the boys from Sperling Beekman will be dressed in tailored splendor, while I'll be in my old JCPenny suit. That jury up there will find a natural affinity for a poor man like me." He chuckled. "And if they fail to notice the contrast, I'll find a subtle way to bring it to their attention." He closed his worn briefcase. "Well, I'm ready to go. If you need me, I'll be at the ever-elegant Eagle Inn in beautiful downtown Gladding."

She shook her head. "I don't know why you take cases like this. God knows you don't need the money. You have nothing to prove to anyone."

"This is not only my vocation, it's my relaxation. Other people take up tennis or golf. Trying lawsuits is my sport. I love it, you know that."

"But why take this one? It's so damn inconvenient."

He nodded, picking up his briefcase. "Yes, but this one has a bit of mystery attached to it. There's something more to this case than meets the eye. I intend to find out what that is."

All she could do was shake her head in bemusement.

"If they have postcards in Gladding, I'll send you one."

"Good luck."

"It's the other side who'll need luck."

Rhonda Janus looked out the airplane's window. They had taxied out behind a Japanese jumbo jet. When it took off, it would then be their turn.

Soft Hawaiian music played quietly in the cabin. The flight attendants wore colorful aloha attire over their usual uniforms. Some of the passengers were sunburned, and all were decked out in fragrant flower leis. Everyone looked exhausted, but obviously sad at having to leave their tropical paradise.

Rhonda Janus couldn't get out fast enough. For her, Hawaii had become a tropical prison. When the phone call finally came, she felt like a convict getting a pardon.

186

The Japanese jet finally took off, and they took their position for takeoff. In a few seconds they were airborne out over the Pacific. In six hours they would reach Denver. From there she would get another flight to Detroit, and then Gladding.

She wondered how it would feel to be back in Gladding. She wondered if the place had changed. She wondered why, suddenly and surprisingly, she found herself near tears.

"May I bring you another drink?"

Rhonda looked up at the stewardess. "Yes please. Another vodka."

The young woman smiled, looking past her at the Pacific. "Hard to leave, isn't it?"

Rhonda smiled. "Not for me."

"Really? You must be going home to something very nice."

Rhonda nodded.

"Romance?" the stewardess asked.

"Revenge," Rhonda said quietly, and then she smiled.

17

Jake had left Detroit sufficiently early for him to arrive in Gladding before nightfall. Except for a short snow squall just past Bay City, I-75 had been dry and clear.

Due to system overload, it seemed as though his brain was about to explode, filled with newly learned evidence rules and trial tactics. He had crammed for the trial as he had for law exams in school. But it wasn't the same. This time it was real. He tried to put the trial out of his mind, but he would find himself thinking of some rule of evidence or trial practice. His thoughts were disorganized, and he wondered if he would remember anything at all when court opened in the morning.

Jake turned off the interstate and found the road to Gladding even more deserted than usual. There were traces of snow that had already collected, and low-hanging clouds were a sure sign of more to come.

Only a few miles from Gladding, he spotted the police car parked at the side of the road. Jake cut back on his speed, the speedometer needle dropping back to near the legal fifty-five miles per hour limit as he passed the police car.

It wasn't the usual blue state-police vehicle, so he presumed it was a local sheriff.

In his rear-view mirror he watched the police car glide swiftly onto the road and speed toward him. Jake checked the speedometer again to make sure he was within the limit, although he assumed he'd been clocked with radar. He expected to see the police lights begin to twirl, but nothing happened. The policeman came up behind him, but stayed back about fifty yards.

Jake slowed, and so did the police vehicle. On impulse he speeded up, bringing his speed up to sixty. Again, the police car matched him, but made no attempt to do anything but follow.

Jake, suddenly anxious, wondered what was happening.

He was relieved to see Gladding. He slowed, found a place near the entrance to the hotel, and pulled in. The police car pulled up behind him.

Jake got out and walked to the driver's side of the police vehicle. He recognized the local sheriff.

"Was I doing something wrong?" Jake asked, as the sheriff rolled down his window.

Sheriff Olsen shook his head, his almost translucent blue eyes fixed on Jake. "No," he said.

"But you were following me."

The sheriff again shook his head. "No. I was providing an escort."

"How did you know I'd be coming that way?"

"It's about the only way to get here from Detroit," the sheriff replied. "Everybody up here knows you drive that fancy Corvette. I just waited at the county line."

"Why?"

The sheriff's face remained expressionless, with nothing to indicate his thoughts or emotions. "It's Sunday. I had nothing better to do."

"Why would you think I'd need an escort?"

The sheriff shrugged. "Some folks up here think you're on the wrong side of things. They know who you are, what you look like, and the car you drive. I thought providing an escort might be a good idea."

"You think I'm in danger?"

The smile was without warmth. "This was in the nature of a precaution, that's all."

Jake stared at him. "Maybe it's in the nature of a threat."

The smile remained fixed. "As they say, a policeman's lot is not a happy one. No one appreciates us." The sheriff put the car into gear. "Be careful," he called as he rolled away.

Jake watched as the sheriff's car slowly moved down the empty street. He felt vulnerable and completely alone. He wondered if the police escort was a subtle way of letting him know the community didn't want him.

He took his bags from the car and locked it. Since the Eagle Inn had no bellboys, Jake carried the bags himself to the registration desk. There was no one there.

"Hello?" he called. He could hear the sound of a television coming from another room. "Hello?" he called again. This time he heard someone stirring in the adjoining room.

A tall, thin man in a checkered wool shirt came out.

"Hello yourself," he said cheerfully. "What can I do for you?"

"My name's Jake Martin. I have a reservation."

He was answered by a grin. "From Sperling Beekman, right? I'm Toby Jenkins. I own this place." He extended his gnarled, weathered hand to shake.

"I kind of thought you folks would be staying out at the Darens', seeing how you people are her attorneys and all. Will that be cash or charge?"

"Do you take—"

The man grinned. "We take everything here."

Jake fished out a credit card and handed it to the man.

He looked at it, then handed it back. "I don't need it now, just when you check out." He reached under the desk and produced a registration card and a key. "You're in room 210. Top of the stairs, third door on your left. If you want, you can leave your bags. My son'll run them up later."

"It's no problem," Jake said, signing the card.

"Oh by the way, there's some messages for you. Your friends said to meet them at the Darens' place. I suppose for dinner, but they didn't say. If it isn't for dinner, my restaurant here isn't half-bad. We close at six on Sundays, but if you want some eggs or something easy, just let me know and I'll open the kitchen and rustle it up. I substitute for the cook when I have to."

"Thanks," Jake said. "Who called?"

"This fellow, Bellows. They checked in earlier. He's got a young woman with him. Separate rooms, but I think she's his girlfriend."

"Cora Simpson?"

His smile became a leer. "Yeah. A little thin, but nice."

"She's a lawyer with our firm, nothing more," Jake said, realizing his tone sounded priggish, even to him.

"Too bad for old Bellows," the man laughed. "Anyway, they're out at Darens' place. Do you know how to get there?"

"Yes," Jake picked up his bags.

"That's not the only message," Jenkins continued. "We're booked up with newspaper types, and they all want to talk to you. Most of them are down at the Northwoods Bar drinking. A lot of them seem half in the bag already, so I suppose if you're going to talk to them, you'd better do it pretty soon. I hear it's developing into quite a party over there. There's going to be some major hangovers tomorrow."

"Thanks." Jake started to turn, then stopped. "I understand I'm not too popular with the local police."

He was answered by another grin, this one not so wide. "Hey, as long as you pay your bill, you're popular with me."

"How do the rest of them up here feel?"

He shrugged. "To be frank, they'd like to see Elizabeth Daren fall on her ass. They're not too happy with anyone who might interfere with that. Nothing personal, just a matter of business. I've heard some strong language on the subject, but it's usually just the whiskey talking. I wouldn't worry, we're pretty peaceful people up here."

"Thanks."

"Of course, there's always a crazy or two around," he added. "But that's true anywhere, right?"

Jake carried his bags to the room. Entering the room was like stepping back in time. An old-fashioned brass bed stood near a tall narrow window. He looked out and saw rusted railroad tracks.

He unpacked. A wooden pole at one end of the room served in place of a closet. An ancient chest of drawers, worn and cracked, was the only other furniture. The wooden floor was covered by a thin, worn throw rug.

An old radiator, its silver paint peeling in spots, hissed merrily.

Jake checked the bathroom at the end of the hall. A small sign with OCCUPIED on one side and UNOCCUPIED on the other hung on the door. Inside, everything looked like the original fixtures. There was no shower, only a large tub set up on four iron claw feet.

He returned to his room, finished unpacking and tossed Sage's old book on the bed. He planned to review it and his own notes once more before morning.

But first he would have to see the others at Raven's Nest.

"Tiger, tell us how you expect to win this son-of-a-bitch of a case?" Sherman Murphy burped unexpectedly, the sound coming like audio punctuation at the end of his question.

T. G. Sage, surrounded by media people, was holding court at a large round table in the rear of the Northwoods Bar. Sage bought each round, but was careful not to match the newsmen drink for drink. He was the only one at the table completely sober and fully alert.

"Murph," he said, smiling, "if I told you, I'd see it in your column tomorrow and then the evil empire of Sperling Beekman would know from where my attack would come and prepare for it. I'm afraid you'll have to wait."

"Are you planning to drag out Elizabeth Daren's past?" The question was asked by Robert Stoneman, a syndicated radio commentator. His deep, authoritative voice rose over the din and jukebox music in the bar.

190

Sage pretended mock surprise. "What past? Are you trying to tell me something?"

"It's all in the divorce records," Stoneman said. "This is the age of the bimbo, and some say she's the champion of that division. You going to put her on the stand?"

Sage raised an eyebrow. "I wouldn't think of it. She's on the other side, after all. Then he smiled slyly. "Of course, if they should call her as a witness, then I'll do whatever I must in order to see justice done."

He was answered by a chorus of loud guffaws.

"Justice, my ass." Bobby Kelman, the *Free Press* reporter blurted out. Kelman, who had been an editor, had been demoted in a recent *Free Press* bloodletting. His sour resentment had become like a physical part of his being. "You'll stick it up her ass if they let you." Kelman was obviously drunk.

"A lawyer does what he must to advance the cause of his client." Sage spoke so quietly that they had to strain to hear him. "Lawyers have to adhere to limits and rules, just like everyone else. However, we can't let pity or even a sense of humanity interfere with what we must do, not if it's legal and it's necessary to protect our client."

"Bullshit," Kelman said. "You fuckers will do anything for money."

Sage appeared unruffled. "Not anything. Although it sometimes looks that way, I suppose." He studied Kelman for a moment, then continued. "Suppose that waitress who you've been flirting with agrees to pop up to your room tonight and then later claims rape, although there was no rape. What then, Mr. Kelman? Would you want me to go easy on the young lady as I questioned her? Would you want me to be sweet and gentle, knowing you could draw a life sentence for something you didn't do?"

"Lawyers twist everything," Kelman grumbled.

Sage smiled. "It depends on your point of view. I do whatever I think necessary for a client."

"You're evading the question, Tiger," Stoneman persisted. "Will you bring out the lady's past?"

Sage gestured to the waitress for another round. "I play the cards as they fall, Mr. Stoneman." He paused. "I have other appropriate clichés, if that one isn't sufficient."

"It could be hot stuff," Stoneman laughed. "I hope she takes the stand."

Sage smiled slowly. "For her sake, I hope she doesn't."

"Well, it looks as if I've arrived just in time." Jerry Casey walked up to the table and grinned. Casey, sandy-haired and pudgy, pulled up a chair across from Sage and sat down. "Think of me as the local truth squad," he said. "I'm here to offset any clever lies Tiger Sage may be providing."

Sage raised an eyebrow. "You wouldn't be accusing me of trying to warp the minds of these fearless journalists, would you, Mr. Casey?"

"Having been a fearless journalist, I know how easy it is to do just that, especially by lawyers buying drinks."

"Where's Lee Stevens?" Murph asked. "I thought he was going to handle the flack work for Elizabeth Daren?"

"He's on assignment, so to speak," Casey answered. "I'll be the representative of truth and justice until he gets up here."

The waitress brought the round of drinks to the table.

Casey looked up at her, gesturing at the men seated at the table. "Do it again, my dear, my treat; and add a vodka and tonic for me."

"What kind of assignment could keep Stevens away from this case?" Murphy asked. "You guys must be getting rich off this."

"Rich, no. A bit more affluent, yes. We are just two former newspapermen trying to get by in a tough world."

"Jesus, both sides are bullshit artists," Bobby Kelman growled. "Truth is going to take one hell of a beating up here before this case is through."

Casey laughed. "Probably. I don't know what Tiger here is planning, but I'll hold a short press conference outside the court-house every day after the court closes down. I'll have press releases and appropriate quotes to hand out. In other words, this is going to be a vacation for you folks. I'm going to do your work for you."

"What about this, Tiger? Do you have a counteroffer?" Murphy asked.

Sage smiled slowly. "Press releases are very nice, but they can't compare with what I'm going to give you inside the courtroom."

Kelman looked up from his drink. "And that is what?"

"Fireworks," Sage replied evenly.

"Chip, how nice to hear from you! Where are you?" Claude deSalle asked.

"We're in this crummy motel in Montmorci. It's a dump, but it's better then those fleabags in Gladding."

"With any luck you won't be there long," deSalle said. "Getting control of the bank is worth at least one week out of your life, wouldn't you say?"

"You might think differently if you were here." Chip Daren's tone was a cross between a whine and a growl. "Gussie is up here, too. God, it's just like when we were kids. She drives me insane. All I have to do is listen to her babble for five minutes and I'm ready to kill."

DeSalle fought against laughing. "Don't do that, it would complicate the case. How is Gussie?"

"If I ever get a word in, I'll ask. She looks fine."

"She understands that no one is to know about my role in this matter?"

"I did manage to get that in. I think she does. You never really know with her."

"Is Sage with you?"

"No," Chip replied. "He's staying over at Gladding, God help him."

"Chip, would you give me a call every evening? I'd like to know what's happening."

"The trial will get front-page coverage. That's what Sage says."

"Sometimes what occurs in a courtroom gets garbled in the newspapers. Editors may inadvertently chop out something important. I'd appreciate the call, Chip."

"At home?"

"That would be best," deSalle said.

"What if you're out?"

"I'll make it a point to be home," deSalle said smoothly, although he felt like yelling at the pompous fool. He paused, wondering if he should risk saying more. Chip Daren was rich but not bright. "If there's any proposal to settle the case, Chip, please talk to me before you agree to any terms."

"I can handle anything that comes up." His tone was suddenly hostile.

"I'm sure you can, Chip. But the result of any settlement could seriously affect the bank's future. I'll merely be your adviser. You will make your own decision, obviously. Even generals consult their staffs, Chip, before making a major battle decision."

"Well, you may be right."

DeSalle smiled. It was the reference to generals that had appealed. An idiot like Chip Daren would like to think of himself as a commander of men.

"Sage says it's unlikely they'll offer any real settlement before the case gets underway," Chip said. "Maybe after we kick the widow's ass around the courtroom, she'll rethink her position. Sage thinks she might."

"Such things have been known to happen," deSalle said. "Good luck tomorrow."

"I don't need luck. I'm just going to sit and watch. From what I hear, Sage makes his own luck. I'll give you that call tomorrow night, deSalle."

"Thanks, Chip."

DeSalle replaced the receiver and shook his head. "General" Chip Daren had once again taken to calling him by his last name. The poor fool was so predictably transparent.

Claude deSalle was surprised at his own unexpected anxiety. Earlier, he had had dinner with friends, just a quiet Sunday supper, but he found he had difficulty paying attention to the conversation.

He felt like a playwright whose masterpiece was about to open and who was denied the right to be present. It was so frustrating. He had put the whole production together. He had arranged for the players, the plot, everything. But he couldn't attend the performance.

He tried to divert his thoughts. He used the remote to turn on the television and searched from channel to channel, but found nothing that could hold his attention. He turned the set off and poured a large brandy.

It wouldn't be long now, just a few days. He had everything ready to go as soon as Elizabeth lost the case.

The Hanover Square board was primed, although they didn't know it yet, to quickly get rid of all the Darens from any connection with the bank. The racy publicity from the courtroom war would leave a sour aftertaste in the collective mouths of all the board members.

The timing was tight, but it would take place just as he planned, if all the actors played their roles as he had designed and directed them to be played. It would be smooth, efficient, almost painless. He would be named chairman, and the deal with the Germans would go through.

DeSalle gulped the brandy. He felt helpless and frustrated. He would have to depend on Chip Daren now for word of what was happening.

Patience, he reminded himself, was not only a virtue, it was a tactic. He was the real general in this battle, and he intended to use every tactic to win. But the waiting, he realized, might become almost unbearable.

The gatehouse at Raven's Nest was lit up. Jake didn't recognize the guard who stepped out as Jake rolled to a stop. There was a cool, professional look about this one.

Jake lowered the Corvette's window. "Jake Martin," he said. "I'm expected."

"Yes, you are. Do you know where you're to go, Mr. Martin?"

"I've been here a few times," Jake said. Even the man's uniform was different. "Are you new?"

"You're one of Mrs. Daren's lawyers, right?"

Jake nodded.

"I work for a national security company," he said. "Mrs. Daren hired us. We're up here while the trial is going on."

"We?"

"There's several of us," he said.

"You look like a cop."

"I was," he said. "This pays better." He stepped back into the little guardhut, cutting off any further conversation.

Jake raised the window and drove on, his car lights shining

194

ahead on the white stone drive leading through the dark pines. Night came quickly in the north.

He circled the main house and parked at the back next to a huge Mercedes. He guessed it belonged to Donald Bellows. Jake noticed another guard standing near the light at the boathouse. His uniform parka was the same as that of the man at the gate. The guard watched silently as Jake walked to the door.

Inside, the maid took his coat and led him to the great room. Huge logs crackled as flames licked about them in the enormous fireplace.

"Well, we were beginning to wonder if you were coming."

Donald Bellows wore a sweater and trousers perfectly tailored to his slim, athletic body. He sat in a large chair near the fire, holding a crystal goblet and looking like the lord of the manor.

"Hello, Jake."

He had never seen Cora Simpson in anything but expensive business suits. She seemed dwarfed by the huge lumberman's shirt she wore over faded designer jeans.

Jake smiled. "I had to check a few things before I left Detroit."

"Did you register at that excuse for a hotel?" Bellows inquired.

"Yes."

"Terrible place," Bellows said. "Well, at least we won't be there long."

He sensed her before she spoke.

"I'm glad to see you, Jake."

Jake turned. He felt a thrill just looking at her. Like Bellows, Elizabeth Daren's casual clothes had been tailored, but she wore them with a model's easy grace. She smiled and Jake wondered if she experienced similar pleasure at seeing him. If she did, she gave no outward indication.

"We waited dinner," she said.

"I'm sorry," Jake said, without offering any explanation.

Her emerald eyes lingered on him for a moment. "Would you like a drink before we go in."

He shook his head. "Not tonight. Thanks."

"Tomorrow will merely be jury selection, Jake. That'll be no problem," Bellows said, grinning. "You look a little anxious. A couple of drinks might help loosen you up."

"Maybe, but I think I'll pass anyway," Jake replied. "I still have a few things to go over tonight. A clear head will help."

Bellows shrugged. "It's up to you." His diminishing smile indicated his annoyance at having his advice ignored.

"Then let's go into dinner, shall we?" Elizabeth said.

She led them into the dining room. Four places had been set at one end of the long refectory table. Elizabeth sat at the head of the table. Bellows and Cora took places on her left. Jake sat at the single place setting on her right.

Jake hardly noticed the food as each course was served quickly and efficiently. He thought he caught Elizabeth looking at him several times. She was pleasant, but only that. Jake ate, but it was mostly a mechanical act.

"Elizabeth, should you ever wish to get rid of your cook," Bellows said, "let me know. Whoever he or she is, could be a world-class chef."

"He is. He comes from Paris." Elizabeth turned to Jake. "What will happen tomorrow?" she asked.

He dabbed his lips with his napkin. "Jury selection. If that goes quickly, we might even get into the proofs."

"What are proofs?" she asked.

Bellows spoke before Jake could reply. "We lawyers tend to make things sound complicated, but this will be an essentially simple process. After the jury is selected and sworn, Jake will make an opening statement." Bellows looked directly at Jake. "It should be simple and to the point, just a short statement saying we offer the will and we'll show it was legally signed and executed in front of witnesses by Gus." He turned to Elizabeth. "That's all we have to show. The presumption that a will is valid is very strong."

"Then you call Dr. Faraday and Rhonda Janus?" Elizabeth asked.

"Yes. We have to show—"

Jake was cut off once more by Bellows. "Rhonda Janus hasn't surfaced, but we don't really need her. One witness is sufficient."

"If she does show up, she may be trouble," Jake said.

"Maybe, maybe not. We'll have to wait and see, obviously." He looked directly at Jake. "If she does show up and tries anything, vigorous cross-examination is the lawyer's best tool to handle such matters."

"She's our witness," Jake said. "We can't cross-examine our own witnesses, at least not for the purposes of impeachment."

Bellows' smile was cold. "There's always a way around petty rules."

"I don't know if the judge would consider it petty," Jake said. "It's a rule of evidence."

"What's impeachment?" Elizabeth asked.

"It's a fancy legal term for showing a witness is lying," Jake said. "The general rule forbids a lawyer from impeaching a witness whom that lawyer has called to give testimony."

"It probably won't come up anyway. We shouldn't cross any bridges until we get to them, Jake." Bellows' smile was icy.

Cora started to speak, then changed her mind.

"Where's Dr. Faraday?" Elizabeth asked.

"He's coming up tonight," Bellows said. "We made a reservation in his name at our so-called hotel. I asked that they give him a room on our floor. They said they would, but you never know. These people up here seem to do what they damn well please."

Elizabeth watched as Bellows busily attacked the filet mignon set before him. "What happens after the jury is selected and Jake makes his speech?"

"We introduce the will. The court already has it on file. Then we call Faraday to show him that Gus signed it in his and Rhonda Janus's presence. And that's it. That's all we're required to do by law." Bellows ladled sour cream over his steaming baked potato. "From there on, it's up to this fellow Sage to try to prove that the will should not be admitted. That," he grinned, "is not only going to be tough, it's going to be impossible."

Jake found he could no longer eat.

"Do you plan on using me as a witness?" Elizabeth asked.

"No," Bellows said.

"Sage can call you," Jake said quietly.

"He cannot," Bellows snapped.

Jake glanced at Cora for support, but she looked away. "Elizabeth was present when the will was signed," he said.

Bellows' eyes froze. "It's your job to keep Elizabeth off the stand. If he tries to call her as a witness, object. The judge will back you up."

"On what grounds?" Jake asked.

Now Bellows colored slightly. "Elizabeth didn't sign the will as a witness, she was merely present. That means nothing."

"If Faraday goes sour and Janus doesn't show up, what then?" Jake asked. "We don't have the videotape anymore."

"Well, we won't call Elizabeth," Bellows said, smiling benignly at her. The smile faded as he put down his fork and turned to Jake. "I understand that you're nervous tonight, Jake, but you're creating monsters that don't exist. These will contests are cut-and-dried affairs. This will be a breeze, believe me."

"Why do you say that?" Elizabeth asked.

Bellows sipped some wine, then spoke. "Judges are a lazy bunch. They'll jump at an easy way out when one is presented. It's to the advantage of this lady judge to keep the lid on this thing." Bellows smiled. "Watch and see. She's a lawyer, she knows how difficult it is to upset a will. She'll start cutting Sage off after a bit. She knows his position is hopeless. She may be a character, but even characters don't like to make work for themselves. Oh, she'll let Sage make some noise, but then she'll contain him. If I were making a bet, I'd wager this thing goes a day and a half, tops."

"This judge doesn't strike me as the kind who would shy away from work," Jake said.

Bellows looked smug. "It may look that way, but you'll see. Judges love to pontificate about how hard they work, but you can't find one in the afternoon unless you go to a golf course. This will be over in the blink of an eye."

"I hope you're right," Elizabeth said.

"When will Craig Dow come up?" Jake asked.

"Craig's caught up in a federal trial in Detroit," Bellows replied. "That one may drag on." He chuckled. "In that case there are no easy outs. The judge is stuck. Our case will be over before Craig's. Anyway Jake, you're prepared, and, as I say, this will be a piece of cake."

"Let's hope," Jake said quietly, meeting Elizabeth's eyes for a moment before looking away.

"A piece of cake," Bellows repeated.

After dinner, Jake excused himself so he could return to the hotel and prepare for the morning. Cora followed him out to the door.

She looked so different dwarfed inside her big lumberman's shirt, smaller, softer, more feminine somehow. Cora Simpson was a beautiful woman, but in the city, with every blonde hair in place and dressed in fashionable tailored suits for work, the beauty seemed more like a formal protective shield. Now, in her oversized casual clothing, she looked more like a teenager, fresh and even a little vulnerable.

"Jake, even if we are competitors, I want to wish you luck tomorrow."

He grinned down at her. Without high heels, Cora was barely over five feet all. He towered over her. "I appreciate it, Cora; I think I'm going to need it."

"Bellows may be right, you know. It could turn out to be very easy."

"Cora, do you honestly think that?"

She slowly shook her head. He noticed that her eyes were very light blue, and he wondered why he had never noticed that before.

"I wish Craig Dow was up here," Jake said, "whether it turns out to be easy or not. That must be one hell of a case he has in Federal Court, if it's more important than this."

She seemed to hesitate, then spoke. "I checked," she said, lowering her voice to just above a whisper. "He's really just along for the ride over there. Howard Rosenfeld is doing most of the work."

"I don't understand. Rosenfeld is one of our top people. Why would he even need Craig?"

"He doesn't, obviously."

"Then why—"

"As I said to you before, Jake, this may mean you've already been selected for the partnership opening. That would make sense."

"But if I haven't?"

"Then, I don't know what to make of it. But I really think you're the one they're going to pick, Jake. I wish it was me, but if not then I'm glad you're the one. I never liked Craig Dow very much."

"I think you're wrong, Cora, but if you aren't, what will you do?"

She sighed. "You know the firm's rules, Jake. I've been there five years. If no partnership is offered I'm out. I have no choice in the matter."

"But—"

She smiled. "I must admit I've had my heart set on being a partner in Sperling Beekman, almost since the time I was accepted in law school." The smile faded slowly. "But, if that's not to be, I'll cry a bit. However, it's not the end of the world. I've had offers from other firms. Being a tax expert does have a certain advantage. We're always in demand. Of course, those other firms are not nearly as prestigious as Sperling Beekman but the money would be about the same. There might even be an advantage in moving to another firm."

"Oh?"

"I've made it a rule never to date anyone in our firm, Jake, no matter what. Mixing business and romance is like smoking near gasoline, a lot of things could go sky-high. If I go elsewhere I can see someone in Sperling Beekman, someone I'd like to know better."

He wondered why he felt a sudden twinge of jealousy. "And who is that?"

"You," she said quietly.

"Me?"

"Is that a problem for you?"

"I'm married, Cora."

"You're being divorced. Or has something happened there that you haven't told me?"

He shook his head. "No. It's just . . ."

"She doesn't deserve you, Jake. She's a fool and she's proving it with Harvey Kellerman." She reached out and took his hand. "Don't be frightened, I'm not proposing; I'd just like to get to know you. That's not so scandalous, is it?"

"Cora, I don't know what to say. Right now, my whole world is upside down."

"It's not the widow in there, is it?" she asked.

"What do you mean?"

"Is something going on between you? She's obviously interested in you, Jake."

"You're wrong there."

She smiled wistfully. "You think so? Women can tell, you know. It's instinctive. Is something going on?"

He laughed. "No. I'm hardly in her league in any event."

"You are, if she sees what I see, Jake."

"Cora, I'm not involved with anyone. Right now, I can't be. Things are just moving too fast. I'm hanging on by my fingernails. I'm not ready for any . . . relationship."

She pulled him down gently and kissed his cheek. "When you are, Jake, do keep me in mind."

She was gone before he could reply.

Back in his room at the hotel he tried not to think of Cora Simpson, Elizabeth Daren, Marie or anyone else. He tried to study Sage's book, but gave it up when he could no longer concentrate. He lay in his dark room beneath a couple of thin, musty-smelling woollen blankets and watched out the window at the distant pine tops dancing in the chilly night breeze.

Faces, like ghosts, danced through his consciousness. Cora Simpson, who tonight had been so different and so surprising. Marie's face was there, too, but it evoked only a painful sadness. He thought about Elizabeth Daren. He wondered if Cora was right. At times he thought he detected a hint of interest, but he couldn't be sure. He was sure of nothing anymore.

Everything had happened so fast. His dream of an idyllic marriage had blown apart. If things didn't go right, his hope for a career with Sperling Beekman would suffer a similar fate. If there had been a decision on the partnership nothing had been indicated to him. Nothing seemed to make sense.

He hadn't been able to get down much of the dinner Elizabeth had offered, which led him to wonder if condemned men ever really ate that traditional last meal.

Sleep would not come. Jake Martin lay quietly, listening to the north wind as it moaned around the old hotel.

18

J ake was slow to waken, having managed only a few hours of restless sleep. He'd allowed enough time to get ready for court, but he hadn't counted on the problems presented by the communal bathroom at the end of the hall. Jake took his place in line behind two newsmen, both of whom were deathly pale. They failed to acknowledge Jake or even each other as they stood staring at nothing, looking like two doomed prisoners waiting their turn for execution. Then each of them spent an inordinately long time in the bathroom. The delay ruined Jake's schedule, so that he was now running late. There was no time for a bath. He shaved quickly, nicking the corner of his lower lip in the process. There was no time for breakfast or even coffee.

It was not an auspicious beginning.

Jake rushed to the courthouse and found the stairway leading up to the courtroom jammed with people standing on every stair. He had to wiggle and squeeze through protesting bodies as he struggled upwards. The sheriff had stationed himself at the courtroom door and was acting as a combination bouncer and usher, allowing only those who had business to pass, while keeping out the mob of prospective spectators who waited in the hope they might eventually get in.

As Jake approached, the sheriff nodded. "Nice of you to make it. The judge wants to talk to the lawyers in her chambers."

"Downstairs?" Jake asked, concerned that he'd have to force his way back through the throng.

"No. There's a small judge's office over there to the left of the bench."

Jake squeezed past the sheriff. He was awed by the sight of the packed courtroom. Over two hundred people occupied every available seat in the arena that was the spectator section. They sat patiently waiting, looking like an audience eager and ready for the opening of a Broadway play. Jake wondered if the sudden grip of panic he was feeling might be the beginning of a major case of stage fright.

The media—both newspaper and television people—lounged around the counsel tables and the empty jury box. Gathered in small groups, they talked and laughed and seemed bored at having to wait for things to get started.

Seated between Donald Bellows and Cora Simpson, Elizabeth

201

Daren sat in the front row of the spectator section. Chip Daren and his sister Gussie were also seated in the front row, but an aisleway provided a separation between them and their father's widow. Chip Daren glowered at Jake with open hostility, while his sister Gussie, who also watched Jake, gave no hint of what she might be thinking.

T. G. Sage sat at the counsel table reading a newspaper, looking completely relaxed and apparently oblivious to the crowds of people milling about and waiting for something to happen.

Jake was painfully aware that every eye in the place seemed to be fixed on him as he walked past Chip and Gussie and over to where Elizabeth was seated.

"Where have you been?" Bellows kept his voice just above a whisper as he leaned forward, his hands on the mahogany railing that separated the spectators from the court. "The judge wants to talk to the lawyers."

"Let's go," Jake said.

"You're the lawyer in charge, Jake. It's your show," Bellows replied quietly. "Besides, we don't want to look like we're ganging up on the other side. You had better hurry in there before she becomes irritated."

Jake nodded. His mouth felt almost too dry to talk. Sage put down the newspaper as he approached.

"Good morning, Jake." Sage's welcoming smile seemed genuine. "The judge wants to see us."

"So I understand."

He followed Sage around the front of the polished magisterial bench. Apparently built as a convenience for the judge to provide a place to rest during court recesses, the little office wasn't much larger than a closet. It contained only a desk and a few chairs.

Judge Lila Vinson, seated behind the desk, was already cloaked in her black judicial robe. She glared at Jake.

"I like people to be on time," she snapped. "From now on get here a half hour early, just in case we need to talk. I don't want this case dragging on any longer than it has to."

Jake was about to protest that he was on time—barely—and that no one had told him to come early, but it didn't seem the time to get into disputes.

T. G. Sage took a seat across from the judge, while Jake remained standing.

"Now, let's get down to business," she said, lighting a cigarette. "The television people want to put a camera in here. Just one; apparently the bunch of them have agreed to share the tape or however they do those things. How do you two feel about that?"

Sage spoke before Jake could even think.

"I have no problem with that," he said.

"You mean they want to televise the trial?" Jake asked.

"What did you think they'd do with a camera? Fish?" she shot back at Jake. "The damn Supreme Court allows cameras if there's no objection and the trial judge allows it. It's all part of their continuing experiment in good government. Well, any objection to the camera?"

Jake wished Bellows had come with him. He hadn't expected anything like this. Jake was nervous enough facing a flesh-and-blood audience, but the prospect of being watched by millions filled him with terror.

"I don't think that would be such a good idea," he said.

"Jesus, I didn't ask you your goddamned opinion," the judge snapped. "Do you object or don't you?"

"I object," Jake said, getting the words out despite his dry mouth.

"Why?"

Jake wondered if he had blundered into some kind of trap.

He swallowed several times, then spoke. "Legally, this is a cut-and-dried matter of the admission of a will," he said quietly. "I think the presence of a television camera could turn this into a media bonanza. Knowing they were on camera, the jury couldn't help but be affected, and the witnesses, too. I think it might cause unnecessary complications and it could disturb the dignity of this proceeding."

Vinson stared at Jake as she inhaled deeply on the cigarette. She blew out a stream of smoke, then spoke. "As a matter of fact, I agree with you. Okay, the cameras are out, but since you're the one who objected, the television people are going to be pissed off at you, not me or Sage. Can you handle that?"

"I'll try to live with it," Jake replied weakly.

She nodded, taking another drag before speaking. "I've got a panel of forty prospective jurors out there. We don't have many jury trials up here so I haven't kept up with whatever refinements the probate courts downstate might have developed; but I like to run the voir dire examination myself. If you want to ask questions, write them out and give them to me and I'll put them to the jury candidates."

"I've got a small problem with that, Lila," Sage said.

She raised an eyebrow. "Oh?"

"Frankly, I prefer to question prospective jurors myself. It helps probe for possible attitude problems that might exist. I have complete confidence in you, Lila, of course, but I know my case as Mr. Martin here knows his. We know what might come up in the testimony. We know what questions to ask. It would better serve justice if you allowed us to put the questions to the jury candidates directly."

Jake suddenly recalled the exact page in Sage's book describing how a trial lawyer could try the case and win it if allowed a full chance at questioning prospective jurors. A clever advocate, author T. G. Sage had written, could turn it into a trial within a trial.

"I think I prefer your way, judge," Jake said.

"You think? Jesus, if you're going to say something, don't pussyfoot around. Do you want me to question the jurors or not?"

"You do it," Jake blurted out.

"Let's compromise," Sage interjected smoothly. "After you ask the usual general questions, Lila, allow us to put anything additional we might have directly to the jury."

Jake realized that the trial had already begun. Sage might look completely at ease and casual, but he was clearly on the attack. If he could set the rules, the case would be over before it began.

"We're both strangers up here," Jake said quickly. "You know these people, we don't. You know what to ask. I think . . ." He stopped. "It's my position that you should do the questioning. Allowing us to submit written questions to you is more than fair."

"Well, perhaps we are strangers, but—" Sage began.

"I'll do the questioning," she snapped. "Is there anything either of you feel should be asked?"

"Lila, I think you're being arbitrary. I've always found that it's important to get a feeling for the people who sit on a jury. As Mr. Martin says, we are strangers, so it's even more important that they get to know us."

Vinson smiled for the first time. "I'll introduce you, Ted. So knock it off. We are going to do it my way. Now, what about questions?" She looked at Jake.

"Oh, I suppose the obvious ones. Have any of them worked for the Darens? Or have they any relatives who work, or have worked for the Daren family? Have they formed an opinion about the case? That sort of thing."

Her eyes narrowed. "Look, I don't want generalities. 'That sort of thing' isn't especially lawyerlike, is it? If some of them have worked for Daren, what then?"

Jake had thought about the possible questions to be put in selecting a jury. It had been a key part of Sage's book. "How did they leave that employment?" Jake said. "Do they have any feelings toward anyone in the case that might interfere with bringing in a fair verdict?" He was about to add and that sort of thing, but checked himself.

"And you, Ted?"

"It would save you a great deal of trouble if you let me do the questioning," he persisted.

"I'm used to trouble, Ted. C'mon, tell me what you want asked."

Sage sat back. "Please make inquiry if any of them ever have had a relative or a friend who suffered from Alzheimer's disease, dementia, or any mental condition that would interfere with the ability to think, or any other disease that impairs judgment."

"Wait a minute," Jake said. "A question like that presumes something that's not part of this case."

"The mental capacity to make a last will is the issue here," Sage retorted quickly.

"But Gus Daren didn't have Alzheimer's, nor was he a victim of dementia."

Sage regarded Jake coolly. "He had suffered a stroke. We will show he lacked the mental capacity sufficient to make a will. That's all I'm inquiring about."

"That's not Alzheimer's, or dementia," the judge said. "If I put that to the prospective jurors, their imaginations will be filled with vivid pictures of some old man tied to his chair and drooling, which I'm sure is exactly what you intended."

"It never entered my mind," Sage murmured.

The judge chuckled. "Yeah, sure."

"Then I must insist you ask them if they have ever known anyone who was mentally crippled by a stroke," Sage said firmly.

"You can insist all you like, Ted, but I'll limit the inquiry to asking if any of them has or had a relative who had a stroke and whether anything connected with those circumstances might prevent them from arriving at a fair verdict. That's as far as I'm going to go. You can try your case when the jury is picked, Ted, not before."

"I will submit proposed written questions," Sage said. "I shall want them made part of the record, especially if you choose not to use them."

Her smile turned frosty. "We've known each other a long time, Theodore. Do you seriously think a threat of appeal would scare me?"

"No threat intended, Lila, but I must protect my client."

"Everything from now on will be on the record," she replied. She turned to Jake. "My ground rules are simple. After the jury is selected and sworn, you will make an opening statement. Just state the facts you expect to prove, no argument. Then Sage can make his opening if he wants to, or he may reserve until the close of your proofs. Whatever, I will want you to proceed with your witnesses in a brisk fashion. When I work, everyone works. You understand?"

Jake nodded.

"After he's done, Ted, you can proceed with your witnesses. When all the testimony is in, Mr. Martin, you can sum up your position to the jury. Then, Ted, you get your turn. I'll then instruct the jury and this thing will be history. Any questions?"

"Am I supposed to go first?" Jake asked. "I mean, he's the one attacking the validity of the will. Doesn't he have the burden of proceeding?"

Vinson frowned. "He can't attack anything until it's in evidence, can he? You set up the will, then he gets his chance. Anyway, that's the way we're going to run things here."

205

"You're forcing me to prove that the will is valid," Jake protested.

She shook her head no. "All you have to prove is that it exists and that it was validly executed according to law. After that, the burden of proof is squarely on the shoulders of the other side."

She looked at both of them. "Let's be clear on one thing. I run a tough courtroom. If I make a ruling, that's it. I don't want any argument. If you don't like it, you can appeal. I like to give attorneys freedom to try their case. But if you get out of line, I'll let you know. And if you don't get back in line, I'm not in the least bit shy about using my contempt powers. I hope that's clear."

Sage smiled. "Absolutely. I have complete trust and confidence in your fairness, Lila."

"From here on, we can cut the Lila business. Until this is over, address me by my title. I don't want you to give the jury the impression that you and I are special friends. Also clear?"

Sage smiled again. "Perfectly clear, your honor."

She crushed out her cigarette. "Okay boys, go to your corners and come out fighting."

Fourteen candidates from the panel of prospective jurors were called to take their place in the large wooden chairs in the jury box. The rest of the panel sat together in a section of spectator seats reserved for them.

Jake sat on one side of the big counsel table. Sage sat opposite him. Both lawyers faced the bench but they turned to watch the responses made by the fourteen candidates to Judge Vinson's questions.

The judge after a short speech about the solemn duty required of a juror, began. One of the jurors, a woman named Schmit, raised her hand when the judge asked if any of them had ever worked for the Darens.

"Did you work for either Mr. or Mrs. Daren?" The judge asked the stout woman, who looked petrified at being the center of attention.

She nodded. "It was a few years back. I was a maid there," she said. "I only worked for a few months. I worked for Mrs. Daren." She paused, blushing. "But not this Mrs. Daren," she said pointing shyly at Elizabeth. "I worked for the Mrs. Daren before this Mrs. Daren."

The spectators laughed. Judge Vinson's grim expression quietened everything but a few muted giggles.

"Why did you leave that employment?" the judge asked.

The woman's blush deepened. "I was fired. That other Mrs. Daren was very difficult. No one could please her."

"Do you bear any grudge toward the Darens because you were let go?"

The woman shook her head. "Oh no, none."

"Would you be able to arrive at a fair and impartial verdict in this case?"

"I believe so. Yes."

Jake wasn't sure what he should do, or if this was the time to do it, but he stood up. "I'd like to challenge the juror for cause." He tried to keep the hesitancy he felt out of his voice, and to speak as if he knew what he was doing.

Judge Vinson glared down at him. "You're pretty quick off the mark. What's the basis for the challenge?"

"Mrs. Schmit worked for the Darens. She was let go. I think that alone would affect her judgment in this case."

"She just said it wouldn't," the judge replied.

"Well, yes, but—"

"You can use a pre-emptory challenge, if you choose, but please wait until I'm through questioning these people. It will keep."

Mrs. Schmit glared at Jake as if he had just called her chastity into question. He knew he couldn't afford to allow her to stay on the jury. If she hadn't been prejudiced before, she was now.

"Judge," Jake persisted. "I have only a limited number of pre-emptory challenges. As I understand it, challenges for cause are unlimited. I believe there is cause shown to excuse this juror."

She half-smiled. "I don't, and that settles that, doesn't it?" She gestured that Jake should sit down. "Now, let's get on with it."

Jake made a mental note to use one of his precious pre-emptory challenges to excuse Mrs. Schmit as soon as the judge was through questioning the people in the box. He hadn't intended to, but he knew he had made an enemy of Mrs. Schmit.

Vinson changed her line of questioning, asking if any of the fourteen people in the box had ever had a relative or friend who had suffered a stroke.

A white-haired man in the back row raised his hand. He was dressed in a lumberman's shirt, clean but worn. He was very thin and had a long, weathered face. His name on the roster provided to the attorneys was listed as Henry Cavett.

"My wife had a stroke," he said, standing.

The judge nodded. "She died from it as I recall."

"She was in the hospital, then the nursing home," he said. "Didn't do any good."

"If the mental capacity of one who suffered a stroke should become an issue here, could you reach a fair and just verdict?"

Sage was suddenly on his feet. "Judge, I don't wish to intrude on the court's prerogative, but I wonder if you could ask Mr. Cavett if the stroke had the effect of—"

"Sit down!" Vinson's sharp words startled the courtroom. "I'll do the questioning, Mr. Sage. I don't want you proposing a question that in effect tries this case."

"Judge," he said evenly, "that's not my intention. I merely want to know—"

She cracked the gavel hard. "Sit down, Mr. Sage. If you have questions, put them in writing to me, as we agreed."

He shrugged, as if to imply he was being muzzled, then slowly and reluctantly sat down.

"Mr. Cavett, my question to you was—"

"My wife was a vegetable." His voice was a whisper, almost inaudible. "She had no capacity for anything. If something like that might come up in evidence, I wouldn't be able to keep the memory of the way she was out of my mind."

"So you might not be able to reach an impartial verdict?"

"That's right," he said.

Jake was on his feet.

But Vinson spoke before he could even open his mouth. "Are you going to challenge for cause?"

"Yes, I am."

Sage got up again. "Judge, I don't think cause has been shown here. Obviously, Mr. Cavett has suffered through watching his beloved wife languish horribly, her mind destroyed. But he is a fair man. I don't think—"

"One more word," she snapped, "and you will be in deep trouble, Mr. Sage. You'll have ample opportunity to make all the speeches you want, but not while we're picking a jury. Have your witnesses do the testifying, not you. This is my courtroom and we will play by my rules. Is that understood?"

Sage bowed ceremoniously. "If I've offended, I apologize. It's simply that the matter is so important to my client. I—" He stopped, as the judge's eyes narrowed into dangerous slits. "Thank you for your patience," he said, sitting down.

"You're excused, Henry," the judge said to Cavett.

Cavett nodded and quickly made his way past the other seated prospective jurors.

She directed her gaze to Jake. "Look, let's not do this piecemeal. Hold your challenges, both of you, until I'm finished."

The clerk called another name. A young, timid woman took the seat just vacated by Cavett. She was sworn by the clerk, stating she would answer all questions truthfully.

"You heard the questions I put to these other people. Would your answers be the same?"

The woman nodded. "Yes."

"Ever work for the Darens?"

"No."

"Ever have a friend or relative stricken by a stroke?"

The young woman shook her head. "No."

Jake, concentrating on what was happening, forgot his anxiety as the selection process continued. He tried to guess the attitude of each prospective juror, if not by their answers then by body language, as they made their responses. After each round of questions Jake was doing most of the challenging, while Sage had challenged only four people. Jake was running out of pre-emptory challenges and he guarded like gold the few he had left. Without the ability to challenge, he would become defenseless.

Earlier, Jake had submitted several written questions to the judge. She used some but discarded others without offering any reason. As the morning wore on, Sage, who had submitted no questions, seemed to grow more relaxed. Jake wondered if he was making some terrible mistake in the jury selection. Sage seemed too much at ease.

Jake finally ran out of pre-emptory challenges when he excused a stout woman whom he thought had glanced with guarded hostility at Elizabeth Daren, although the woman verbally assured the judge she had no prejudice toward anyone in the case. He looked at his watch. It was just a few minutes after twelve. He was surprised at how fast the morning had gone.

The stout woman was replaced by an even larger woman, but at least the new candidate didn't throw daggers at anyone. She seemed pleasant enough, and was obviously thrilled to be called to the jury box. Her answers were all quite innocuous.

When the judge was finished, she looked directly at Jake and then at T. G. Sage, as Jake wondered if Sage might now exercise some of the challenges he had so carefully hoarded.

The courtroom became strangely hushed. Fourteen people waited quietly. Eight women and six men. Most of them were middle-aged but there was one young man and one young woman. Dressed neatly, but plainly, they seemed like ordinary, hardworking people. They were serious, almost solemn, and gave no clue as to what they might be thinking.

Sage stood up and slowly walked to a point directly in front of the proposed jury. Jake watched as Sage studied them as someone might inspect a painting at an exhibition. Sage took a few silent seconds looking at each juror in turn. Some of them looked away, embarrassed. Sage nodded slowly, then turned to the judge.

"I find this panel quite acceptable," he said, his firm voice echoing slightly.

"Well?" Judge Vinson stared at Jake.

Jake debated imitating Sage, but decided he couldn't carry it off. He had exhausted his pre-emptory challenges, and he knew he could not challenge for cause without a good legal reason.

Now it was Jake's turn to stand. "We accept the jury."

"Swear 'em," the judge commanded her clerk. The fourteen stood as the clerk read off the juror's oath from the small card she held in her hand.

"Sit down," the judge commanded as soon as the clerk finished.

"Fourteen of you have been selected, but only twelve will ultimately decides this case. Two of you, so to speak, are along for the ride. Like spare tires, we swear two people extra to serve as alternate jurors in case someone gets ill or for some other reason has to be excused. Presuming that all fourteen of you are still aboard when this case is completely finished, we'll hold a drawing. The clerk will draw two names and those two people will be excused. The remaining twelve will have the duty of deciding the facts in this case."

She paused. "We will start every morning at nine o'clock sharp. You will come directly to this courtroom and assemble in the jury room over there." She indicated a doorway at the other side of the bench. "Unless I tell you otherwise, we'll have an hour for lunch and then we'll work until four every afternoon."

She paused, then continued. "Eagle County isn't large and I think most of you know me and you know I mean what I say. I don't want you discussing this case at home, no matter how tempting that might be. If your friends or relatives want to know what's happening, tell them to come down and watch. And I don't want you talking about this case among yourselves or reading about it in the newspapers. If anyone approaches you in connection with this case for any reason, I want you to tell me immediately. Otherwise, just mind your own business and listen to the testimony. Don't jump to any conclusions until you hear the whole thing. When all this is over and all the evidence is before you, then you'll have all the time you need to meet and decide. But nothing until then." She glared at them. Some of them nodded in response.

Vinson glanced at her watch. "It's twelve-thirty. I want everyone back here by one-thirty, sharp."

The clerk rapped the gavel and everyone stood as Judge Vinson got up and left the bench, leaving the courtroom to erupt into conversation, noise and muted but nervous laughter.

Jake felt the panic return as reality hit him: the trial was actually about to begin. In precisely one hour he would have to address a jury for the first time in his life.

Sage looked over at Jake and grinned. "There's something absolutely exhilarating about the start of a trial," he said, with great good humor. "Don't you think?"

"That's one way of looking at it," Jake replied, noticing that once again his mouth felt exactly like cotton.

The crowd milled about as they slowly made their way out of the courtroom, again reminding Jake of a Broadway audience, this time leaving the theatre during intermission. They chatted quietly among themselves, an audience that had just been pleasantly entertained.

Elizabeth, Bellows and Cora Simpson had remained seated. As

he approached them, Jake met Elizabeth's eyes for an instant. He couldn't possibly imagine what she was thinking.

"That was awfully quick," Bellows said, his tone slightly disapproving. "I'm rather leery of the looks of some of the people on that jury."

"I ran out of challenges, as you could see."

Bellows stood up and stretched. "Well, you did your best, Jake," he said. "Like it or not, we're stuck with them."

"What do you think of the jurors, Jake?" Elizabeth asked.

"It's hard to say. They look like they'll take their job seriously, or at least most of them do. They reflect this community. Up here, people are used to a hardscrabble life, and it may be hard for them to relate to the kind of money involved in this case." He smiled. "Fortunately, both sides are rich, so if there's any prejudice against wealth at least it's balanced."

"Elizabeth has been kind enough to have invited us all to lunch," Bellows said, ever the well-mannered gentleman.

"I think I'll take a pass," Jake replied, looking at Elizabeth. "I'd like some more time to prepare for this afternoon."

"Don't be silly, Jake," Bellows said. "Just tell the jury that Augustus Daren signed his will according to law. That's our case. Don't try Sage's case for him. Keep it simple. After that, you call Dr. Faraday."

"I still think I need some time."

"As you wish." Bellows smiled, but his eyes were cold.

Cora Simpson waited behind as Bellows escorted Elizabeth toward the door.

"It's amazing, Jake. You actually looked like you knew what you were doing."

He smiled at her compliment. "I'm like a blind man in a sandstorm, Cora. But if I give off an impression of competence I consider that an honest-to-God miracle."

"Well, miracle or not, I'm impressed."

"Thanks."

She paused, looking around the empty courtroom, unsure if she should say more. When she spoke, her voice was barely audible. "Maybe I shouldn't tell you this, but Bellows is second-guessing everything you do, as if he disapproves."

"Oh?"

"He doesn't say anything to me, but I can hear him whispering to Elizabeth."

"If he doesn't like what I'm doing, why doesn't he try this case himself?"

"Don't get sore at me," she said. "Just be careful. Okay?"

"Yeah. Thanks, Cora."

"Good luck," she said as she hurried to join the others.

Jake waited until almost everyone else had left. The sheriff was still posted at the courtroom door.

"Most of what passes for restaurants up here will be filled," the sheriff said as Jake prepared to leave. "If you want to get back here in time, Jenkins over at the Eagle Inn will send a sandwich up to your room."

"I'm going to skip lunch."

"Nervous?" The sheriff grinned.

"No," Jake lied. "I seldom eat lunch."

The sheriff closed the courtroom door after him. "Be back in an hour. The judge can be real fussy about that."

"I'm just going for a walk."

"Mind you stay in town, eh?"

"Why?"

The sheriff shrugged. "Just a precaution."

"Did you warn T. G. Sage too?"

"I didn't think he needed it, given all the circumstances."

The smile had vanished from the sheriff's face.

"See you back here in an hour."

"This place hasn't changed a single bit. God, what a dump," Gussie said as T. G. Sage escorted both Darens into the Eagle Inn's restaurant. "How can you bear to stay here?"

Sage politely nodded his appreciation to the hotel owner, who had saved them a table in the crowded restaurant. Sage held a chair for Gussie.

A waitress took their order and then departed.

"Gussie's right," Chip Daren grumbled, looking around. "This joint was a wreck when I was a kid and it's just gotten worse. I'll get a room for you where we're staying. It's early American tourist, but anything would be better than this."

Sage chuckled. "My temporary lodging here is not without purpose. Trying a jury case in a strange place is a lawyer's nightmare. Every town has its own set of taboos, quirks, preferences and prejudices, and a jury reflects each and all of them. By staying here, I'm soaking up a little of the true essence of Gladding, so to speak."

"Maybe you should have hired a local guy to help you," Chip said, scowling. "You still could."

"Fortunately, the other side is as foreign to this place as I am. And the elitist lawyers of Sperling Beekman aren't the kind to hang around the local bar, buying drinks and wiggling their way into the natives' confidence. Something that I'm not above."

"When do you think this'll be over?" Gussie asked. "It's so utterly boring."

Sage eyed her for a moment, then smiled. "I think I can promise you that it won't be boring from here on in."

All three fell silent as their meals were served.

"I don't like the look of that jury," Chip said, after the waitress departed.

Sage bit into the hamburger, chewed a bit, then spoke. "A jury is always an intriguing enigma, a mystery. I don't care how much investigation is done or background checks made, you can never really predict what a jury will do."

Chip glared at him. "I thought you were supposed to be the Merlin of juries, goddamn it."

Sage munched on his hamburger then sipped his tea. "Merlin, at least according to legend, had help: stars, bones, the whispers of woodland spirits. Even with all that, his powers weren't boundless. I have no spells or powders to help me along, just my own nimble wits." He took another bite. "In a lawsuit, there are never any guarantees."

"I hope you realize what's on the line here," Chip almost shouted, managing to whine and be impudent both at the same time.

"I do," Sage replied, smiling, "and I'd keep my voice down if I were you, unless you want to solicit the opinion of the people at the surrounding tables." This time the smile was gone. "I will do my very best. You insisted on my taking this case, as you'll recall, and you also insisted that we hurry to trial without benefit of discovery. With an order for discovery I would have been able to look into their documents, examine their proposed exhibits and interview their witnesses. Now, as per your instructions, I am flying blind. I told you then, and I'll tell you now: any risk is entirely yours. I have the statement you signed to that effect, in case your memory needs refreshing."

Chip glowered at his food, but didn't reply.

"I don't see why in hell you need me up here," Gussie said. "This is an enormous waste of my time."

"It helps if the jury can see you at your brother's side," Sage said. "The concept of family can be critical. This jury may not understand the fine points of international banking or the control of billions of dollars, but families are something they know about."

"So, what happens now?" Chip asked.

"Jake Martin will introduce your father's will."

"Can't you stop that?"

Sage sipped his tea. "It's merely put into play, so to speak. He then has to establish your father's signature, through the witnesses to the will. Dr. Faraday is in the courtroom, so we'll proceed with him, since the elusive Ms. Janus seems to have disappeared."

"She's at our motel," Gussie said.

Sage raised an eyebrow, then turned and looked at Chip.

"She just turned up," Chip said, his tone falsely innocent. "I got her a room where we're staying. I have a car and driver standing by there. I told her to wait in her room until I called."

213

"Why?" Sage asked.

Chip looked away. "It just seemed like a good idea."

"Obviously, Mr. Martin is denied the opportunity of talking to her before she takes the stand this way." Sage nodded to the waitress and signaled for the bill. "Should the judge discover that you have hidden away a key witness, you and this case will be in a great deal of trouble. Putting ethics side, what you're doing isn't very smart. I want you to make that call immediately."

"You know what? You worry too much," Chip said.

Sage stood up. He was smiling so that anyone watching him would think it was just the end of a congenial lunch, but his quiet words cut like steel. "Get Rhonda Janus here," he said. "I don't know where she's been, and I don't want to know. That's your business. But I know where she is now, and I am demanding that you get her here as quickly as possible."

"Look, Sage—"

"Or get yourself another lawyer," Sage said, cutting him off. "Is that clear enough?"

"Chip, stop being an asshole for once in your life. He's only asking you to make a telephone call."

Chip Daren's face flushed with anger, but he said nothing. Then, reluctantly, he nodded his agreement.

"Shall we get back?" Sage said, cheerfully. "I rather look forward to a very interesting afternoon."

19

Time, Jake thought, had passed much too quickly. He had attempted to focus his mind on the task ahead, to plan out exactly what he would say to the jury, but somehow nothing definite had seemed to jell.

Now he returned to the courtroom, which was once again filled to capacity. His heart began to race. He tried to remember when, if ever, he had spoken in public. All he could recall were the few times the professors in law school had required him to stand and discuss an assigned case. And all he could recall about those experiences was feeling extremely uncomfortable.

He was acutely aware of the throng of seated spectators. Media people were clustered around the assigned press table and in extra chairs set out for them around the perimeter of the courtroom. Judge Vinson was on the bench and all fourteen jurors were seated.

The air was charged with an unnaturally hushed expectancy.

"You may begin, Mr. Martin," the judge said.

Jake stood up and walked a few steps in front of the counsel table, fully aware that his palms were clenched and moist. He forced himself to turn to the jury.

Each of them was watching him with fierce intensity. It was as if they expected him to perform some unusual trick, one they didn't want to miss by looking away at the wrong time.

"Your honor," Jake said, glancing at Judge Vinson, then turning to the jury. "Members of the jury. In this case —"

"Speak up!" The judge's voice cracked like a cannon shot in the surprised silence of the packed courtroom. "It won't do you any good to talk if no one can hear what you have to say."

Jake wondered if his face was as red as it felt. He took a deep breath and began again, this time in a voice that sounded to him artificially loud. "Ladies and gentlemen of the jury," he said, "we are presenting to you the last will and testament of Augustus J. Daren—"

"Mr. Martin," the judge snapped. "These people aren't deaf. Do you only have two settings—whisper and shout?"

Jake saw that all the members of the jury grinned, and the heavy woman, the one last selected, giggled.

"Try something in between those two extremes, Mr. Martin."

Jake swallowed hard and nodded. "As I began to say, we are presenting Augustus Daren's last will for probate." He paused, wondering if the judge might make another comment. Nothing was forthcoming, so he continued. "A testator, that's the person who makes the will, must be shown to have intended the offered instrument to be a will; that is, the direction of what is to be done after death with the property he or she possesses."

As Sage's book suggested, Jake tried to look directly at each one of the jurors as he spoke, moving from one face to another.

"The law in this state requires that a will, in order to be valid, must be signed by the testator in front of two witnesses. The law also provides that these two people sign the document as witnesses to the signature."

Jake tried to read from their faces what kind of a reaction he might be having, but their expressions could only be seen as opaque, as though they'd been painted on.

"We will show you, ladies and gentlemen, that Augustus Daren intended the document we offer to be his last will and testament and that he properly signed it in front of two witnesses who also signed as required by law. We ask you to so find, so that the will can be admitted into probate and that Mr. Daren's property be distributed according to his directions."

The statement, given what was at stake, seemed inadequately short, but Jake couldn't think of anything more to say. He was required to stick with the facts and not argue. Jake tried to smile.

"Thank you," he said. He was aware of muted whisperings in the audience. To him, it sounded not unlike the buzzing of insects.

Jake was painfully aware of how awkward he felt as he returned to his seat at the counsel table.

"Mr. Sage," the judge said, "Do you wish to reserve your opening statement until you are ready to present your witnesses?"

Sage stood up. Jake noted that unlike himself Sage seemed entirely at ease. He walked slowly to the front of the bench and looked up at the judge.

"Usually, your honor, I would reserve my remarks until later, but I think Mr. Martin has deliberately attempted to mislead this jury, so I feel I must speak now."

Jake was on his feet, even though he didn't know exactly what to say. But he knew he couldn't let Sage's remark pass unchallenged.

The judge held up her hand. "Mr. Martin is about to object to those remarks of yours as being improperly argumentative," she said to Sage. "And I will sustain him even before he opens his mouth. If you wish to make an opening statement, Mr. Sage, just say so. Reserve any speeches until the proper time."

"Your honor, I am just trying—"

"Either make your opening statement or sit down!"

As he turned to the jury, Sage's smile was sad, silently expressing his sorrow that truth and justice were being unfairly denied. He stood before them, arms folded across his chest, slowly, almost imperceptibly rocking on the balls of his feet. Sage was no longer smiling.

"Allow me to tell you a little something about myself before I begin. The judge introduced both myself and Mr. Martin, but all you know about us, of course, is merely our names. I am T. G. Sage, an attorney. I have a one-man law office in Detroit. I was born in Michigan and I worked my way through a Detroit city law school. I take all kinds of cases in my practice: criminal, civil, anything and everything. You can see that I'm not a young man. I've been trying cases all my adult life. Win or lose, I try to do my best in every case I try."

Sage gestured at Jake. "My opponent is with the prestigious and very large law firm of Sperling Beekman, arguably the best firm of attorneys in Michigan, perhaps even the country. They employ only the cream of the crop, from the best law schools the country has to offer. Mr. Martin, originally from New York City, is a graduate of the celebrated Ivy League college, Columbia University.

"Sperling Beekman and Mr. Martin, their star trial lawyer, represent the Daren estate, an estate I might add that totals over a half-billion dollars. Of course, Sperling Beekman and Mr. Martin are accustomed to representing clients with that kind of money."

Jake suspected that Sage's remarks were probably improper, but he didn't know exactly what to say to stop him.

"I am just one man," Sage continued, and I represent the son of Augustus J. Daren, just one of the heirs. Obviously, I don't have the vast legal resources that Sperling Beekman can command. So I ask you that as this trial progresses you remember that, and make allowances for the rather unequal contest that you are about—"

"Objection!" Jake was on his feet. "This isn't exactly David and Goliath. Mr. Sage earns more in one year that I expect to make in my lifetime. I don't know what he's trying to pull—"

"You see," Sage interrupted, "how clever these New Yorkers can be? They will try to twist—"

The judge's gavel cracked into life like a rifle shot.

"Both of you will be silent. I want a side bar conference and I want it now!"

Sage gave the jury another sad look and a shrug, then he followed Jake to the far side of the bench. Vinson wheeled her chair forward so that she could be close to the attorneys and their conversation not overheard.

"I want this business stopped," she said.

"I thought it pretty outrageous," Sage whispered.

"Not him, Ted. You!"

"Why, judge, I'm just a poor lawyer trying—"

"You're a bullshit artist, Ted. I want this two-bit stuff cut right now. You might be able to get away with that 'poor lawyer' crap in Detroit, but not here."

She looked at Jake. "From now on, young man, you will state a legal reason for any objection you make, and you'll state it to me; not the jury, not Sage, nor anyone else. I rule on objections here. Got that?"

Jake nodded.

"All right," she growled. "Let's go back to work."

Jake returned to his seat and Sage took his place in front of the jury.

"Let the record show that Mr. Martin's objection is sustained," the judge said evenly. "Proceed to something else, Mr. Sage."

Sage's saintly expression seemed to indicate that despite the judge's words, he had at least won some kind of moral victory. He bowed slightly to the jury and then spoke.

"Mr. Martin described the Michigan law covering the making a will correctly, but he skipped by a very essential point; perhaps the most important point of all."

Jake remembered reading Sage's book about opening statements. He stood up. "Objection," he said. "This isn't a statement of what Mr. Sage expects to prove, this is pure argument, nothing else,"

"Sustained," the judge snapped.

Sage seemed entirely unruffled by the interruption. "We will prove to you, members of the jury, that the most essential element of all is missing in what my opponent claims to be a last will. We will

217

show you that when the late Augustus J. Daren signed the claimed will he was mentally incompetent to do so. We will show by sworn witnesses that the once healthy, robust banker had been so devastated by a major stroke that he had been robbed of the mental capacity to make a will."

"Objection," Jake said, standing. "He was competent."

The judge threw up her hands. "Now you're arguing, Mr. Martin. I won't tolerate objections that are used to circumvent the rules. Sit down."

Jake eased himself back into the chair.

"That objection, if you can call it that," the judge said, "is overruled."

Sage turned to the judge. "Thank you, your honor." Then he looked again at the jury. "We will show you, with the witnesses who saw him and with medical experts, that on the day the will was signed, Augustus Daren no longer knew what he was doing."

Sage paused, again rocking slightly on the balls of his feet. "It's sad, isn't it, when a vibrant, intelligent man suffers what amounts to an explosion in the blood vessels of his brain? We call that a stroke. Some of you may have seen what terrible things a stroke can do. Oh, sometimes, for the lucky ones, the damage isn't extensive and they make a complete recovery. But some strokes rob the victim of his very personality and take away the power to think. We will show you," Sage said, his voice becoming suddenly sharp and dramatic, "that Augustus Daren had lost the power to think when he was helped to make a scrawl that is being passed off here as a signature."

"Objection," Jake said, then added, "argumentative."

"Sustained."

"Perhaps I might state it another way," Sage said, in a calmer voice. "We will show that Augustus Daren had no idea what he was signing on that day." He paused. It lasted so long that Jake wondered if he had stopped. Then Sage spoke again. "Then why go through this charade of making a will, if the man didn't know what he was doing? It's a reasonable question, isn't it?"

Sage stopped, walked to the counsel table and poured a glass of water from the carafe provided, drank some, then spoke from where he stood. "We will show that an evil conspiracy existed, a conspiracy designed to steal control of one of this nation's major banks, a conspiracy to use the hand of a dying man as the chief tool to carry out that attempted theft."

"I object," Jake shouted, standing.

"To what?" Sage rasped. "The truth?"

The judge rapped the gavel like a machine gun. Sage bowed to her, then the jury. He frowned at Jake and then sat down.

"That's quite enough, Mr. Sage. I caution you both." The judge's voice was so strained by anger that her words were barely audible. "Any more of this bickering and I will deal with it in the harshest terms. Understood?" Vinson glared at both lawyers. "We'll take a ten-minute break," she said, then hurried from the bench.

Everyone stood and the jury was escorted to the jury room.

"What the hell are you trying to pull?" Jake angrily demanded of Sage.

T. G. Sage's face split into a wide grin. "Pull? Why, my dear young man, this is what they call an adversarial proceeding. And, I might add, this is only the beginning."

"You're doing a good job, Jake." Bellows' tone carried no genuine enthusiasm as Jake walked back to talk to Elizabeth during the break. Elizabeth's smile seemed tentative, as if she were unsure of the job he was doing for her.

Most of the courtroom spectators had remained during the break, afraid to leave and risk losing their seats. Jake followed the gaze of some of the spectators and watched as a redheaded woman was escorted to a seat in the front of the courtroom by the sheriff. Her tan was so deep that her skin tone rivaled the rich mahogany of the courtroom. Her yellow and red summer dress was more suited to the beach than to the northern Michigan autumn climate.

It was then that Jake recognized her. "Rhonda Janus just came in," he said.

Bellows smiled. "I told you she'd show up."

Rhonda Janus glanced briefly at Elizabeth and then quickly turned away.

"I had better go talk to her," Jake said. "Excuse me."

"Miss Janus, do you remember me?"

She smiled coldly, as if responding to an unwelcome intrusion, then shook her head.

"I'm afraid not."

"I'm Jake Martin. I was the attorney who came up to Raven's Nest to have Mr. Daren sign the will."

She inspected him with new interest, then nodded. "Oh, yes. I didn't recognize you. You seem older than I remember."

Jake shrugged. "That's what comes with fast living. We've been trying to reach you."

"I've been on vacation," she said.

"Who contacted you?"

Her smile was just a trifle too bright. "No one. I read about it in the newspapers. I knew I'd probably be wanted as a witness, so here I am."

"No one contacted you?"

She shook her head. "No."

"Have you talked to anyone about this case?"

"No."

"Not even T. G. Sage, the attorney for Chip Daren?"

"Sage? No, I don't even know the man."

"How about Chip? Did you talk to him?"

She frowned. "Are you being unpleasant?"

"No. Just curious."

She looked away. "I haven't talked to anyone. I'm just here to do my duty, that's all.

From the stirring in the courtroom, Jake sensed that the clerk had taken her place in front of the bench, a signal that the judge was about to come back in.

"May I talk with you when we're finished here today?"

"I'm exhausted," she said. "Perhaps some other time."

"It won't take long," Jake persisted.

She paused, then she turned and looked directly at him. "Maybe tomorrow," she said.

"You'll probably be on the stand tomorrow. It's important that we talk before that. Can you see me for a few minutes tonight?"

The gavel announced the entrance of the judge. Everyone stood.

Rhonda Janus did not answer; she just smiled. It was a forced smile.

"Bring in the jury," he judge said.

Jake was surprised when T. G. Sage made no objection to the introduction of the will as an exhibit. Jake thought that offering the will into evidence would have provided an excuse for some dramatic theatrics from Sage, but he merely glanced at the will, then handed it back as though the document had no real meaning or importance.

The clerk marked the will as an exhibit.

"It's your party at this point, Mr. Martin," the judge said. "Let's get going."

Jake nodded. "I would like to call Doctor Milo Faraday, who was a witness to the will."

Faraday stood up, eased his way past several of the spectators and then crossed the courtroom to the witness stand. He moved with slow dignity, as if performing some priestly rite. The clerk, who looked more nervous than Jake felt, swore him in, and then Faraday settled himself in the witness chair.

Jake, uncomfortable once more at being the center of attention, took a deep breath to steady himself.

"What is your name?"

"Milo Faraday."

"You are a medical doctor, is that correct?"

"Yes."

"Doctor, allow me to show you a document." Jake took the will from the clerk and handed it to the doctor.

Faraday examined it carefully, slowly turning the pages, then he looked up.

"Have you seen that document before?"

"I have."

"And is that your signature on the last page?"

Faraday nodded. "It is."

"And did you witness the late Augustus J. Daren sign that document on the date it bears?"

"I did."

"And did you sign it in his presence and the presence of Rhonda Janus, the other witness?"

"I did." Faraday said.

Jake decided not to risk any more questions. He had shown that the will was signed according to law, nothing more was required. He turned to Sage, remembering the suggested ritual words contained in Sage's own book on trial procedure. "You may take the witness."

Sage nodded, then got up slowly.

"You said you are a medical doctor. I presume you are licensed to practice in the state of Michigan?"

"I am," Faraday replied.

Sage slowly walked to the end of the jury box, then faced the witness again. "Do you have a specialty, Doctor?"

"I do. I am a board-certified neurologist."

"And what is a neurologist?"

Faraday looked over at the jury. A superior smile indicated he was about to impart vital knowledge. "A physician who specializes in diseases of the nervous system is called a neurologist."

"Diseases of the nervous system. Would strokes, to use a lay term, come under your jurisdiction, so to speak?"

Faraday nodded. "Yes."

"Did you treat Augustus Daren prior to his death?"

"Yes."

"In fact you were hired to do that full time, isn't that correct, doctor?"

Jake stood up. "I object. This is all very interesting but it isn't relevant. Doctor Faraday is here to testify merely as a witness to the execution of the will."

Sage looked up at the judge. "The competency of Augustus Daren is an area that is most relevant, if the court please. Mr. Martin has brought the treating physician—a specialist—here as a witness, and his observations could be very helpful to the members of the jury on the key question of whether Mr. Daren knew what he was doing or not."

"Dr. Faraday was called as a witness to the will. Mr. Sage is trying to use him for another purpose."

The judge shook her head. "There's no law against that, at least none that I know about. Objection overruled."

"You were hired to treat Mr. Daren full time, is that right?" Sage repeated.

"Originally I was one of a team of physicians who treated Mr. Daren when he was first admitted to the intensive care ward for what you term a stroke. Later, Mrs. Daren asked me to consider staying with her husband after he was released from the hospital."

"And did you?"

"Yes."

"Up here? At the Darens' home, Raven's Nest?"

Faraday nodded. "That's correct."

"Did you live with the Darens?"

"Yes."

"Doctor, did you see Augustus Daren every day while you lived at Raven's Nest?"

Faraday paused. "Well, I attended two medical conferences during that period, just a few days each time. I was away then, but other than that, yes, I saw him every day."

"And Mrs. Daren, too?"

"I saw her every day, with the exception of those two short conferences I mentioned."

"How about holidays?" Sage asked.

Faraday shrugged. "I spent them up here. I'm single and I have no children. My brother and sister live in other states."

"Did you exchange gifts with the Darens at Christmas?"

Jake stood up. "Objection. This line of questioning has absolutely nothing to do with the issues in this matter."

"How about that, Mr. Sage?" the judge asked. "You do seem to be wandering a bit."

Sage chuckled. "At my age, I do wander once in a while, but this isn't one of the times. I want to establish that Dr. Faraday was considered almost a member of the Daren family while he lived with them up here. He saw Augustus Daren not just in the doctor-patient relationship: he had an opportunity to observe him much more frequently and closely than that, and in much more depth."

Judge Vinson frowned. "Well, I'll overrule the objection at this point, but unless you try to get quickly back to the issue I will shut you off. Understood?"

Sage nodded. "Thank you."

He turned once more to Faraday. "Mr. Daren suffered a second stroke, did he not? More serious than the first?"

"Yes," Faraday said. "They were about a year apart. The second cerebral vascular accident left Mr. Daren in a completely comatose state."

"Was he able to communicate after that second stroke?"

Faraday shook his head. "No. As a matter of fact, he couldn't function without the help of machines. He was in a coma. We provided nourishment, oxygen, everything necessary to life by tube and machine."

"He was, was he not, clinically dead?"

"Objection," Jake said, rising. "None of this pertains to what's at issue here. It isn't relevant."

"Sustained," the judge said. "Mr. Martin is right. What might have happened after the execution of the will has no bearing on the questions you raise."

Sage paused, as if he was considering arguing the point, then he nodded and looked again at Faraday.

"All right, Doctor, let's talk only about Augustus Daren before that second stroke. Was Daren on medication after the first stroke?"

Faraday nodded. "Yes. We had him on blood thinners, and tranquilizers."

"Tranquilizers?" Sage asked.

"Valium, mostly," Faraday answered. "Mr. Daren often became agitated. That, by the way, isn't an unusual condition in stroke patients. We kept the Valium dose at five milligrams, no more than three times a day."

"You say 'we'. Were other doctors involved?"

Faraday smiled. "Sorry. No, it's just my manner of speaking. I was his only physician during that time."

"Did Mr. Daren drink alcohol after the first stroke?"

Faraday paused before speaking. "Well, I advised against it, but he insisted on two martinis before dinner. Sometimes he had an after-dinner brandy."

"Even while he was on the medication?"

"Well, I wasn't in favor of it, of course. But I was his doctor, not his keeper."

"Did it affect him?"

"Objection," Jake said. "That's calling for an opinion."

Sage snapped at Jake. "He was the treating physician. If he can't give an informed opinion, who can?"

The judge sat forward. "Mr. Sage, if you have something to say, say it to me. It's my job to make rulings, not Mr. Martin."

Sage looked up at her. "Dr. Faraday is a nationally known neurologist. He was in daily contact with August Daren, watching him for the purpose of monitoring his physical condition. The doctor obviously knows the effect that drugs may have on people. He was there. I want to know if Augustus Daren's mental capacity was affected by either tranquilizers, alcohol, or the two mixed together."

The judge shook her head. "There's nothing in evidence yet upon which to base an opinion. I'll sustain the objection until you have laid a proper foundation."

Sage's expression, usually placid, now reflected irritation. "You mean you want me to question him about what Daren did? Did he stagger, slur his words, is that what you mean by a foundation?"

The judge's eyes narrowed. "That's exactly what I mean, and you know it. Get on with it or surrender the witness."

Sage sighed. "During your time at Raven's Nest did you ever see Augustus Daren stagger?"

Faraday nodded. "Almost all the time. The man had suffered a partial paralysis on the left side of his body. He dragged his left foot. Some days the degree of impairment seemed worse than others. However, walking was always a problem for him."

"Did these impairments ever become worse after taking those two martinis you spoke of?"

"Wait a minute?" Jake said. "The witness just got through saying it happened all the time. Mr. Sage is suggesting an answer to the witness."

Judge Vinson peered down at Jake. "Has the phrase 'wait a minute' replaced the word 'objection'? Or is that what you meant?"

"That's what I meant," Jake said. "If Mr. Sage is going to testify, let him be sworn."

Jake secretly rejoiced in remembering the phrase in Sage's book.

"I'll sustain the objection, if that's what it was."

Sage merely nodded. He looked again at Faraday. "Doctor, did you ever see any physical change in Gus Daren after he had the martinis?"

"He got a little tipsy."

"Objection," Jake said, enjoying his newfound power. "That's too subjective to have any meaning."

The judge smirked. "I know what being tipsy is; so does the jury. That's good enough for me. Overruled."

Sage walked slowly forward. Each member of the jury watched him as he positioned himself directly in front of the witness.

"Augustus Daren was the chairman of the board of Hanover Square Bank, was he not?"

"Yes"

"Did he run the affairs of his bank while you were living up here with the Darens?"

"Mrs. Daren ran everything," Faraday said.

"Objection," Jake said. "This has no bearing on anything before this court."

"Your honor," Sage said, this time speaking with vigor. "I will show that Mrs. Daren ran the bank because Augustus Daren was mentally incompetent to do so. I will show this court and this jury that he lacked the ability to conduct his own affairs, including making any will or other testamentary deposition."

The judge stopped him by raising her hand like a crossing guard. "Hold your argument for the end of the trial," she said to Sage, then turned to Jake. "You got off the mark too slow for a timely objection. The question has been answered. Anyway, I would have overruled you, so I'll let it stand." She nodded to Sage to continue.

"Doctor," he said, turning back to the witness, "did you ever observe Mr. Daren having problems with his concentration?"

"Objection," Jake said, standing. "That's a leading question."

The judge raised an eyebrow. "He's cross-examining. He can ask leading questions on cross-examination. Overruled."

Sage waited for Faraday's answer.

Faraday shifted slightly, then spoke. "Mr. Daren didn't watch television because he said he couldn't follow the story line. A half-hour show seemed beyond his ability—he couldn't remember the characters or what had happened. Even sports seemed too much for him. This inability to concentrate and the failure of his memory—sometimes he couldn't even remember who I was—frustrated him terribly. It made him so irritable that he sometimes came to the point of tears. That caused him to become more and more withdrawn."

"These . . . ah . . . failures of concentration and memory, did they improve or sometimes became worse?"

"At times he would become almost childlike," Faraday said.

"How was he on the day he signed the alleged will?"

Faraday shrugged. "It was not one of his better days. I think he thought we were gathering for a birthday party for him."

"Was it his birthday?" Sage asked.

Faraday shook his head and smiled. "No, not even close. It was a delusion."

"A delusion? How often would he have delusions?"

Jake jumped to his feet. "Just a minute, Doctor." He turned to the judge. "I object. He's asking two questions at once. We won't know which one the doctor might be answering."

"Sustained."

Sage's only response before he continued was a noncommittal shrug of his shoulders. "What's a delusion, Doctor?"

"It is a persistent belief for which there is no evidence."

"Like a hallucination?"

"No. A hallucination usually implies seeing something that isn't there or hearing a nonexistent sound. A delusion is quite different. If you believed you were the king of France, that would be a delusion. A delusion adversely affects judgment. A deluded person loses the grip on reality we all must have."

"So if Augustus Daren believed he was at a birthday party, he was suffering from a delusion?"

"Yes."

"Did you ever observe him when he suffered other delusions?"

"Yes. He believed he was in the process of building an international banking network. It preoccupied his thinking."

"Well, he was a banker," Sage said.

"But he wasn't running his business," Faraday continued. "His wife, acting in his name, took full charge of all his business

225

activities. Mr. Daren sincerely believed he was in charge, but that was a delusion."

"On the day he signed the will, did he know what he was doing?"

"In my opinion, he did not."

Sage paused, his silence serving to emphasize the doctor's damaging answer. Slowly he walked back to the counsel table and took his seat. "Your witness," he said quietly.

Any nervousness Jake had felt before was now eradicated by rising rage. He stood up and stalked to a place directly in front of Faraday.

"You signed the will as a witness, did you not?"

Faraday smiled. "Yes."

"Even though now you claim you knew Augustus Daren was suffering a delusion?"

"Objection, if the court pleases," Sage said, "He's cross-examining his own witness."

"Judge—"

Jake was cut off with an impatient wave from Judge Vinson. "The doctor was called as a witness to the will, nothing else. I don't think it would be fair to Mr. Martin to characterize the doctor as his witness. Objection overruled. Proceed, Mr. Martin."

Jake was flooded by a sense of relief. Direct examination limited the scope and style of questions. Cross-examination allowed much more latitude. Jake knew he lacked the experience to proceed if he had had to adhere to the narrow range allowed in direct examination.

"You did sign the will?" Jake asked.

"Yes. I already testified to that."

"Did you express to me, or to anyone, your reservations concerning Mr. Daren's mental competency?"

"No one asked me," he said. "Certainly you didn't."

"What held you back, Doctor? Shyness?"

Faraday's smug smile revealed him at the pinnacle of his sense of superiority. "I'm a doctor, not a lawyer. I presumed you people knew what you were doing. Mr. Daren's problems were patently observable that day. Anyone watching him knew he was incompetent."

"The signing of the will was videotaped. Do you recall that?"

"I remember a person with a video camera, yes. That tape would have clearly shown Daren's confused mental condition. I understand it's missing, unfortunately."

"Are you implying that we're withholding evidence?"

Faraday looked at Jake with a cold eye. "I'm not implying anything."

"Who told you the tape was missing?"

"You did," Faraday said.

"I don't recall that, Doctor."

"Objection. He's not questioning the witness," Sage interjected, "he's arguing with him."

"The question, if that's what it was, is argumentative," the judge said. "Sustained."

Jake recalled Sage's book regarding the tactics in cross-examination. It advised approaching a vulnerable side, a side where the witness might not be prepared or coached on what to say.

"You testified that you were a single man when you agreed to come up here and treat Mr. Daren. Is that true, Doctor?"

For the first time, Faraday's expression was briefly uncertain. "Well, perhaps I misspoke in a technical sense; I was being divorced at the time."

"What were you paid to attend Mr. Daren full time?"

"Objection," Sage said. "That's hardly material or relative to the issue here."

"It might be," the judge replied. "Overruled for the moment, Mr. Sage."

"What were you paid?"

"You must remember that I am a specialist, a board-certified—"

"What were you paid?" Jake raised his voice.

"Three hundred thousand a year."

Jake heard the audible gasps from the spectators.

"Was that in addition to room and board?"

The question provoked laughter from the spectators, but Judge Vinson ignored it.

Faraday was no longer smiling. "I lived there at Raven's Nest, if that's what you mean."

"Was anything additional promised you in the way of compensation?"

Faraday's face tightened. "There was a bonus."

"A bonus?"

"Objection," Sage said. "This isn't at all relevant to the issue here."

Judge Vinson shook her head. "We'll see. Overruled. Go ahead," she said to Jake.

"Tell us about this bonus, Doctor."

"It was an inducement to me to stay up here for a year," he said.

"Oh? And how much was this inducement?"

Faraday hesitated, then spoke. "Three hundred thousand."

Jake heard a new series of gasps from the spectators.

"Did you collect the bonus?"

"I did."

"You said you were going through a divorce at the time; did you declare the bonus as an asset in that proceeding?"

"Objection," Sage's voice had some real anger in it. "The doctor's divorce has absolutely nothing to do with this case."

"You aren't planning to try that case too, are you, Mr. Martin? I don't have jurisdiction over divorce." The judge's smile was without a trace of humor.

"I can tie it up with this case," Jake said. "Just a few more questions will do it."

Judge Vinson pursed her lips. "We'll see. Go on."

"Did you declare the bonus in the other matter?"

Faraday smirked. "No. Since it was not due me unless I put in a full year, according to my attorneys it wasn't an asset."

"When Mrs. Daren let you go," Jake asked, "were you given severance pay?"

"I wasn't let go, as you put it," Faraday snapped. "There was no reason for me to stay on."

"What were you paid, if anything, in addition to what you already received?"

"You must understand. I had given up my practice, and—"

"How much were you paid?" Jake interrupted.

"Three hundred thousand," Faraday said.

"You were at Raven's Nest almost two years, is that correct?"

"Yes."

"You were paid for both years?"

"I was."

"As I figure it, Doctor, you came away with over one million dollars for less than two years' employment, is that right?"

"I've already said that I gave up my practice. I was being compensated for that."

"Did anyone pay you anything to come here and testify?"

Faraday's eyes narrowed. "No," he said sharply. "No payment of any kind was made."

"How about a bonus? You seem to be rather fond of that sort of thing?"

Sage was shouting as the judge cracked her gavel.

"That will be quite enough, Mr. Martin. The objection is sustained."

Jake turned and walked to his seat. "Your witness," he said to Sage.

T. G. Sage sat for a full moment, intently studying Jake, who completely ignored him. Then he rose from his chair.

"Do you have anything more of this witness?" the judge asked.

"A bit more, if the court please."

"How long is a bit?"

Sage laughed. "Well, you know how those things are, your honor. It's always hard to predict. It could be a few minutes or perhaps an hour."

"It's after four o'clock," she said. "Can you return in the morning, doctor?"

Faraday nodded reluctantly. "If necessary."

"Good," the judge said, looking over at the jury. "Okay, we'll break for the day. Everyone will be back here tomorrow morning at nine sharp."

The clerk rapped her gavel as the judge left the bench.

Jake thought he had done well with Faraday until he turned and saw Donald Bellows glaring at him. Jake walked back to where Elizabeth, Cora and Bellows sat.

"What were you trying to accomplish with that little piece of business?" Bellows demanded in an angry whisper.

"I was trying to discredit him," Jake replied.

"You sounded like a cheap shyster," Bellows snapped. "We at Sperling Beekman never sink to that sort of thing." He stood up, pointedly turning away. "Well, I could certainly use a drink," Bellows said in a normal tone of voice. "Shall we adjourn to somewhere we can relax?"

20

Jake drove slowly out to Raven's Nest, where two uniformed guards now manned the entry station, both looking very military and alert. One of them waved him through.

The day had been unseasonably mild but, as darkness approached, the air had once again turned chilly. Much to his surprise, he saw Donald Bellows leaning against his big Mercedes. Bellows was obviously waiting for him.

He walked up as Jake climbed out of the Corvette.

"Jake, I'd like a word with you. Let's take a walk down to the lake, shall we?"

In his tailored overcoat, Bellows looked snug, but Jake felt the bite of the cold wind through his thin raincoat. He wished he'd remembered to pack the liner that went along with it, but at the time he'd had too much on his mind to think of such small details. He jammed his hands into his pockets and joined Bellows as he walked slowly down toward the water.

"I think Faraday may have done terminal damage to us today," Bellows said.

"I told you he might be an adverse witness," Jake replied. "Although I didn't think he'd change his story so radically. He came on a lot stronger in the witness chair than he did when I talked to him."

Bellows turned his collar up against the cold. "The problem is the delusion business. Did Faraday say anything about delusions to you?"

"Nothing."

"Delusion—this is the torpedo that may sink our ship. The law will wink at questions of questionable competency. If it didn't, every old person's will would be open to attack. A wandering mind, memory problems, concentration difficulties, the law will still generally presume a will valid even when that can be shown."

Jake nodded. He had read all the cases.

"But in Michigan, an insane delusion constitutes sufficient reason to declare a testator incompetent." Bellows was behaving as though he were telling Jake something brand-new.

"I know," Jake reminded him. "I was surprised Sage didn't make more of that."

"He will," Bellows said.

"Someone got to Faraday," Jake said. "He slipped in that business about delusions before Sage even mentioned the word. Faraday's been carefully coached."

Bellows looked at Jake. "You don't know that and it's unwise to assume it. Perhaps Gus really was suffering from delusions. As lawyers, Jake, we don't want to get so involved in our case that we lose our objectivity."

"You were up here and took the information from him when he decided to change the will. I presume he was all right then?"

They had reached the water's edge, where small waves lapped against the sand.

Bellows gazed out at the far shore. "In retrospect, I'm not entirely sure. He was very quiet, a condition extremely unusual for Augustus Daren. As I recall, Elizabeth did most of the talking. Of course Gus would occasionally spew saliva around, so talking was embarrassing, I suppose. At the time, I thought that was all it was. Now, I'm not so sure. Elizabeth did the talking, and Elizabeth got the benefit of the change made. Undue influence is another reason to toss a will out in this state, as I'm sure you know."

"At least Faraday didn't say anything about that."

Bellows smiled. "He's not through testifying, is he?"

"Faraday is a liar."

"Objectivity, Jake. We have to maintain objectivity in order to advise our clients properly. You don't know that he's lying, and even if he is, we have no way to prove it."

Bellows carelessly kicked a stone out into the water. "Also, we have no idea what Ronny Janus might say. If she supports Faraday about the delusion business, I'm afraid the ball game is really all over."

"And if she doesn't?"

Bellows shrugged. "The jury would be inclined, I think, to give more weight to a skilled physician's opinion, if there were a conflict."

Jake watched the breeze ripple the dark waters of the lake. He felt chilled to the bone.

"I asked to talk to her when we finished today, but she ducked out."

Bellows nodded. "I may have been wrong about her. I honestly believed she would be supportive. But given all the indications, I suppose we have to presume her testimony may also be adverse to us."

Bellows turned to jake. He studied him for a moment before speaking. "I apologize for speaking so harshly back there in the courtroom. I was angry about Faraday and I suppose I was taking it out on you. It won't happen again. I know you're doing your best."

"Maybe you or someone from the firm should take over," Jake said. "After all, I'm not a trial lawyer."

"To be frank, I don't think it would make much difference now."

A low-flying gull swooped close by.

"Jake," Bellows said, "you're being considered for partner." He smiled. "I know that hardly comes as news. However, the firm looks for that little something extra in the persons selected to join Sperling Beekman as full partners. It's a quality difficult to define, but I like to think of it as a 'can-do' attitude."

All at once Jake forgot about the cold.

"You see," Bellows continued smoothly, "it's not enough to be a competent technician. A partner must possess abilities beyond that. You are an exceptionally competent lawyer, Jake; we all agree on that. But what we need is someone who can seize the moment, as it were, and who knows instinctively when that moment has arrived. The firm requires people who can not only recognize a problem but who can make the key decision to solve it."

"I'm not sure I follow you."

Bellow's jovial chuckle was almost paternal. "I do tend to get a bit obscure at times. Let me make myself a trifle more clear. I believe, based on what happened today, that we will lose this contest."

"I don't think—"

"Hear me out. We, Sperling Beekman, don't like to lose. It's bad for business. Other firms start thinking they can beat us, whether it be a trial or negotiation. A firm's reputation in these matters is more valuable than gold. We can't afford to lose this case. I think it's time to propose a compromise to Elizabeth."

"I personally don't think she'd agree to any compromise, but you can try."

Bellows shook his head and smiled. "I think the lady is—how did we used to say it?—sweet on you, Jake. I doubt if she'd listen to me, but I think, based on my observations today, your words would carry much greater weight than mine."

"The main thing up for grabs here," Jake said, "is control of the bank. Under this will, if it's admitted, she'll have absolute control—fifty-one percent of the voting rights. She might be open to any compromise as long as that remained intact."

Bellows looked up at the brooding clouds. "That's indeed what this is all about—control. But there's still room to negotiate. Why don't you propose a compromise whereby she'll have forty-nine per cent? It's not a majority, obviously, but she'd need only a few votes to keep control. Elizabeth is reasonable. I'm sure she'd go along with that."

"I doubt it, but even if she did, what about the other side?"

"As far as I can determine, they'd be satisfied with a symbolic victory. Despite their ages, both Chip and Gussie are still children. That small change in percentage, in addition to forgetting about Chip's share being forfeited, would be all the victory they'd need. As I say, it would be merely symbolic, but Chip and Gussie would feel they'd be getting back at dear old dead daddy, which is really what this is all about."

"Are you sure? I think it goes deeper than that."

"Let me worry about the other side. I've known them for years." Bellows turned and looked directly at Jake. This time his expression was solemn. "If you can get Elizabeth to agree, I can promise you the partnership."

"Just like that?"

Bellows smiled openly. "It's that extra ingredient I spoke of. If you can pull off a face-saving settlement, the firm would know you've got the kind of stuff we're looking for."

"And if I don't pull it off?"

"Never cross bridges until you get to them, Jake. I'll take Cora aside for a while tonight. That will give you a chance to talk to Elizabeth."

"I'm not sure that I should."

"You owe it to your client. Things didn't go well today in court, we both know that. She has to be put in the picture, as they say. We have a duty to keep the client informed."

"Well, I can tell her what we discussed, but—"

Bellows clapped him on the back. "You'll do it, I know. And it will give me the greatest pleasure to welcome you into our ranks as a full partner." He thrust his hands into his impeccably tailored pockets. "Damn, it feels like it's going to snow. Shall we get back?"

Jake was trembling, but he wasn't at all sure it was entirely due to the weather.

After dinner was over, Bellows announced that since Sage had raised the issue of insane delusions, he and Cora had to get back to the hotel to review some cases.

Jake stayed behind. As the wind outside moaned, he sat with Elizabeth in front of the fire, the two of them sipping coffee laced with whiskey. They sat without speaking. Jake wondered what she really thought about his performance in the courtroom, but he was too uncertain of himself even to bring up the subject.

"May I ask a favor?" he asked her.

"Certainly."

"A line for the communal bathroom forms at the hotel very early in the morning, which makes bathing a major scheduling problem. Could I use one of your bathrooms to take a shower before I go back?"

She laughed. "Of course, Jake. I still think you all should stay here. Raven's Nest is infinitely more comfortable than the old Eagle Inn."

"Bellows made the right decision about that. It keeps everything perfectly professional. Staying here might appear a little cozy to the local people."

He sipped the coffee. "By the way, Bellows had a few things on his mind when we strolled down to the lake."

"I thought you did a very good job today, Jake," she said.

He shook his head. "It wasn't like that. It was no trip to the woodshed. He wants me to propose a settlement to you."

"Why didn't he say something to me himself?"

"He thought you might be more receptive if I proposed the settlement."

She arched an eyebrow. "Why are you telling me this, Jake? Why didn't you just go ahead as he asked?"

Jake shrugged. "I don't think it's part of my job to deceive you."

"What kind of a settlement did Bellows propose?"

"Apparently, you would retain forty-nine percent of the total voting rights. Everything else would be the same." Jake finished his coffee. "Bellows thinks Faraday's testimony may sink our case. If that's true and we lose, you'd end up with just the seventeen per cent voting power your stock would give you."

"Do you think we might lose?"

"Elizabeth, this is my first jury trial; I have no prior experience upon which to base an opinion. It's true that Faraday hurt us, but the presumption that a will is valid is very strong legally. I think it's too early to tell, one way or the other."

"What about Chip Daren? He won't settle. He's clearly out for blood."

"Bellows says he thinks he would settle, that he would accept a symbolic victory."

"Has he talked to him?"

Jake paused. "Lawyers are allowed to approach opposing lawyers, to sound out settlement possibilities. But without Sage's permission, Bellows would have no right to discuss anything directly with Chip Daren."

"Do you think he might have anyway?"

"It would be unethical," Jake replied.

She smiled serenely. "That's a nice answer, Jake; it artfully avoids the issue. Tell me, was there a little bait put out for you so that you'd advance the settlement idea?"

He nodded. "Yes. But that makes no difference."

She studied him for a moment. "You've told me what Bellows thinks, now I'd like to hear your opinion."

Jake watched the flames dancing about the glowing logs. "My opinion obviously isn't worth much, Elizabeth."

"Should I settle on those terms?"

He thought of the partnership. It had been the focal point of his life for five years, his only ambition. If he was turned down he would have to forget about other law firms; he was too old to start from the bottom. He would have to move back to New York and scratch around for whatever law work that might be available. The dream of security and wealth would vanish. Oddly, all that seemed almost inconsequential now. It was a matter of duty to the client.

"If it was me," he said, "I wouldn't even talk settlement at this point. I presume Rhonda Janus' testimony will also go against us, but it's too soon to know." He smiled. "There's an old saying: The hawk only gets the rabbit that runs."

She laughed. "What does that mean?"

"I'm a New Yorker not a woodsman, remember, but I think it means that the hawk can't see a rabbit that has the nerve to stay still. The hawk sees motion, so a terrified rabbit leaping for its life becomes a visible and easy target. Anyway, it's hardly profound."

"It might be. Another Irish coffee, Jake?"

"I shouldn't, but I took a hell of a chill out there by the lake. One more, and that hot shower, and I'm on my way."

The maid was summoned and the fresh drinks prepared and served.

"Do you know what would happen if I gave up that two percent and accepted forty-nine percent, Jake?"

"What?"

"Hanover Square would be the target of a takeover before the ink even dried on such a settlement. There are several Japanese banks that are circling out there, just like your hawk, watching for an opportunity. Germans, too; but I don't know if they'd have the stomach for a bidding war with the Tokyo people."

"But you'd have forty-nine percent. Maybe Bellows is right. You'd only have to get a few votes behind you to block a takeover."

"The money offered would be too good, Jake. They would spend whatever was necessary. I couldn't match what they would offer. I would lose the bank. There's absolutely no doubt in my mind."

He nodded. "I take it then you'll consider no settlement that would affect that majority voting control?"

"That's right. As far as I'm concerned, it's all or nothing."

234

"You'd make a tough gambler."

She smiled. "I am a tough gambler. We'll stay in this game until the finish."

"I'll tell Bellows."

"No, tell him I said I'm thinking about it."

Jake sipped the coffee. It seemed stronger than the first cup, but he enjoyed the feeling of warmth it provided. "I'm not much for lying."

"I am thinking about it, Jake. Maybe not about accepting it, but I am thinking about why it was made. So on that basis, it's really not a lie, is it?"

"I suppose not."

"Besides, that's my price for using my shower." She laughed.

"You're the client. And I do really need the shower."

"Jake, it's late. Why not stay the night?"

He looked away. He wondered if she suspected how strongly he was attracted to her. He wondered at it himself. "That wouldn't look too good," he said. "Everyone in that hotel knows everything about everyone else—when people come in and what they've been up to. I think the owner runs the place more for the gossip than the money. I truly wish I could stay, Elizabeth, but I had better go back."

She said nothing, but her eyes were fixed on him. Then she spoke. "I'm glad I have you as a friend, Jake."

"Sage, where the hell have you been?" Chip Daren's whining voice was accentuated by the arrogance of drunkenness.

T. G. Sage had driven over from Gladding to the Montmorci motor inn that Chip and Gussie had made their headquarters. Gussie sat on a bed in Chip's room, and a redheaded woman, whom Sage presumed was Rhonda Janus, sat at a small table opposite Chip.

"I had to spend some time with our friends in the media," Sage answered. "These days a lawyer has to try two cases: one in front of the jury and the other in front of cameras and on the front pages. Juries are easier."

Chip waved his hand as though the answer was acceptable but annoying. "You want a drink?" Chip gestured toward an array of bottles and mixers crowded on a dressing table.

Sage crossed the room and extended his hand to Rhonda Janus. "I saw you in court today," he said. "I'm T. G. Sage."

"Ronny Janus," he said, looking quickly away.

"I regret we haven't had a chance to talk, but I didn't know where you were or how to contact you."

"So what?" Chip said. "She's here now. That's all that's important."

Sage tossed his coat on the other bed, then began mixing himself a highball with ginger ale and just a touch of bourbon. From the bottle levels he assumed that the Daren children had been doing some world-class drinking during the short time they had been in the north.

"Faraday kicked that bitch's ass today," Chip said. "The fucker may look like he has a stick up his ass, but he came through nevertheless."

Sage sat at the edge of the other bed. He smiled at Gussie.

"Did you ever meet Dr. Faraday before today?" Sage asked Chip.

"Once. I talked to him about what he might say on the stand."

"You never mentioned that to me," Sage said, tasting his drink.

Daren laughed a little drunkenly. "You said there were some things you didn't want to know."

Gussie smiled, her eyes appraising Sage in a frankly sexual way. "You were very good today."

"I'd better be, considering the fee I'm charging you people."

"You ought to give most of that back," Chip said. "You're just the front man. I'm doing all the work."

Sage chuckled. "Attorneys try never to do such a repugnant thing. It goes against our sacred code." He looked over at Rhonda Janus. "Would you like to hear what I'm going to ask you tomorrow?"

"Don't fuck around. Just tell her what to say," Chip interjected. "We don't want any mistakes."

Sage completely ignored him. "I shall ask you about Augustus Daren's mental state."

"You mean about the insane delusions?"

Sage raised an eyebrow. "Apparently I'm not the first person to discuss this matter with you."

She looked at Chip, who almost imperceptibly shook his head. "I haven't talked to anyone," she said quickly.

Sage studied her for a moment. "Miss Janus, you seem to know what will be required for you tomorrow. I will polish witnesses if I have to—rather artfully, if I say so myself. I never tell them what to say—that's quite unethical—but I do indicate subjects that might come up and responses that might be made. It's a fine line sometimes, but I never tell them what to say."

"Bullshit," Chip said.

"I tell them that the truth is what we seek. And truth is best even beyond ethical considerations. If a witness lies it creates a possible line of attack. If a witness is caught in a lie, the testimony, no matter how useful, is instantly destroyed."

"I don't think I understand," Janus said.

Sage stood up, finished his drink and grabbed his coat. "Tell the truth tomorrow," he said. "We don't want any manufactured testimony. You tell the truth, and leave the rest to me."

"Listen, Sage," Chip growled. "I've got a lot hanging on this. Not only billions, but control of the bank. So cut out this ethical shit and get down to business."

"If you've lost confidence in me," Sage said as he stepped to the door, "I will be happy to turn the case over to a lawyer of your choice."

Gussie spoke sharply. "Chip, just shut up. You're loaded." She raised her eyes upwards in disgust, then smiled apologetically. "Pay no attention to him. We're delighted with what you're doing. We wouldn't think of replacing you."

Sage nodded, noting that Gussie Daren had much more class, despite her reputation, than her brother. He then looked at Janus. "We should finish with Dr. Faraday tomorrow. Then you'll be the next witness to testify."

Rhonda Janus tried to smile, but somehow it didn't quite come off. She looked frightened. "I'm ready," she said.

"Apparently," Sage replied, as he let himself out the door.

Jake felt better after his shower, although his hair was still damp, but once he was outside the Corvette seemed as frosty as the interior of a refrigerator. As he pulled away from Raven's Nest, he waved at the uniformed gate guards.

The road to Gladding was dark and deserted, his headlights providing the only light. He was as alone as if he were traversing the moon. When it began to mist, a combination of snow and rain, he turned on his windshield wipers. It was then that he noticed a car's headlights behind him.

He slowed so that the other car could catch up and pass. But as he slowed, so did the other vehicle. He wondered if it might be the sheriff again. He speeded up, and so did the other car.

It occurred to Jake that it might not be the sheriff this time. Suddenly the few miles to Gladding seemed like a hundred. Despite the wet road, he pressed down on the accelerator and the Corvette answered instantly, its powerful motor roaring with a smooth surge. Surprisingly, the other car kept pace easily.

Gladding, tiny as it was, seemed like welcoming civilization. The streets were deserted, but the bars were still open and their neon signs looked oddly comforting.

Jake looked into the rearview mirror as the car following passed beneath one of the town's few streetlights. It was the sheriff.

Finding a parking space near the hotel, Jake pulled in. The sheriff pulled in next to him and rolled down his window.

"I should give you a ticket," the sheriff said. "Ninety miles an hour is even more than I let the local people do. You could have hit a deer and gotten yourself killed."

"Why were you following me?"

"Just making sure nothing happened to you."

Jake felt his pulse returning to normal. "Why don't I give you my schedule so you can let me know when I should expect you?"

"Scared you, did I?" The sheriff's face catching the reflection from a red neon sign looked somehow threatening. "I'll let the speeding charge go this time. Just be more careful from now on," he warned, as he pulled out and sped away down the deserted main street.

The mist had turned into a snow shower and Jake, alone in the street, was freezing. He felt cold, alone and very vulnerable as he turned and hurried into the Eagle Inn.

T. G. Sage, with traces of snow on his coat, was waiting for him just inside the front door. "What was that all about?"

"The sheriff caught me speeding. I got a warning."

"About the speeding, I presume." Sage chuckled. "I had just come in when I saw you park. Can I buy you a drink?"

"It's late," Jake said.

"It is, but the friendly saloon down the block is still open. I could use a quick nightcap."

"Wouldn't that look odd, the two of us drinking together?"

"Perhaps it might in a big city, but up here they know lawyers hang out together. Abraham Lincoln was a circuit rider, which meant that he and all the other lawyers rode the circuit with the judge. They stayed at the same country inns, took their meals together and spent their evenings in each other's company. It isn't odd, it's expected; at least in places where lawyers are a tad rare."

"Okay, but just one drink."

Sage smiled. "I haven't yet sunk to getting opposing counsel drunk. I've thought about it several times in the past, but I've always risen above temptation. Come on."

At that time of the night the Northwoods Bar was almost empty. Two men sat at the bar, separated by three stools, their attention riveted to an old television set's grainy picture. Four men Jake recognized as newspaper reporters sat at a rear table. They were talking loudly and didn't notice Jake and Sage's entrance.

Sage chose an old-fashioned wooden booth near the front of the place. The high partition of the booth shielded them from observation by the men at the back of the bar.

The bartender wiped his hands on a towel and came over.

"What's this, a peace treaty?" He grinned, exposing stained, uneven teeth.

Sage shook his head. "Merely two gladiators saluting each other before the battle. I'll have a beer. Anything you have on tap will do."

"A brandy for me," Jake said.

Sage extracted a cigar and lit up. "Finding a public place where one can smoke in peace without the risk of encountering some crazed fanatic is becoming more and more rare. I may move up here. I rather like this spirit of live and let live."

"Smoking's bad for you."

Sage emerged from the cloud of smoke and grinned. "Almost all of life's pleasures are, if you think about it." He leaned back against the wooden partition. "You said, I believe, this is your first jury trial?"

Jake nodded his affirmative response.

"I find that surprising. You're doing very well for a novice."

"I have a coach."

Sage smiled. "Oh, who?"

"When the trial is over, I'll tell you."

"Is this coach of yours up here?"

"Yes."

Sage inhaled on the cigar. "Odd. I haven't noticed anyone serving in that capacity. Certainly not Donald Bellows. From what I can observe, he's letting you sink or swim pretty much on your own."

"I'd say that's about right."

The bartender brought the drinks. Waving away Jake's attempt to reach for his wallet, Sage paid the tab.

"The widow's a very attractive women, isn't she?" Sage sipped his beer, leaving a foam ring above his upper lip.

"Yes, she is."

"Intelligent?"

Jake nodded. "Very."

"Beautiful, smart and rich to boot. Ah, to be young again."

"Are you married?" Jake asked.

"Once, years ago. It was a painful experience for both of us. I learned my lesson, but she eventually remarried. Several times." Sage grinned. "Since that sobering experience there has been a succession of lady friends. However, as soon as I see that unmistakable marriage light in their admiring eyes, I move on to someone else. That's not as ungallant as it sounds. Being a trial lawyer leaves no time for a family. Marriage under those circumstances would be unjust and unfair. Besides, I rather like coming and going whenever I choose and never having to account to anyone." Sage puffed on the cigar. "How about you? Married?"

"Yes, but I've just been sued for divorce."

"Children?" Sage asked.

"No. My wife's a lawyer too. She thought children would interfere with her career."

"The divorce your idea or hers?"

"Hers," Jake replied.

Sage nodded. "Painful. I should know. But, like most traumatic things in life, it passes. Obviously, it comes at a very bad time for you."

"There's never a good time for that sort of thing."

"True." Sage sipped his beer. "Are you planning on calling Rhonda Janus as a witness when we get through with Faraday?"

Jake smiled. "She's a witness to the will. How could I avoid it?"

239

"The law says you need call only one witness to a will," Sage said.

"And if I didn't call her, you'd jump all over me in front of the jury, then call her yourself."

"You can bet on it."

"I haven't talked to her," Jake said. "We tried to find her, but I suppose you had her hidden away."

Sage shook his head. "Not me. That isn't my style. I talked to her for the first time tonight. For only a few minutes, I might add."

"Just long enough to tell her what to say."

"Not this time."

"Well, what kind of a witness will she be?" Jake asked.

Sage finished his beer, dabbed his lips with his handkerchief and stood up.

"She's a fascinating specimen. If she takes the stand, I think tomorrow will prove to be a very interesting day," Sage said. "Well, it's been a pleasure, Jake, but I'm at an age where I really need my sleep. I'll see you in the morning."

Sage walked a few steps away from the booth, and then turned. "Whoever your coach is, he's pretty good."

Lee Stevens climbed into a cab at Chicago's Midway airport and gave the driver the address.

The driver, a black man in his mid-fifties, looked back at Stevens. "You sure you got the right place? That's a rough neighborhood, you know what I mean?"

"It's a hotel, right?"

The cabby laughed. "It ain't the Palmer House. Man, this joint's just one step above a flophouse. I don't think you'd like it much there."

"I won't be staying. I'm looking for someone."

The driver put the cab into gear and sped toward the airport exit.

Stevens listened with only half an ear as the cabby talked nonstop about putting ungrateful children through school, which evolved into an essay about today's youth, society's change and the driver's philosophy in coping with his world. Stevens mumbled sympathetic noises as they were caught up in the slow-moving traffic on the Dan Ryan. After pulling off the expressway, the man drove down back streets to a run-down, crumbling area just a few miles away from Chicago's Gold Coast.

The McKenzie Hotel had once been a stately structure. "1924" had been cut into the building's cornerstone. In 1924, during the Roaring Twenties, a six-story brick hotel so near to Chicago's center had probably been a posh address. But no more.

The block looked like a backlot set for a movie depicting the Great Depression. Most of the cars parked were either rusted or wrecks. The people, the few that were on the streets, were poorly dressed and moved with guarded watchfulness.

"You want me to wait?" the driver asked. "Getting another cab around here might be pretty close to a miracle."

"That's a good idea."

Stevens walked through the doorway, or what was left of the doorway. It had once housed a revolving door, but that was gone and a plywood partition had been hammered up to fill up the space and provide support for what looked like a reclaimed house door.

The lobby, a cavern thick with a sour odor of stale urine, decay and death, contained no furniture. Tiles were missing from the filthy floor and paint peeled from the walls, thick with grime. More unpainted plywood had been used to form a makeshift hotel desk. A flabby young man seated behind what passed for the desk eyed Stevens suspiciously. He was swarthy and a gaudy earring dangled from one fat lobe, the bauble almost concealed by his long stringy hair.

"Whaddya want?"

"I'm looking for Leon Clooney."

"He ain't here."

"He lives here, right?"

The young man lifted his shoulders. "Maybe."

"Where is he now?"

"How should I know?" The smile exhibited a gold tooth, gleaming in contrast to its stained mates.

Stevens took out the twenty-dollar bill he had in his topcoat pocket and held it up.

"Information costs money. I understand that," Stevens said quietly. "Where can I find him?"

The young man's arm shot out like a striking snake as he grabbed the bill.

"He's working at a book and video store down the street. But don't tell him I told you, all right?"

Stevens nodded. "What's the address of the store?"

"Hey, I don't know the number, but you can't miss it. It's got a big black cat painted on its sign. It's called Pussycat World. Stupid, no?" He grinned. "You a cop or what?"

Stevens didn't reply but turned and hurried to the cab.

"Shithole, ain't it?" the cabby said. "Mostly old guys on welfare and burnouts live there. Where we going now?"

"There's an adult bookstore down the street. The man I'm looking for works there."

The driver shifted and looked back at Stevens. "Say, this is all legal, right? And nonviolent? Nonviolence is sort of a religion with me."

"You have nothing to worry about. That's my church, too."

"Good."

Pussycat World had been a store, but what once had been display windows were now bricked in by cement blocks. The sign, as garish as the name of the place, was outlined in flashing lights. Several of the bulbs had burned out but had not been replaced.

"Wait for me, okay?"

The driver laughed. "If you're into that kind of stuff I can take you to some much better places."

"Just trying to locate someone," Stevens said, getting out of the cab.

Harsh fluorescent light glared down from ceiling fixtures. The front of the store consisted of a barricade of large racks containing standard magazines. The narrow entrance to the rear of the store was guarded by a cracked glass counter.

"Cost you a buck to look. It's refundable if you buy something."

He looked older than the photographs Stevens had seen, and thinner. He was six feet tall and looked no more than a hundred and thirty pounds. Leon Clooney's blond hair was receding and he had grown a straggly mustache, apparently to compensate. He sat in a high wooden chair, a piece of battered furniture once common in pool halls. A worn brown cane was cradled between his legs. He had the sallow unhealthy look of a drunk.

Stevens flipped him a dollar and walked through the opening into the back part of the store. He was confronted by rows of racks stacked at every level with adult magazines. Directly behind Clooney were bookcases filled with videos.

"Hey, if you're interested, we just got in some good animal stuff. South American stuff." Clooney snickered. "The real thing for the right kind of customer."

"How do you know I'm not a cop?" Stevens asked.

Clooney grinned, showing smallish gray teeth. "Look at the way you're dressed. That topcoat is quality goods. No Chicago cop would walk around in anything that expensive, not if he was working." He shrugged. "We get a lot of people like you in here. People interested in speciality items. Kiddies, animals, the kind of stuff that's out of the ordinary."

"And you supply it?"

The grin spread and glittering greed was reflected in Clooney's washed-out blue eyes. "Hey, whatever you want. Even snuff films." He lowered his tone. "Look, if it isn't here, I can get it for you on the sly, you know? Special deals, special prices, without my boss even knowing. Sound good?"

"I've come a long way to talk to you, Mr. Clooney."

The greed was suddenly replaced by fear. "Hey, get the fuck out of here! I ain't got no money. I ain't got nothing. So whatever you're after, I ain't got it!"

"No need to get yourself excited, Leon." Stevens watched Clooney's paranoid reaction. "I'm here to talk a little business."

"Look, you fuckers ruined my business, you ripped off my stock and you smashed up my fucking leg. I haven't got anything left and I'm working here for minimum wage. We got no business to do, so just get the fuck away from me."

"Relax, Leon. You're mistaking me for someone else. But I am here to talk about your old business back in Michigan."

"Oh fuck! It never ends," Clooney said, his voice weak. "Who are you?"

"My name is Stevens, Lee Stevens. I'm from Detroit."

"Some kind of investigator?"

Stevens just nodded. "What happened back there in Michigan?"

Clooney settled himself back on the high stool. He seemed to study Stevens for a moment, as if deciding whether to tell him anything. Then he spoke in a soft, almost inaudible voice. "You know much about this business, the porno business?"

"Not much."

"Neither did I." Clooney lit a cigarette. His hands were shaking. "I was in the Navy. They trained me as a photographer. When I came out I decided to make it my business. You know, graduations, weddings, that sort of thing. It was a good idea, only up in northern Michigan no one has much money to waste on photographers. I was mortgaged to the hilt and sinking fast. I tried everything just to make ends meet. I got into video work and that's when I heard about the Hammer Brothers from Detroit."

"Who?"

"The Hammer Brothers. They were supposed to be two guys who ran a porno factory out of their home in downriver Detroit. I heard they were making a fortune." He inhaled on the cigarette, taking the smoke deep, then continued. "I lined up some girls, turned my basement into a small movie studio and started cranking out budget flicks. Nothing fancy, just bar bums and hookers. You don't need much acting ability in porno work, at least not in the kind I made. I bought a duplicating machine and everything."

He smiled at the recollection. "I started to make money, real money. The distribution was no problem. I just contacted porno shops like this one and they took all I could deliver."

"So?"

"There are no Hammer Brothers," he said ruefully. "That's just a made-up name. The fucking mob owned the business. See, I didn't know that. Anyway, they viewed my stuff as competition. They warned me off, I got to give them that; but I'm from Bay City, Michigan, what the hell do I know about gangsters?

"Anyway, one night they came to my place, broke every camera and light, tore the fuck out of everything, and demolished my expensive duplicating machine. They they took a baseball bat and smashed my right knee like it was glass. They said if I started up again they'd be back and take care of the other leg."

He crushed out the cigarette in a scarred metal ashtray. "I believed them. I owed everybody I knew, so I had no option but to skip town. That's hard to do when you're hobbling around in a cast. They tell me they can fix the leg but it would cost a fortune. Anyway, I drifted around and I finally ended up here."

"What about the Veterans Administration doctors?" Stevens had managed to trace Clooney through his contacts with the VA, but he didn't tell him that.

"I don't trust them. They treated me, but the surgeon was some jerk who could hardly speak English so I said no to the operation they said would fix me up. At least I still got a leg. Someday I'll get enough money to get the best specialist to do it." His laugh was hollow. "Anyway, you asked. That's what happened to me back home."

"You did some video work for lawyers, didn't you?"

"Yeah, some. Not much. A few depositions, a couple of wills. I kind of let that go when the porno business started getting good."

"Did you videotape Augustus Daren when he made his will?"

Clooney's eyes became wary again. "Is that what this is all about?"

"Did you do the camera work?"

"What if I did?"

"Did you make copies of the legal work you did?"

Clooney hesitated, then shook his head. "No."

"Too bad."

"Why too bad?"

"You might be able to make a lot of money, enough to get the leg fixed, and then some."

"What do you mean?"

"We need a copy of the Daren will video."

"I saw it in the papers that he finally died," Clooney said. "You know, if I wasn't scared shitless I could make a lot of money. They tell me dead people can't sue for libel or any of that shit."

Stevens arched an eyebrow. "Do you have that tape?"

"What kind of money are we talking about?"

21

Jake had managed to avoid Donald Bellows during the morning. He rushed to the courtroom, arriving just a few minutes before trial was scheduled to begin. Bellows immediately hurried forward as Jake entered the courtroom, taking him aside to ask about Elizabeth Daren's reaction to his proposal for a possible settlement. Jake had debated using Elizabeth's suggested ploy to put things off, but decided the issue was far too important for any deception.

When Bellows was told that Elizabeth had turned it down, his manner turned frigid. He ordered Jake to try again. This time Bellows left no doubt as to Jake's future. Everything was dependent on his getting Elizabeth Daren to settle. If she didn't, not only was his chance for partnership gone, but his present employment could also be terminated.

Before he could protest, the judge entered the courtroom. Bellows, his face grim, returned to his seat as the judge commanded the attorneys to proceed. Jake was confused; conflicting emotions boiled within him, but he forced himself to concentrate as Milo Faraday took the stand and Sage continued his questions.

Sage stood back, near the rear of the jury box, leaning against it as he gently questioned Faraday. With his half-glasses perched on his nose, he assumed the pose of a kindly old gentleman trying his best to understand the scientific answers Faraday made to his simple but probing questions.

Jake felt like a jack-in-the-box as he popped up again and again to object to the inadmissable conjecture Sage was drawing from Faraday.

At first, Jake had little success with his repeated objections, and he wondered if the jury was beginning to consider him a nit-picking nuisance. But then the tide seemed to turn and the judge began to rule for Jake, shutting down Sage's line of attack. Finally, even Sage gave up. He looked at the jury as if silently imploring their aid in seeking justice, despite a heartless judge, then he turned the witness over to Jake.

Jake walked to the exact spot Sage had occupied and questioned the witness from there.

"Dr. Faraday, who did you talk to about this trial?" Jake asked.

Faraday's smile was almost a smirk. "You."

"I remember it well, Doctor, perhaps even better than you."

Sage half-stood. "Objection. Not only argumentative, but it's not even a question."

"Sustained," the judge snapped.

"Besides myself, Doctor, who else did you talk to about this case, if anyone?"

Faraday shrugged. "Some newspaper people last night. I tried to answer their questions as best I could."

"Before the trial, Doctor, did you discuss this case with anyone besides myself?"

"No."

"Not even with Mr. Sage?"

Faraday hesitated, then spoke. "No."

"Did anyone from Mr. Sage's office speak to you about this matter, at any time?"

"No."

"Did you talk to Mrs. Elizabeth Daren about this matter?"

Sage started to stand, as if preparing to object, but then changed his mind and sat down.

"No," Faraday answered firmly.

"You testified that you lived with the Darens here at Raven's Nest for over a year, isn't that correct?"

"Yes, that's right."

"You told the jury yesterday that you ate with the Darens, socialized with them all during that time, in addition to being Mr. Daren's physician; also correct?"

"That is so."

"And you didn't call or discuss this case with Mrs. Daren?"

"No," Faraday answered quickly, but suddenly, his manner was wary.

"Are you sure?"

Sage stood. "The question's been asked and answered."

"Sustained."

Jake was getting mad, his rage directed not only at the smug Faraday, but at his firm and the whole disastrous situation in which he found himself. He forced himself to remain steady, but he hoped that his fury might help sharpen his thought process.

"Well, Doctor, if you didn't call her about this case, did you discuss anything else with her?"

"No."

"After Augustus Daren finally died, did you send flowers, or offer condolences of any kind?"

"Objection," Sage said.

The judge waved him to sit down. "Overruled. I'll take the answer."

"Well?"

Faraday's expression was no longer so confident. "He was

246

hardly alive, not in the usual sense of the word. It wasn't as if he fell over dead in the prime of life."

"That isn't what I asked, Doctor. When Augustus Daren was declared dead, did you contact his widow in any manner—flowers, a phone call, even a sympathy card?"

"As I—"

"Answer the question!" Judge Vinson commanded.

"No," Faraday said.

"Have you spoken to Mrs. Daren here in court?"

Faraday shook his head.

"You have to answer verbally, Doctor," Jake said.

"No."

"Are you hostile toward her?"

"Objection," Sage said. "This had nothing to do with the issue here. It doesn't have any bearing—"

"Overruled," the judge said, frowning at Sage. "Mr. Martin has the right to make inquiry into a witness's possible bias or prejudice."

"Well, Doctor?" Jake continued.

Faraday spoke in a tone so low it was almost inaudible. "I have no hostility toward Mrs. Daren."

"Oh? Isn't it strange that you spent all that time with the Darens and haven't even said hello—"

"Objection," Sage snapped. "Argumentative."

The judge nodded slowly. "Sustained." She looked down at Jake. "I think you've made your point, Mr. Martin. I would suggest you move on to something else."

Jake nodded his agreement. "Have you received any money or other consideration for giving testimony here?"

Faraday hesitated for just a split second. "No." The single-word response was spoken tentatively.

"Have you been promised any money, or anything else, in the future, contingent upon your testimony here?"

"No money," he said.

"How about anything else?"

"Objection," Sage said. "This is merely a fishing expedition."

"I'll take the answer," the judge replied, looking over at Faraday as if seeing him for the first time.

The doctor paused. His eyes darted around the courtroom for a moment. "No."

"Are you as sure about that as you are about bearing no hostility toward Mrs. Daren?"

"I must object," Sage protested. "This is going too far. I—"

"Sustained," the judge said, cutting him off.

"I have no further questions," Jake said, walking back to his seat at the counsel table.

The courtroom seemed unnaturally quiet as Sage remained

standing but said nothing. He seemed to study Faraday for a moment.

"Well?" the judge said.

"We have no additional questions at this time. We would like to reserve the right to recall the witness if it becomes necessary."

The judge nodded. "All right." She looked at Jake. "Call your next witness."

Jake stood up and looked back at the spectators. Rhonda Janus was seated near the exit.

"We would like to call Rhonda Janus, the other witness to the will. We are calling her for that purpose only," he said.

Rhonda was once more dressed in tropical, casual clothing, this time in an apple red blouse worn over a multicolored skirt. Despite the season she wore open-toed sandals.

Jake went through the same obligatory questions as he had with Faraday. When he handed her the will he detected the odor of alcohol on her breath as she identified her signature.

"Your witness," Jake said.

Sage had wandered to the rear of the courtroom. He began his questioning almost from the spectators' section.

"You were the private secretary to the late Augustus Daren, is that correct?"

"Yes."

"And how long were you so employed?"

"Seven years."

"Was that before Augustus Daren married Elizabeth Daren?"

She nodded. "He was married to Gussie's mother then." Rhonda smiled at Gussie. Gussie Daren's expression remained remote.

"As part of your employment, were you provided with living quarters?"

"I was. I had my own little apartment in their house when Mr. Daren lived in Bloomfield Hills—that's when he was still working in Detroit."

"And did you move up here to Raven's Nest when Mr. Daren relocated here?"

"I did. I didn't have an apartment up here, though. But I had a lovely room with a private bath."

"Did you take your meals with Mr. and Mrs. Daren during that time? I refer, of course, to Elizabeth Daren."

"I did, usually."

"Mr. Daren moved up here after his first stroke, is that correct?"

"Yes it is."

"So you had the opportunity to observe him closely both before he had that stroke and after, is that correct?"

Jake knew the form of the question, more a statement than an inquiry, was objectionable, but he also knew that if he objected, Sage would just ask it again in proper form, making him look foolish

248

in front of the jury. That maneuver was specially covered in Sage's book on trial procedure. Avoiding the trap, Jake remained silent.

"I saw him every day," she answered, "both before and after the stroke."

Sage had drifted back to his favorite spot at the rear of the jury box. In his book, Sage had described this position as being the best place to conduct examination, since it forced the witness to speak up and the jury could then hear everything clearly.

"Tell us how he was before the stroke."

Rhonda Janus began hesitantly but gained confidence as she talked. The Augustus Daren she was describing began to sound like a cross between Albert Einstein and Clint Eastwood.

"And after the first stroke, were there any changes?"

Jake expected the worst, but even in his imagination he could never have conjured up what she was now telling the hushed courtroom. She described in lurid language a man who had lost almost every semblance of human mental and physical ability. She lingered over her own role, picturing herself as a combination of Mother Teresa and shadow chief executive of an international bank. Warming to her self-serving narrative, she vividly told of nursing the crippled Augustus Daren's twisted body while cleverly managing to run the banking business in Daren's name.

But she had gone too far. Her testimony had become bizarre and patently unbelievable. Sage desperately tried to cut her off without appearing to do so. But she continued on and on like a runaway locomotive. Finally, when she paused to ask for a drink of water, Sage managed to lead her into some less volatile territory. Then he quickly turned her over to Jake.

Jake glanced at the courtroom clock. It was almost time for the lunch break, but he wanted to get in a few questions to underscore her failed credibility, giving the jury something to think about while they ate.

"That's a pretty nice tan you have, Miss Janus," Jake said, smiling.

"Thank you."

"Have you been on vacation?"

She preened just a bit. "Yes."

"Oh, where was that?"

"Hawaii," she answered.

"A lovely place," Jake said kindly. "Where exactly were you in Hawaii?"

"Maui."

"Stay there with friends?"

"Objection," Sage said. "This is obviously irrelevant and immaterial."

"I'll take the answer," the judge replied.

"I stayed at a resort."

"Which one?" Jake asked.

"The same objection," Sage snapped.

"The same ruling," Judge Vinson harshly retorted. "At least for the moment. I'll take the answer."

Rhonda hesitated, then spoke quietly. "Golden Shore," she said.

Jake had read about the luxury megaresort in magazines, one of the newest and most expensive vacation spots in the world.

"A very nice place, I understand. How long were you there?"

She seemed nervous. "A while."

Jake smiled. "Well, it might help if you could be just a little more specific."

One of the jurors snickered.

"A couple of weeks," she said. "It's difficult to remember exactly."

"Didn't you go there only a day or two after the announcement of Augustus Daren's death?"

She glanced over at Sage and then stared at a spot at the back of the courtroom to avoid looking at Jake. "I suppose I did."

"When did you return from Maui's Golden Shore?"

She answered quickly. "The day before yesterday."

"Did you come directly here from Hawaii?" Jake asked.

She nodded. "I had a stopover to change planes in Denver and Detroit, but other than that, yes."

"So, that would mean you were there longer than just a couple of weeks?"

"Time flies when you're in Hawaii."

"I presume it does. How much did all that set you back, Ms. Janus?"

"Objection," Sage said, standing. "Room rates in Hawaii are not the subject of this inquiry."

Jake looked up at the judge. "They might be, if someone else was paying the freight, someone with an interest in this case."

"Now, just a minute," Sage snapped. "There isn't a scintilla of proof to even suggest anything of the sort."

"Overruled," the judge said. "However, this is looking like it might take a while, so I think we should break now for lunch. Everyone be back here at two o'clock sharp."

The clerk rapped the gravel as the judge left the bench.

Rhonda Janus scurried from the stand as if escaping. Sage watched her go, the look on his face grim.

Jake stood as the jury was escorted out, feeling a radiating sense of pleasure run through his body. Despite his inexperience, he knew no one could deny the fact that he had done well with the witness.

Donald Bellows approached, took him by the arm and spoke in a voice low enough to be audible to Jake alone.

"You're fired, Martin."

"I'm disappointed Jake couldn't come," Elizabeth Daren said as they finished lunch. "I didn't have a chance even to speak with him."

Bellows, who had left the table several times to use the telephone, smiled at Cora Simpson. "Cora, I wonder if you'd mind? I'd like to talk to Elizabeth alone for a few minutes."

Cora obeyed instantly.

"What's up, Donald?"

Bellows sipped his coffee before answering. "I'm extremely concerned about the turn this trial has taken," he said quietly. "I had hoped we could have prevented it from sinking into personal matters, but that's impossible now."

"I don't understand."

"Of course not," he said, smiling indulgently. "You're not a lawyer. However, things have taken an increasingly ominous turn, I'm afraid."

Elizabeth frowned. "Everything seems to be going very well. No one in his right mind could possibly believe Rhonda Janus. She made a fool of herself. And I thought Jake did an excellent job on Milo Faraday."

Bellows toyed with his coffee cup. "It only looks that way. Unfortunately, young Mr. Martin opened the door to T. G. Sage. Everything is fair game now."

"In what way?"

"Elizabeth, if this trial continues, you will have to take the stand. I warned young Mr. Martin not to get sucked into anything that would allow such a thing to happen, but he charged right into Sage's trap anyway. Now, no matter how things might appear at the moment, legally someone has to refute the allegations made by Faraday and Janus that Gus was, well, deluded."

"He wasn't, as you know, Donald. I'll be happy to testify to that."

He sighed. "Ah, if it were only that simple. But it isn't. If you take the stand, Sage will dredge up the whole business of Gus's divorce to marry you."

"What bearing could that possibly have?"

"It gives Sage the chance to allege you exerted undue control over Gus. In Michigan undue influence is cause to throw out a will. Obviously, this judge is letting everything in, even gossip. I think she's just amusing herself. I can tell you it won't be so amusing if all that divorce business is rehashed and spread all over the world's front pages."

"If it is, it is. I don't have any alternatives," Elizabeth said.

"Oh, but you do." Bellows' smile was benevolent. "Elizabeth, Gus's children aren't looking to win really, they just want some sort of token victory, just something to save face. If we give up only a few percentage points, say, cut back your controlling vote to forty-nine percent, I'm sure they'd call the whole thing off."

"I won't—"

"Elizabeth, lawyers have a solemn duty to advise their client fully, no matter what the consequences to the attorney." Bellows was no longer smiling. "If this goes all the way, even if you win, you'll be smeared internationally. If you take the stand you'll end up as a laughingstock, the subject of nasty little magazine pieces, your name will become a dirty joke used by smutty comics. Using everything from that old divorce case, Sage can do just that. And should that happen, would anyone pay any attention to you, even if you did have absolute control of the bank? I'm afraid not, Elizabeth. You'd be completely discredited as a banker. Even if you win, under those circumstances you would actually end up losing. You'd be ruined."

He reached over and patted her hand. "However, if I can work out this token compromise, you'd have no trouble picking up a couple of votes to add to your forty-nine percent. You'd be in control, and none of this nasty business would happen." He smiled benignly as if he had just bestowed a kindly blessing.

Elizabeth drew her hand away. "If the compromise you propose did happen, a raider—either Japanese or German—would swoop in and grab Hanover Square Bank in the blink of an eye. Money talks, Donald, and there are some powerful people out there with extremely loud voices."

He shook his head. "I think you're overreacting."

"No, I'm not. I know exactly who they are. And they are perched and ready, should the opportunity present itself."

"But—"

"The answer, Donald, is no; absolutely no." She stood up. "We should start back to court."

"I'll have to ask for a recess," he said.

"Why?"

"As I've just outlined to you, I have a solemn duty to see to your best interests. Jake Martin ignored my specific instructions, and by doing that he has put you and this case in jeopardy. To protect you, I fired him. I've notified the other managing partners at the firm of my decisions. I have another lawyer, a skilled trial man, coming up."

"Shouldn't you have discussed this with me first?"

Bellows shook his head. "Oh, if the decisions had to do with the merits of the case, I certainly would have. But, despite my initial appraisal, I'm afraid Martin wasn't the man for this case, or for our firm, for that matter. But don't worry, Elizabeth, we'll take care of everything handily."

"But—"

"Don't concern yourself, my dear. This is nothing more than an internal matter concerning Sperling Beekman." He glanced at his watch. "Oh, we will have to hurry at that."

"You go ahead, Donald. I'll have my driver bring me."

"As you wish. As a matter of fact, you don't really need to be there. A substitute of lawyers is just a procedural matter. It shouldn't take very long."

"I'll be there," she said.

Chip Daren, uncomfortably warm in the close confines of the antiquated wooden telephone booth in the hallway of the Eagle Inn, finally got put through to Claude deSalle.

"Where the hell have you been?" Chip demanded.

"Lunch," came deSalle's even reply. "Where are you?"

"I'm in a phone booth in this lousy little craphole they call a hotel up here," Chip snapped. "They've got Rhonda Janus on the stand. She started testifying this morning."

"This is an odd hour to call. Is this some kind of emergency?" deSalle asked quietly.

"I've got a hundred million dollars riding on this, deSalle. I'll call when I feel like it. Anyway, this is a goddamn emergency."

"Even if you should lose, which you won't, your sister's agreed to split with you, so we're talking fifty million," deSalle said, trying to keep the disgust out of his voice.

"Is that all? Shit, why am I worried, eh? Fifty fucking million dollars is a lot, deSalle. It's more than you'll ever see in your goddamn lifetime."

"Don't get yourself worked up, Chip. What's the emergency?"

"Rhonda Janus," he said. "You kept her under wraps. You should have continued keeping her under wraps."

"What's happened? She's supposed to testify that your father was clearly incompetent mentally."

"Oh boy, is she! She's cooked up an absolutely bullshit story. Sage says the jury doesn't believe her, not a fucking word."

"So? There's still Faraday."

"But they aren't through with Janus. Sage says they're going to ask who paid her Hawaii bills and who told her what to say."

"Tell him to stop them," deSalle snapped. "He's your lawyer. Tell him to start doing his job."

"He'll try, but if he doesn't succeed, the shit's going to hit the fan. How were those bills paid?"

There was a pause. "By credit card."

"Yours?"

"No," deSalle answered. "It's a corporate account."

"Well, that's good."

"If they try," deSalle said slowly, "they could eventually trace that company and that card to me. But that would take time. Tell Rhonda to keep her head and to keep my name out of it. That should be easy enough."

"It would be if she wasn't a lush," Chip replied. "She drank her

253

goddamned lunch here at the hotel. I watched her. Besides, I don't want to talk to her. That would look bad."

"Have Sage do it."

"He doesn't know about you. Anyway, I don't think he'd go for the idea of telling a witness exactly what to say. Especially a drunk. You can't trust them."

"Well then, Chip, you'll have to do it, won't you? Tell Rhonda to say she paid her own way with cash from her savings. Unless they have the resort records, they won't be able to prove anything else. It would take a court order and a lot of time to force the resort to hand over records like that. I know Elizabeth wants this case over in a hurry, as do we. Just tell Rhonda to say she paid her own way, and keep her mouth shut about the rest. It will all work out. You have nothing to worry about."

Claude deSalle sounded confident, but his hands trembled as he hung up the telephone.

Jake walked along the roadway, oblivious to the freshening wind and the dropping temperature.

It was all over. He had lost on every count, his marriage, his career, everything.

He found it peculiar that despite his personal situation, he couldn't concentrate on his own problems. His mind was filled with the questions he would have asked Rhonda Janus, if he had been permitted to continue trying the case. It was as though his brain couldn't accept the bitter truth that he had been fired.

Jake wondered what a lawyer did when he was removed during a trial. Perhaps something procedural was required of him. There might be a standard form to be signed, or perhaps there was a statement to be read into the record. Tiger Sage's book had nothing in it about lawyers removed in mid-trial.

If there was something required, he supposed he should go back to the hotel. They'd know he could be contacted there. Reluctantly he turned around and began to walk back, still thinking of how he would have questioned Rhonda Janus.

"Hey, you're going to be late," Jenkins, the hotel owner, said as he came in. He handed Jake a phone message. "That's from Mrs. Daren's maid. She says her boss wants to talk to you in the courthouse before the trial. Better hurry."

"Did she say what she wanted?" Jake asked.

"Nope. But you better hop over there. Lila Vinson is a nice woman, but she's got a very short fuse."

Jake paused. Perhaps Elizabeth wanted to say goodbye. Or maybe she had persuaded Bellows to change his mind, although that seemed extremely doubtful.

Maybe she wanted to say that firing him had been her idea.

254

He shoved the note into his coat pocket and hurried out the door, toward the courthouse.

Once again, he had to squeeze through the people collected on the stairway leading to the courtroom. The sheriff nodded a hello as Jake pushed past him.

He had just stepped in the door when Cora Simpson rushed up to him. "Oh Jake, this is so awful. I tried to find you at the hotel but no one knew where you were."

"I was out walking."

"This is so damned unfair. I'm going to resign in protest."

Jake could see tears forming in Cora's eyes. "Don't do that, Cora. That's foolish. I appreciate the thought, but you have your own career to think of."

"But—"

"Besides, I may need all the employed friends I can find. So please keep your job."

"I'd do anything to help you, Jake. I hope you know that."

"I do know, Cora. It means a lot."

The clerk rapped the gravel. Everyone stood as Judge Vinson made her way to the bench.

Donald Bellows hurried forward and took a position directly in front of the bench.

"Your honor, I am Donald Bellows, one of the partners in Sperling, Beekman, Howe, Woods and Simon. Our firm represents the estate of Augustus Daren."

Jake had intended to find Elizabeth, but the sight of Bellows made him stop cold. He stood with Cora in the aisle and watched.

"If the court would indulge us," Bellows said, "I would like to request a recess until tomorrow in order to make a substitute of attorneys."

"I object." Sage stood up at the counsel table. He walked quickly forward until he was standing right next to Bellows. "This has the distinct aroma of a delaying tactic."

Bellows turned and peered at Sage with obvious disdain, then he again looked up at the judge.

"We are as anxious as Mr. Sage to dispose of this matter. There is no intent whatsoever to delay this proceeding."

"Why do you need to substitute attorneys at this point?" Judge Vinson asked.

"We, the firm, believe it's in the interest of our client."

"I see Mr. Martin back there among the spectators," the judge said. "He's here: why can't he proceed?"

"He no longer works for our firm," Bellows said. "I've notified our office in Detroit and a trial lawyer is already on the way up here. However, he won't arrive until seven or eight o'clock tonight, so we ask that this matter be recessed until tomorrow morning."

Jake watched as Elizabeth stood up and walked forward. She stood only a few steps away from Bellows.

"Your honor, I would like to say something." Elizabeth sounded calm, fully in control and totally self-confident.

"Mrs. Daren," the judge said, looking down at her. "It's best to have your attorneys do the talking."

"That's the point," Elizabeth said. "I'm discharging the firm of Sperling Beekman as my lawyers."

Bellows jerked as though someone had sent an electric shock through him. He stared at Elizabeth, then turned to the judge. "If I might have a few minutes, your honor. I believe there's been a failure of communication between myself and my client. I'd like to—"

"Hold it," the judge snapped. "Let's do this in chambers." She peered out at the spectator section. "You," she barked, pointing at Jake. "Whether you've quit or whether you've been canned, you had better get in on this too."

The small side office had not been designed for conferences. Elizabeth stood against one wall, with Bellows between her and Tiger Sage. Jake took a position at the door.

The judge sat behind her desk and lit a cigarette. "Now, what the hell is this all about?"

"It's simple enough," Bellows said. "We don't think Martin here is doing the job properly, and we want someone else to take over."

"You fired Mr. Martin?" the judge asked.

"To be blunt, yes," Bellows replied.

The judge squinted up at Elizabeth. "Are you serious about dumping these people?" She gestured toward Bellows.

"I am."

Vinson shook her head. It was all too much for her. She looked at Sage. "Well Ted, surely you must have something to say about this?"

Sage shrugged. "I don't care who tries this thing. I just want to get on with it."

"Mrs. Daren," the judge said. "Both sides have pressed for an early trial date and I set this up to accommodate all parties. I don't want to force you to go forward with lawyers you don't want. But on the other hand, I can't allow something like this to be used to delay this matter, since Mr. Sage informed everyone at the beginning that he has other commitments he must honor in the near future. It would be unfair, you see, to put this off now for any extended period of time."

"I won't need any time," Elizabeth replied. "I can—"

The judge held up her hand. "You might not need time, but a lawyer coming in at this point would. He or she would need time to learn what the case is about, what the witnesses have said thus far, and otherwise prepare to continue the trial."

256

"I don't think that will be necessary," Elizabeth said firmly. "I will ask Mr. Martin to continue on as my lawyer for this case."

"You can't do that, Elizabeth," Bellows said. "He works for us."

"You fired him, you just said so," the judge interjected.

"Well, maybe I said that, but that's not what I meant. Mr. Martin is an employee of Sperling Beekman and cannot take a case unless the firm approves."

The judge looked at Jake. "What about that, Martin?"

Now they all turned to look at Jake. Bellows looked confused, half-frowning, half-smiling.

"I was fired," Jake said.

"I acted in haste, Jake," Bellows said. "Anyway, you can't take the case. It would be unethical to do so. It would amount to client stealing, and if you went ahead Sperling Beekman would have to take steps to have you disbarred."

"Hold it, hold it," the judge commanded. She took a deep drag on her cigarette, then studied it for a moment. She looked up at them. "Here's how it goes. I don't give a damn who represents the estate of Augustus Daren. You people can thrash that out among yourselves; I'm going to recess for the day. But we are going to start tomorrow at nine o'clock sharp. If there's no lawyer here to represent the estate, then I'm going to see that someone becomes a resident of our little jail up here." She glared at each of them in turn. "If you think I'm whistling Dixie, try me."

"Judge, I must insist—"

She cut Bellows off. "Are you hard of hearing? You people get out of here now and get this straightened out. Send in my clerk when you leave."

Sage was tight-lipped and looked grim, but he surreptitiously winked at Jake as he passed.

"Elizabeth, let's go to your place and talk this out," Bellows said to his now ex-client.

"I've done my talking. Your firm no longer represents me."

"We've been representing the Daren family for generations," Bellows said, with a nervous smile. "I realize now I should have handled this more diplomatically but, believe me, I was acting only in your interests."

"Submit a bill," she said crisply. "If your firm is representing me in anything else, or the bank, I am ending that right now. You can submit a final bill for whatever may be owing."

"You're overreacting," Bellows said, taking her arm.

Elizabeth pulled away sharply and turned to face him. "Am I? You seem strangely interested in having me settle this on terms unacceptable to me. The manner in which you've handled this case from the beginning seems strange. How do you lawyers say it? I've lost confidence in you, Donald, and in your firm."

"Elizabeth, I'll have our head of litigation come up here tomorrow. Don't do anything foolish."

"Why wasn't he here from the beginning?" she snapped. "Why did you proceed with a lawyer who'd never tried a jury case before?"

He tried to smile, but it didn't quite work. "I thought he could do the job. However, I must admit I made a mistake. But, thank heavens, it's not too late. Tomorrow—"

"There's no tomorrow for you, at least not as far as this case is concerned," she said firmly.

His expression was no longer ambiguous. He was angry. "Young woman, don't let all this go to your head. I don't know what's been going on between you and Martin, but Sperling Beekman will not play the fool—"

"Will you take the case?" Elizabeth asked Jake.

"I still don't have any experience, Elizabeth. You'd better get someone else."

"You heard the judge; it's too late for that. Will you or won't you take the case?"

Jake shrugged. "If you want me to."

Bellows' face was turning bright crimson. "If you even walk back into this courtroom to get your hat," he snarled at Jake, "I'll have you disbarred, you unethical son-of-a-bitch."

Jake realized that the spectator seats were still filled. Everyone in the courtroom seemed delighted by the scene they were witnessing. He started to laugh. "I started the case. I might as well finish it."

Bellows was almost out of control. "Martin, I hope you have other skills, because you're through as a lawyer. If you think you're the first snot-nosed associate who tried to steal a client from his firm, you're not. The state bar's grievance committee will make short shrift of you."

Jake knew the firm's power within the bar association, and he knew this was no idle threat.

"Take your best shot," he said to Bellows, sounding much more courageous than he felt.

22

A mob of media people were waiting for Jake outside the court-house. Jerry Casey, the public relations man, tried to keep them back but they blocked Jake's way, thrusting microphones in his face as television crews sighted their cameras on him.

"Donald Bellows said you're a disgrace to the legal profession," a woman shouted at Jake, holding a tape recorder close to his lips. "What have you got to say?"

"Are you and Elizabeth Daren lovers?" another called.

"Is she any good in bed, Jake?"

"Bellows said you're a thief."

"Tiger Sage says you're a jerk. Whaddya got to say about him?"

"C'mon, say something; you gotta talk to us sometime."

Jake tried to remain calm despite the taunts. He knew they were trying to get him to explode. Jerry Casey pushed in front of Jake and spoke with crisp authority. "Mr. Martin will have a statement tomorrow morning, here in front of the courthouse."

"Do it now!" one of them shouted at Jake. "Whaddya, afraid?"

"Tomorrow," Casey said.

Jake pushed his way through the newsmen. Some of the more aggressive reporters followed him all the way to his car, still trying to goad him into an angry response, something dramatic that would look good on the six o'clock news.

He backed up slowly, a cameraman tried to block his way, but the photographer jumped out of the way just in time. He watched in his rearview mirror as a television truck pulled out into the street to chase him.

Jake waited until he cleared Gladding's city limits, then he hit the accelerator and the Corvette left the pursuers far behind.

Reaching Raven's Nest was like finding a safe harbor in a storm. The guards waved him through. Once inside, the maid showed him into the great room where Elizabeth was waiting for him.

"Have a little trouble with the press?"

"It was like Hitchcock's *The Birds* back there. No matter what I did they kept coming. How did you get through?"

"My driver is very good about those things. He's specially trained. He had me out and into the car before anyone realized what was happening. Can I get you a drink?"

"Yes. Whiskey."

The drink was instantly produced. He sipped and found it

strong. "I'm flattered that you want me to continue," Jake said, "But I shouldn't have even started this trial, Elizabeth. You should bring in someone who really knows what he's doing."

"And face the wrath of Judge Vinson? Besides, she's right. If we brought in someone new, he or she would have to have some time to orientate themselves. I can't afford that kind of delay, Jake. No matter what happens, this has to be accomplished quickly."

Jake gulped down the rest of the drink. "Did you mean it back there? About firing Sperling Beekman?"

"Absolutely." She signaled the maid to bring Jake a refill. "We haven't discussed your fee, Jake. What do you have in mind."

He chuckled. "If I'm paid what I'm worth I'd end up with nothing. Let's think about the fee after this is all done."

She shook her head. "That's not businesslike, Jake. What were you making at the firm?"

"A little over a hundred thousand." He suddenly realized with shock that he was now entirely without income of any kind.

"How about a $25,000 retainer?"

"That's far too much. This should all be done this week."

"You can bill me on whatever basis you decide. Deduct it from the retainer and return any excess. That seems fair."

Jake took the fresh drink offered by the maid. He realized he would need the money. "Okay."

"You did quite a job on Rhonda Janus," she said.

"It isn't over yet. Sage may be able to repair the damage."

"I doubt it," she said, looking out at the lake. "I think you'd better plan on staying here for the rest of the trial."

"No, I don't agree. I think we should keep things the way they are. Those news people were already trying to needle me about a personal relationship with you."

"Jake, unless you want a daily repeat of *The Birds* it would be better if you stayed here. My people are experienced. We can get you in and out of Gladding with minimal wear and tear."

The whiskey was beginning to take effect. "I don't think my staying here would be very smart."

"Are you talking personally or professionally?"

He studied the glass without replying.

"We might as well be frank with each other, Jake."

He nodded. "Putting gossip aside, I am attracted to you."

She smiled. "Is that so awful? I'm flattered."

"At the moment, Elizabeth, I really don't need any more complications, not even a schoolboy crush. My life, at least at this moment in time, seems to have come apart."

"Things aren't that bad, Jake."

"I'm being divorced, and I'm not sure now whether I want that or not." He sipped the drink. "I've been fired. I'll probably be disbarred. I've never tried a jury case before and I find myself in the middle of a court battle with the state's top trial lawyer, in a case involving millions of dollars." He looked at her and smiled wryly. "I hate people who whine. I suppose I sound like some kind of prime jerk."

"You don't, Jake; not at all. And we're sort of in this together, aren't we?"

"It's not quite the same thing."

She shrugged. "I wonder? Donald Bellows said if I continue the case, Sage will put me on the stand and ruin me by digging up all that stuff from Gus's divorce case. If he's right, everything I've worked for will be destroyed, including my reputation. So, you're not the only one with a lot at stake."

Jake looked at her. "Sage might have been able to call you if the two witnesses to the will hadn't shown, but if he tries to do that now, I believe I can stop him. Bellows knows that."

"Jake, let me tell you what I really have riding on this case."

"You mean control of the bank?"

"Not even that; nor the money."

"What then?"

She again looked out at the lake. "I loved my husband. That may sound trite, but I never really knew what it was to truly love another human being, not before Gus. And he loved me. That was a first, too." She smiled. "Oh, there had been a number of romances, but never real love. Until Gus came along I never knew what it was like to have someone feel so deeply about me."

She spoke so softly he had to strain to hear her.

"Some people never have that experience. Most never do, I think. I am extremely grateful for what I had and I shall never forget it."

"In time, you'll—"

She shook her head. "That kind of love is rare. He was everything to me; he was my world. And, truthfully, I was his world too. We were like one person. That's what this case is all about, Jake."

"I don't understand."

For a moment he thought she might begin to cry, then she continued to speak. "What do you do to honor a love like that? Endow a college? I have the money to do that several times over, but it wouldn't be much of a monument, would it? Gus's name on a building or a library. That sort of thing didn't mean much to him in life, nor does it to me." She smiled. "The best monument, the best thing I could ever do for my husband, and the best way to celebrate what we had together is to fulfill his dream, to make Hanover Square what he had intended it to be."

She looked at him. "You must understand, Jake. It's not for me that I have to win this case. It's for him." She looked away. "For what we had together."

She looked away and he saw a single tear begin to slide down her cheek. "If I lose, I lose my one real chance to show the world just how much my husband meant to me. So you see, the stakes for both of us are somewhat considerable."

She turned to him. "I understand what you're going through. I promise not to be a complicating factor."

Elizabeth Daren was so stunningly beautiful, he could hardly speak. "I'll do my best for you, Elizabeth." Her face reminded him of a classical sculpture. He smiled. "Do you have any idea of the effect you have?"

"On men? I've known about that since I was thirteen. But it's always been a double-edged sword, frankly." She looked away from him. "It still is."

Lee Stevens returned to Pussycat World, but Leon Clooney wasn't at his post. A man with a narrow face, who appeared youthful until you got up close, watched Stevens approach.

"Where's Leon?" Stevens asked.

"Why?"

"I'm supposed to meet him here."

The man's eyes narrowed with interest. "I don't know what Leon is into, man, but I can probably help you out. Whatcha got in mind?"

"Where's Leon?"

The thin man leaned nearer to Stevens, and spoke in a low voice. "Look, whatever it is—a little nooky, babes, boys or even sheep—I can probably get you a better price than Leon. Everything is available in this neighborhood. Gambling, dope, sex, whatever you want. If I can't get it for you I can direct you to a place where you can make your own deal."

"Where's Leon?"

"Is your name Stevens?"

"Yes."

"Leon's scared shitless. He doesn't want to see you. Are you going to hurt him?"

"No."

"It's no skin off my nose either way."

"This is strictly business," Stevens said. He took out a twenty and held it out. "Where's Leon?"

The smile became wider. "Hey, do I look like the kind of a guy who'd sell somebody out for twenty lousy bucks?" He laughed as he reached out and took the bill. "But then, why not? Do you know where he lives?"

"At the hotel."

"If you could call it that, yeah." The man's grin became an evil leer. "Look, if he can't come through for you, c'mon back. You name it, I can get it." His voice dropped low. "And watch out for that fucking Leon. That gimp can be a tricky son-of-a-bitch."

262

Sherman Murphy had been absolutely right about the north country; it was a treasure-trove of unbelievable oddballs. He had discovered an abundance of local characters ranging from the eccentric to the clearly committable.

There was only one problem. His editors didn't believe they really did exist.

Murph had written a memorable column on Frederick Flying Crow, an Ojibway Indian who lived just outside of Gladding. Although Flying Crow had been blinded as a young infantryman during World War II he still liked to hunt. His grandchildren would drive him out to a secluded northern glen, seat him on a stump, give him his bottle of whiskey and his rifle and run for the car. Flying Crow would wait until he heard them drive away. Then, for two hours as he sipped the liquor, he shot at anything he happened to hear. His grandchildren, returning, would start blowing their car horn a mile away to signal Flying Crow to stop firing. They then collected their happy grandfather, checked the clearing to make sure he hadn't actually shot anything or anybody, and then took him home until the next time.

The paper's features editor—who didn't like "Murph's Turf" in the first place, or Murphy—accused him of inventing the entire Indian business as well as his column about the retired madam, an ancient crone who was well over ninety and who was still called the Queen of the Lumberjacks by all the locals. A woman with a croaking laugh who, despite her age, still had a bright-eyed lust for life. The editor told Murph that the paper's readers weren't interested in fictional Indians or withered ex-madams.

The editor reminded Murph that he had gone up there to dig up juicy inside stuff about the Daren family. That was what sold newspapers. He did not have to remind Murph that his readership was slipping or that his contract was coming up for renewal. He didn't have to. That remained the primary concern in Sherman Murphy's mind.

T. G. Sage had fed Murph some interesting items, but none substantial enough to inspire a full column. Everyone else, even Gussie Daren, was refusing interviews. Murph had done a few pieces on the trial, but it was mostly a rehash of the stories already sent in by the paper's star reporter who was doing an outstanding job in covering what was happening in court.

Things were boiling now. Donald Bellows had fired Jake Martin, and in turn was fired by Elizabeth Daren. Martin was back in as trial counsel, but he was under the cloud of possible disbarment proceedings. There was a rumor that Martin was Elizabeth Daren's lover. This was juicy, but it was already being trumpeted on the front page. Unless he wanted to sound like a weak echo, Murph desperately needed something fresh, something no one else had.

Tiger Sage was available, holding forth as usual at the local Gladding bar, but he was on the wrong side of the case to supply inside stuff about Elizabeth Daren's lawyers.

Murph was frustrated. He decided to drive to Montmorci once more to try again to talk to Gussie. It was unlikely that he would get anyone to talk, but it was better than just sitting around getting sloshed.

When he got to the motor inn at Montmorci, Murph decided to fortify himself with a drink at the little bar in the lobby of the place. It would help buffer him against the rejection he expected. Murph often joked that he couldn't work on an empty liver.

She was seated at a table in the back, all by herself, the only other customer in the place. Murph took his drink from the bartender and walked over.

"Hi," he said. "My name's Sherman Murphy. I saw you testify in court today."

Rhonda Janus looked up, squinting, trying to focus. "Who?"

"Everyone calls me Murph," he said. "I write a column for *The Detroit News*. May I join you?"

She squinted again. "Murph's Turf?"

He nodded.

"Hey, I used to read you all the time when I lived in Michigan. That stuff you used to do about dogs and kids always made me cry."

"Thanks." He sat down. "Can I buy you a drink?"

"Sure." She smiled. "It's nice to talk to someone who isn't mad at me."

"Who's mad at you?"

"Who isn't? Jesus, you would have thought I sold state secrets or something today the way they acted."

"Who?"

"Chip and Gussie."

Murphy reached inside his coat and brought out his mini recorder. "Do you mind if I tape this? I have the worst memory in the world."

"Let's just talk," she said. "I don't want to have to watch what I say. That's too much like being in court."

"Whatever you say." Murph made a show of putting the compact recorder back in his pocket, but as he did so he switched it on. The expensive recorder, the size of a pack of cigarettes, was sensitive enough even inside a pocket to pick up everything she said.

"Tell me about Chip and Gussie," he said, signaling the bartender to bring her another drink. "They look like a couple of assholes to me."

She smirked. "You don't know the half of it. The whole goddamned family is nuts. Today, I do my best. I tell it just the way I was told to tell it. But are they satisfied? Hell, no."

264

"So what? They're not paying for it."

"No, not directly, but I think it's probably their money."

"Oh? How much are you getting to testify?"

"They paid for Hawaii. You wouldn't believe that place I stayed at. It cost a fortune. And they paid off the balance that I owed on my condo, plus I'm supposed to get ten thousand when this is all done. Now I don't know about that. Chip is so angry I don't know if they'll pay me. Even though I told it just the way they wanted."

"Chip and Gussie told you what to say?"

She looked away wistfully. "I should have been Gus's widow, you know. He loved me."

Murphy smiled sympathetically. "Tell me all about it, Rhonda," he said softly as he stole a glance at his watch. He still had plenty of time to get everything into the paper. This was more than just a column, this was national front-page stuff, the kind of thing that people remembered when contract time came around.

"Tell me everything," he said. "I just hate to see people ill-used."

Jake was not surprised to see the sheriff's car as he pulled out of Raven's Nest. As usual, the car had been parked on the shoulder of the road, lights out and concealed by the darkness of the evening. But this time he had driven only a short distance when the sheriff flicked on his rotating red light and quickly closed the distance between them.

Jake pulled over. The dark forest bordering the roadway seemed particularly ominous as red rays from the scout car lights flickered against the trees. The effect reminded Jake of dancing flames. He rolled down his window and waited.

"Get out," the sheriff said as he came up to the Corvette.

"What the hell am I supposed to have done?"

"Get out," the sheriff repeated.

Jake felt the sudden grip of fear. They were completely alone in a desolate, isolated part of the woods.

He looked up at the sheriff, whose facial features were strangely accented by the revolving red lights. "Look, if this is some kind of scare tactic—"

"Someone wants to talk to you," the sheriff said.

"Oh yeah? Well, I don't—"

"The judge wants to see you. Privately." He emphasized the last word.

Jake was taken by surprise. "Okay. I'll follow you."

"She doesn't want anybody seeing your car. I'll drive you and bring you back. Your car's safe enough here. Out here the only thing you have to look out for is skunks. Four-legged ones. Let's go."

Jake hesitated, then got out and followed the sheriff back to his police car. He got in on the passenger side. "What's this all about?"

he asked as the sheriff turned off the warning patrol lights and pulled out into the deserted road.

"I don't know," the sheriff replied, indicating by his tone that he considered the subject closed.

Judge Vinson's house was located near the town, but it was isolated, standing alone among dark trees, well back from the road. Except for one lighted window at the rear, it was dark. Jake followed the sheriff up some backstairs and into a large kitchen. The judge, dressed in a faded shirt and worn jeans, sat at a kitchen table.

"Sit down," she commanded. "Do you want a drink?"

Jake shook his head. The sheriff, looking very much at home, poured himself a drink from a bottle on a sideboard and joined the two of them.

"I got a call from Stanley Thornbeck. You know him?" the judge asked Jake.

"I've heard of him," Jake replied. "Thornbeck and Ross."

She nodded. "The number one political law firm in the state. Thornbeck is a former president of the State Bar. He takes care of the Republican end and Ross handles the Democrats."

"What's that got to do with me?"

"Thornbeck is still active in the bar association. He was calling about you."

"I don't think I understand."

"Thornbeck is so smooth adhesive tape wouldn't stick to him. I've only met him a couple of times but you'd think from that phone call we had been friends from childhood. God, but he was charming and gracious. I've never received a threat in a nicer way in my life."

"Threat?"

"He said he was calling as an officer in the state bar. I suppose he still serves in some capacity. He told me—strongly suggested, were his words—that I remove you as attorney from the Daren matter."

"Why?"

"He said—and I'm merely telling you what he said—that you were acting in an unprofessional manner, in violation of the code of ethics. He said that if I didn't do something, the bar association would get the Supreme Court to step in and take the case away from me and remove you. He said that 'we' didn't want to expose the legal profession to any unnecessary and harmful publicity, so he had some suggestions to offer."

"Like what?" Jake demanded.

She smiled for the first time. "Thornbeck said he understood you were a young man and inexperienced. He said that if you were removed, he'd promise that nothing would happen to you, that you wouldn't have to face disbarment proceedings. Then, to sort of top it off, he suggested that I try to get Elizabeth Daren to accept a reasonable settlement. To get this messy thing disposed of quietly, that's how he put it."

"Why tell me all this?"

"First of all, it's your career that's in jeopardy, not mine. If it had been anyone but Stanley Thornbeck calling I would have told them to fuck off. But Thornbeck is a powerful figure in the bar and well connected. I imagine he's probably fronting for your former firm and Donald Bellows, but I think he means what he says."

"I've already made my decision."

"I know. But you might want to rethink things. By pulling out now you can make sure you save your license."

"I've done nothing wrong or unethical."

She sighed. "God, I'm glad I'm not young anymore. There's a lot of injustice in this world, Jake, whether we like it or not. These people can tie you up with hearings and proceedings until you're either bankrupt, nuts or both. After a while being disbarred will begin to look appealing, if only to bring the torture to an end."

"If I don't agree to quit, will you remove me?"

"No."

"And if they take this case away from you?"

"If it happens, it happens. If they try anything beyond that, they'll find I have a few friends too, so don't worry about me."

Jake studied her for a moment, then spoke. "Why even tell me any of this?"

"Am I in on it, is that what you mean?" She shook her head again. "No, I'm not. I'm not going to remove you even if I could do it, but I thought you should know what was happening in case you wanted to grab a last chance at escape while you still had the opportunity."

"I'm staying on as trial counsel," Jake said.

"Okay by me," she said. "But remember, courage sometimes can carry a stiff price tag."

Jake shrugged. "You do what you have to do."

"Those probably rank as someone's last words, but if that's the way you want it, it's okay with me." She studied him for a moment, then spoke. "We can forget this conversation ever took place. And don't get the idea that you and I have formed some kind of alliance by this. You're on your own in my courtroom, sonny; I just did this as an act of Christian charity."

"I appreciate it."

The sheriff finished the last of his drink. "Let's go."

"I'll see you in court," the judge said, once again speaking in her usual official tone.

Jake and the sheriff headed back toward where the Corvette was parked. "Are you going to continue to follow me around?" Jake asked.

"Some people would be delighted to get this kind of service," the sheriff said.

"I'm not."

"Okay. I never really thought you were in much danger. It was more to let you sweat a little. I don't have much chance for fun up here. But you're on your own from here on."

They rode in silence until they were almost to where Jake had left the Corvette.

"Are you banging the widow?" the sheriff asked without looking over at him.

"What a thing to ask," Jake said, surprised. "I'm not."

The sheriff slowly shook his head. "I was kind of hoping you were."

"Why?"

"It's a sin for something like that to go to waste."

When he got back to the Eagle Inn, the owner handed him a stack of telephone messages. Jake glanced quickly through them. One message was from the head of the state bar's grievance committee, a man known as fair, but who had the fearsome reputation of being totally without mercy. All Michigan lawyers tended to tremble at the mere mention of his name. Jake laid that message aside. Most of the others were from newsgathering organizations who wanted interviews.

Lee Stevens had called several times from Chicago. The messages were all marked urgent. Jake went to his room and called the Chicago number. It was answered on the first ring.

"Stevens, this is Jake Martin. What's so urgent?"

"Where the hell have you been? I've been penned up in this goddamn hotel room for hours."

"Things have gotten pretty hot up here. I just got back. What's up?"

"How bad do you think the widow wants to win this case?"

"Real bad. So?"

"Where are you calling from?" Stevens asked.

"The Eagle Inn. The finest hotel in Gladding. As a matter of fact, the only hotel in Gladding. Why?"

"Let's be a little cautious about what we say, okay? You never know who might be listening in."

Jake laughed. "Maybe we should have figured out a code."

"I don't think you're going to think this is so damn funny," Stevens said. "I found the guy who made that you know what."

"Does he remember making the you know what?" Jake laughed.

"I think he's got a copy. He says he has."

Jake was suddenly completely alert. "Have you seen it?"

"No, so I'm not sure it really exists. He won't show it unless we come up with some very heavy money."

"Like what?"

"One hundred thousand. In cash."

Jake whistled. "If he wants that without proof, he's nuts."

"He reads the papers," Stevens said evenly. "He's got a pretty good idea what's at stake here. He won't bargain. It's all or nothing. Do you think the widow would pay?"

"If it's what he says, yes."

Stevens sounded tired. "This guy is not exactly a high-rent type, you understand? I found him working in a porno store. He may be lying for all I know. He says he'll produce what we want when we have the money here for him. He says we don't have to pay unless he does produce."

"That sounds safe enough."

"Oh yeah? This guy lives in a neighborhood where they'd kill you for your shoes. I hate to think what they'd do for a hundred grand. If this goes down, I want armed bodyguards."

"I'll talk to the widow," Jake said. "And I'll get back to you."

"Don't forget, be careful about what you say over the phone. Safe phone is maybe as important as safe sex. At least in this case."

"I'll get back to you."

Jake hung and dialed Raven's Nest.

Claude deSalle sipped a brandy as he listened to Donald Bellows, who was pacing up and down the length of deSalle's long living room as he talked.

"As soon as the courts open tomorrow," Bellows said, "we'll file a motion for superintending control with the Supreme Court. Our people are drafting it as we speak. We'll have that case jerked away from that ignorant woman and get it into a court of our choice."

"I don't think so," deSalle said quietly.

"And I've already put the machinery in motion to have that insolent young bastard's law license taken. They'll suspend him tomorrow and disbarment will follow. I'll see to that. Sperling Beekman will not be trifled with, believe me."

"What you're talking about, Donald, will take time."

"Not the suspension; that will be done tomorrow. Of course, the Supreme Court will have to review what's happened before they assign the case out to another judge."

"That could take weeks, maybe months, even if the court agreed to do what you ask," deSalle said. "Time is the one thing we don't have, Donald; you know that."

"But—"

DeSalle shook his head. "You're allowing your emotions to interfere with your judgment. Everything is progressing nicely. Elizabeth is saddled with an inexperienced lawyer who's up against the best trial man in the state. Even if Rhonda Janus did make a bad impression, the doctor's testimony will more than compensate for that. Then when Sage puts the local people on the stand, it should be all over except for the shouting. I don't want you to do anything that could interfere with that."

"It's a matter of pride," Bellows said. "Sperling Beekman can't afford to look like a fool. The other partners are upset about losing the Daren business. I have to take strong action now, otherwise I'll look weak and vacillating, and that would invite more criticism. This is important to the firm's reputation. We have to—"

"You'll be leaving the firm, Donald, so what the hell do you care what happens with Sperling Beekman? There is just too much at stake here. I'm afraid you'll just have to swallow your pride for a while."

"But Jake Martin must still be removed. I've set everything up to do just that."

DeSalle's tone of voice reflected his loss of patience. "If you should have this young man suspended, Elizabeth will then hire an experienced top-line lawyer and things may not end up the way we want. Do you understand that?"

"Claude, I could end up looking like a damn idiot."

"You'll be a rich idiot—a very powerful idiot—if all this goes through, Donald. I promised you that." He finished the brandy. "Your firm's mandatory retirement would have forced you into a wasted life of endless bridge games, and you couldn't stand even the thought of that, could you? I offer you years of power and wealth. That's why you agreed to do what you've done."

DeSalle stood up. "We're so close to pulling this thing off, I don't want anything to upset it. If something does, Donald, then all our agreements are off."

"Well, I wouldn't do anything—"

"You certainly would be an idiot if you did," deSalle said. "After this is all over, you can take whatever revenge you wish. However, right now I'm sure you'll want to rush back to your office. You had better call off whatever dogs you've unleashed. We can't risk having any loose ends dangling."

"But we're preparing to go into the Supreme Court tomorrow. The firm's lawyers are drafting—"

Continuing to smile, deSalle took Bellow's elbow and escorted him toward the door. "Just tell them you have decided to think things over. Lawyers are forever doing that; it will sound natural enough." He patted the other man's shoulder. "You've been an integral part of this from the beginning, Donald. We are an inch away from victory. Don't do anything now that might cause you bitter regrets." DeSalle paused. "And do give my love to your lovely wife, will you?"

Jake picked up the phone on the first ring. He wondered if it might be Lee Stevens again, or Elizabeth.

270

"Jake? It's Cora."

Her voice sounded a little odd.

"Where are you?" Jake asked.

"My little apartment," she answered. "I was at the office but I had to leave."

"Why?"

"Oh, Jake, I don't think you want to know."

"Try me."

"That bastard Bellows has a crew of lawyers preparing charges against you. I talked to him, but he's so enraged there's no reasoning with him. I understand the other partners are less than thrilled that the firm's lost the Daren business. Bellows is trying to make that your fault." She seemed to slur the last word.

"Cora, have you been drinking?"

He was answered with a sigh. "I've had a few since I walked in the door. It's not my usual way of handling things, but I needed something to try and lift my spirits. I feel so sorry about all of this, Jake."

"There's no reason to get stiff over it, Cora. What charges are being prepared against me?"

"I was too angry even to ask. If Bellows goes through with it, I am going to resign. I wouldn't want to be a part of a firm that would do such a lousy thing."

"That's nonsense, Cora. You've worked very hard to get where you are. Don't give it all up now."

"You did."

Jake laughed. "Not voluntarily, I didn't. Stick around, Cora, at least until the partnership thing is settled. Otherwise Craig Dow wins by default."

"He's a louse. He purposely dodged coming up there for the trial. I don't know how he did it, but he did. He shouldn't be allowed to be a partner. He has no guts."

"Cora, could you send me up your notes on the probate cases you researched? Unless I'm removed, this trial will be over very quickly and I really should have those cases ready to cite to the judge."

"Bellows took the whole file, everything—including my notes. Even the copies. He demanded them, as a matter of fact. God knows why. Anyway, everything pertaining to the case is under lock and key in his office."

"Damn. I wonder why he'd do that."

"I don't know." She sighed again. "I'm a little fuzzy now, Jake. Drinking isn't my thing, I guess. Maybe tomorrow I'll be able to remember some of the citations. If not, I can go back to the firm's library and start digging up those cases again."

"I don't think there's that much time left, Cora."

"Jake."

"Yes."

"Can we date?"

He smiled. "Let's put that on the back burner, Cora. You have to admit, I've got my hands full right at the moment."

"Think about it, Jake."

He laughed. "Okay, Cora, I'll think about it."

"I will too," she said. "Goodnight."

He heard the sound of a kiss and then she hung up.

Sherman Murphy had the night copy editor read back what he had called in; the golden words that would be tomorrow's column. The front-page story he had already dictated would also carry his byline, but it didn't require the literary style that he liked to flash in his column. The story could be in standard reporting language, but the column had to sing.

Murphy closed his eyes as he listened, smiling with delight at the musical flow of the words being read back to him. "Murphs' Turf" would be dynamite. Prize-winning dynamite.

If the newspaper's lawyers, or even the boss, tried to change one precious word, Murph was prepared to kill.

He glanced at his watch. He'd met the deadline to make the first edition. Tomorrow, Sherman Murphy's coup would be the story, not the Daren case. That would be merely secondary.

The thought was so nice it was like being a little drunk.

23

If anything, the crowd waiting outside the courtroom door had grown even larger. Jake realized he had become something of a celebrity as the people jammed together on the stairs cleared a path for him as he approached.

The sheriff winked at him as he passed through the courtroom door. Inside, as usual, every available seat was occupied.

T. G. Sage was reading the *Free Press* and looked up as Jake put his briefcase down on the counsel table.

"The judge wants to see us before we start," Sage says. "How do you feel?"

Jake shrugged. "I'm okay."

Sage followed him into the judge's cramped chambers.

Judge Vinson, too, was reading the *Free Press*. She put the newspaper down as she took a final sip of coffee from a plastic cup.

"Well, what's the situation?"

"I'm ready to proceed," Sage replied.

"I don't mean that," she snapped. "Has either one of you been served with anything from a higher court?"

Jake shook his head as did Sage.

"Odd," she said. "I figured this place would be crawling with injunctions and court administrators. Maybe they can't find us."

"What were you expecting?" Sage asked.

She grimaced. "I figured the Supreme Court might order this trial stopped until they had time to look into the matter. I had a few telephone calls last night from some people who have the power to pull off something like that. But so far this morning, no calls, no injunctions, no nothing."

"I think we should go ahead," Sage said.

"You bet your ass, we will," she snapped. "At least we will until I'm ordered to stop." She looked at Jake. "Is the Hawaiian maiden out there?"

"I saw her when I came in."

She stood up. "Well, then, let the perjury begin."

Sage chuckled. "Are you casting aspersions on the witness?"

"Everyone lies a little," she said. "It's usually just a matter of degree."

The clerk rapped the gavel bringing everyone to his feet as the judge led the way into the courtroom. Judge Vinson mounted the three stairs to the bench, while Jake and Sage returned to their places at the counsel table.

"Bring in the jury," she said.

The jury, looking properly solemn, filed in.

"Okay," the judge said to Jake. "You may continue with Rhonda Janus."

Rhonda, attired in yet another colorful tropical outfit, walked to the witness stand and sat down.

"You've been sworn, Ms. Janus," Jake said. "Yesterday, you testified that—" He was aware of a whispered commotion among the newsmen. Jake turned to look, wondering if the order the judge anticipated might have arrived. He saw the rotund columnist, Sherman Murphy, frantically waving a copy of *The Detroit News* at him. Other reporters were clustered together reading copies of the paper with great interest.

"Quiet," the judge snapped.

"If I might have a minute, your honor," Jake asked.

"If you can quiet these people down, fine."

Jake hurried to where the grinning Murphy was sitting. "What is it?" Jake whispered.

"You better read this before you ask little Rhonda any more questions," he said, thrusting the newspaper into Jake's hands. The story was on page one. Jake scanned it quickly.

"My column is in the B section," Murphy said. "That's the best part."

Jake, although he was aware he was the target of the judge's irritated scowl, took the time to read both the story and the column.

"Mr. Martin," the judge's voice cracked with anger. "This isn't a library. If you want to read, do it on your own time."

"Yes, your honor. I apologize." He took the newspaper with him as he approached the witness stand.

"Ms. Janus," Jake said. "Do you know that gentleman seated back there at the press table, Mr. Murphy?"

She nodded. "I met him last night."

"And did you discuss this case with him?"

She frowned. "We talked about a number of things."

"Did you tell him you were paid to come here and testify?"

"Objection," Sage shouted. "This is outrageous. There is nothing in evidence upon which to base such an insulting question."

"Sustained," the judge said. "If you wish to impeach the witness, do it with testimony and not innuendo."

Jake nodded his assent. "There's a story about you in today's *Detroit News*. Perhaps you'd like to take a minute to read it?" He handed the paper to her.

"Just a minute," Sage said. "If he's going to try to introduce that as an exhibit, he hasn't laid the proper foundation."

"Maybe he will," the judge said. "Overruled."

Rhonda Janus studied the story, her lips moving silently.

"Now," Jake said when she was done, "did you tell Mr. Murphy there, or anyone else, that you were paid to come here and give testimony?"

Sage started to rise, but the judge merely shook her head.

Rhonda's eyes first went to Sage, then she looked at the shocked Chip Daren. Finally, she turned to the judge.

"I really don't want to answer that," she said quietly.

"Answer the question, witness," Vinson commanded.

Rhonda's face contorted and for a moment Jake thought she might burst into tears. "I don't have to," she said in a voice just barely audible. "How do you say it? I'm taking the fifth. I think that's what you're supposed to say."

The judge arched her eyebrows. "You can only refuse to answer if it might tend to incriminate or degrade you. That's what the fifth amendment to the constitution says. Since you didn't evoke the fifth amendment yesterday when Mr. Sage was questioning you, it's a little late to do so now. I strongly suggest you answer Mr. Martin's question."

"I can't," Rhonda said, looking down at her lap.

"What do you mean, you can't?"

"If I do, I'll be arrested and maybe put in jail."

"The jury is excused," the judge said.

Judge Vinson waited until they had filed out and the jury room door was closed. Then she looked down at Rhonda Janus.

"You might get into jail quicker than you think," she said. "Refusal to answer can be contempt of this court. We have a very nice little jail up here, but I'm sure it's not quite what you're accustomed to." She paused. "Now, will you answer Mr. Martin's question?"

Rhonda shook her head. "I can't." A single tear trickled down one cheek as she looked up at the judge. "I thought the constitution protected everyone."

The judge threw her hands up in the air. "It does, but you can't pick and choose what questions you'll answer."

"Yesterday, I didn't know about this." She held up the newspaper.

"Let me see that."

The judge carefully read the story, then the column. "Have you seen this?" she asked Sage.

"Just now. Someone gave me a copy."

"Mr. Martin," the judge said, "I'm going to bring the jury back in. You can ask the witness a question. If she refuses to answer, I will order her to do so. If she still refuses and claims constitutional privilege, I will formally reserve the question of contempt and you can proceed to your next question."

"Your honor," Sage said, walking up to the bench. "I must object to such a procedure."

She smiled. "I thought you might."

"This isn't the Inquisition," Sage protested. "The witness has a right to refuse if she reasonably believes her testimony may incriminate her. She can't be forced to testify against herself."

The judge pursed her lips. "No one's forcing her to do anything. If she refuses to answer a question, she assumes the risk that the constitutional protection may not apply. Your objection is noted and overruled."

Sage was not about to give up. "If the jury is subjected to listening to a list of questions, each one being refused, they will tend to discredit not only this witness, but perhaps others. That, I submit, is just not fair."

"Whatever it is, that's how we're going to do it," she said.

"I must object strenuously."

"Overruled." She nodded to the clerk. "Get them back in here."

In the courtroom the process became almost mechanical. Jake's question was followed by Rhonda's refusal, followed by the judge's order to answer, and then Sage's objection. The process was repeated over and over again.

Jake carefully worded each question so that the jury would get the full impact and implication of Rhonda Janus' refusal to answer.

275

Rhonda had to be instructed repeatedly by the judge to keep her trembling voice up as she recited what had become for her a litany, declining to respond to each question on constitutional grounds. She refused to answer Jake's questions about whom she had talked to about the case, what had been paid her and by whom.

Jake paused and walked to the back of the courtroom.

"Do you recall giving testimony in this matter yesterday?"

She nodded. "Yes," she whispered.

"I'm sorry," Jake said. "I can't hear you."

"Yes!"

Jake paused for effect, then spoke in a loud voice.

"Yesterday, on the stand, is what you told the jury the truth?"

Sage was rising when she answered. "I refuse to answer the question on the grounds that it may incriminate me. I take the fifth amendment."

Judge Vinson stared at her with narrowing eyes. "You testified here under oath yesterday. Did you commit perjury?"

Rhonda Janus seemed to shrink away from the judge; she did not look at her. "Same answer," she said in a voice just audible. "I refuse to answer the questions on constitutional grounds."

"I order you to answer Mr. Martin's question. Were you lying yesterday?"

Rhonda's voice faded as she once again said her little litany about invoking the fifth amendment.

The courtroom became very still as Jake stood motionless, intently studying the witness. Then he looked over at the jury and spoke in a voice cold with disgust. "I'm through with this . . ." he paused ". . . witness."

"Mr. Sage?" The judge said.

Sage didn't even stand. "No questions," he said.

The judge looked down at Rhonda Janus. "Witness, this isn't over," she said. "I will take the various legal options open to me under advisement. In the meantime, I order you not to leave the state."

Rhonda merely nodded. She got up and began walking, unsteadily at first, but then she began to pick up speed as she headed for the courtroom door. Like a school of feeding fish, the newsmen rushed out in pursuit.

Jake waited until the noise of their exit diminished.

"We have introduced the will," he said to the judge. "And we have offered the two witnesses to that will. We rest."

Sage stood up slowly.

"If you're thinking of making a motion for a directed verdict or anything similar," the judge said, "let me advise you it would be a waste of time. Are you ready to proceed?"

"We are, your honor. However, I wonder if I might ask the

court's indulgence so that I might have a few minutes before I call my first witness."

She frowned. "Look, I'm not the one in a hurry. But I warned both you lawyers that if this matter lasted beyond this week I would adjourn because of the hunting season. You can take all the time you want, as far as I'm concerned, but just keep that in mind. This is Wednesday. If we haven't finished, and I mean completely finished, by Friday night, this matter is going to be set over for at least two weeks."

Sage bowed slightly. "I'll do my best," he said, smiling.

"Fine. We'll take a twenty-minute break."

Sage found a spot in the county clerk's office where the three of them could be alone.

"I'll kill that brainless bitch," Chip snarled. "You can never trust a goddamned drunk."

"Ronny did her best," Gussie said.

"If that was her best, I'd hate to see her worst," Chip snapped at his sister.

Sage perched himself up on the edge of an ancient wooden desk. "Someone should be grateful to Rhonda Janus." he said evenly.

What the hell are you talking about?" Chip demanded.

"She protected whoever paid her," Sage said looking at Chip. "Was it you?"

Chip colored slightly. "No!"

"But you know who did," Sage replied. "She may not be too bright, but our Rhonda is certainly loyal. However, loyal or not, I trust you both realize she's badly hurt our case. What she did was absolutely stupid. The jury may begin to think about a conspiracy. That could taint the entire case. Her display may cast a cloud of doubt over the rest of our witnesses. It's absolutely essential that the jury believe those witnesses beyond question. We carry a heavy burden of proof."

"What are you saying?" Chip demanded.

"I'm perfectly content to continue," Sage said. "But perhaps you two might wish to reconsider."

"Settle?" Gussie said.

"Settle, my ass!" Chip exploded. "What's to settle? Do you think that bitch would give up control of the bank?"

"That's doubtful, I agree," Sage said, serenely unperturbed by Chip's anger. "However, she might be persuaded to forgo enforcing the will's forfeiture provision. As you continually remind me, that involves a considerable sum of money."

"This isn't about money, Sage," Chip snapped. "It never has been. We want the bank. Nothing less than that!"

Sage looked at Gussie. "Do you feel the same way?"

She shrugged. "Not really. But this is Chip's little game after all,

277

isn't it? It's his decision. Do you think there's still a chance of winning?"

"Anything's possible."

"Jesus! You can't let that bitch walk away with the money and the bank. What are you, a wimp? You're supposed to be a fighter."

Sage raised one eyebrow. "From the beginning you've chosen to keep me in the dark on a number of important matters. The payments to the lovely Rhonda, for instance. Someone has been directing the strategy for the conduct of this case. Who that someone is, I don't know. But if you have any complaints, I suggest you take it up with your secret adviser."

"But you—"

Sage stopped Chip by holding up his hand. "I rather expected there would be trouble over this rather strange arrangement, and that's why I drew up the agreement between us. You agreed, in writing, that any risk in conducting things in this manner would be entirely assumed by you."

Chip was about to reply, but his sister put a restraining hand on his arm. "He's right, you know."

Chip's mouth curled downward in anger. "There's going to be an army of hunters up here in a few days. Maybe I'll just shoot that scheming bitch. That would settle things."

"It wouldn't give you control of the bank."

"What do you mean?" Chip growled.

"Under the will, if Elizabeth Daren dies, the voting power would go to the trustees of your father's Foundation."

"I could work with them," Chip said.

Sage smiled. "Not from prison, you couldn't. And believe me, that's where you'd be for the rest of your life. There's no first class section in Michigan prisons, so I doubt that you'd like it a whole lot."

"With all the bullets flying in the woods up here, they'd never know it was me. It would just be a hunting accident."

"He was the same as a child," Gussie said, smiling. "Always full of wild schemes. Fortunately, he never had the nerve to actually try any of them."

Sage nodded, his eyes steady on Chip Daren. "In this case, it would be just as well. Mrs. Daren is surrounded by security men. They look competent to me. And in case they didn't shoot you first, you'd be the absolutely number one suspect if anything happened. You wouldn't need a lawyer then; you'd need a magician."

Chip's face trembled with anger, but he made no reply.

"Since there won't be a settlement," Gussie said. "What happens now?"

"We'll proceed with the other witnesses. Unless there are some more major surprises—" he looked at Chip "—we shall present an extremely strong case that your father was not legally competent when he signed the will. The local people are angry that the Daren

278

land hasn't been opened up for development. That resentment will be reflected in the jury's attitude, and it should work to our benefit." He smiled. "Also, I'm not exactly unskilled when it comes to persuading a jury to see things my way."

"This is one case you had better not lose," Chip said, still furious.

Sage sighed. "I don't know how much success you've had with threats in your life, but they seldom work, especially if you can't back them up."

Gussie smiled. "Don't pay any attention to Chip. He threatens everyone. It's just part of his effervescent charm."

Chip glowered at her.

Sage rose. "I believe we all understand each other." He glanced at his watch. "It's time to go back to work."

Lee Stevens' anxiety level was high as the driver guided the big Chrysler through the dingy Chicago backstreets. The driver, as well as the two other security men, were all armed so he wasn't worried about the safety of the one hundred thousand dollars in his briefcase. Stevens was worried that after all his work, Leon Clooney might not be able to produce the promised videotape, or worse, that Clooney, in terror, might have hidden himself away into the murky depths of his sordid world.

"It's just ahead there," Stevens said to the driver. "In the next block, on the left."

The driver and the other two men were all about thirty, and although they were well-dressed, they had the unmistakable, hard-eyed look of cops.

The driver pulled into a vacant parking space just in front of Pussycat World. Although it was midafternoon, there was no one on the shabby street.

"Mr. Stevens," the driver said, "I suggest that you and Rayburn go into the store. Leave the money here. If your man has what you want, you can have him come out and we'll make the exchange right here in the car. It's safer that way."

Stevens nodded and got out. Rayburn, the security man, followed him. Leon Clooney was sitting in his usual place. He was alone in the store.

Clooney's eyes were fixed on Rayburn. "Who's he?"

"A security man," Stevens replied. "I'm not about to walk around alone in Chicago with all that money."

Clooney's face glistened with sweat. "You got it?"

Stevens nodded. "It's out in the car."

"Bring it in," Clooney said.

"Not until I know you have what I want," Stevens said.

Rayburn was looking at the magazine racks with their garish displays of flesh. His hands were thrust deep into his topcoat pockets and he seemed to be paying no attention to Clooney or Stevens.

"Don't you trust me?" Clooney asked.

"If you want to see the money, you can go out to the car and take a look. There's a couple more security men there."

"If I—"

Rayburn, who had been studying a stack of group sex magazines near Clooney, suddenly whirled around, pulled out a revolver and brought the muzzle up close to Clooney's head.

"I'll take that," Rayburn said quietly, reaching down and coming up with a small automatic pistol that Clooney had had concealed in his lap.

Now Clooney's eyes were wide with fear. "Hey, I wasn't going to do anything," he protested weakly. "I had that thing for protection, that's all. I don't know you guys. I didn't know what you might do."

Rayburn put Clooney's automatic in his pocket. "I'll return this to you when we leave," he said as he replaced his own weapon into his other coat pocket.

"Do you want to see the money?" Stevens asked.

Clooney, who looked even more pale, shook his head. "No," he said, his voice slightly tremulous. "I'll get the tape."

He eased himself down from the high bench behind the tall counter. Using his cane, he hobbled out and crossed the store to a glass cabinet displaying sexual toys. Once there, Clooney took out a key and unlocked the cabinet's door, then reached beneath a stack of rubber dildoes and took out a videotape hidden in the pile.

"This is it." He held it out to Stevens.

"I want to see it before I make payment."

Clooney nervously glanced at Rayburn, who had positioned himself back at the opening in the partition that divided the store. He hesitated for a moment as if unsure of his next step, then he shrugged.

"We got a jerk-off booth," Clooney said. "I'll set it up there."

He hobbled to what looked like an old-fashioned instant photo booth, pulling back the curtains to expose a chair facing a television set above a VCR machine.

"We charge five bucks to use this," he said. "It's supposed to be for previewing a tape before you buy, but guys come in here and whack off while they watch." He expertly inserted the tape and flipped on the television. "It's kinda funny sometimes. They get carried away, talking to the screen and moaning."

The screen was full of dancing gray snow, which then cleared and a garish red logo appeared announcing "Bay Brothers Productions."

"I'm the Bay Brothers," Clooney said. "I thought it sounded more professional that way."

Softly throbbing rock music played as big orange letters proclaimed, *The Hot Tycoon's Last Will.*

The title faded and a bosomy brunette was shown sitting behind a desk and polishing her nails. She picked up the phone on the first ring.

"Screw, Cheatem and Lust, attorneys at law," she said into the phone. She chewed her gum for a moment. "I'm sorry, Mr. Lust can't come to the phone right now. He's busy making August Daren's will." She smirked. "That's our biggest client. We call him big Gus." She rolled her eyes as she emphasized the word *big.*

Steven looked up at Clooney. "What the hell is this?"

"Wait a minute. You'll see."

The camera panned to a door just past the girl on the screen. Then there was a fade-out and Augustus Daren appeared on the screen.

"We are here today to . . ."

Immediately, Stevens recognized the off-camera voice as belonging to Jake Martin. He turned to Clooney as Martin's voice continued while the camera was on Augustus Daren. "What have you done?"

Clooney looked at the screen fondly. "Hey, it was easy. I spliced hot studio stuff into the Daren tape. Some of it's pretty funny. See, when he says he's leaving something to someone, I spliced in some suck and fuck segments. I don't like to brag, but you'd think the whole thing was shot just to make a porno movie."

"Don't you have the original Daren tape?"

Clooney shook his head, his eyes still on the screen. "Nope. That will thing ran about fifteen minutes. I used most of it, but there's a couple minutes of the original missing. I tossed the other one away," he said. "It was of no use to me."

"And you think this damn thing is useful to us?" Stevens snapped.

Clooney shrugged. "What I spliced in, I can splice out. It's no big deal when you have the right equipment and you know what you're doing."

Stevens looked back at the screen. A thin young woman was being pawed by three men.

"That's supposed to be the Daren trustees," Clooney said. "This isn't exactly Academy Award stuff, but the people who watch these things don't care. They know what they want to see. It's a little like kabuki. You only need some excuse for a plot; it's the action they want to see, the good old in and out."

"You were the cameraman who shot the actual Daren will footage?"

"Yeah."

"And you edited this, whatever it is, yourself?"

Clooney nodded. "I was operating on a shoestring. I did all my

281

own work; I couldn't afford to hire it done." He looked wistfully at the screen. "I woulda made a lot of money eventually if those sons of bitches hadn't come and busted me up."

"How did you think you could possibly use this?" Stevens nodded toward the screen. The girl and the men were now naked.

"A novelty item. Hey, Daren was pretty well known. I wouldn't market anything like this in the usual way. I'd make up a flock of copies and sell them in one lot. Someone else would do the distributing. That way they couldn't trace it back to me. I had a lot of fake names; the Bay Brothers, Little Pine Productions; all kinds of names." He sighed. "I could have made a bundle, but I suppose there's something to be said for being alive."

Clooney looked at the screen. "I was waiting for the old man to finally die. You can't sue for libel if you're dead. When he croaked, I was tempted to try and sell it. But if I started to show it to some distributors, I might have had another call from the guys that did this." He tapped his knee with his cane. "So I did nothing. Then you came along."

Stevens shook his head. "This isn't what you said it was."

"Hey, most of it's there. You wanted old man Daren making his will. You got it. I can just cut the dirty parts out and it's almost as good as new."

"If you did that, spliced the original, or what's left of it, together, could you keep this copy?"

Clooney leered. "Not bad, huh? I mean I always got top action in my stuff. Hot, but still good art, you know?"

Stevens looked at the screen again. Two different women were making love to each other. "If we can get any of this into court, we'd have to show what happened at every step of the way. We'd have to have both the before and after tapes."

"Hey, no problem. We can get that done at a place right here in Chicago. We just have to rent their equipment. I'd do it and it would take only a couple of hours."

Stevens nodded. "Even if you could, you'd have to come back with us. We'd need you as a witness to get the court even to consider it."

Clooney eyes almost popped from his head in fright. "Screw that! I can't go back to Michigan. I told you that!"

"You want the money, don't you?"

"You agreed—"

"I agreed when I thought you had the original tape. I don't even know if this is of any use. We're not paying a hundred thousand for something we can't use."

"I'm not going to Michigan," Clooney said firmly.

"If you come with us, I'll see you get a first class ticket out to wherever you want to go. And if we can't use the tape in court, you won't get all the money, but I'll give you five thousand for your time."

Clooney looked as if he might break out in tears. "But you promised—"

"If we can use it, you'll still get the money." Stevens looked toward Rayburn. "And we'll protect you. You have nothing to lose, Leon."

"Maybe. Come back tomorrow—"

"Now, Leon," Stevens said. He turned to Rayburn. "How long would it take us to get to Gladding if we drove straight through?"

Rayburn thought for a moment. "Ten hours, maybe a little longer. We could fly, but by the time we made the arrangements it would take as long, and we couldn't bring along our weapons."

Stevens nodded. "Get your coat, Leon. We'll get you to that photo lab, then we'll hit the road for Michigan. It's three o'clock now; if we hurry, we can get up there before court starts tomorrow."

"But I'll have to pack," Leon protested.

"We'll buy you whatever you need. Grab that tape, lock this hole up and we're on our way."

"What's the fucking hurry?"

Lee Stevens smiled. "We have to get up there before the trial is over, Leon. That's the fucking hurry. Let's go."

24

Jake listened, forcing himself to maintain a neutral expression to conceal from the jury the horror he felt as every word of the expert's testimony seemed to cut into his case like a scalpel's thrust.

The doctor, a nationally know neurologist who specialized in problems of the elderly, had an easygoing manner, but he spoke with a quiet authority that was almost hypnotic. Sage was playing him as skillfully as a master violinist might stroke a Stradivarius.

Jake had fought to keep the doctor off the stand on the basis that, expert or not, he had never seen Augustus Daren and therefore could not give an opinion based merely on what others had said. He had argued with such vigor that Judge Vinson had finally threatened him with a citation for contempt. She had coolly demanded that Jake validate his argument with supporting Michigan cases. But he had none to offer. They were under lock and key with Bellows. The doctor was not a surprise witness, so the judge refused to stop the proceedings to allow Jake time to look up the law or even to call Cora to see if she could remember the case citations.

Sage quoted several Michigan cases, which was good enough

for the judge, although she restricted his inquiry to hypothetical questions based on Dr. Faraday's findings.

But that was more than enough for Sage. He led the doctor through a discussion of insane delusions and their effect upon mental competency. The doctor smiled knowingly at the jury as he explained the workings of the human brain in relation to possible stroke residuals. The jury, all of them, smiled back like eager pupils anxious for the brilliant illuminations of a beloved teacher. Any gains he had made by discrediting Rhonda Janus were fading fast, and Jake sensed his case slowly sliding away.

When Sage finally finished questioning the doctor, Jake rose and stood at his seat, without approaching him. He knew he had to be careful. The jury really liked the doctor. Sage's book had cautioned care with such a witness.

"Doctor, these opinions of yours are based solely on the information proposed to you by Mr. Sage here in the courtroom, is that right?"

The doctor nodded pleasantly." "Yes."

"If that information was incorrect, then would your opinions also be incorrect?"

"If data is faulty, obviously any conclusions based on such data would be equally faulty."

Jake could hope for no more than that. Anything else might be a fool's trip into dangerous territory. "Thank you," he said, and sat down.

Sage's second witness was also a doctor, this time a psychologist from Harvard, an expert in rehabilitation for stroke and accident victims. Again, Jake fought a battle to try to keep the expert off the stand, but he was equally unsuccessful.

The psychologist did not have such a winning manner, but his opinions were just as damaging. This time, knowing that the members of the jury weren't so impressed, Jake boldly probed to try to score some points on cross-examination, but the psychologist was unshakable. Sage had managed to weave a skillful web of medical testimony to convince the jury that Augustus Daren had been in the grip of an insane delusion at the time he signed his last will.

The doctor was excused.

"We call Phil Hunt as our next witness," Sage said, his voice reflecting his growing confidence.

The judge stood up. Jake suspected she was dying for a cigarette. "We'll take a fifteen-minute break," she said, "then we'll continue with the next witness."

Jake walked back to where Elizabeth was sitting.

She looked up at him. "Not good, is it?"

He tried to smile. "We got hurt," he said without elaboration. "This next witness is your former gamekeeper, right?"

She nodded. "He was very close to Gus. That was well known up here."

"Can he hurt us?" Jake asked.

"Not if he tells the truth," she replied.

If Phil Hunt was lying, he nevertheless sounded quietly convincing. Hunt, a small, wiry man, was relaxed on the stand, and when he spoke to the jury he seemed like just an ordinary guy talking to his neighbours. He spoke with calm dignity, answering Sage's questions as if reluctant to reveal the shame of his former employer's sad mental state. His testimony, coming on the heels of the doctors', gave eyewitness support to everything the medical men had said.

Jake, when his turn came, tried to shake the former Daren gamekeeper, but without success. He tried to bate Hunt into anger, but the only person Jake seemed to irritate was the judge.

He looked over at the jury and noticed that each of them avoided his gaze. That, according to Sage's book, was a bad sign. The courtroom had turned quiet, the kind of ominous absence of noise found in funeral homes or hospital waiting rooms.

Jake walked back to the counsel table, then decided to try one more line of attack.

He picked up a sheet of paper and pretended to study it. "You seem to have come into some money recently, Mr. Hunt. Isn't that so?"

To Jake's surprise, Hunt's self-assurance gave way to a look of distress, but for only a moment.

"Objection," Sage said, getting to his feet. "The question isn't material or relevant."

"Overruled," the judge said, her eyes fixed on Hunt. "Answer the question," she said quietly.

"I took out a loan recently," Hunt said. "A loan to fix some things around my place."

"What kind of things?" Jake asked.

Sage was about to object, but sat back down as the judge shook her head.

Hunt's confidence was deserting him, his expression suddenly guarded. "Oh, a new roof, a few things like that. A new truck."

"How much was the loan?" Jake asked.

"If the court please," Sage was up, "this has no connection to this case. I object to this line of questioning."

Vinson looked at Jake. "If you can connect this up, you had better do it. For the record, the objection is overruled."

Jake walked back near the spectator section, then turned and faced Hunt squarely.

"When did you get this loan?"

"A month or two ago."

"How much was the loan?" Jake asked again.

Hunt's eyes shifted nervously. "A couple thousand."

"How many thousand?"

Hunt hesitated, then spoke. "Forty thousand."

There were gasps from the spectators.

Jake debated continuing, but he knew his bluff might be called and then he would lose more than mere advantage. His own credibility would be destroyed. Even asking who made the loan could explode if someone had had the foresight to launder the money through a mortgage to a corporation.

"Boy, Mr. Hunt, someone must have just discovered they like you an awful lot," Jake said.

"Objection!" Sage roared.

"Sustained," the judge snapped.

Jake shrugged. "I think I've made my point. I'm through with the witness."

"Look," the judge snarled, "any more of those cute little asides and you'll be making them over at the jail. Got that?"

Sage quickly led Hunt back into the safe area of Gus Daren's last hunt. He ignored asking about the loan. He too recognized its explosive potential. Jake hoped the jury noted Sage's reluctance.

Hunt's answers this time were a bit more muted and did no real harm. When Sage finished, Jake offered no additional cross-examination.

Phil Hunt's testimony had hurt, but Jake hoped the legacy from Rhonda Janus had spilled over, at least enough to make the jury suspicious of Hunt's description of Gus Daren.

But there was no way to tell if it had.

T. G. Sage's next witness was a stout, pasty-looking woman who had once worked as a maid in the Daren house.

She dutifully answered his questions but, like Rhonda Janus, she couldn't resist painting too vivid a picture, describing Augustus Daren as a drooling, demented man who cringed in terror at his hallucinations.

Jake glanced over at the jury. They weren't impressed. Sage, apparently sensing the jury's attitude, quickly finished and turned her over to Jake. He walked up close to her.

"Did anyone talk to you about this case?"

"Mr. Sage. Today."

"Did he tell you what questions he was going to ask?"

"No, he just told me to tell the truth."

"Did you talk to anyone else?"

She hesitated. "Ah, no."

"How did you come to be a witness here today?"

"Pardon me?"

"Did you just wander in off the street?"

"Objection," Sage said.

"Sustained."

"You must have talked to someone," Jake said. "I was given your name as a witness. Someone must have talked to you."

She nodded quickly. "I forgot. Phil Hunt talked to me."

"What did he say?"

"Oh, he just asked if I had been working at Raven's Nest when Mr. Daren had the stroke."

"And that's all?"

She nodded. "Yes."

Jake paused. "You sure? You forgot before."

"Objection," Sage snapped.

The judge sighed. "Sustained. Get on with it."

Jake walked to the back of the courtroom, then turned and spoke. "Did anyone pay you to come here and testify?"

"Objection," Sage said.

"Overruled. I'll take the answer."

"Well? Were you paid?"

"No."

Jake smiled. "Have you taken out any loans recently?"

There was a smattering of laughter behind him.

"No."

"How about a bonus to be paid after you testify?"

She shifted uncomfortably and hesitated.

"Did you hear me?" Jake asked.

She nodded.

"Well?"

She seemed to be silently debating what answer to give, then in a voice close to a whisper she said, "No."

Sage's book cautioned against asking any questions when the answer wasn't known. It wasn't always possible, the book said, but it was a wise choice when applicable.

Jake looked over at the jury, and wondered if they thought she was lying too.

The answer would come only in their verdict.

"That's all," Jake said.

The witness was excused.

"It's almost quitting time, Mr. Sage," the judge said. "Do you have any more witnesses?"

He stood up, paused for a moment, then answered. "We may offer additional testimony in the morning."

"Okay. Then we'll break for the day." She looked at Jake. "Do you expect to have any rebuttal witnesses?"

Jake nodded. "Yes."

Vinson frowned. "We're running out of time. I caution you again. If this isn't done by Friday, I'm going to set it over until after deer season. I'm not going to like that, and the jury isn't going to like that." She looked at Sage and then Jake. "So, I'd strongly advise you both to hurry this thing along."

The newspeople outside the courthouse were more interested in Tiger Sage, and Jake found he was able to get to his car with comparative ease, fending off just a few reporters.

A light rain, combined with fading daylight, cut the visibility as Jake drove out to Raven's Nest. He was surprised to see a large helicopter parked on the grass in front of the main building. Jake parked and went in.

As usual, the maid escorted him into the great room. Two well-dressed Japanese men stood as Elizabeth introduced Jake.

The younger man, Mr. Icura, spoke impeccable English. The other, Mr. Yamashita, older and clearly the boss, spoke English to be understood, but with a definite accent.

"Mr. Icura and Mr. Yamashita are here to make me an offer I can't refuse, Jake. Or at least, that's what they'd like me to believe."

"We understand you are doing an excellent job in court," Icura said to Jake. "We also understand you are losing." It was said with a smile.

Jake sat down near Elizabeth. "I wouldn't agree."

Yamashita nodded. "No, of course not. It is not the way of the warrior to acknowledge possible defeat."

Jake laughed. "I'm no warrior, just a run-of-the-mill lawyer."

Yamashita turned his attention to Elizabeth. "Let me be frank," he said. "We have obtained options on much of your bank's stock. We will offer to buy you out now at the price we previously quoted. That way, we will take control of the bank and you will make a very handsome profit."

"And if I don't?"

Yamashita's face remained expressionless. "When you lose the case, we will have sufficient stock to gain control easily. We will not need to buy your shares. When that happens, your stock won't be nearly as valuable, as I'm sure you realize."

"Who sold out?" Elizabeth asked. "Gus's children?"

Yamashita shook his head. "We didn't even approach them. They seem much too unreliable, anyway."

"Then it must have been the trustees," she said.

"Do not think ill of them," Icura interjected. "They are frightened at the prospect of the children getting control. They have a duty to protect the trust. We have agreed upon a price to be paid when you lose the case here. The trust will be greatly enriched."

"Only if I lose the court case," she said.

"You will lose," Yamashita said flatly. "We have had observers here every day. I regret to say they assure us that all is lost for you."

Elizabeth smiled. "If that is so, Mr. Yamashita, why are you

288

here? If what you say is true, you have only to wait a few days and pick up my bank at bargain rates. Why don't you do that?"

Icura laughed loudly, but stopped quickly when Yamashita glanced irritably at him.

Yamashita sighed. "The cards have been stacked against you. Let me assure you we had nothing to do with that, but we know about it. Of course, there is always the outside chance the jury might be foolish. But we don't like to take chances, however slight. You would be wise to accept our offer now. It won't be made again."

"I appreciate your position," she said, "but I am determined to see this through to the end. If I lose, I lose."

Yamashita's expression was grim. "As you might well imagine, we have had people infiltrate your banking organization."

"Spies?" Jake asked.

Icura smiled. "I hope you're not shocked, Mr. Martin. It is common practice in business today. It's even taught at some of your better universities. We like to think of it as information gathering."

"It's still spying," Jake said.

Icura nodded. "It is a common practice among our competitors. We have to protect ourselves."

"And what have your information gatherers found?" Elizabeth asked.

Yamashita spoke. "I am reluctant to tell you this, but in order for you to make a wise decision, you must know where you stand. It seems one of your main people has been sabotaging your efforts right from the beginning."

"Claude deSalle," Elizabeth said.

"You knew?" Yamashita was not able to disguise his surprise.

Elizabeth shrugged. "He is a very able banker," she said, "but in areas involving personal ambition, he is not to be trusted. I take it he's the one who is responsible for building this case against me?"

"We understand that is so."

Elizabeth nodded slowly. "Well, I appreciate your candor, but my answer is still no."

Yamashita merely bowed his head politely.

"Will you stay the night?" Elizabeth asked.

"We must get back, regrettably."

"At least stay for dinner," Elizabeth said.

"Our pilot tells us we have to avoid the weather front moving in, so we must decline."

"I won't keep you then." Elizabeth stood up. "If I should lose, you can still expect a fight for control."

Yamashita smiled. "You would have made a wonderful samurai, Elizabeth; a warrior willing to perish for a cause."

"If I don't perish," she added, "and I win this case, you may find I can be an especially skillful opponent."

Yamashita bowed with dignity. "You are already."

The pulsating roar shook the house as the helicopter rose into the dark sky. Jake went to a window and watched it speed across the lake, its whirling navigational lights making it look like a movie version of an alien spaceship. It was soon out of sight.

Elizabeth was watching the fire.

"Just out of curiosity," Jake said, "what did that decision cost you?"

She looked up at him. "You mean turning them down?"

"Yes."

A burning log broke, sending up a shower of glowing sparks that fell back into the flames in the fireplace. Elizabeth watched the display as she talked.

"My share—one third of the bank's stock—is worth perhaps two hundred million. Yamashita offered to double that."

"That's almost a half-billion dollars," Jake said, his tone reflecting the awe he felt at the thought of such an amount.

"More, actually," she said. "If we lose, Yamashita will buy the trust's share. It's usual in these kind of takeovers that the remaining stock becomes depressed. It would probably be worth only half of what it is now."

"My God! Are you sure you made the right decision?"

She didn't answer immediately, then she shrugged. "The money, at this point, means nothing," she said quietly. "I made a solemn promise to Gus that I would carry out his plans for the bank. As I told you, Jake, the bank will be his memorial. Everything in life that's important to me is bet on the outcome of this trial." She looked at him. "I made the only decision possible under the circumstances."

"But Yamashita said the cards are stacked against you."

She nodded slowly. "After all this began I knew it had to have Claude deSalle's fine hand. I was prepared for that. It was Donald who surprised me."

"Bellows?"

She looked at him sharply. "We wouldn't be in this mess if it wasn't for Bellows. He's deSalle's man. I knew it when he tried to use you to get me to settle. It also explains who stole the original videotapes from your office."

"I can't believe—" Jake started to say.

But he was interrupted by the arrival of Lee Stevens.

Jake didn't recognize Leon Clooney, who looked much older than he had when the Daren will had been taped. He had become almost emaciated and had a defeated, seedy appearance.

The cash in Stevens' briefcase was deposited in the house safe, along with the extra copies of the videotapes Stevens had brought up. Jake wanted to see the tape, but Stevens drew him aside.

"We got a few problems with the tape," Stevens said, whispering.

290

"Like what?"

"That asshole Clooney spliced porno segments into it."

"What?"

"The original is gone, but most of the footage is still in the remake. We got here late because we had to stop at a studio and have Clooney make copies and splice out the sex stuff. He said it wouldn't take long, but Clooney's so scared he kept screwing it up. I have the porno version, but I also have the copy after he spliced out the crotch stuff. The new version isn't bad, but you can tell it's been cut up a little."

"Oh, God," Jake said. "I won't be able to get that into evidence."

"You can try." Stevens shrugged. "I promised to pay Clooney five grand, no matter what. He's to get the rest of the money only if the tapes can be used in court. He knows that."

Jake looked over at Clooney, who sat nervously on the edge of a chair, as if he were afraid he'd be asked to leave at any moment.

"He looks like a bum."

"Yeah. If I'd had the time I would have cleaned him up a bit, but I knew you needed the tapes right away."

"No matter how he looks, I'll have to use Clooney as a witness," Jake said, shaking his head slowly. "This whole case may turn on him."

"Couldn't you get the tapes in some other way?"

Jake sighed. "No. Someone has to testify to what happened to the tape, explain about the alterations and how they were done. He's the only one who can tell about that."

"You'd better take a look at the tapes. I have both the hot and the restored versions."

"Let's see them."

Lee Stevens frowned. "I wouldn't show the porno to Elizabeth. It's pretty raunchy."

Jake looked at him. "I just found out in dollars how much she has riding on this. I'll tell her what we have and leave it up to her."

"In the meantime, I'm starved," Stevens said. "Could we get something to eat first?"

"I want to see the tapes," Jake said.

Stevens shook his head. "You might not have an appetite after that. Believe me, Jake, what you're about to see ain't *The Sound of Music*."

25

Tiger Sage finished his case with two additional witnesses. Jake was finding it difficult to concentrate, his mind preoccupied with how he would approach the question of the videotapes with the judge.

Both witnesses were local women who had worked at Raven's Nest, and their testimony was almost identical to Phil Hunt's of the day before, a fact Jake brought out on cross-examination. In his questions, Jake intimated that the witnesses had been coached, although they both denied it.

After the last woman left the stand, T. G. Sage announced that he was resting his case.

The judge looked down at Jake. "You said something yesterday about rebuttal?"

The moment had come. Leon Clooney was sitting in the spectator section under the close guard of Lee Stevens, who had both videotapes in his briefcase.

"Judge, I wonder if I could have a short conference?"

Her expression indicated her annoyance, but she reluctantly nodded, then looked over at the jury. "Take ten minutes," she said.

Jake waited until the jury had gone and the door to the jury room had been closed, then he spoke. "Could counsel talk in your chambers?"

She grimaced. "Well, all right, but let's make this fast."

Jake and Sage followed her into the cramped office.

"All right," she said to Jake, "you've got my attention. What do you want?"

"I'm about to offer some videotapes into evidence," Jake said. "And I'm not sure how you might want to handle that."

Sage raised an eyebrow but remained silent.

The judge lit a cigarette. "You're the lawyer, sonny. I'm not going to try your case for you. Do what you want to, and I'll rule then. Got that?"

"I think you had better see these videos first." Jake said.

Sage crossed his legs, casually running a finger over the crease in his trousers. "And just what are these tapes?"

Jake decided to be candid. He told the story of tracing Leon Clooney and finding what had happened to the original videotape.

"I have the tape as we found it in Chicago," Jake said, "complete with all the sex scenes. We had Clooney edit out the sex, and that edited tape contains most of the footage shot when Daren executed the will."

"Most?" Sage asked.

"Some of it was lost, but probably ninety percent is there."

Sage pursed his lips as he slowly shook his head. "What you propose is clearly inadmissible. It's altered evidence, and even without seeing it, I will object."

"We had better take a look at these videos before we go on the record," the judge said. "How do you propose to show these things?"

"We have a television and a VCR in the car outside. We can set it up in a matter of minutes."

"I insist that whatever we see be kept private," Sage said. "I don't want any one of the spectators to get even a hint. Jurors can hear things from family and friends. I mean to keep this from them in any form, including second-hand."

"Have the sheriff help set up the television in my office downstairs. I'll hold off any ruling until I see just exactly what you've got."

"It's pretty raunchy stuff, judge," Jake said.

She scowled. "Set it up and I'll be down to see it. And step on it, unless you want to spend part of the winter up here."

Sage walked out with Jake. "I'm glad for your sake you found the tape, but I can't allow you to use it here." He smiled. "It will, however, come in handy if your old firm does bring charges against you before the bar. You can make a pretty strong case now that someone in the firm was sabotaging your efforts in this case from the beginning."

"You think so?"

"There's nothing like a bit of graphic evidence for effect, smutty or not. That's why I have to keep this out."

"You won't," Jake said.

"Don't bet on it."

They watched both tapes in silence. The judge, still in her judicial robe, sat smoking a cigarette, her face as expressionless as though her features had been carved from stone. Sage's mouth was set firmly, grimly prepared for battle. The sheriff seemed amused during the crude sexual scenes shown in the first tape. The security man who had set up the television was as unreadable as the judge. Jake felt his heart thudding within his chest, unable to determine what the judge was thinking or what she might do.

The second video finished and the security man began rewinding the tape.

Judge Vinson stood up. "I've seen them," she said. "Let's go up to the courtroom and put all this on the record."

They followed her up the stairs and back into the crowded courtroom.

Judge Vinson took her accustomed place behind the high bench. "Let the record show that on the request of Mr. Martin, the court has just viewed two videotapes he proposes to submit into evidence. He has informed the court he plans to offer them through the testimony of the man who made the tapes. Is that correct, Mr. Martin?"

Jake stood. "It is, your honor."

She looked at Sage. "I presume you object, Mr. Sage?"

He slowly got up and walked to a spot just in front of the bench. "I object most strenuously," he said crisply. "What is being offered is a hodgepodge of altered videotape footage. We have no way of knowing what the deleted parts might show. The claim is made that those missing parts were excluded by accident, but we don't know that. They might have been conveniently lost for an entirely different purpose. They might have revealed a man in the throes of an insane delusion, we might have seen a man whose mind was so crippled by a damaged brain that . . ."

Sage continued smoothly, citing ruling case law as if he had just looked it up. He was confident and persuasive. Jake listened with a sinking feeling.

". . . the law is clear," Sage was finishing up. "Doctored evidence is just too risky to be permitted. I respectfully ask the court to keep this record clear and clean and to sustain my objection."

Jake was about to reply, although he really had no firm idea of what he might say, when the judge held up her hand to restrain him.

"The issue in this case is relatively simple," she said, as the court reporter busily took down her words. "It boils down to whether Augustus Daren was legally competent when he executed the will offered here for probate. I agree that the tapes are questionable; however, they might be of some help to the jury in determining the key issue here. If Mr. Martin can establish their history through his witness, I'll let them in for what they may be worth."

"Wait a minute," Sage snapped. "I must protest this ruling. The law is—"

"I've ruled," she growled. "There are appellate courts. If you quarrel with my findings, you know where they are."

"I want an adjournment so I can bring an emergency appeal on your ruling."

"You're the one who is in such a hurry, Mr. Sage. We will not stop now. If I'm wrong, you can have me reversed by an appellate court. In any event, we aren't going to waste any more time; we are going ahead."

"But—"

"I've ruled."

"I take an exception!"

"Exceptions aren't required anymore in Michigan, Mr. Sage. Your objection is noted and overruled."

Tiger Sage was about to speak but she raised a warning eyebrow, then turned to Jake.

"Call your witness," she commanded. "Bring in the jury."

Leon Clooney was not a good witness. Sweaty and halting in speech, he kept looking around as if trying to escape. Jake carefully led him through the story of the two tapes. Then, as he had instructed Clooney he would, he asked him about the money. Jake knew the payment for the videotapes might sour the jury, but he also knew it would be better to bring it out first than let Sage do it. Jake could hear the soft whisperings behind him in the courtroom as Clooney told of being promised a hundred thousand dollars for the tapes.

T. G. Sage's cross-examination was merciless. Clooney turned as red as if he were barbecued as Sage took him through his sleazy history as a small-time pornographer. Jake glanced at the jury. He wondered if trying to get the videos in might backfire. The jurors were obviously appalled by Clooney.

Over Sage's renewed objections, Jake offered the tapes after Clooney hobbled from the witness stand. Judge Vinson directed that the television be set up directly in front of the jury. The newsmen flocked to that side of the courtroom, crowding against each other, trying to sneak a look at what the jury was seeing.

Jake watched the jurors as they viewed the first tape. Some of the women had looked away at first, but they seemed to overcome their squeamishness and by the end of the tape all of them were glued to watching the television. The second, edited video, seemed anticlimactic. This time the jury watched more comfortably but with less intensity.

And then it was done.

"Do you have anything additional to offer?" the judge asked Jake.

"No, your honor."

"Mr. Sage?"

Sage rose, but was silent for a moment. He studied the jury, and then looked up at the judge. "We believe we have established our case."

"Good," the judge said. She looked at the jury. "We'll take a short lunch break. When we get back, the attorneys will make their final arguments to you. Then I will instruct you in the law you will apply in this matter. After that, it will be all up to you. We'll take thirty minutes."

It had turned too cold to walk comfortably, so Jake got into the Corvette and found a deserted road near town and parked. The pines on each side of the sandy road rustled in the autumn wind, but all else was silence. He tried to think of what he would say to the jury. There was so much to be said, it seemed like a jigsaw puzzle that he would somehow have to piece together in a logical way. He would have to talk about Rhonda Janus and the implications of her refusal to answer questions about payment for testimony. He would have to attack the doctors whom Sage had produced. He would have to tell the jury that they shouldn't trust opinions from medical men who had never seen the patient. He would have to cover the testimony from the former Raven's Nest workers who . . . It all seemed quite impossible. There was just too much.

Jake felt overwhelmed by what he had to do, his mind becoming more numb as the minutes slipped by. Too soon, it was time to go back and all he could muster was a foggy outline of what he wanted to say.

When he returned to the courtroom, he was so nervous he wondered if he'd be able to talk at all. He watched as the jury filed in, then rose and took his place in front of the jury box.

He remembered Sage's book and the advice on beginning an argument to a jury. "Ladies and gentlemen," Jake said. "I want to thank each of you for the attention and interest you have shown . . ."

Jake continued, knowing that he was missing key points and feeling that he was proving just how completely inept he was. He faltered several times, trying to say what he so desperately wanted them to believe.

The jurors watched him coolly, without any evident response. Jake wondered if what appeared to be reserved politeness really might be concealed hostility. He spoke for only a short time. It seemed to him that his closing argument had gone entirely too fast, but he had nothing more to offer.

He stopped for a moment. He decided to abandon a formal style and just talk to them normally. He took the time to look from one juror to another, making eye contact with each of them.

"I'm going to be frank with you," he said in a conversational tone. "Somebody is lying here. And not just a little. This thing can't be both ways, can it? I mean, Augustus Daren was either incompetent when he executed the will, or he wasn't.

"Now you've heard all the testimony from the flesh-and-blood witnesses. And you've heard strange tales indeed. You've heard versions of Mr. Daren's condition varying from a man with memory problems to a drooling, mindless wreck."

Jake smiled. "People can vary on what they saw, but not that much, not if they're telling the truth. And you've heard about loans and paid vacations and bonuses. Kind of strange, isn't it? I mean, all that easy money being made, all of a sudden, and none of it in connection with this case. Do you believe that?"

Jake again paused and searched each juror's face for a moment.

"The old saying is that dead men don't tell tales. Well, that's not true anymore, is it? The most important testimony you heard in this case was given by a dead man. You don't have to rely on anyone else to decide if Augustus Daren was competent when he made the will. You saw him yourselves. He talked to you. You may not trust those other witnesses but you can trust your own eyes and ears."

Jake didn't realize his voice was raised as he approached the finish. "You saw there was nothing wrong with that man's mind! You saw he knew exactly what he was doing! You saw with your own eyes that he was in complete control!"

Jake paused for only a second, then continued. "Augustus Daren is our witness! We don't need anyone else. He was legally competent when he signed the will; you saw that for yourselves. The will, ladies and gentlemen, is absolutely valid, and we respectfully ask that you so find!"

Jake turned and walked to his seat at the counsel table. Around him he was aware of an almost strange silence in the courtroom.

Tiger Sage waited just a moment, then stood up, smiling congenially at the jury.

As if in sharp contrast to his own sometimes awkward performance, T. G. Sage was brilliant. Jake listened as the older lawyer wove humor and drama together, artfully using parts of the testimony to wave a tale of sordid greed. He described Augustus Daren as a senile prisoner who performed like a mindless puppet in the hands of his selfish wife. The jurors, to Jake's horror, were responding to Sage, smiling at his wit and nodding as he made more serious points.

He finished with a flourish.

"My young friend," Sage nodded at Jake, "tells you that his case depends entirely on that videotape. I think he's right; that does represent what this is all about." Sage walked back a bit and raised his voice slightly. "That videotape illustrates exactly that I've been talking about. This case stinks like a long dead fish and so does that so-called tape!"

"Sleaze!" His word echoed in the courtroom and he paused as if waiting for the echo to end, then continued with vigor. "They bring in a low-life photographer. You saw exactly what he was and what he did, and how much he was paid for coming here. Mr. Martin, in his remarks to you, conveniently skipped past just how much his star witness was paid to bring in that filth. One hundred thousand dollars! And for what was he paid?"

Sage walked two paces closer to the jury, his face coloring with emotion. "For a disgusting, doctored, spliced, altered piece of junk. You saw it; you know it was junk! But they paid one hundred thousand dollars for that junk! Why?"

He paused and stepped almost to the jury box rail. "Because it had been cleverly doctored so that you couldn't see what the other witnesses described, that Augustus Daren didn't know what he was doing. That so-called tape was carved, cut and edited, ladies and gentlemen, until it became worth one hundred thousand dollars!" He looked intently at each of them. "It is nothing more than an elaborately constructed electronic lie. It can't be trusted any more than the man who made it."

Sage's voice dropped to a softer tone. "You know, all these people—the Darens—won't be out a nickel if you throw this so-called will out. This isn't about money—all of them have plenty of that. This is about power."

His voice was now almost at a whisper. "Elizabeth Daren used a sick old man in a sleazy grab for power. Don't let her succeed. This whole case is just as sleazy as that tape they presented. Show this grasping, greedy woman that justice still rules in Eagle County. Do your duty, toss this alleged will into the garbage can where it so justly belongs!"

Tentative applause rippled through the spectator section when Tiger Sage finished. It was silenced by the judge's gavel. Jake looked at the jury, wondering what they might be thinking after Sage's impressive performance.

The courtroom settled down as the judge prepared to charge the jury, giving them the law they would use in deciding the facts of the case. Sage had submitted some proposals to be included in the judge's charge to the jury. Jake had had none. Things had moved too fast and he hadn't prepared anything.

Judge Vinson read from a set of model instructions, altering them as she went along to suit the circumstances of the Daren case.

Jake watched the jury. They seemed riveted to what she was saying, paying much more attention to her than they had to either him or to Sage. The judge explained to them the definitions of insane delusion, undue influence, fraud and the other causes Michigan law gave for discrediting a signature on a will.

She proceeded slowly, like a teacher, explaining the law, the presumptions and how they were to be used in reaching a verdict. Although she had admitted the tapes, she warned the jury against relying on them alone, almost as if refuting Jake's main point.

The judge, in closing, told the jury that their decision had to be based on all the evidence, but that only one of two verdicts could be rendered. She said they must find the will either valid, or they must find it not valid. Having finished, she then directed that two names be drawn so that the jury's number would be reduced to twelve.

Jake was dismayed. An elderly man he thought might side with them was excused, along with a woman who had shown no indications of partiality, real or imagined.

The jury was sworn and then sent into the jury room to reach a verdict.

As Judge Lila Vinson walked off the bench, Jake Martin sat

completely still. As the buzz of animated conversation rose around him in the courtroom, he looked at no one.

It was over.

Elizabeth returned to Raven's Nest. Lee Stevens asked Jake to stay on and talk with the newsmen Stevens had lined up for interviews. Stevens had resumed his duties as spokesman for Elizabeth Daren, and he seemed to be genuinely enjoying himself. Leon Clooney, together with the bank security man, was heading back to Detroit to get a plane to Key West, the location he had selected to relocate and enjoy his newfound wealth.

Everyone in the courthouse seemed at ease, telling stories and joking as they waited, but as each minute passed Jake began to think that he could no longer bear the suspense. He had to get away.

Jake asked the sheriff to call him at Raven's Nest if the jury came in with a verdict, then he left.

It was just past five o'clock, and the little town seemed to reflect the excitement and tension Jake felt. Despite the chill, people were out on the street, gathered in clusters and busily talking. There was traffic on the usually deserted main street. Everyone seemed to be waiting.

Ronald, the butler, greeted him when he arrived at Raven's Nest and escorted him into the great room. Elizabeth had changed into slacks and a sweater. Jake gratefully accepted her offer of a drink.

But even the healthy jolt of expensive whiskey didn't help to ease his anxiety.

"Jake, be candid. What do you think?" she asked.

They sat in the great room. Again a fire was going in the huge fireplace. The heat felt good.

"I can't tell."

"Can't or won't?"

Jake smiled. "Elizabeth, I have nothing to compare it with. You were there, how do you think we did?"

"I'm a novice too," she said. "But if I were a juror, the video would have persuaded me."

Jake laughed. "Let's hope, although the porno business may have soured any favorable impression." He looked at her. "Have you decided what you're going to do about deSalle?"

"Are you changing the subject?"

"If you don't mind. Otherwise, I may end up screaming."

She laughed. "We wouldn't want that. All right. What will I do about dear Claude deSalle? If I lose, not much, obviously."

"Fire him now," Jake said.

"Whoever takes over the bank would just rehire him."

"Yes, but at least people would know him for the snake he is."

"Revenge is a bitter cup. Gus taught me that."

Jake played with the ice cubes in his drink, twirling them around so they caught the fire's reflection. "If you win, you will."

"Will what?"

"Fire him."

"Probably not."

"What!"

Elizabeth laughed. "Claude is a very skillful banker and he has essential international contacts that will be beyond value in any expansion."

"How could you ever trust him?" Jake protested.

"I wouldn't," she replied. "I never have, although I never fully realized just how enormous his ambition is. Now that I do, I can make a better judgment on what to assign to him."

"Elizabeth, you can't be serious!"

"Claude is like an attack dog. Very valuable for what you need done, so long as you never expose your own throat. Claude, if used properly, can help me rip out the throats of my competitors. I will just have to protect my own neck and always and forever keep my eye on him."

"You'd actually keep him on? After what he did? We wouldn't be here, any of us, if it wasn't for that son-of-a-bitch. He has to go."

She smiled. "If I fire him, one of my competitors will pick him up and he'll be in a place where I can't watch him. He's very good, Jake, even if his ethics are nonexistent."

A maid refilled their drinks.

"Jake, a good executive takes a long view. You can't run something as large as Hanover Square and evaluate things in a personal light."

Elizabeth smiled. "Besides, I plan to use Claude to ruin Donald Bellows. He has to be put out of business. I don't need Bellows, and if I'm any judge, Claude will have no sense of loyalty. He'll be happy to help destroy Bellows. If we win, Sperling Beekman will have another opening for partner."

"Bellows deserves anything he gets, I agree, but you can't keep deSalle on. You'll be up here and he'll be downstate and free to do whatever the hell he wants."

She shook her head. "Win or lose, I'm leaving here."

"But, I thought—"

"Raven's Nest has been my university, Jake. I was taught the banking business here by a master. But we can't stay in school forever, can we? Besides, if we lose, I couldn't just sit around up here wondering what might have been. And if we win, I'll have to spend every waking moment working at the bank. I have such wonderful plans."

"Are you going to sell Raven's Nest?"

She shook her head. "No, are you familiar with the Swedish developer, Ingmar Svenson?"

"The guy who builds the resorts?"

"He's going to put in a recreational development here. Raven's Nest will become a resort hotel, and he'll build a condo complex on the lake, complete with a golf course and everything else to attract the top tourist dollars. It will be glorious."

"When did you decide all this?"

"Almost a year ago."

Jake felt a flash of anger. "You might have told me. If the people up here knew that, and knew of the jobs it will bring, they'd have had a much different attitude toward you. It would have helped us with the jury."

"It would have hurt," she said firmly. "People would have thought I was doing it merely to curry favor for the trial. They wouldn't have believed it, Jake. And if they thought I was capable of that kind of deception, they'd have no question in their minds that I might have deceived Gus about the will."

"Maybe," he said, grudgingly.

They sat in silence for a moment, the only sound the crackling of the burning wood.

A maid hurried into the room. "Mr. Martin, the sheriff is asking to talk to you." She handed Jake a portable phone.

"Yes?"

"The judge says you're to come as quickly as possible. The jury's got a verdict."

The packed courtroom was unnaturally quiet. Except for an occasional nervous cough, there was no other sound from the tense spectators. Everyone seemed frozen in expectation, the faces in the courtroom as defined as if they were all part of a large ornate oil painting.

As they waited for the judge to make her entrance, Jake glanced over at Tiger Sage. The older lawyer seemed almost serene, looking a bit like an old man on a park bench, happily oblivious to the cares of the world. If Sage was anxious, he gave no hint of it.

Jake looked at the closed door of the jury room. In minutes they would come out and render their decision. Although it was a rustic courtroom located up in the deep woods of Michigan, that decision would have worldwide financial effects. He wondered if the jury fully realized just how important their verdict would be.

But it would hold no final resolution for him, Jake knew. It would make no real difference in his life. The divorce would go on to completion. His career with Sperling Beekman was over forever, even if no steps were taken to have him disbarred.

Not only had his world been changed drastically, he himself was different. Utterly different. The experience of the trial had been like an ordeal of fire and he had come through it finding out more about himself than he had ever realized.

301

Win or lose, he had been tested, and like raw metal thrust into flames, Jake felt he had been turned into something stronger, more enduring. He had surprised himself. He felt he had finally become a lawyer, and if not that, he knew he was a better man. Stronger, tougher, no matter what the future might hold.

But even that soothing thought didn't help ease the rising tension within him.

Everything seemed to be taking so long.

Finally, Judge Vinson strode from her office and mounted the bench. Everyone stood.

"Sit down," she barked. She looked at the sheriff. "Okay, bring them in."

Sheriff Olsen knocked on the jury door and opened it. "The judge is ready," he said.

They marched out slowly, their faces surprisingly stern. Jake noted they avoided looking both at him and Sage. Each juror took his or her place but did not sit down. Jake tried to read the decision from their faces, but each face seemed chiseled from stone.

The courtroom became even more silent as everyone waited.

"Have you reached a verdict," the judge asked. "And if so, who shall speak for you?"

The stout woman, the one Jake thought might be hostile, tentatively raised her hand. "We have, and I shall speak," she said, her voice betraying nervousness.

Now, not even a cough could be heard. Jake thought it was like being suspended in time.

"We, the jury," she said, "find that the will is valid."

26

Jake had somehow managed to push his way through the crowd and get to the street.

The whole episode had the quality of a fevered dream to him beginning the minute the jury's foreman had announced the verdict. He wondered if he would clearly remember any of it, except as a distorted montage of strange faces and fragmented noise.

T. G. Sage had said something to him, but in the uproar he couldn't make out what it was. Sage and the two Daren children were being engulfed by a horde of newsmen as Jake left.

He walked, unmindful of the cold, trudging along the dark street, trying to sort out what had happened and trying even harder to think of what was to come. He found he couldn't concentrate on anything. His mind was filled with pictures, like small unedited snippets of film, of faces, of talk, of testimony.

He had not really expected it.

He had won.

The Augustus J. Daren will was upheld and Elizabeth Daren was now the undisputed ruler of her deceased husband's empire.

Jake stopped and turned back. A car full of hunters drove by. They would be arriving now by the thousands in anticipation of Sunday, the opening day of the annual deer season.

Despite the late hour, little knots of people still huddled around the courthouse. He looked for her car but it was gone. He got in the Corvette and drove to Raven's Nest.

The gate guards congratulated him on the victory.

Ronald, the butler, a wide smile on his usually reserved face, greeted him at the door. "Hail, the conquering hero," he said. "A job well done, Mr. Martin."

"Thank you." Lee Stevens rushed to meet him. "Where have you been? I've got a flock of radio talk shows that want to interview you. Tomorrow I've lined up Elizabeth with Ted Koppel on Nightline. We're hot, Jake, real hot!"

"Where's Elizabeth?" Jake asked.

"In her office over there," Stevens said, grinning. "There was no time for celebration for her. She hit the ground running. She's one hell of a woman. She's on the phone, telling people what to do, giving orders. There are more telephone lines in here than at the Pentagon." Stevens laughed. "She reminds me of a field commander sending troops into battle. She honest-to-God loves power. She's a tough cookie, that one; I don't think I'd want to get on her wrong side."

Jake poked his head inside the door of the surprisingly small office. Elizabeth waved as she talked with authority into the telephone. "I don't care about that," she said. "The meeting will be at two o'clock tomorrow and no one is excused."

She pressed a button to hold the call. "I have Yamashita on another line. I think he's about to agree to everything I want."

"Go on, then," Jake said. "Talk to him."

"It'll do him good to wait," She smiled, but she was obviously eager to return to what she was doing. "Jake, I can offer you a job with Hanover Square. We'll figure out a title and duties later. The money will match anything you might have made with Sperling Beekman."

She was incredibly beautiful. But looking at her, Jake felt nothing but a surprising sense of loss. "I know nothing about banking," he said. "Thanks, though."

She frowned, surprised. "Are you angry?"

Jake smiled. "No, not at all. You're busy. We can talk later."

"I'm leaving tonight, Jake. Come with me."

"No, Elizabeth. You said it before. I'm a little foggy about the future. I'm going to put everything on the back burner for a while. Okay?" He knew he was really saying goodbye.

"As you wish." She pushed the telephone button. "If you're serious," she said, obviously speaking to Yamashita, "I can have the papers drawn immediately. However, this will be a joint venture, not a partnership . . ."

Jake left the office and walked past the dying embers in the huge fireplace.

Stevens was talking excitedly into a portable phone. He put his hand over the mouthpiece. "Hey, where you going?" He grinned. "What about those radio phone interviews?"

"Not tonight," Jake said.

"You're passing up a golden publicity opportunity, Jake. You could be famous if you want, you know that?"

"I'll see you back at the hotel."

Stevens laughed heartily. "Not me, Jake. You're looking at Hanover Square's new Vice President for Communications." He grinned broadly. "and with a salary to match the title. She's hired Jerry Casey, too. I have to go back to Detroit with the boss tonight."

"Good luck," Jake said.

But Lee Stevens was already back in frantic conversation on the telephone.

Outside, Jake eased slowly into the Corvette and headed for Gladding.

When he got back to the hotel there were messages waiting. One from Cora, another from Marie. He went to his room and called her. This time her secretary put him through without hesitation.

"Jake," she said, "we heard that you've been fired. How very dreadful for you."

"It might be for the best, Marie; you never know." He added, "I won the Daren case, by the way."

"How nice, but does that really matter now that you've lost your chance at partnership?"

"Everyone up here seems to think it mattered."

"Up there, Jake, every little thing matters. I've talked to Harvey Kellerman. He was very concerned about you. I was touched."

"I'll bet you were."

"Harvey thinks he might be able to help you get a job: not with our firm, of course, but he thinks he can get you something with the city's law department. It wouldn't pay much at first, but—"

"Marie," he snapped. "Tell Harvey to take his job and stick it up—Oh, to hell with it. Tell him thanks, but I have other plans."

"Jake, I find your attitude offensive. Harvey is trying to help."

He shook his head and laughed. "Speaking of attitudes, Marie, yours could do with a little improvement. Tell Roger Bartlett I'll sign

304

whatever divorce agreement he wants. When are you and Harvey getting married?"

She didn't answer immediately, then she spoke. "That's up in the air. Harvey may have some difficulty with his divorce. His wife is such a bitch."

Jake said. "Maybe that's for the best, too, Marie. That way when you do get hitched, Harvey won't have too big of an adjustment problem." He hung up as she was making a sputtering reply.

Cora's message was marked urgent and asked him to call her at Sperling Beekman no matter what the time.

She answered the phone herself.

"Jake! Congratulations! We just heard. It's wonderful. You must be walking on air."

"I feel pretty good."

"Jake, there's big news here, too; really big news. All the partners spent almost the whole day in a closed-door meeting. Bellows is out."

"Really?"

"I don't know all the details yet, but they forced him to resign as partner. I understand they may even want to go to the bar association and get his license. They apparently have something on him. How's that for justice?"

"Not bad."

"Jake, I was notified after that meeting that I'll be made partner."

"That's wonderful, Cora. Congratulations. That must have broken Craig Dow's heart."

"He may be out, too. They think he might have been in cahoots with Bellows. Anyway, he's under a cloud here. I think any partnership aspirations he had are finished."

"I'm glad it was you who won, Cora."

"There's more, Jake; the really important part. They talked to me about you. They asked me to talk to you, to ask if you'd come back here as a full partner. You would take Donald Bellows' place. How's that for irony? Of course, it would be contingent."

"On what?"

"They say you can have the partnership if you can bring back the Daren business to the firm. I told them I didn't think that would be a problem. I know Elizabeth Daren likes you. And now that you've won the case, she'll surely say yes. How's that for news?"

Jake felt no elation, and that surprised him. "They'll only take me back if I bring back the Daren account with me, right?"

"That shouldn't be a problem, should it?"

"Depends on your definition of problems. I'm not sure I would want to come back that way."

"Jake, don't be a fool. This is just a business thing. You've always wanted the partnership and now you can have it."

305

"I don't know—"

"It's the opportunity of a lifetime. all you have to do is talk to Elizabeth." She paused, then spoke. "We could work together, Jake. Would that be so bad?"

He smiled. "I thought you never got involved with anyone in the firm?"

"All rules can be broken."

"I'll see you again, Cora, whether I'm in the firm or not."

"I'm glad of that. Very glad."

Trading Elizabeth's good will for a partnership seemed like something Donald Bellows would do. "Cora, tell them I'm not interested in coming back to the firm. At least, not that way."

"Jake!"

"I'll call you when I get back to town, okay?"

"Of course, but don't do anything hasty. Let me tell them you're thinking it over, at least."

He nodded. "Okay." He looked out the window for the last time. "I need to think things out a bit. Everything has happened so fast."

"Call me as soon as you get back. Please?"

He hung up.

The prospect of being a full partner at Sperling Beekman had been his goal for five hectic years. Now, with it in his grasp, he wondered why he didn't really want it anymore.

He stood up and started to pack.

Jake packed quickly, and checked out as a party of four hunters checked in. As he passed the door, Jake glanced in at the hotel's taproom. The newsmen were gone. They had been replaced by hunters all dressed in field clothing, boots and the orange caps and markings required by Michigan law.

The hunters were loud and boisterous, the noise level close to deafening.

Tiger Sage, seated by himself at a small table, waved and motioned for Jake Martin to join him.

Sage stood and extended his hand. "Congratulations again," he said, raising his voice to be heard above the din. "It's a trifle noisy here. I have some excellent scotch up in my room. We should have a drink together. It's customary."

Jake was anxious to leave. Despite his win and his new self-awareness, he associated Gladding with the worst time of his life. He wanted to get far away from the little northern town, and as quickly as possible.

"Thanks, but some other time," Jake replied.

Sage guided him out to the relative quiet of the hotel's hallway. "Come now, it's a courtesy between lawyers to have a drink after a combat. You wouldn't deny me that, would you? Besides, I'd like a word with you."

Jake shrugged. "Okay. But just one. I really have to go."

Tiger Sage's room was a duplicate of his own. The older lawyer poured out the scotch into two plastic glasses, and raised his own glass to Jake.

"You did a very nice job, Jake. It's not often that I'm beaten in court."

Jake allowed himself a smile. "I didn't beat you. The videotape did that."

Sage took a large gulp of the scotch. "You told me you had a coach. I think he did an excellent job, and my curiosity is getting the best of me. I'd like to know who he is."

"His name is T. G. Sage."

"No. I mean, really. Who is he?"

"I have your book on trial practice," Jake said. "I've almost memorized the damn thing. So, you see, you really were my coach throughout the whole trial. If it hadn't been for your book I would have been lost."

Sage raised an inquisitive eyebrow. "That little tome of mine is long out of print. How did you get hold of a copy?"

"I bought it at a used-book store in New York years ago while I was still in law school."

"Hoist by my own petard, by God." Sage finished his scotch and poured out some more. "What are you going to do now?"

"I don't know. I was thinking of going back to New York."

"Do you have prospects there?"

"No, but it's home, or at least it was." Jake sipped the scotch. "But I also just learned Sperling Beekman will take me back as a full partner. Of course, I have to bring the Daren legal business back with me."

"The widow seems fond of you. I don't think that would be a problem. However, I hear a tone in your voice that indicates you are filled with something less than wild enthusiasm by that offer."

"Something like that," Jake said, accepting some more scotch.

Sage ceremoniously lit a cigar, instantly filling the room with a cloud of acrid smoke.

"I'm a single practitioner, Jake, one of the last of a vanishing breed. However, times are changing and I keep finding myself in scrapes because I often have to be in two places at once." He studied the cigar. "I've been thinking about forming a firm, but I haven't ever found the right person." He looked over at Jake. This time the friendly manner vanished. "Trial practice demands a certain type, you see, a fighter, someone who likes it and won't give up. You've demonstrated that quality rather dramatically."

Tiger Sage studied him with narrowing eyes. "You've sacrificed your job, your career, and even risked dishonor for the sake of your client. I doubt many of the new breed of lawyer would even consider taking a risk like that, Jake."

"It was just the circumstances," Jake said. "Believe me, I'm no hero."

"For a novice, you did a remarkably fine job in court. I think you have a real feel for the work. I would like you to come in with me."

"I appreciate the offer, Mr. Sage, but I'm . . . well . . . confused about what I should do."

"Let me unconfuse you," Sage snapped sharply. "This kind of opportunity doesn't come along every day. I'll offer a partnership: you get a straight third of our profits, more if things work out between us."

"But—"

"Damn it, Jake, that's almost a half-million dollars a year. That's not exactly minimum wage, although, believe me, you'll earn every dollar. People come to me for my own unique skills and because of my reputation. In the beginning, I'll have to continue doing the main trial work, obviously, but I'll bring you along and you'll handle most of the lesser jobs until you're fully seasoned. That won't take long. People already respect the man who beat me in the Daren case. In fact, if you're willing to sign aboard, I have a case for you."

"That's very generous, but—"

"If you do come with me, Jake, it won't be an easy existence. You have to have the heart of a warrior for this job. And it's lonely. There's really not much time for a private life. It's tough—I wouldn't kid you—but if you have the guts for it, it becomes the only acceptable way of living."

"Mr. Sage, you don't know anything about me."

"Call me Ted, and I know everything about you except your hat size. Do you think I'd go into a contest without knowing what and who I was up against? Do you accept, or not?"

Jake started to laugh. "You don't give me much time."

"Yes or no?"

"All life is a gamble, I suppose." Jake said, "Okay, yes."

"Good. You know our client. And he certainly has reason to respect you."

"Oh?"

"It's Chip Daren. He brought the action up here knowing that if the will was admitted, he would forfeit his share. His sister Gussie verbally agreed to divide what she is to get with him in case of loss. She was acting, so to speak, as his insurance underwriter."

Sage smiled. "Gussie, it seems, has had a change of heart. She told Chip, just after the verdict, that the deal was off. He wants to sue her on the basis of a verbal contract. The amount that's up for grabs—over a hundred million—is not chicken feed. Chip will tell you about it. By the way, he's not going to appeal this trial. All his rage is presently directed at his darling sister. I'd go over to the jail and see him now."

"The jail?"

"He punched Gussie in her lovely mouth. The sheriff has him in custody at the moment."

Sage reached into his pocket and pulled out a roll of breath mints. "Here, take these. We're like surgeons. The customers tend to lose confidence in us if they smell liquor on our breath." Tiger Sage's smile was genuine. "Better get along, partner. I don't know how late they keep the jails open up here."

"What about the criminal charge against him?"

"Assault," Sage said. "Handle it, get him out on bond, but make sure he understands the fee to defend on the criminal charge will be in addition to our charges in the other lawsuit."

"I've never had a criminal case."

"You do now. As a trial lawyer, late-night visits to jails are something you'll learn to live with."

Tiger Sage raised his glass and grinned. "Welcome, brother, to our small but rather select fraternity."